A Sinner in Paradise

a novel

DEBORAH HINING

Copyright© 2013, by Deborah Hining

Deborah Hining
dhining@lightmessages.com
dhining.lightmessages.com

Published 2013, by Light Messages Publishing
Printed in the United States of America
ISBN: 978-1-61153-057-5

ALL RIGHTS RESERVED

No part of this publication may be reproduced, stored in a retrieval system, or transmitted in any form or by any means, electronic, mechanical, photocopying, recording, scanning, or otherwise, except as permitted under Section 107 or 108 of the 1976 International Copyright Act, without the prior written permission of the publisher.

*In memory of Marynell Wells Griffitts, my mother,
who believed that love really is all you need.*

Acknowledgements

When a book has been over 25 years in the making, there are many, many people who have had a hand in it. I started writing it, oh… around 1987 or so, and between fits of furious scribbling and long stretches where it languished in a drawer, I scattered bits around to friends I could sucker into reading it. I read portions of it aloud to my students, some of whom were brave enough to perform a scene or two in public. I begged fellow writers to critique it; some were kind, some were not, rightly so. I even foisted manuscripts onto gracious clients who, astonishingly, agreed to read the draft of a novel written, by all people, their financial advisor. They didn't even ask what I thought I was doing. Many went to the trouble to edit portions, and one even offered to serve as an agent for me. I asked my husband to read draft after draft and always felt a thrill when I caught him laughing or tearing up. What I discovered during this long process was not that I had the makings of a great novel, but that I have wonderful, caring, intuitive friends and loved ones who are willing to do far more for me than I deserve.

All this is in the way of thanking those of you who were a part of my life during this process, which did not seem so terribly long at all. We all were just living and creating and sharing and loving, and somehow, in all this jumble of goodness, this novel came into being. I am grateful to you all, and you all know who you are.

But I owe a big and specific thank you to my editor, Elizabeth Turnbull, who actually became enthusiastic about the story and made me finish it, made me rewrite it, and made me do things I never wanted to do. Thanks to her, her constant encouragement, and her hard work, this sloppy piece of fiction was whipped into shape until it became something I am proud to put my name on.

One

Geneva hated cats. She didn't know why she had so many of them. Four had been bad enough, but now here she was sitting in the floor of her closet in the middle of the night, watching Evangeline squeeze out her third kitten. This would make seven cats altogether. *Damn!* She hadn't even known the cat was pregnant.

This had to be Howard's doing. All Geneva's toms had been neutered, and she had always made sure none of the cats had ever gotten out, but knowing Howard, he had let them escape while she was away. That would be just like him, the passive-aggressive, undermining, conniving prick. He had hated her cats, even though they had never done anything to hurt him, ever—except for the one time Dr. Zhivago had pooped in his shoe. But that didn't warrant letting out—or more likely, throwing out—Evangeline so she could get pregnant. No doubt the father was some ugly, scraggly tom, and Geneva would never be able to get rid of the kittens.

Kitten number four was making its appearance. It was ugly, all right. *Men. They can ruin your life even after you've gotten rid of them.*

Not that Geneva had actually "gotten rid" of Howard. As a matter of fact, it had sort of been the other way around, and his leaving had been one of the worst moments of her life. No, actually the worst moments came later. Right after he had committed the awful treachery *(I think we ought to postpone the wedding, darling. Maybe call it off for awhile. You know, so we can be really sure… blah blah blah.),* she had the fleeting pleasure of throwing things at him and watching them splinter around his cowardly head.

Fortunately she had had the presence of mind to throw the cheap wine glasses she had gotten free for subscribing to a romance book club and not the Waterford. And that had felt good. It also had felt good to abandon the rarified façade she had so carefully cultivated over the past few years and unsheathe her native West Virginian tongue slashing Howard with a few modified nouns he had never heard before. She smiled at the memory. *How he had cowered, throwing his arms up to protect his pretty face!* Fueled by his mincing and ducking, she hadn't stopped until she had thrown all seven glasses at him. The eighth, unfortunately, was not yet in her arsenal. It wouldn't appear for a couple more weeks, when the next installment was due.

But the sweetness of that little episode had been short lived. After that, and for the longest time, she gulped misery with her coffee every morning and slept in the arms of misery every night. She was lost, devastated, and haunted with pain. Heartache became her constant companion.

She pondered the alliteration. *Haunted by heartache. Devastated with despair.* Tears sprang to her eyes, and she thought, *tears trickling.* No, that was overused. *Waterfalls washing.* Nah, the image wasn't good. *Tears tumbling.* Hmm, yes, that was better. *Tears tumbled down her wan, beatific face….* She nodded to herself. That image fit the situation nicely.

The pink nose of kitten number five emerged, pulling her thoughts back from the literary. *Oh, God!* There was something wrong with it. It was smaller than the others, and even after

Evangeline had licked it thoroughly, it just laid there, barely moving. All the other kittens had already vigorously attached themselves to Evangeline's underside, but this one remained limp and pitiful. Geneva felt her stomach heave. *Oh, please don't die, you poor little thing!* She nudged the other kittens aside and tried to nuzzle the tiny creature against a choice-looking teat, but it would not suck. It shivered and gave a weak mew, and the sight made Geneva more miserable than ever. She wrung her hands, then cried, and finally threw herself on the floor and sobbed violently.

Why had Howard forsaken her? What was wrong with this kitten? It was dying, and it was all his fault! She had been the best thing that ever happened to that man! Her sobs subsided a bit as she remembered how glorious their past had been.

Four months ago her life had been perfect. She searched for a metaphor to express it: *Love had alighted, folding its gossamer wings and nesting in her soul.* After a lifetime of searching (and searched she had, diligently, industriously) she had finally found the perfect mate, practically made to order—the one she had constructed in her imagination years earlier. Howard Whittaker Graves III was handsome, educated, sophisticated, and wealthy. Well, she hated to admit that wealth was important, but all that stuff Howard had given her had been nice. And she really needed the new car he had promised. A BMW. Her old Mazda was getting cranky, and she didn't know what she was going to do about getting a new one.

She watched Evangeline struggle and strain, and she watched the sick kitten shiver.

Oh, God, she prayed. *Don't let this kitten die! And help me get through this night.* The prayer was sincere, one of a long string she had uttered since Howard had left her. Remembering the solace of her childhood conversations with God, she found it comforting to send her pain and her requests heavenward once again.

She had at one time been one for long and diligent daily prayer, but somewhere along the line she had abandoned this habit after she had realized that she was bright and beautiful and ambitious enough to get whatever she wanted without divine intervention.

But now she was a broken vessel, and she needed all the help she could get.

Not long ago, she had prayed for Howard to be struck dead by some awful, agonizing malady (*What Biblical character had died with his bowels gushing out?*) but later, when she realized that she really just wanted him back, she prayed that he would come crawling, repentant, and begging for forgiveness. Neither prayer had been answered, but that didn't stop her from taking her grievances before the Lord on a daily basis.

Kitten number six, large and greedy, had made its way into the world and managed to shove aside the runt. He latched onto the teat Geneva had tried to reserve for the little guy. She poked around to find another teat and, cradling the weak kitten, mashed his face up against it. He whimpered and coughed, then wobbled his head a little and laid it down. The other kittens pushed it aside, wiggling against Evangeline's milk bar like the last call had been rung. Knowing that the poor thing would surely die if it didn't get some nourishment soon, she threw on her clothes with panicky hands and rushed out to the all-night pharmacy for baby formula.

Aside from the pimply, slack-jawed cashier there were three people in the store, and Geneva reckoned there might have been enough brainpower among them to maybe pass a basic literacy class. She grabbed a canister of *Babies Only Milk-Based Formula* and raced to the cash register. Too late. The three intellectual giants had already beaten her there. Talking to the cashier was a ragged man with trembling hands and a week's worth of growth on his face.

Behind him was an extraordinarily tacky looking blonde couple. Well, she thought he was blonde—his eyebrows were, anyway. His actual hair was purple and spiked into what he surely thought of as a magnificent mohawk. The girl had streaks of purple and red in her ratty do. Each of them clutched a box of condoms, and they were intensely arguing over the merits of the different brands. She wanted the pink ribbed ones, but he was adamant that they should get the ones designed for a more "natural" experience. Geneva wanted to rip out his purple troll hair spikes, and she hoped they would choose ones that would render them both sterile for life.

The sad-looking man in front of the line was having trouble coming up with enough money for the bottle of prescription pills lying on the counter.

"I'm a little short," he said sadly, looking at his dirty cuticles.

There was silence. The girl in front of Geneva snorted and slouched, elaborately crossing her arms over her chest. The cashier looked at the man without interest.

After a long moment, Geneva groaned, "Oh, for Pete's sake." Then, when nobody responded, she spoke again. "How short are you?" she asked, too loudly. The girl with the pink condoms snickered. Geneva glared at her and asked again, but more kindly, "How short are you?" The girl snickered again, and threw over her shoulder, "Oh, I'd guess about five or six inches right now, from the looks of him." The guy with her guffawed, and the girl looked pleased with herself.

Geneva elbowed her way to the front of the line, plunked down her formula and said, "Here, I'll pay for it, and this, too," and threw two twenties on the counter. The cashier gave her an idiotic stare, but rang up the sale while Geneva turned and smiled wickedly at the couple behind her. It was worth it to spend an extra $24.95 to break in front of them. Scooping up her change, she turned to go, then recoiled when the ragged man pulled at her sleeve.

"Thank you, Miss. God bless you," he said softly, haltingly. He had tired, kind, brown eyes, with deep wrinkles radiating out like star bursts. When he smiled at her with genuine gratitude, Geneva suddenly felt her throat constrict and a vast chasm open up in her heart. *The world was a cruel, cruel place.* She managed a tight little smile and nod, then impulsively thrust the change she still held in her hand into his grimy one and rushed out the door before the tears began.

She was so distraught and in such a hurry that she tripped on the curb outside her apartment, ripping the bag and dropping the cardboard cylinder full of dehydrated formula on the sidewalk. As she fell, she felt the insubstantial container give way under her knee and then the soft, powdered grains impressing themselves into her kneecap.

There was a moment of pain followed by indecision. Should she go back for more? The kitten could die in the meantime, and besides, she didn't want to run into the condom couple again. They may have figured out by now that she had broken in line in front of them. Swiftly, she searched her purse and found a small, plastic Ziploc bag containing bobby pins and elastic bands and another that held the brooch she had planned to have repaired. These accessories she dumped into her purse, then she carefully scooped as much of the formula as she deemed still sterile into the bags. It was plenty for a three-ounce kitten.

By the time she made it home, the poor little fellow was off by himself in the corner, cold and shivering. With a breaking heart, Geneva mixed the formula from one of the bags, picked him up, and gently and painstakingly squeezed dropperful after dropperful into his miniscule mouth. All the while, she fumed at Howard. Here she was losing sleep over a cat that she didn't want, and he was at home, sleeping peacefully without an inkling of the misery he had caused. And when the kitten died at sunrise, she sobbed passionately, stroking his tiny body and trying her best to comfort Evangeline. Evangeline was such a sweet, sensitive kitty. Her favorite, really, and Geneva knew the poor thing would grieve over this loss.

After a while, she realized that Evangeline was taking it pretty well, so she turned her consolations toward herself, telling herself that she hated cats anyway—*but this one was exceptionally pretty—all white with black paws.* He reminded her of a snowy dancer wearing black ballet shoes. And the loss of such beauty was horrible to her. It seemed that everything fine and beautiful and delicate was shattering all around her. *It was not fair! Life was not fair!* Only the ugly and painful seemed to survive unscathed, survive and grow and multiply, despite how carefully she crafted and nurtured the things she found beautiful. Before she knew it, she had cried herself to sleep.

She awoke to the Saturday sun streaming through cat hairs floating in the air. They refracted the light curiously, even beautifully. Her pillow was soggy from last night's tears, and the first thing Geneva thought was that she was going to have to quit crying into it because she was sure all that salt was affecting the condition of her hair. Then she thought about Howard again, and the kitten, and began to cry anew. After awhile, she forgot why she was crying and thought only that it felt good to cry. But then she realized that it was beginning to feel less good than it had the night before. That confused her.

She rolled over and mused about how she had been betrayed, until her growling stomach drew her attention. There was, she realized, a small recompense for the broken heart in the fact that she had lost ten pounds within a month of Howard's departure. *Well, actually, a largish recompense in that,* she decided. *No great loss without some small gain,* she thought, remembering one of her mother's homespun expressions. No, in this case, a great loss *and* a great loss. *Hey, that was pretty good.* She could tell her mom that. She tossed cats and covers off her slender frame and smiled down at her concave stomach and her delicate, tiny wrists.

As she thought about her mother, a sudden wave of homesickness swelled and engulfed her heart. She wanted her loved ones around her right now to comfort her, and she wanted to be home among open spaces and green mountains and to feel clean wind on her face. She missed her mother's arms and her father's smile; indeed, she missed her whole family scattered over the mountains like stands of study hickory and fragrant spruce. At home in the dappled shade and clean sunshine, she might be able to renew herself, to gather strength from the mountains, to forget Howard, and to learn how to live all by herself, celibate, the surface of her life smooth and untroubled by the vagaries of men.

She made a sudden decision: she would go home! She would quit her job, give away her cats (*well maybe not Evangeline, since she was a new mother*), rent out her chic apartment, and spend the summer, perhaps the fall, among her high, clean mountains. She knew that such a respite would equip her to resume her life and her brilliant career when she returned.

As for Howard, ha! She would show him! He would no doubt realize how foolish he had been; consumed with guilt and regret for his loss, he would spend months searching for her. When he finally found her, he would throw himself at her feet and beg for forgiveness. Then she would straighten her spine, give him her strong, sure smile and tell him to take a flying leap off Buttermilk Knob.

She lay very still, considering the image, and decided that she liked that scenario much better than the one she had been mulling over since February, which placed Howard sobbing bitterly at her bedside as she lay pale and dying, her heart mortally wounded. Besides, she had relived the scene so often, embellishing it with each recounting, that she had run out of possible accoutrements and had worn it to a thin, no longer comforting, shred. She sat up with dignity. *So long, little Eva. Hello Brunhilde!*

Rolling to the edge of the bed, she dialed her parents' number in Tucker, West Virginia, and waited with pounding heart, formulating the most effective salutation. Perhaps, *Mom, I've had it in this awful city. I'm coming home!* Then her mother would gasp, and say, *Oh, honey!* and make those nice little motherly, comforting noises that Geneva liked to hear whenever she was feeling small and wounded.

The phone rang until Geneva finally admitted that there would be no answer. *And no answering machine, either. Dammit.* She'd given her parents an answering machine last Christmas, but they never bothered to turn the thing on, claiming they could not figure out how to work it. But she knew they just didn't like anything that intruded upon the serenity of their lives. Sometimes they even turned the ringer off for days at a time when they wanted to enjoy a particularly serene autumn or a spectacular thunderstorm season. Impatiently, she let it ring once more, then slammed the phone down, bitterly complaining to herself about the way events always seemed to conspire to thwart her most romantic impulses.

Still, she would not let the inspiration of the moment go wasted. Immediately, she phoned her sister who lived on a farm tucked into a mountain valley ten miles from the town where they had grown up. Her sister was more considerate, answering after two rings.

"Rachel, I've had it in this awful city. I'm coming home."

Satisfied with her delivery, Geneva slipped into the kitchen and opened the cupboard door quietly. It would not do to let the cats hear her rustling around in the kitchen.

Characteristically, Rachel did not sense the drama of the moment; she did not gasp, but merely drawled into the receiver, "Well, I wondered when you'd come to your senses. What happened? Did you finally realize that you've made enough of a fool of yourself over that bookie?"

"He's not a bookie. He's a stock market analyst," Geneva replied coldly. Rachel, like her whole family, had the tendency to belittle those professions that did not require the use of one's hands, a tendency Geneva invariably thought terribly working class. "And yes, I have decided to come out of mourning. I'm coming home and I'm giving up men. Not necessarily in that order."

That out, she tried to think of something noble and brave to say, but after an awkward moment, she merely burst into tears and sobbed, "Oh, Rachel, I'm sick of everything here. I don't have any friends, and the men are all either mean or gay, and I miss everybody, and it's already hot and sticky here, and I'm so blue I feel like throwing myself in front of a train." She continued thus for several minutes telling various lies and slandering the city which, two years earlier, had glimmered like a beacon in the wilderness. At last, when her list of miseries and wrongs petered out, she ended her final sentence with a little sob and gasp. "Where's Mom, anyway?"

"Geneva, you know she and Daddy went to Pennsylvania. Remember Mom has a quilt in a show there? And they're going to visit the Jorgansonns for a while and help the Gunter's son build his house. He's getting married this fall. I doubt they'll be home before July. But don't worry, honey, come on down and stay with us. We'd love to have you, and it's so pretty here now. The rhododendrons are really going to be fabulous this year."

Geneva grunted in response. What had she done with the can opener? Evangeline had followed her into the kitchen and was crazily running around her ankles in anticipation of breakfast.

"You'll feel a lot better once you get out of DC," Rachel continued. "Besides, I could use you. I'm starting to get big now, and Wayne keeps threatening to hire someone to take care of me. Mom offered, of course, but she's slowing down some. Gosh, don't tell her I said that. And I don't want her cutting her trip short to chase after all of us."

While considering the invitation, Geneva picked up Evangeline to quiet her mewing and searched through the silverware drawer for the can opener. It would be nice to spend the summer at the farm in the high meadows where Rachel, her husband Wayne, and their two small daughters made their home. It was a farm in the picturesque rather than practical sense, although they did keep a small garden, a few sheep and chickens, and a couple of horses. Since Rachel liked to weave, the sheep were not entirely for effect. But they hired the shearing and lambing done every spring because Wayne was too busy as a general surgeon to do any real farming. Both Wayne and Rachel, however, always were on hand to help with delivering the newborn lambs, for this couple reveled in fecundity. There were always babies on the farm: chicks, ducklings, goslings, lambs, puppies. It was fitting that after six years of marriage, Rachel and Wayne already had two children and were expecting twins in four more months. It was clear they planned to fill up the big, rambling farmhouse they had just built.

No can opener. By this time the other cats had joined Evangeline and were meowing hysterically. "Get away," she muttered, cupping her hand over the phone, "Evangeline, shut up. All of you, get way. Get away. I SAID, GET AWAY!"

"What?" came Rachel's voice.

"Nothing. These cats are acting like starved alley cats and I can't find the can opener."

She finally found it and succeeded in getting the cans opened, the food in the bowls, and the bowls on the floor, suffering only one scratch on her forearm in the process.

Geneva turned her attention back to Rachel, magnanimously accepting the job of caring for her during the last part of her pregnancy. As she hung up the phone, she felt her sister's calming influence steal over her like a rosy twilight. She breathed deeply, then, feeling profoundly selfless and resolute, she immediately set about preparing for her departure.

The first thing she did was to pull out her financial records to determine how long she could live without working, and decided that thanks to Howard's genius concerning the intricacies of Wall Street, she could practically retire, provided she could rent her apartment to cover the mortgage and her car held out. *Screw Howard.* She would have bought herself a new car if he hadn't made those noises about the BMW. She considered having the ancient Mazda serviced, but decided that it could wait until she returned home. Her experience had taught her that big city mechanics were all wolves, bent on fleecing unsuspecting women. A mechanic at home would cost about half, she reasoned in her economical way.

Mentally arranging her list of priorities, she began calling friends to see how many of them wanted a cat or two. Nobody wanted a cat, but several offered to take over her apartment, which Geneva found a little disquieting, despite the fact that she had hoped she would find a renter quickly. Of course, it pleased her that she was well known for her splendid decorating prowess. She had found this apartment a year earlier—a gutted horror just a block away from the most fashionable side of Georgetown—and had bought and refurbished it with the money and antiques Granny Morgan had left her. She had always loved showing it off, but now she was piqued that everyone seemed more enchanted by her dwelling than with her person. Although nearly all of them protested that they would hate to see her leave, they were just a shade too quick to offer to move in. She began to wonder if she could stipulate that the cats came with the apartment.

By Monday morning, she was chafing to get on the road, but she thought that the least she should do would be to give the store where she worked as a display designer a month's notice since she knew it would be next to impossible to find someone qualified enough to do her job. When she placed her resignation on her boss' desk with just a hint of a flourish, her thrilling heart expanded in anticipation of Sally's anguish over her departure. But Sally's polite speech about how much Geneva would be missed but that she would not dream of standing in her way, did not quite measure up to Geneva's expectation. Then Sally further irritated her by ending the speech with a too casual, "By the way, are you going to sell your apartment?"

Geneva suffered greater disappointment when faced with the chore of interviewing for her replacement, she found a pile of applications on her desk for a dozen or so hopefuls who displayed an eagerness for her job that she personally found excessive and downright tacky. Then, as she discovered that some of the applicants were surprisingly talented, with excellent resumes, she secretly began to feel a little deflated, even harboring the slightest suspicion that she might have been lucky to have landed the job in the first place. The thoughts nibbled like little minnows. *Would it be wise to leave after all?*

She chased them away with a restless gesture. *Yes.* She needed this vacation. She would not abandon her resolve because of a few tremors of unfounded doubt.

That evening, she mentally checked off her list the considerable number of people she had called about relocating her cats. Joyce, a friend of her friend Carlos, who had once attended a party at Geneva's place, would surely take one. Carlos had informed her that Joyce usually kept a menagerie. Now Geneva remembered that Joyce had made a point to compliment her on her cats' exceptional beauty (they had all been extraordinarily well behaved that evening), so Geneva tracked down the number and prayed as she waited for Joyce to answer. Fleetingly, she hoped that all of Joyce's cats had died during the last few weeks.

"Joyce! This is Geneva... Geneva LeNoir." She spelled and pronounced her name in the proper French way, Le-*noir*, unlike everyone else in her family who always had made it one word and said "*len*-or." *Leave it to a bunch of hillbillies to mutilate a perfectly good French name.* "Carlos' friend... You came to a party at my place last fall? Geneva, on Taylor Street..."

There was a long pause, and then, "Oh, *Yes!*"

Relief washed over her and she rushed on. "Well! However have you been? Isn't it awful the way we haven't gotten together recently?" Well, they never actually had, but they'd said they meant to.

Joyce was equally appalled that they had let their friendship lapse for so long and (after Geneva prompted her) asked about Howard, which led to a lengthy discussion about the flawed nature of men in general and wound up some forty five minutes later with Geneva announcing her departure and asking Joyce to take a cat or two. Or several.

Joyce thought briefly, then replied, "Er... Jenny—"

"Geneva," corrected Geneva.

"Geneva, you know I'd love to, but I just can't take another animal. The ones I have are eating me out of house and home. I sure hate it that you're leaving, though." She paused one infinitesimal fraction of a second. "By the way, I might be willing to take over your apartment while you're gone."

For the rest of the month, Geneva packed and interviewed applicants. In her spare time she read feminist literature and shopped for new clothes—all black. She rented her apartment to a stranger at nearly twice the monthly mortgage rate, made arrangements to store her furniture, and placed ads for free cats. She called friends of friends who might be interested in having a nice cat. There were no takers.

She thought about leaving a basketful of kittens on Howard's doorstep but reconsidered when she remembered he had thrown his shoe at Petrarch after he discovered the cat poop in it. She knew that Dr. Zhivago had been the culprit, for he had always shown a distinct dislike for Howard, and she was outraged that Howard could be so stupid and callous as to pick on poor, gentle Petrarch who was nothing but a gentleman all the time. Howard had known he was her favorite when he threw that shoe. That was an insult to her directly! *No, Howard would probably drown them or something.* So she sighed and resignedly named them. The female names she lingered over lovingly, and after days of pondering, finally settled on Simone (after deBouvier) and Scarlet (after O'Hara). The males' names sprang, like Venus, full blown from her lips: Larry, Moe, and Curly Joe.

The next day she loaded her car and said farewell to the city as she tore up the ticket she had gotten for parking beside a fire hydrant while she ran in for one last check. "Who needs it?" she shouted defiantly, then she cranked up the car, headed for the interstate, and floored it, mindful of the fact that she was running away, sans fast-track career opportunity, sans chic apartment, sans fair-weather friends and lovers, but with nine cats. Her mind seethed with the turmoil of a woman scorned and, in general, dumped on.

But as she cleared the perimeter of the city noise and exhaust fumes, heading into the clear blue and silver June morning, her heart gave a little leap. She felt freer and happier than she had since the day Howard had finally overcome his reluctance and had asked her to marry him. And suddenly she found herself singing about freedom and pressing her small, delicate foot mercilessly down on the accelerator, saying goodbye to her sophisticated life in the city without a regret. She suddenly liked her cats again, laughing out loud when Petrarch perched on the back of her seat, draped his forelegs over her shoulder, and purred louder than the little Mazda's engine.

As she caught sight of the first line of hazy blue mountains,

Geneva repeated over and over again, "Home at last! Why did I ever leave?" And when she began the long ascent into the high country and felt the temperature drop, she breathed the air in deep gulps, as one thirsty from long labor in the fields drinks from a sweet well.

She arrived at the rich meadowland where Rachel and her family lived just as the sun was beginning its initial descent and spreading gentle fire over the warm, green land. It all looked just as she remembered: the crystalline light swirling under the big, sapphire sky; sheep grazing in the field; the horses in the pasture who were stunning examples of bad offspring of champion bloodlines. Because they were slow out of the gate and adamantly refused to jump anything higher than a gopher hill, Wayne had gotten them for a relative bargain at auction. A horse breeder would have scorned them as lazy and virtually worthless, but they were beautiful, perfect for cantering through the rolling fields Rachel had sown with wildflowers, and serving the family as beloved, pampered pets.

Geneva saw her sister as soon as she turned into the drive. Beautifully pregnant and carrying a basket of strawberries and roses from the garden, Rachel was shading her eyes and laughing at her children as they romped across the wide expanse of lawn with Sammy, their gleaming Irish setter. With their red and gold hair, the four of them looked like jewels in the gilded air. Geneva roared into the drive and leaned on the horn, scattering chickens that flurried and fussed. She bounded out of the car to catch her sister in a tremendous hug, marveling at how perfect she looked with her hair and skin glowing in the rich sun.

"Rachel, Rachel! You look just like a Renoir! No, better that that. A Titian! How wonderful to be here! Home at last! How I have missed you all! I feel as if I have come from the wars! Oh, Phoebe! Hannah! How you have grown!" She lifted each of her small nieces high into the air and squeezed them until they shrieked and choked her with their fierce little hugs.

Rachel, a serene madonna, glowed at her sister. "Geneva, darlin'.

So good to have you here. You poor thing," she added suddenly, holding her at arm's length and frowning at her. "You look so sallow and sickly. Never mind. We'll fatten you up and get some blood back in you. I bet you haven't had anything decent to eat for weeks."

This was true. Mostly diet colas and granola bars, but Geneva most certainly did not enjoy the critical observation concerning the new body for which she had suffered so much.

"Well, come on in," Rachel continued. "You must be tired after that drive. Mama and Daddy won't be home for a while yet, but they're really glad about your coming home. Mam-ma can't wait to see you, too."

The Mam-ma to which Rachel referred was their one surviving grandmother, Hannah Morgan Turner, the only child of Granny Morgan, whose genetic and material legacy had insured Geneva's perfect aesthetic sense and her well-furnished apartment. Now ninety years old, Mam-ma Turner, like her mother before her, had long enjoyed health, energy, and a handsome face.

Mam-ma Turner had borne nine children, all dead now save one, Gaynell, the mother of Rachel and Geneva. The others had died early, before they had produced heirs, lost to gaping black mines, to unfruitful childbed, to war, to the ravages of ignorance and disease, and one to the treachery of capricious weather high in the shadowed hills. Only Gaynell had survived, and for many years it appeared that she would be the last of Granny Morgan's bloodline.

She, too, had been—indeed still was—considered a legendary beauty, but acquainted with sorrow and death as she was, she virtually ignored that gift to live her days along the practical lines of survival and the driving need to procreate. Her beauty had helped her to marry young and happily, and although the twenty two years with her first husband, Gerald, had been pleasant ones, she had felt eternally impoverished with the absence of sons and daughters. "What good is a pert little nose and all this yeller hair if I don't have me any younguns to pass 'em along to?" she had often repeated as she wandered through her empty house.

Then her husband, a union organizer among the miners, was killed during a riot over the issue of child labor practices, and two years later she remarried, not anticipating the ironic turn of events precipitated by Gerald's death. She told herself that she might as well spin out her last years in the company of a good man and not mourn what might have been, but shortly after the new union with Ray Lenoir, Gaynell had found herself suddenly and inexplicably (she thought) pregnant. At the age of forty-five she was, after all, able to pass along the pert nose and yellow hair to her first daughter, Rachel. Geneva followed three years later, just as pert and just as golden, and proclaiming her fertility at her advanced age a miracle, Gaynell threw herself into motherhood with the same surprised delight that Abraham's Sarah surely had with the product of her late-blooming womb.

And so, Rachel and Geneva had grown up under the wrinkled caresses of old people of the Morgan line who doted on them, who called them "little miracles," "blessings," "the joy of their lives." It was no wonder that they passed through their rainbowed youths feeling they were destined to grace the world in a way that it had never seen before. They were treasures beyond price, more special than their adult cousins and their children on their father's side. Those children had become so numerous that the Lenoir name was as familiar as redbud over the West Virginia valleys and hills.

Not only were Rachel and Geneva loved, they were also well taught—bone bred with an abiding respect for the venerable mountains and the ways of "old timers" who gave them a love for tradition and unbroken custom. Like leggy tulips standing by a support, Rachel and Geneva never stood completely alone as long as they remained near home. Thus, they unquestioningly had given themselves to the music of the green and blue mountains around them. But in her unsettled teens, Geneva listened to another distant song, for in her restless heart, she knew she would break away from the cloying sweetness of too much family love. Sensing something shimmering over the horizon, she left to find it, and when she did, she loved it, too. It was glamour, it was independence and self-expression, it was sophisticated, articulate friends who taught her how to pretend to be sleek and polished, and it made her happy.

Yet, despite her senses' delight with her new life, Geneva's soul soon became parched and uneasy in the blinking lights. Too often she felt the clash between cultures when she recognized that her new life existed at a solitary extreme from her upbringing, and her heart was too often fragmented with the business of trying to reconcile her past with her future. Always attuned to the rhythm of the Appalachian tongue, the safety of old custom, the comfort of rugged politeness, she became acutely aware that those ways were different, substandard, and laughable according to the values of her new world.

She did her best to conform, to strip away the wilderness that marked her upbringing, but each time she tried, she hurt as if she were stripping away her own skin—the flesh, and the sinews holding her bones together. So instead of changing on the inside, she manufactured a gleaming façade, which she layered over the surface of her vulnerable core. She changed her speech and shifted such nonessentials as her politics to mirror those of her contemporaries. The sophisticated artists, merchants, and political hangers-on in Washington, DC found her perfectly correct.

But whenever she came back to the mountains, the comfortable, downy rags of her past rushed to clothe and bind her, and she realized anew that she was irrevocably connected to the aged roots lying beneath her feet. The tears stung her eyes when she realized how long it had been since she had seen Mam-ma Turner.

"Oh, I see you brought the cats," Rachel was saying. "Good grief. How many are there? Oh, and kittens!" She reached into the car to catch up each of the kittens, now cute and rambunctious as only kittens can be. Geneva watched her fondle them, not trying to hide her pride in them. "Well," Rachel sighed as she set the last one down, "I guess the barn will hold them all." She laughed, "I just hope we can keep them in mice and cat food."

Alarm flashed in Geneva at the idea of her cats sleeping in the barn. They had been used to sleeping on pillows all of their lives. Not that Geneva had encouraged them—they always just moved into the most comfortable places without feeling the need for an invitation, but Geneva worried that since she had gotten used to hearing them purr (and nine of them going at once could take some getting used to) the silence might be maddening. Then she remembered that Wayne was allergic to cats, so she smiled and said brightly,

"Oh, great. I couldn't stand all these cats around me in my apartment. I tried to get rid of them before I came home."

Rachel insisted that Geneva have something to eat, then she put the children down for a nap, and the two sisters wandered through the garden bedecked with flowers and small, yellow squash, then around the rambling farmhouse. At last they ambled onto the porch, settling into the swing after Rachel had brought out a nearly-empty bottle of wine.

"I'll join you in a glass of this if you promise not to tell Wayne. He thinks I shouldn't drink at all, but right now I think I need it—or rather these two do," she said, patting her rounding belly. "Every once in a while, they get into a soccer game with my spleen as the ball. Maybe this will calm them down. Put the little beggars to sleep." She poured the wine.

Geneva giggled as she picked up her glass. "These look just like the glasses I threw at Howard the night he left."

"Did you hit him?" Rachel asked mildly.

"Nah. Just scared the hell out of him. You should have seen him ducking! His eyes got as big as millwheels, and he kept hollering, 'Geneva! Control yourself!' And I said, 'I am controlled! If I really wanted to hit you, your nose would be paté!'"

"Guess he didn't know you had the best fastball in the entire eighth grade."

"If he had, he'd have gotten out a lot faster."

They settled into the porch swing, laughing, sipping the honeyed warmth and admiring the angle of the sun, the abundant wildflowers, and the thin, sweet mountain air. They talked together as only sisters can, of common memories, and with the acceptance born of years of shared confessions. Geneva's brooding dissipated into the flawless, living sky, and she began to forget about the last two years in DC, to nestle down into the old sense of family and place. For long moments she even forgot that she had been jilted, and when the talk turned to Howard, she found only a hollow ache where the shattering pain had once been.

"I never did know what you saw in him, anyway," complained Rachel after listening to Geneva's grievances concerning her ex-fiancée. "I couldn't stand him from the beginning."

"Oh, Rachel," sighed her sister. "Who knows why anybody loves anybody? But I do—did—love him. He really was sweet—and romantic. He'd read poetry out loud to me, and once we read all of *Romeo and Juliet* together. He treated me like a goddess or something."

"Yeah, 'something' is right. Old worship 'em and leave 'em Howard. I liked that guy—Pete—the guy you dated your senior year a lot better. Wasn't he going to be a dentist?"

Geneva groaned. "Not my type. Do you know what he gave me for my birthday? A case of Colgate and a lifetime supply of dental floss that he got free from a vendor at a dental convention. Howard sent two dozen roses, one for every year for my last birthday."

"Well, you still have something worthwhile to remember Pete by."

"Six miles of waxed string."

"What about the cute guy from Norway? With the sailboat? You seemed pretty taken with him for a while," said Rachel. "And he seemed to like you, too."

"Oh, he was all right," sighed Geneva. "But he wore these really stupid clothes—you know, white pants and black socks with sandals. Once we went to a nice restaurant, and he wore a tie with a knit shirt. I was embarrassed to be seen with him. And he was too short."

"Well, Howard was no giant," reminded Rachel.

"Yeah." Geneva thought about his. If she wore heels, they

stood at exactly the same height, so she generally had stuck to flats around him. This had always irritated her—her legs never looked quite right in flats. "But he was special to me," said Geneva, her eyes filling with tears. Yet, even as she let the ache take hold of her, spinning her around and making her head swim, she looked slyly at Rachel and asked, "How come you didn't like him?"

Despite Geneva's apparent fussiness about the men she chose to let into her life, she was really only an apprentice in her ability to detect flaws in a body. Rachel had always been the master, and although Geneva had never before fully appreciated her skill since it had often been turned upon her own person, she now was glad to see how Rachel could ply her tongue to avenge her baby sister. In a few moments, she had reduced Howard to the butt of a number of vulgar and hilarious jokes.

"His lisp drove me nuts!" Rachel said.

"No! He doesn't have a lisp!"

"Oh, yes he does. Last time we were there, he kept telling me how 'thweet' he thought you were. 'Oh, you are tho thweet! Tho thpethal!' Lord, I was glad your name wasn't Susan. Can you imagine him calling you his 'thweet Thuthan? Come on, Thweet, Thpecial Thuthan! Thtep down here below me on the thtair tho I won't look tho thort!'"

"You're kidding. I never noticed it."

"Your brain was on hold. Fried, no doubt, from the toxic waste they call air there in the city. And didn't you ever notice his fat rear end?"

"Well, yes, I did notice that it was a little, er —plump," admitted Geneva. She had meant to encourage him to take up jogging or something since her master plan had always included a man with an athletic body. "I guess that's from all that sitting around doing his Wall Street thing."

"That's Wall Thtreet, thweetie," said Rachel, languidly reclining against the arm of the swing." Thoth big invethtorth do have a tendenthy to get big atheth, don't they? And his nose holes were big, too!"

"Nose holes!" You mean nostrils?"

"Nothtrilth, noth holth, who cares? I felt like I was looking up a horse's nose."

Catching Rachel's malice, Geneva corrected, "Horth'th noth."

"Horth'th ath," countered Rachel.

"*Biiiig* horth'th ath," said Geneva, imitating Sylvester the Cat and spraying Rachel with saliva.

"*Thupendouth* horth'th ath," slobbered Rachel. "Jutht a minute. I'm going to get uth thome more wine."

Rachel went into the house and returned with a new bottle of cold wine and six more wineglasses. "I hope you're in the mood to do some sweeping," she announced, "because I am going to make a toast." She splashed a small amount in each of the eight glasses, and very solemnly, she stood and held up the first one.

"Here's to Howard's lithp." She drained the glass and threw it against the side of the house, where it splintered. Then she ceremoniously handed Geneva one of the remaining glasses. She rose and lifted it. "Here's to Howard's fat ath," she intoned, then drank and heaved the glass with her whole, angry self. It crashed resoundingly.

Rachel picked up two more. "Here's to Howard's noth holth. Both of them." Not bothering to drink, she turned and tossed a glass over each shoulder, splashing wine against the wall and littered floor.

"Here's to Howard's lack of integrity." Crash.

"Here's to Howard's inability to recognize a good thing when he sees it." Crash.

"Here's to Howard getting my cat pregnant." Crash.

"*What?*"

"Never mind. You're up."

Rachel cleared her throat, and lifting the final glass, declaimed with dignified authority, "Here's to the total, utter, unredeemable collapse of the stock market!" She drank and drop kicked the glass into the side of the house. They both fell into the swing, hooting and screaming until Rachel grabbed her stomach and begged to stop.

Cleaning the mess took considerably longer than it had taken to create it, but Geneva derived sublime satisfaction as she swept and dumped glass shards. She smiled broadly as she searched for missed splinters. She'd be damned before she let Howard cause her nieces to suffer cut feet.

The following morning, Geneva and Rachel took the children out to gather the eggs and feed the livestock. They watched the horses canter into the pasture, their chestnut flanks and high-bred legs flashing in the sun. Geneva longed to be astride one of them and asked Rachel about riding.

"I can't ride," said Rachel, "since I've gotten so pregnant. For the past few months, our new neighbor, a veterinarian, has been coming over to ride with Wayne a couple of times a week. But I haven't seen him for a while. Maybe he's been too busy. Why don't you and Wayne go out this evening?"

So Geneva began riding every day. With the daily chores, which she found to be considerable, and the exhilarating rides and the summer splendor, she forgot about her wan, pale beauty and began looking vibrant and healthy, though she halfheartedly bemoaned the two extra pounds that had come from nowhere. She hadn't been aware that fresh vegetables could be so fattening. But halfway into the second week, when Rachel and Geneva went to visit Mam-ma Turner, Geneva was pleased when her grandmother, after the appropriate exclamations and hugs, commented on how thin she looked. She did not mention that Geneva was pale, however, so Geneva decided to give up on wan and try for a more wholesome effect.

She put aside the black outfits she had bought in her pique and delved into Rachel's closet for the sunny yellows and poppy reds. Looking in the mirror, she decided that she really did look better than she had three weeks ago, and she hummed to herself as she thought that if Howard could see her now, he would surely fall on his knees and sob into her skirt. *He would suffer for her yet, she determined.*

Yes. She felt her strength returning, returning as surely as the spring thaw fills the banks of the brook.

Two

Geneva settled into Rachel's family as gently and easily as a leaf settling onto a peaceful stream. Once she became acclimated to the business of caring for Rachel's family, she quickly melded into its harmony and rhythms, although she was surprised at the amount and the kind of work Rachel did. Together, the two women stripped the garden of ripened vegetables and spent day after day canning and freezing. Wayne, an earnest, cheerful bear of a man took pains to make Geneva feel welcomed and appreciated, and the girls let their Aunt Geneva know how much they loved having her with them. Every day Rachel's serenity and her joy over the upcoming birth of her babies reminded Geneva of the importance of fundamental life. Geneva was content, but sometimes she found herself thinking about the night Howard proposed to her, and then she would sit by the window, gaze out at the hazy mountains, and sigh.

Three weeks into her visit, just when Geneva was beginning to feel that life had become one long lullaby, Dr. Zhivago came to her looking droopy and coughing badly. As she picked him up, wondering if she should find a veterinarian for him, Esmeralda limped around the corner of the barn on three paws. Blood oozed from her torn left ear. Horrified, Geneva whirled and ran into the house.

"I need a vet," she said breathlessly to Rachel. "Dr. Zhivago sounds like he has pneumonia, and something has attacked Esmeralda and has torn her all to pieces. I knew they shouldn't have slept in that barn, and now I don't even know where the others are. I just hope something hasn't carried them off. Poor babies."

Rachel glanced out at Esmeralda and smiled, remembering how frequently Geneva forgot that she hated her cats. "Let's see," she said unhurriedly. "Today is Friday. John should be in. He's just next door—that is, on the other side of the pasture. He keeps a practice in Tucker, but on Fridays he stays home and opens a clinic at his house. He's a wonderful vet, and I daresay he'll fix them up just fine. You may want to take the kittens, too, for a once-over. Get them wormed and vaccinated." She paused a moment, then added mysteriously, "I think it's time you met him anyway. He's very eligible, and I think you'll find him interesting."

Geneva decidedly was not in the mood to meet any eligible men, interesting or not. All she wanted was to get her poor cats attended to. Certainly she was not in the mood to listen to any treatise on the virtues of the bachelors in the neighborhood. Hillbilly bachelors especially did not interest her. She gave Rachel a withering look, but she merely beamed her big-sister smile again and looking somehow deceitfully benign, calmly explained that while the clinic was within walking distance, it would be easier to carry two critically ill cats and five frisky ones in the car.

It took half an hour of everyone's time to round up the kittens, but after several escape attempts, all the cats were bundled into the Mazda. At last, Geneva roared off, shouting directions to Rachel to find the other cats to make sure they were all right.

The drive lasted perhaps two minutes, but during that time, Geneva managed to invoke a surprising number of possible scenarios that placed her cats in grave danger. Her heart's penchant for drama encouraged her to imagine tragedy, but in her practical mind, she knew they were not really as bad off as she wished they might be. Not that she really wanted them to be sick, but the novelty of returning home was beginning to wear off, and she found herself wanting something... well... kind of exciting to happen. Drifting around the farm with Rachel and the sweet children was certainly charming, and riding the Morgans each evening held its own exhilaration but that was always short-lived. Besides, her energies and artistic temperament demanded more than cooking and canning and waiting for Rachel's babies to arrive. She needed to throw herself into something that would require all of her passionate soul and concentrated energy. So she tried very hard to imagine how grief-stricken she would be if one, or both, of her two beautiful cats died, and then she remembered that two others could be missing as well. *Perhaps even now their poor carcasses had already been gnawed to bits by mountain lions.* A little shiver danced up her spine as she wondered how sympathetic this "wonderful, interesting vet" would be.

The sign on the entry drive said, "John Smith, DVM."

Whoa, thought Geneva. *Prosaic name. He'll have to be exceptional to overcome that!*

She saw him as soon as she pulled into the drive so had the advantage of a good scrutiny well before she got out of the car. He was certainly good looking—tall, clean-limbed, and well muscled, with (unlike Howard) a cute rear end. She had noticed this part of his anatomy first, not because she necessarily looked, of course, but because he happened to be bending over petting some sort of an animal when she first turned into his driveway. The second thing she noticed about him (aside from the broad shoulders, the perfect chin, and the curly, honey-colored hair) was that he was wearing a cast on his right leg from foot to thigh. By the time she stopped her car, she found him interesting enough after all, so that she momentarily forgot her cats, which were at this moment contentedly licking each other's faces.

"Hello," he said, turning and standing to his full height.

Gosh, he looks kind of like the guy in the paper towel commercial, but with a friendlier mouth, Geneva thought. His eyes, Geneva noticed, were beautiful—green, as alive as fire. She stared at him for a long moment before she realized that he was waiting for her to speak. Flustered, she turned to haul out her cats.

"What's the matter with them?" he began, then noticed Esmeralda's ear. "Oh, I see, a torn ear. Poor girl, we'll get you fixed up in just a minute. Let's go into the surgery and have a look at you." He tucked Esmeralda under his arm and strolled to the door of the house, scratching her under her chin. Geneva caught Dr. Zhivago up into her arms as the good doctor called over his (*decidedly broad,* Geneva thought) shoulder for her to follow.

As the veterinarian anesthetized Esmeralda's ear and stitched her up, Geneva watched the process with interest, for the muscles in Dr. Smith's arms had the most charming habit of rippling as he moved his hands. Howard had not had such arms. His had been thin and sinewy, capable in their way, but not flagrantly masculine as these arms were. Geneva lost herself in the contemplation of what those arms might be capable of. Inwardly, she giggled as she found she had constructed an entire trashy romance novel revolving around herself and this gorgeous body who was stitching up her cat. After a while, she began to feel a little guilty for taking such intimate liberties with a total stranger, but the guilt dissipated shortly. He was just a good-looking, good-old boy. Nobody to take seriously, and it certainly did him no harm to appreciate his beautiful physique. She smiled and dropped her eyes, feeling superior and deliciously in control.

He was speaking to her. Geneva dimly perceived that he had said something, "What is her name?"

Oh, he must be referring to the cat in his hands. "Esmeralda," she replied after an extended moment. She really didn't expect him to catch the connection between the cat and her namesake, but he gently stroked the cat's head and said, "Well, Esmeralda, I have a Quasimodo around here someplace. He's a badger, but now that you've got that disfigured ear, maybe you won't be so choosy." He dropped his voice to a loving whisper," and you'll still be a good mom, won't you?"

Geneva was pleasantly surprised. She hadn't met many people with her good taste in literature, fewer still who could recognize the literary implications of her cats' names, and she certainly had not expected any good-old boys from the hills of West Virginia to catch on. She gave the man the benefit of her most delighted smile, but when he returned it, she found herself suddenly and inexplicably flustered. To cover her embarrassment, she asked, "What happened to your leg?'

Looking soberly at the cast, he replied, "Well, I was on an errand of mercy, chasing a runaway horse with a damsel in distress on his back. I got hold of the bridle just as we all jumped a fence and got knocked off and sort of stepped on."

Geneva suddenly came tumbling from her own runaway high horse. Caught completely by surprise that this fellow had just described something similar to what she had just been thinking, she gasped, "Really? How awful!" But really, she meant, *How wonderful!* The thought of a modern paladin, risking life and limb, literally, for a woman on a runaway horse thrilled her to the ends of all her nerves. She had never met anyone in real life who had done such a thing, but ever since she had read *Thundering Love* last year, she had fantasized about being on a huge black stallion, wildly out of control, nearly fainting from the rush of wind, her hair streaming behind her like the subject of a pre-Raphaelite painting. *She would be wearing a floating, white gown. No—something in virginal blue, in layers of silk chiffon cut on the bias, with a tight bodice that would accentuate her heaving breasts. And then from nowhere would come the thunder of galloping hooves, and a tall, broad-chested stranger would encircle her perfect waist with his muscular arm and pluck her lightly from the dangerous steed...* She looked at John Smith more carefully. He certainly was shaping up to be far more interesting than she had expected.

"Well, now," he said briskly, "Esmeralda is all fixed up, practically as good as new. I'm afraid she'll have a bit of a nick in that ear from now on, but that will just be a part of her charm. And what's up with this old boy?" He plucked Dr. Zhivago from Geneva's arms and scratched him under his chin. Dr. Zhivago purred so loudly that Geneva laughed.

"This is Dr. Zhivago," she said proudly, knowing how much this name would be appreciated by the literary veterinarian. "He has a cough, so I thought I'd bring him, too."

The vet's response surprised her. "Well, old chum. You can't help your name, though I daresay you're not much better than the original. Let's listen to your chest here."

Geneva was stung. "What's wrong with his name? I like it."

"Hmm. Actually, now that I think of it, it is a very good name, very fitting for a tom cat."

"What do you mean?" Geneva bristled. Was he making fun of her hero, the man who epitomized the tragedy of unrequited love? She looked at Dr. Smith warily, through narrowed eyes. He could be one of those Rambo types who scoffed at tenderness in a man. If so, she'd have nothing to do with him.

He smiled again. "Dr. Zhivago was an old tom cat himself. Left a perfectly lovely wife and pretty babies and lit out after another woman. Some people think the story is romantic, but I think it's a bunch of claptrap."

"Oh," said Geneva, chastened. She hadn't exactly seen it in that light before now, but she thought rakishly that he sure had a lot of concern over names. Must be because his own was so prosaic.

"I suppose," she said with exaggerated innocence, "that your name means something special?"

"Oh, yes. John Smith," he said proudly and somberly. "Smith is a venerable old name, a proud family, a noble profession. We are the sons of Vulcan, the fearless handlers of the most powerful of elements: fire and steel."

"Right," said Geneva after a pause, wondering if the man were serious. "And what about John?"

"John, beloved of Christ. Saint, apostle, visionary. The steadfast one, but with the greatest gifts." He sighed and shook his head. "I have been burdened with a weighty name."

After another long pause in which Geneva decided it would not be appropriate to giggle, she gave him a sidewise glance and said with a self conscious little smile, "You sure know a lot about names. Mine's a little different. Geneva. Geneva LeNoir," she said, pronouncing it carefully. Of course, she was proud of her (properly pronounced) name. Not as proud as John Smith seemed to be of his, but she did like the sound of it. To her, it sounded exotic and mysterious, made more so by the fact that she had never set foot in the city for which she was named.

"Ah, Geneva." He locked his beautiful eyes upon hers and seemed to look into their depths with what appeared to Geneva an intense longing. It made her mouth water. "Beautiful alpine city, all cool and green," he smiled. "Clean as a glacier. I like that."

"Oh, you've been there?"

"Nope," he said cheerfully. "But it sure provokes the imagination."

She laughed. "What about LeNoir?" she pressed, expecting a discussion about mystery and velvety darkness and midnight passion. She wanted that look again.

He wrinkled his brow. "LeNoir. Noir. Let's see. Blackness. Dark? Hmm. Doesn't much suit you, does it?" Then he brightened. "Well, you can change it when you get married. I believe your cat here has bronchitis."

Geneva was torn between the desire to challenge his abrupt censuring of her name and concern over her cat. She felt more inclined to continue with the name issue, but John Smith obviously had turned his attention to Dr. Zhivago and was asking her questions about how long he had been coughing, and whether he had been out at night. He gave him a shot of antibiotics and gave her some pills to administer, then he leaned pleasantly against the counter and offered Geneva a cup of coffee.

She didn't quite know how to respond. John Smith made her feel full of contradictory emotions. On the one hand, he seemed to personify the literary (and her own) ideal: honorable, romantic, dashing, and handsome. Yet, he had glibly insulted her twice over something that seemed trifling but in such a way as to thoroughly rile her. The worst part of it was that she couldn't think of a single comeback to sting him as smartly as she would like. So she accepted the coffee, then looked for an opportunity to needle him, perhaps embarrass him for his impudence. She wondered how he would fare if she declared outright war.

She gave him a steely smile. "What makes you think I'm not married?" *Ha!* Now he would have to admit to looking at her left hand, which meant she had caught him thinking about her in a less-than-professional way. She hoped he would blush.

"I asked your sister two weeks ago," he replied cheerily.

"I beg your pardon?"

"Yep. Saw you riding one evening and fell flat in love with you first thing. The way the sunlight fell on your hair gave you a halo, and I thought you were the most wonderful thing since penicillin. I went straight to the phone and called Rachel and asked her who that beauty was riding on Fairhope. She told me all about you." He looked straight at her and grinned.

Geneva was the one to blush. Normally she relished such compliments from men, but this man made her uncomfortable. He was too big, too handsome, too straightforward, too—everything. She realized that she was not in charge after all, and she was feeling more and more certain that she probably would not take charge today. She directed her attention to the kittens to change the subject.

"These little guys were born eight weeks ago. I brought them in for all the necessary shots and such," she said briskly, lifting each of the kittens from the basket. "This one is Simone, and the feisty one here is Scarlet. And these are the Three Stooges. Larry and Moe, and the fat one, of course, is Curly Joe."

John Smith laughed. "Interesting choices," he said, then fell silent as he examined and vaccinated them. When he tried to replace them in their basket, they became uncooperative, so Geneva helped him, then closed the lid and swiftly scooted toward the car.

But before she got there, Larry and Curly Joe got out, clinging precariously to the outside edge of the basket before they flopped to the ground and fled. Geneva stamped her foot and started to swear at them, but noticing Dr. Smith chuckling, she threw her head back and smiled saucily.

"I'm afraid you have just inherited two kittens, Dr. Smith, unless you want to go under the house and get them out. They're half wild by now, because they've been living in Rachel's barn since we got here." That ought to wipe the grin off his face!

The vet remained leaning against the doorway and drawled, "Well, okay, but I hate to break up the set. Can I have Moe, too?"

Geneva tried not to gape. Was he really willing to take three of her cats? She paused a moment, collecting her thoughts so she could reply casually. He might change his mind if she followed her first impulse to squeal and jump up and down.

Apparently he misunderstood her silence, for he continued, "I need some mousers around here, and I figured you really didn't need this many cats, especially since Esmeralda will be giving you a new batch in a week or so."

"What?" said Geneva in a small voice? "Esmeralda?"

"Sure," he smiled. "You mean you didn't know?"

"No," she said faintly. There was a silence while she counted backwards. *Damn that Howard!* "I always kept her in."

"Well, I'm reasonably certain she's pregnant. Congratulations."

An uncomfortable image leapt into her mind. She saw herself as the victim in an Ionesco play, surrounded by cats, inundated, suffocated by cats, meowing, purring, hissing, scratching cats. Hundreds of them, burgeoning and growing bigger until they popped, spewing more cats out in every direction. "Rats," she muttered, eyes dilated.

"Does that mean I can have Moe, too?"

"Yes," she replied, breathing hard. "How much do I owe you?"

"Let's call it an even swap. But this will be the last time," he warned. "I usually don't accept kittens in exchange for services."

Geneva picked up Esmeralda, who was rubbing against her

legs, probed her stomach gently, and she did feel the swelling there. Carefully, she pushed the cat through the half open car window and placed her beside the basket.

"This womanizer needs to come back in a week so I can check him again," Dr. Smith said as he lightly gathered up Dr. Zhivago and tucked him under his arm. "Esmeralda should come, too and I'll take out the stitches." He walked awkwardly to the car. "Just call me Richard the Third," he added, apologizing for his halting walk with a wink. "I'll grow a hump next week. I bet you'd like that."

Surprised and a little riled at his misplaced intimacy, his insinuation that he knew what she liked, and piqued about the new information concerning Esmeralda's impending multiplication, Geneva straightened her back and said good-bye to him with as much dignity as she could muster, then used her practiced walk getting to the driver's side. She had intended to appear regal and confident, but the effect was lost on John, who raced ahead of her as well as he was able in order to open the door for her.

What a bizarre man! He seemed so contradictory, flickering between solemnity, gallantry, lightheartedness, and what seemed like mockery. But her distrust of him vanished as he reached across her to claim Moe and gave her a radiant smile, his marvelous eyes once again turned upon hers. Geneva thought he looked as if a laurel wreath belonged on his head. His face was very close, so close she could smell his skin, clean and real. It reminded her of the smell of spring rain and a warm, dry hayloft. Geneva could swear she fibrillated. She felt herself grow warm and dizzy, then once again she blushed, angry with herself for appearing so foolish.

Violently, she cranked up the car, intending to cavalierly spin out of the drive; unfortunately, the car died before she could get her foot onto the accelerator, then it lurched drunkenly forward and died again on her next attempt. She finally got the car going, and drove rather sedately and sheepishly down the driveway, cringing in her humiliation and watching John Smith in her rear view mirror the whole way. She didn't notice that she had veered off the drive until she had driven into the ditch flanking the main road.

It was impossible to discreetly extricate herself; with a sinking stomach and with hot chills working their way down to her fingers and toes she got out of the car and watched as John Smith hobbled toward her, his white cast swinging out in a wide arc with each step he took, his arms flailing upwards as the arc reached out and downward as it swung in again. Even in her humiliation, Geneva saw the absurdity of their situation, and she began to laugh. At first it was only a suppressed snort, but the closer John grew, the funnier he looked, with his earnest face growing larger with each ridiculously balance step, so that she began to laugh outright. She held her sides and threw back her head, and all but pointed at him as he came closer and closer.

"Laugh all you want," he grinned at her. "Meanwhile, Esmeralda and Tomfoolery are absconding."

Geneva whirled in time to see the cats darting off through the pasture toward home. Simone and Scarlet were trying to wriggle out the half-open window to join them. Dr. Zhivago did not look nearly as peaked as he had earlier in the morning.

John began to laugh, too, and the two people who had been strangers, awkward at their first introduction, stood gasping helplessly, pointing at each other, at the car in the ditch, and at the long-since disappeared cats. Geneva felt as if a door were opening and she was standing on the threshold of something startling new and fresh. The misty morning air hummed and danced around her, and the silvery light swarmed with energy, sweeping her up and making her feel drunk with exhilaration. *There was something to this John Smith*, she decided. She would get to know him better. For the moment, she had forgotten that other guy's name.

"Come on," he said. "I'll tow you out with my Jeep." And then, much to her relief, for she was still embarrassed at her incompetence behind the wheel, he added gently, "That ditch is an awful problem. I've driven into it a couple of times myself."

Geneva walked slowly beside John, trying not to giggle at his ungainly stride, and suddenly she felt awkward again, caring very much that she might say the right thing. So far, everything he had said to her had taken her off balance, and she was more afraid than ever of sounding foolish. All the façades she had so carefully cultivated over the years, the masks among which she instinctively could pick to impress a variety of people, had mercilessly deserted her. She did not know whether to flirt, to be coy or shy, or bold or frank. For the first time in her life she was afraid to open her mouth.

John was quiet, too. She kept giving him sideways glances, but noticed only that he seemed uncomfortable with his damaged leg. She began to feel guilty that she may have caused him to hurt it again, and then she wondered who the woman was that he had rescued. Perhaps she should not be so capable astride a horse in the future.

"I hope you didn't hurt your leg running like that. Shouldn't you use a crutch or something?"

"Well, to tell the truth, I guess I shouldn't be running on it. But it's pretty close to mended by now."

"Just can't keep from running after a damsel in distress, can you?"

"Like a moth to the flame."

After John's Jeep had pulled the car out of the ditch, he waved at her and called out the window, "See you in a week, provided you catch them."

"Thanks," Geneva replied. "They're probably back at the ranch by now." She drove off carefully, not caring to repeat her earlier attempts at a dramatic exit. All she wanted to do now was to think about the way she felt when John Smith leaned close and looked at her, smelling so warm and alive. She remembered with a smile the fact he had said he loved her.

Geneva liked the notion of men being in love with her, and in fact, had pretty much become an expert at finding ways to coax such admissions from them. She had always had admirers, usually several of them at a time, and had always enjoyed watching them jockey for position among themselves, challenging one another like boyish rivals over a rich prize. Geneva understood that the games she played with them often made her seem superficial, particularly to less beautiful women, but it had never bothered her enough to stop her from playing them. Until Howard, she had never really given her heart to any of them. Perhaps that's why he had been so attractive—he had been so damn hard to get—and why his desertion had wounded her so severely.

Of course, this business of love at first sight was only a joke. She had learned long ago not to become too excited over such pretended gallantry. Once a gorgeous Canadian actor named Terrance had asked her to marry him immediately after they were introduced. She had been flattered, even though she knew he was jokingly referring to the green card she would be able to provide for him. She had made light of it, but secretly she had toyed with the idea of getting a real proposal from him (at that time in her more frivolous past, she had been keeping an informal tally of proposals). To that end, she had flirted outrageously with him for a week before a mutual friend gently pulled her aside and informed her that Terrance was homosexual.

Yes, she sighed, *Renaissance poets may have believed in love at first sight, but modern men only make jokes about it.* Still, it might be fun to see if she could make John Smith stop joking and love her, not seriously, of course, but enough for an interesting diversion while she recovered from Howard's treachery. She began humming to herself as she drove into Rachel's driveway.

The children were playing with the runaway cats when she arrived. Rachel came from the house with flour on her hands, her golden hair pulled up into a loose braid, and Geneva could not help but hope that she was as pretty as her older sister. Craftily, she wondered how well Rachel knew John Smith. She got out of the car smiling.

"Well, what did you think of the good doctor?" asked Rachel, barely suppressing a smirk.

"He's exasperating, but cute, and he kept the Three Stooges," returned Geneva. "And why didn't you tell me the two of you have been talking about me behind my back?"

"Oh, I didn't want to influence your first impression. I thought you might like him. Come on in the house and tell me all about it. By the way, your cats showed up five minutes ago."

Geneva was eager to talk about John Smith, DVM, more eager still to find out more about him. She decided to get the facts straight first. "He's not gay, by any chance, is he?" she asked offhandedly. No use turning herself inside out for a man with suspicious tendencies.

"Good grief, no! He's been seen with half the women in the county, and the other half is lined up waiting their turn. Gosh, I thought he'd be just your type. What makes you think he's gay?" Rachel was visibly disturbed.

"Oh, no reason. I just wondered. Lots of eligible men are." Geneva did not wish to pursue this line of conversation and be forced to explain her folly concerning Terrance the actor. "He has a broken leg. I guess that's why he hasn't been riding."

"Oh, yes, I know, but he said he hopes he can go riding with you when it's healed, you lucky thing."

"Well," Geneva replied ruefully. "I guess I'll have to work on being a little more helpless if we do."

"What do you mean?"

"He didn't tell you how he broke it?"

Rachel looked at her slyly. "What did he tell you?"

"That he was rescuing some woman on a runaway and took a fence badly. Have you ever heard of anything more romantic?" For the first time, Geneva allowed her sister to see how interesting she found Dr. Smith to be.

Rachel gave her a strange smile. "Oh. Yes. That is romantic." She looked off toward the mountains, and smiled again, murmuring, "Yes, he's very good." She turned conspiratorially. "Well! Why don't we do something about getting the two of you together? Shall we hatch a plot?"

Geneva laughed. Like herself, Rachel also was an incorrigible matchmaker and schemer who had no scruples about arranging and rearranging situations and facts if it meant that somebody, particularly if that somebody happened to be one of themselves, might end up in more interesting or advantageous circumstances.

"You're awful!" laughed Geneva. "Remember how we stalked Wayne for a month so that you could 'accidentally on purpose' run into him up on Jacob's Mountain?"

"It worked," beamed Rachel. "There's magic on that mountain, I tell you, and I bet if we could get you up there with John… Well! Just wait until I drop these twins before you walk down the aisle. I want to look good in the pictures."

Geneva hugged her sister, simultaneously chiding her for her unabashed attempts to manipulate Geneva into moving back home permanently. Still, she appreciated Rachel's line of thinking; besides, after Howard, she felt she needed a boost. John Smith might prove to be rather fun.

After dinner that evening, Geneva and Wayne went for their usual sunset ride while Rachel put the children to bed. When the riders returned, Rachel was sitting at the loom, working in subtle reds.

"Hi," she said, absorbed in the pattern. "Did you have a good ride?"

"Yes, but we missed you," replied her husband as he rubbed her shoulders and nuzzled her hair. Geneva remembered when Rachel had decided that Wayne was "The One" and had gone to astonishing lengths to get his attention. At that time, Wayne was a shy, quiet, gangly man, not comfortable with his own body and less comfortable with women. He had just moved into the area to join a practice in Tucker, and Rachel, already attracted to him for reasons no one could fathom, had determined to marry him when she discovered how much he liked babies and horses. Rachel recruited Geneva, and together they devoted an entire summer to snaring him, although it had turned out to be more difficult than they anticipated. Wayne had been distant with Rachel, perhaps frightened by her beauty, perhaps too busy to notice that she was pursuing him.

But Rachel had honed in on him as confidently as queen to drone, and the poor man never knew Rachel's plans for him until he was at the brink of the hive. Geneva smiled to herself. *There must have been some magic up on Jacob's mountain.* Within a year after his "accidental" meeting with Rachel, Wayne had been transformed into a confident, loving husband, and he seemed to grow more contented as his family grew larger. Geneva did not want to spend her life turning out a brood of children up here in these hills, but she sure wanted what Rachel and Wayne shared. If only Howard would come to his senses…

No, it is too late for that, she decided morosely. *In fact, there's probably no one out there who will be to me what Wayne is to Rachel.* The exhilaration of the morning's meeting with John Smith turned to bitter, choking dust in her heart, and she turned her head away from the nuzzling couple, mourning for her lost future.

But early the next Friday, the day she was to return her cats to John's office, Geneva woke, surprised at how warm and excited she felt at the prospect of seeing the handsome veterinarian again. She had spent some days lecturing herself about the irresponsibility of her unbridled dreams of the week before and had told herself that she had outgrown her infantile desire to collect men's hearts like a string of trophies. But today those self-chastising thoughts evaporated as she washed her hair and dressed.

Oh, you're baaaad, she hummed to herself, thinking about how much fun it was going to be to flirt with the guy down the road. She actively calculated the strength of her arsenal as she rounded the cats into her car. She knew John liked her hair, so she would show up early, while the sun was still low enough to shine straight through it and show off all the gold. Confident of her beauty, she now wondered what it would take to make John think she was witty and bright as well. She went through her memory for jokes about animals, weighing them, determining which ones were clean enough to tell.

As she slipped behind the wheel, Rachel gave her a wink and a smile and said with mock innocence, "He likes spunky women."

"What are you grinning about?"

"Just thinking about Jacob's mountain."

"Rachel, you cut that out. You know I have no intentions of luring that poor man up there. What would I do with him after I caught him? Can you see a country veterinarian in Washington, DC?"

"I'm sure you'd think of something. You always were able to manage dichotomies. And duplicities," she muttered under her breath.

"I heard that!" yelled Geneva out the window as she cranked up the car.

When she arrived at John's house, Geneva found a note on the door stating that he had been called out and would be back by eight o'clock. Since it was nearly that time now, she decided to wait for him. She glanced back at the cats lolling in the back seat preparing themselves for a nap, then she got out of the car, leaving the windows down so they could enjoy the cool. She wandered around the yard, admiring the pearly morning, the dew-laden Black-Eyed Susans, and the blue chicory growing with exuberance along the fencerow. She breathed the flavor of the honeysuckle, then peeked into the outbuildings, the office, and then, after a half-moment's struggle with her conscience, decided to check out the main house where John obviously lived.

There was a large window that might look into the living room, but it was high, and enormous holly bushes grew densely in front of it. Undaunted, Geneva mounted the porch steps, then swung her legs over the railing. She stood on the outer edge of the porch, hung on to the rail, and leaned out far enough to peep through the window.

The view was both more and less than she expected. She had thought she would see something of some masculine luxury, like a lazy boy recliner and a big television, but this room was spare and minimally furnished with Shaker furniture and a sisal rug on the hardwood floor. A plain bookcase brimming with books stood against one wall; two simple prints of English hunting dogs graced another wall. There was one large potted schefflera in the south window, but nothing more. There were no curtains. It was a nice beginning, she decided, clean and unpretentious, but much too Spartan, and it needed softening. Some sort of window treatments and more furniture—maybe a better bookcase. Pillows, an oriental rug for more warmth… Geneva became lost in what she would do to make the room more attractive and interesting. Slowly, insidiously, a Master Plan began to take shape in her head.

She tried to push it away, telling herself that the last thing in the world she wanted was to be the wife of a hillbilly veterinarian, but no sooner did she find the two halves of her mind in agreement over this than she began remembering John's eyes and wishing that the man they belonged to belonged to her. Finally, she gave up the battle and allowed herself to indulge in the game of Siamese Twins, which she often played whenever she felt twinges of homesickness.

In the Siamese Twins game, Geneva fantasized that she was two people with different bodies but whose minds were interconnected. One of them could be home among her restful green hills; the other would go about her daily work and continue her climb in social and artistic circles in the city. Each could enjoy the experiences of the other, and they even occasionally might change places. They were so identical that no one could tell them apart. The country twin would go to the city for a bit of excitement; the city twin would come home to rest and ride and enjoy solitude among the craggy rocks. Geneva delighted in the game, frequently diverting her mind to it no matter where she happened to be, but particularly in traffic and in crowded elevators, and although she knew she was silly to indulge in such an impossible fantasy, it often seemed to be the only thing to keep her going the days she felt overwhelmed by the suffocating noise of the city.

Today she imagined that she was the country twin who happened to be married to a handsome veterinarian who read sonnets aloud to her in the evenings after they had returned from a thrilling ride on half-wild horses. *They would make love in front of the fireplace, and her hair, the same color as the flames, would splay out over the carpet, and the scent of jasmine and sweet olive would perfume that air. She would...*

Suddenly, she heard a car turn into the driveway. Panic rose up like a hot hand and grabbed her stomach, jolting her so violently that Geneva lost her grip on the rail and fell to the soft, damp earth. Falling through the holly, she caught her elbow on something hard and pointed on the way down. With pain searing her arm, a moment or two passed while she gasped and writhed on the muddy ground before she managed to collect herself enough to scramble behind the bush. She crouched there watching John's Jeep approach. As the immediate pain began to subside, her mind clicked into focus. First she thanked God that she had worn a green shirt, then she pulled her bright hair back, tucking it into her collar. With a pounding heart, she made herself as small as she could and focused her attention on the man who stood barely ten feet away.

John was looking at her car, then he turned and surveyed the yard area calling, "Ms. LeNoir?" Geneva hunkered down lower, underarms stinging from sweat screaming to get out through the antiperspirant, and watched him hobble directly toward her. She held her breath momentarily, releasing it carefully only when he seemed to change his mind and walked back to her car. After he circled it once, he looked up again, searching the horizon.

"Ms. LeNoir? Geneva? Are you around here?" Geneva prayed, shutting her eyes tightly and promising all manner of things to the Almighty if He would just get her out of this mess. She pushed away the fog threatening to cloud her mind long enough to formulate a plan, then she sat back and waited for a miracle.

It happened. John walked around the side of the house. As he passed out of view, Geneva made her break, ignoring the claws of the holly in her hair and across her face. After a moment of panic, she cleared the bushes and dashed for the car. Breathing hard, she yanked open the car door, grabbed the sleeping Dr. Zhivago, then ran madly toward the open field. She ran as low and as fast as she could while looking over her shoulder for sight of John. By the time he came into view again, she had made it about twenty-five yards, well into an exuberant thicket of brambles. Immediately she turned and stood, then casually began making her way back toward him.

"There you are!" he called. "I thought that was your car." He hobbled toward her, then stopped, surprise and shock in his face. Fearing the worst, she looked down at herself to ascertain what kind of damage she had sustained to cause his reaction. It was not a pretty sight: a large tear had left a hole in the arm of her shirt; blood oozed from her elbow, and her hands were scratched and dirty. Her pale linen shorts were caked with dirt, and more blood ran down from the scratches on her legs. Slowly she became aware that she was gasping for breath and that her heart was pounding. She gave a little moan when she realized that she was also sweating.

"Good grief, what happened to you?" exclaimed John. Geneva concluded that her face must look awful, too. Frantically she searched her brain for a way to make the lie convincing.

"Dr. Zhivago got away from me and took out toward home. I, uh, chased him, and, uh, tripped. I think I must have landed on something hard," she concluded lamely, looking woefully at her wounded elbow.

"Oh, you poor thing," said John, but his eyes showed admiration. "But I'll be darned if you didn't catch the cat and hang onto him. You've really got spunk." He beamed at her with frank pleasure. "Come on, let me help you into the house and see if there's anything I can do. Here. He can find his own way home, and we'll look at him later." He lifted Dr. Zhivago from her arms and set him down, then he took her good arm and gently led her toward his house. When Geneva realized how close a call she'd had, she began to tremble. Black spots swam before her eyes; she felt so dizzy that she stumbled through the long, golden grass.

"Careful. Goodness, you're awfully pale. Does it hurt bad?" John looked at her compassionately.

She managed a weak smile. Thank God for the injury. It

explained her distress. "It does hurt some. I guess I feel a little lightheaded."

"Do you think you can make it back to the house? You can lie down there, and I'll take a look at the arm." He tried to put an arm around her waist, but his bulky cast came between them and prevented them from walking. Then he tried to support her from the other side, but she winced when he touched her injured arm.

"Aren't we a pair," he laughed. I think the least you could do is tear up the other arm. How am I supposed to rescue if you if I can't get near you?"

Geneva began to recover. There was no suspicion in his wonderful green eyes, and she realized that an unparalleled opportunity shimmered before her. *If John liked spunk, he'd get it.* She put on her brave face and said cheerfully, but with a hint of expressed pain, "We'll just hobble back together. I can make it— it's just a few scratches."

As John took her hand, she became aware of his scent again and felt a sudden and powerful desire to bury her face in his neck and hair. The country twin relaxed. She began to enjoy this moment of victory as she felt her smooth palm press against John's work-rough one.

But her smug confidence splintered when, just as they negotiated the steps to the porch, she glanced off to the right where she had fallen. There, halfway between the porch and the ground, was a nail sticking out of the wood siding. On that nail was a square of bright green linen, exactly the same shade of Geneva's shirt. She stumbled again.

"Hang on, we're almost there," said John, carefully guiding her through the front door. "Let's go into the kitchen. You can sit down and we can take a look at that arm, wash it off a bit."

In the kitchen, he gave her a drink of cold water and sat down to see to her elbow, but when he touched her, his hands, so capable and gentle with the cats, suddenly shook and looked too big and cumbersome upon her slender arm. He tried, awkwardly, to push the snug sleeve of her shirt up above her elbow, and after one unsuccessful attempt, his face clouded. "I'm just bumbling here," he said sadly. I can cut it off just above your elbow here, or if you like, I can give you a shirt to put on—that is, if you think you can get this off by yourself.

Geneva hesitated to consider her options. What she really wanted was a shower and a mirror. It was embarrassing to have all this sweat, grime, and blood all over her, and she knew she looked frightful. On the other hand, her elbow really did hurt enough to make her dread the prospect of driving the half mile back to Rachel's house. If she could get John to drive her back, that would get her home and keep him away from his house, or more precisely, from the sight of the green linen fragment stuck to his house.

"This is my favorite shirt," she lied. "I'd like to mend it if possible, but I don't think I can get it off by myself. Would you mind driving me back to Rachel's house?"

"Of course. I should have thought of that. I could call Wayne to meet us, and he can look at your arm. Are you strong enough to walk?"

"Certainly," she said brightly, giving him her hand and letting him guide her back out the door. She carefully diverted his attention as they passed the fateful nail.

Rachel gasped when she saw Geneva's disheveled appearance. "Geneva! What happened?"

John answered for her. "She chased Dr. Zhivago through the field and fell on something. Looks like she's hurt her elbow pretty badly."

Noting her scratched face and legs, Rachel queried, "What did you land in, a blackberry thicket?" but Geneva stopped her with a grimace. There was an old family joke Geneva did not particularly want to hear at this moment. It concerned one Fourth of July family picnic when Geneva was learning to water-ski and had planned a dramatic landing by holding onto the tow rope until the last moment so she could glide right onto shore for a dry landing. Unfortunately, she forgot to let go of the rope until she had skied well inland and through a blackberry thicket. Ever since that day, everyone in the whole damn clan had joked about her being accident prone. Every time she showed up with a Band-Aid on her knee, they asked her how she liked her blackberries.

"Ow, this hurts, Rachel," she said, trying to elicit enough sympathy so that Rachel would stop with the blackberry bit. "Would you help me into the house?"

Once in the bathroom, Geneva took one look into the mirror and wailed softly, "Oh, Rachel, I look like an ad for World Vision. Some impression I must be making on John!" Her golden hair was streaked with cobwebs and mud, and her face was pale, dirty, and covered with scratches. There was a network of dried blood on her once-beautiful legs.

"You'll look better once you're cleaned up and you get some makeup on. Besides, those welts will clear up by tomorrow. But what on earth happened?" Rachel asked as she peeled off Geneva's shirt.

Geneva told the whole miserable story in whispered gasps, ending it with, "So you've got to get over there and get that piece of my shirt off that nail while John's over here."

"Geneva, I can't do that," hissed Rachel. "In case you haven't noticed, I'm seven months pregnant with *twins!* I'm not supposed to walk fast, let alone run over and climb behind some bushes to rescue a little bitty piece of your shirt. If you couldn't get out of there without tearing yourself all to pieces, how do you expect me to get this through?" She slapped at her belly.

"Okay, okay. Maybe I can run back over there if you can keep him occupied."

"Geneva, you're crazy. If he catches you sneaking across the field, he'll really think something's up. You've led him to believe that your elbow is all busted up."

"Well, what can I do?" whispered Geneva, turning on the bath water. "If he sees it, he'll figure it out. Oh, Rachel, why didn't I tell him I was chasing the cat off the porch?"

"Why didn't you refrain from peeping into his house in the first place? Geneva, you're awful."

"No worse than you." Irritated and humiliated, Geneva fought back. "You remember the time you stole the 'Dear John' letter of out of Jimmy Kramer's mailbox when you changed your mind after you mailed it?"

"That was my letter. I was only getting it back," flared Rachel.

"It was a federal offense," retorted Geneva.

Rachel got prissy. "Well, you should talk. I remember the time you picked Carole Summerland's locker so you could put a snake in there just because she wouldn't admit to having fouled you in a basketball game, and you got a technical because you stomped on her foot."

"I was fourteen years old, Rachel, and we lost the championship because of that technical, which you and I both know I didn't deserve. Besides, you sure put your share of frogs and snakes in people's beds," hissed Geneva, remembering a few slithery reptiles between her own cool sheets on summer nights. She finished stripping and stepped into the tub.

"All right, Geneva," sighed Rachel. "You finish your bath, and I'll drive over there while you keep John busy. You can manage that, can't you? And if I miscarry right there in the holly bushes, it'll be all your fault."

"Oh, never mind," grumbled Geneva, trying to lather her hair with one hand. "Maybe I can sneak over there tonight when no one can see me, that is, if he doesn't notice it before then. I couldn't stand the guilt of premature twins."

Rachel put her hands into the suds, scouring Geneva's head with her nails. "How bad is your elbow anyway? Can't you lift your arm?"

There was a knock on the door. "Is everything all right? Do you think I should call Wayne?" came John's voice.

"Oh, gosh, hurry, up," said Rachel. "Here you are, supposed to have a broken elbow, and you're taking a beauty bath, having your hair done."

"Rachel, tell him not to call Wayne," whispered Geneva through gritted teeth.

"How's the arm?" John asked, the anxiety evident in his voice.

"Just a minute, John," called Rachel sweetly. "We're checking it out now." She turned to Geneva and lowered her voice. "Let me see your elbow," she whispered, grabbing Geneva's arm and twisting it around to look at it. Geneva shrieked with pain.

Just outside the door, John responded, "I'm going to call him."

"No!" came Rachel's quick reply. "I don't think he needs to come. Just a minute, and we'll let you look at it." She prodded gently at the injured elbow. Geneva winced.

"Geneva, it does look pretty bad. It's still bleeding, too. You'll probably have to get stitches. Do you think it might be broken?"

"I don't think so, but I hope it's sprained at least. The way I carried on, I hope it's everything short of broken, or John will think I'm an awful wimp."

John's anxious voice came through the door again, "Rachel? Geneva? How is it?"

"We'll be right out, John," called Rachel. "Geneva's getting cleaned up. I think we might ought to get some stitches, though."

Geneva finished her bath quickly, but insisted on putting on some makeup before she faced John again. The scratches and welts on her face refused to be concealed, however, so she gave up and came out for Rachel and the animal doctor to prod at her arm and murmur together over it. John thought it might be chipped, but Rachel believed it was only sprained. They agreed, however, that it needed stitches, so they bandaged the area, then John insisted on driving her to the hospital.

As they made their way down the front steps, she gave one last, appealing glance at Rachel, who, suddenly experiencing a change of heart, sidled up to her sister to whisper, "Don't worry about a thing. I'll take care of everything while you're gone."

"I love you, Rachel," sighed Geneva.

John behaved very nicely while Geneva was admitted to the hospital, opening doors for her, looking concerned and appropriately ruffled. He insisted on staying with her as they wheeled her into the emergency room, pretending to be an important person in her life, and then he sat by her bed and stroked her head, told her jokes, compared injuries, and made up funny stories she could tell people about how she hurt her arm.

"Of course you don't want to tell anyone you tripped while chasing a cat," he insisted. "You won't get any fun out of that. You could tell them you were tangling with a mountain lion, or how about you got in a fight with a guy in a pool hall who wouldn't pay up his bet with you."

Geneva giggled, feeling a little cocky. "I'm going to say I fell off your front porch, and then I'll sue the pants off you," she said recklessly. "Where's a lawyer when you need one?"

John brightened, then laughed suddenly and leaned toward her, his eyes dancing as if he was about to tell her a secret. Geneva bit her lip, wondering if he had caught on to her deception. But before he could speak, Wayne walked in with his best friend, Joe Fuller, the plastic surgeon Geneva knew well. He and his beautiful wife had been to the house for dinner a couple of weeks earlier. Joe was amusing, but overbearing, with something of a God complex. Geneva thought she liked him, provided he really was kidding, as he seemed to be every time he opened his mouth. He had a licentious tongue, which she found both funny and obnoxious.

"Hi, Geneva. What have you done to yourself?" asked Wayne. "Rachel says you busted up your elbow pretty badly and will need stitches. I brought Joe just in case."

"Yes, only the best will do when it comes to your delectable elbow, you gorgeous piece of work. If it has to be violated with stitches, best to let me be the one."

Geneva groaned. "Oh, Lord, will somebody shut this guy up? The last thing I need is for you to be coming on to me when I'm in pain."

"Don't look at me," replied Wayne. "I can't do a thing with him, and he keeps trying to seduce Rachel right in front of me. You wouldn't know the guy was married to the most gorgeous woman in the universe."

"You leave my gorgeous wife out of this, Wayne," said Joe

mildly. "This is just my bedside manner."

"That's what I'm afraid of," replied Wayne.

"Oh, tsk tsk tsk," murmured Joe as he peered at Geneva's elbow with a magnifying glass. "But it looks clean." He let the magnifying glass rove over Geneva's upper arm, then across her shoulder and toward her breasts. Geneva slapped his hand away.

"Cut that out! Are you going to stitch me up or leer at me?"

"Can't I do both? I do my best work leering."

Geneva looked at John with mock pleading. "Can't you do something? You're bigger than he is."

Joe snatched a scalpel off a tray and brandished it. "Don't even think about it. I'm so quick with this scalpel that you won't know what's been altered until it's too late. Now stand back and watch me ply my most excellent trade. Geneva, too bad stitches in this elbow are all you need. I'm wasted here."

John crossed his arms. "Sorry, Geneva. Last time I tangled with him, he threatened to turn me into Miss America," he said, shuddering and putting his hand to his forehead in mock horror. "It was horrible. I spent six months in therapy over it."

As it turned out, Geneva's arm was very badly sprained, *thank goodness,* and Joe put in eight tiny, neat stitches. She also had to get a tetanus shot. Joe offered to do the deed, claiming that his offer had nothing to do with getting a glimpse of her "beautiful peach of a behind." She bore it all bravely, with a pale smile and an occasional witticism. John never left her side, praising her stoicism and her cheerfulness, and when they were left alone again, Geneva caught him looking at her strangely, as if he wanted to say something but felt too shy. She felt her confidence building, and before the morning was out and they were returning to the mountain, she felt that she had evened the score between them. If he had won the first round at their initial meeting, she certainly had won this one. She sat back and smiled up at the white, sudsy clouds floating in the perfectly blue sky. It was going to be in interesting game.

When they returned that afternoon, Geneva's car sat quietly in the driveway, and Rachel was relaxing serenely on the front porch, sipping iced tea, surrounded by all of Geneva's cats. She and Wayne were waiting for them and had already prepared a lunch of fresh gazpacho and turkey sandwiches. Geneva sat down ravenously, happy in the knowledge that John surely liked her, and after lunch her smile brightened considerably when Rachel pulled her into the kitchen conspiratorially, to flourish a small, green fragment of fabric. Geneva hugged her sister, her eyes sparkling with mirth, then she returned to the dining room to flirt with John.

After a delightful hour, Wayne went back to work and John prepared to leave as well, explaining that he should get back to his clinic. He asked Geneva to walk with him to his car, and as she matched her stride to his, she hoped he would take the opportunity to ask her out. After all, she felt that after what she had been through today, she deserved a romantic evening. Unfortunately, John's mind suddenly seemed to be turned to his patients.

"I know your arm is hurting," he said, "so I need to get out of here. But I intend to come over tomorrow and check on your cats."

Geneva started to protest that her elbow did not hurt nearly as much as he imagined, but she bit her tongue. Better to let him see how bravely she bore her suffering. So she cradled her arm and smiled wanly. "Would you do that? That's awfully sweet of you."

"It's the least I can do, considering you hurt yourself in my field."

"You mean wrestling with your mountain lion, in your pool hall."

"Which happens to be on my front porch."

"OK. You come check my cats and I won't sue you. But watch it from now on, buddy. I don't cotton to mountain lions running loose in the pool halls I frequent. Runs down the reputation of the joint."

"It was an accident, ma'am. From now on, I'll make sure Wild Joe and the other critters don't try to hustle you. They didn't know you was quality folk."

"You do that," she laughed, then thanked him again for rescuing her and walked slowly into the house. She had him figured out, she thought triumphantly. He likes smart, spunky women, and she had already impressed him. *From now on, she would play this role to the hilt, and consequently, play this good looking rube like a fiddle.* She bet herself that tomorrow he would ask her for a date.

Three

The next day, John returned before lunchtime to round the cats onto the porch and examine them. Evangeline's pregnancy was progressing nicely, he declared, and he added that the Three Stooges were fit and happy in their new home. They had already been neutered, too, so Geneva could stop worrying.

Geneva was not worried about the cats. At this moment, she was more concerned about figuring out a way to entice John to stay a little longer. He picked up Dr. Zhivago to listen to his chest, and suddenly, his face sobered and darkened. Pressing his fingers along the side of Dr. Zhivago's neck, he cocked his head as if listening or thinking hard.

Geneva's heart plunged. "What is it?" she demanded.

"I'm not sure," said John slowly, his forehead furrowed with concentration as he withdrew a blood pressure cuff from his medical bag. Solemnly and deliberately, he wrapped the cuff, which seemed absurdly large for the cat, around and around Dr. Zhivago's foreleg and pumped it up. Geneva watched anxiously as he placed his stethoscope against the cat's paw and listened intently.

"What is it?" queried Geneva again, her voice a little unsteady.

"Oh, nothing really… uuhm. Dr. Zhivago seems to have a little blood pressure problem."

"*Blood pressure?*"

"Not bad, just a little high. What have you been feeding him?"

"Regular cat food. And I bet he catches things around the barn." She wondered guiltily if mice and frogs were bad for cats.

"Hmm." Pause. "Hmm," again. "Well, that shouldn't cause it. May be a fluke. Tell you what, I'll come back tomorrow evening and check again. His bronchitis seems to be gone, though."

"Oh, will you? Thank you! What do you think it is? Will he be all right?"

"I'm certain he'll be fine. Really, nothing to worry about," John said briskly. "I just want to give him a chance to calm down. He's pretty excited right now."

Geneva peered closely at the cat who was at the moment flopped over on his side, one leg in the air, industriously licking his bottom. He didn't look too excited to her, but then again, she didn't know much about cats; she had never bothered to learn much about them since she disliked them so much.

"Is there anything I can do?"

"No. Just make sure he gets plenty of exercise." He produced a catnip mouse and dangled it in front of Dr. Zhivago. The cat leapt at it, snatching it from John's fingers, and tore out across the yard, frisking his tail and flinging the toy high into the air. Geneva stared after him. He might seem just a little more nervous than usual. It was hard to be sure. Dr. Zhivago had always been pretty rambunctious. He disappeared around the barn with one last shake and toss.

John stayed a little longer to inquire after her arm, and when he noticed Geneva's anxious glances toward the barn, he reassured her again. "Please don't worry about Dr. Zhivago. I honestly don't think there's anything wrong with him. I bet tomorrow I'll find everything perfectly normal."

Nevertheless, Geneva worried all that night and all the next day, and felt insulted when she expressed her concerns to Wayne and Rachel. Rachel pretended to ignore her. A funny look passed over her face, then she walked out of the room. And Wayne! Well! Wayne actually snickered! Geneva knew her brother-in-law didn't care for cats, but his cavalier attitude made her temper flare. Obviously, they did not recognize the significance of the problem, so she finally chose to ignore their callousness and turned her energies into thanking her lucky stars that John had come along and noticed Dr. Zhivago's condition. What other vet would take such meticulous care?

When John arrived at the door shortly before twilight the next day, Geneva was waiting for him with Dr. Zhivago on her lap. Getting him and keeping him there had proved to be more difficult than she had anticipated when she was calculating the best pose for effect. She had hoped the sick cat would lie languidly in her arms, but he kept wanting to play with the runners on the rocking chair. Geneva finally had to stop rocking and sit perfectly still to get him quiet.

"Thank you for coming," she sang out to John as he limped onto the porch. "I've noticed he does seem a little feverish. What do you think?"

John looked at her with a stern, solemn face, so different than the one he had greeted her with less than two weeks ago. Geneva's face prickled with anxiety. He was not the sort of person to let her worry needlessly. Surely there must be some terrible prognosis for Dr. Zhivago, and he was hiding it from her in order to spare her hurt. Gently, he picked up the cat and checked his blood pressure, wrapping the cuff around and around his foreleg once again. There was a long silence as he listened intently into the stethoscope. Geneva held her breath until he released the pressure.

"Well, what it?" she demanded.

The light came on behind John's eyes. "Just as I thought. He's perfectly fine. I guess he was a little nervous around me yesterday."

Geneva almost sobbed with relief. Although she did not like cats in general, she had favored Dr. Zhivago ever since she had found him, a shivering, ice-covered kitten sitting by a city gutter, the sleet coming down hard on his tiny head. He had mewed so pitifully at the passersby who ignored him that Geneva could not help but stop and pick him up. Despite the fact that he was nearly frozen, he had begun to purr loudly the moment she held him under her coat, and he had snuggled so wonderfully that she resolved then and there to take him home with her, despite the fact that her apartment already was home to three other stray cats.

That had been his last grateful moment. Once he got into her home, he had taken over as alpha male, thoroughly intimidating the other cats, demanding the best spot on the bed and the best cat food available. But Geneva never forgot that initial purr, and she always felt a special softness for the fat, greedy adult tom that he had become. He had remained her favorite to this day.

She turned her shining eyes to John's and breathed, "I'm so grateful," and then, because she knew she could stop worrying about Dr. Zhivago, she turned her attentions to the charming veterinarian. Certainly, this latest development had caused him to become even more attractive.

John sat heavily in a chair and exchanged pleasantries for a while, then he looked intently at her and after a short pause cleared his throat. "Say, er, Geneva," he began earnestly. "I don't know if you'll feel up to it by Saturday night, but if you aren't busy, maybe we could do something."

Geneva's heart leaped; a flush warmed her to the scalp. Her arm troubled her so little that she was ready to yank the sling off then and there and ask John to dance, but instead she looked at her lap and said demurely, "I think I'll feel just fine by Saturday. What would you like to do?"

"Well, there's a new stock theatre in Tucker, and they've got a pretty good repertoire. I think tomorrow night they start *Midsummer Night's Dream*, and they're staging it at the amphitheatre in the botanical gardens. Would you enjoy that?"

Geneva glowed at him. She couldn't imagine a more wonderful evening than sitting among the flowers in the clear mountain night, watching a play about magical love with the devastatingly handsome John Smith. "I'd love it," she sighed.

"Good," he smiled. "Rachel told me you majored in theatre. I sort of minored in it, at least I hung around as much as possible. As a matter of fact, I once played Oberon."

Geneva laughed. "I played Puck."

"I think the role was written for you! I'll pick you up about six for dinner."

She walked him to his Jeep, watching as the engine roared to life and the car spun out of the driveway the way she had hoped to do instead of driving into the ditch. Muted thunder grumbled softly in the west; a flash of lightning lit the clouds building black against the pink and silver sky. *Rain all you want tonight*, she said to herself, *but please, please give us a clear night Saturday!* And she took the porch steps more sedately than she felt.

The first part of the new week crawled by like a sloth. Geneva combed through her wardrobe, debated about cutting her hair, and rode more than usual, hoping to catch a glimpse of John near his house. She never did, and soon she began to think she would grow old and die before Saturday arrived. She thought about manufacturing some ailment for her cats so she would have an excuse to go see him in the middle of the night. Ooh, wouldn't that be romantic? *She would bang on his door, perhaps in the pouring rain with a gasping cat in her arms. Her nightgown would cling provocatively, and she would be fainting with anxiety. And he would come, shirtless, of course, and resuscitate the cat, and maybe her, too...* Her mind went feverish with possibilities.

Sometime during the night, Evangeline's kittens were born. Geneva found the five greedy newborns in the barn, and she was just calling Rachel to come admire them when their parents arrived, full of news and excitement. The quilt had placed third in the prestigious competition, and the Gunter's boy and his bride would come home to a fine house after the November Amish wedding. Not seeing the need to stay when they were anxious to see their errant daughter as well as their pregnant one and their grandchildren, they had cut their visit short.

"I'm going to stay for a few days," said their mother. "Missed my babies and thought I'd come up and spend some time with you." She put her arm around Geneva and hugged her. "Besides, I bet you could use some help canning beans. Are they in up here?"

"You're a godsend," smiled Rachel. "We're inundated with them."

Their father, Ray, stayed through dinner, and afterward they all sat on the porch to be entertained by a thoroughly satisfying thunderstorm. Evangeline left her voracious babies long enough to snuggle in Geneva's lap; the rest of the cats scattered themselves about the porch, batting at the ghostly moths fluttering in the golden pool of light from the porch lamp. Wayne and Rachel sat in the swing, Hannah's downy head between them, while Phoebe snuggled in her grandfather's arms.

Geneva surveyed the scene, remembering her own childhood and the silken cocoon of her parents' love. Thunderstorms, where the lightning fractured the sky and reminded mortals of their frailty, were special to her because, like Phoebe, she had watched many of them from the warm safety of Ray's hard, capable arms. She sat quietly, watching the fire split the sky, wishing she were three years old again and life was not so demanding or hurtful. But then she thought about next Saturday and amended her thoughts. Life could still be pretty good.

When the storm passed, Ray rose to look at the washed sky. The striated sun was already half sunk into the nearest mountain, its long rays slanting horizontally through the clouds. "I'd better get on back down the mountain and open up the homestead," he said. "Get the dogs back from over at the Wilkenses'. Gaynell, you take care of these girls, and keep them out of trouble. Wayne, don't let these women gang up on you." He hugged both his daughters and his wife, then caught his granddaughters up to snuggle with them for a moment. They squealed and giggled as he rubbed his rough chin against their baby cheeks.

"Granddaddy! Don't beard us!" laughed Hannah, her face bright red from rubbing against his whiskers. Ray's family crowded around to watch him as he climbed into this car and waved as he drove out of sight.

"Well," said Gaynell after he had turned the corner." I reckon Geneva and I'll work on the dishes. Rachel, you're strictly ornamental from now on. All you have to do is lie around on that porch and love on the children. Wayne, you just sit right there. We don't need you in there messing things up." Wayne smiled gratefully at his mother-in-law, and Rachel blew her a kiss as they headed for the kitchen.

Once apart from the others, Gaynell turned to her daughter. "Geneva, honey, we came on home because the family wants to throw Rachel and Wayne a surprise shower Sunday afternoon. You and I have to get the house in shape and negotiate all the business of getting them away from the house and so forth."

"What fun!" exclaimed Geneva. "It's about time something exciting happened around here."

"You're going to think exciting once those twins get here. There won't be a good night's sleep among you!" But Geneva did not hear her. At the word "exciting" her thoughts had turned once again to the small farmhouse on the other side of the flowery pasture.

For the rest of the week, Gaynell rose early and scoured the house while Geneva and Rachel stood aside helplessly and watched their seventy-two-year-old mother haul around chairs and sofas. Geneva's injured arm prevented her from doing much more than getting in the way, and Rachel was absolutely forbidden to work. At last, feeling too guilty to watch another minute, Geneva went outside to gather wildflowers from the fields, then made huge arrangements for every available table in the house. Afterward, she sat on the hearth and scrubbed out the fireplace with one hand.

Rachel felt equally purposeless, but finally, after she and Gaynell had fallen into a half dozen altercations concerning the state of each others' health, Gaynell finally relented. "If you have to do something, polish the silver," she instructed. "You know everybody in the county will drop in to see the babies after they're born, and you'll need something to serve them with."

Rachel sighed and donned her gloves. "I feel like a queen termite. Totally useless, except for procreation," she grumbled.

By lunch Saturday, the house was spotless, but then Gaynell went to work in the garden. Geneva gathered more flowers and straightened the pictures. Rachel, caught up in the frenzy, polished their glass surfaces. Wayne, not interested in housecleaning, took the girls out to look at the lambs.

Late in the afternoon, Geneva threw down her rag and declared, "Time for someone to wave a wand and turn this sooty lass into a princess. Wish me luck, fat, ugly sister!"

Rachel sneered, snapping at her with a towel. "Okay, poof!" she said. "Oops, wrong spell. You've turned into a hippopotamus. But it is an improvement."

"Har har. Just wait until you see my spell. I shall create such a vision, you poor, dowdy, enormous thing! You cow! You blimp!" She darted to the bathroom, barely avoiding another snap from Rachel's towel.

Geneva spent an hour bathing and styling her hair. After several false starts at dressing, she finally selected a simple, pale blue, flowing cotton dress with a lightweight jacket, and she knew she looked perfect. Tonight was going to be special for the country twin. She could tell by the way the arteries in her temples throbbed.

John arrived in a bright red vintage Mustang convertible. "Where did you get this?" Geneva asked, delighted at the prospect of flying under the waxing moon, the wind whipping her hair and brightening her face.

"Borrowed it from a friend. I'm thinking of buying it," replied John, looking smug, but Geneva barely noticed his expression.

She couldn't wait to jump into the car and be off. "I figured the occasion warranted more than a shockless old Jeep."

"Excellent idea," smiled Geneva. This John Smith seemed to be clairvoyant, or else he had exactly the same ideas as she for a romantic evening.

The evening was, indeed, perfect. They drove into the haze of the dying day, up to the top of the mountain, then through the glorious sky along the ridges until they turned to descend into Tucker. Despite his immobile right leg, John managed the straight shift well, handling the switchbacks, straightening the curves as one irons a silk ribbon. They drove to a small restaurant with a terrace high atop a hill overlooking the town and sat there, eating and talking, but never ceasing to admire the mountains and the mist as it crept into the valleys and softened the sky's maiden blush. Geneva leaned her head on her hand and gazed out over the royal mountains. She sighed happily, but even as the breath escaped her, the tears sprang into her eyes.

"I know how you feel," said John softly, reaching across the table to take her hand. "It is heartbreakingly beautiful. Sometimes I feel like we really haven't the capacity to absorb the intensity of how the sky wants to make us feel. It's like having a god for a lover. It's wonderful, but sometimes it just provokes too much feeling."

Geneva sighed again and sipped her wine, enjoying the respite from the eternal struggle between the reality of who she was and what she was supposed to be, or what she thought she wanted to be. Right now, she felt complete, her soul mended by the healing mist lying low in the purple valleys and the life in John's eyes. She looked at him with renewed appreciation. She liked the way he took her nebulous romantic ideas and shaped them into form and clarity. But then she found herself wondering if she were allowing herself to be foolishly led into a fresh heartbreak, if John might at this moment be laying plans for her conquest and rejection. Then she remembered that she was the one who had toyed with such a plot, and she felt herself blush with shame. He did not deserve the treatment she had surely planned to hand to him, and she resolved that she would not be so manipulative, that she would treat him with respect for his transparent integrity, his obvious sensitivity.

They talked about the goodness of the green mountains around them, about the aura of mystery of the more distant blue ones. They talked about their families and what each of them hoped for. Like Geneva, John had grown up in a backwater to working class parents, and like Geneva, he had decided early on that he would break away from the ignorance and poverty he saw in his small, western North Carolina hometown.

"I got away, or at least part of me did," he admitted, "but not for long. After I graduated from vet school, I joined the army and managed to get out of going to Vietnam. They didn't need vets there, but I got to go to South America to work with cattle. Don't ask me why the army was interested in cattle. Anyway, after my discharge—gosh, three years ago, in nineteen seventy-four—I joined a small animal practice in New Orleans, which was a lot of fun, but something always bothered me when I was there. I kept feeling like I was going to fall off the edge of the world. It was too flat, too loose in so many ways. And I got sick of french poodles and society ladies after just a few months, so I ran away and volunteered as an adjunct to the Peace Corp for a year and got to travel around to a lot of different places.

"It wasn't until I came home for a visit in the fall that I realized that I missed—." He laughed apologetically. "What I *needed* was the mountains, and not just this," he said, indicating with a wide sweep the vast, foreboding hills around him, "but the people, the values, the spirit and stoic soul."

"Yes, the stoic soul and the redneck attitudes," replied Geneva, understanding his speech more than she cared to admit. "Sure it's great being here if you don't mind being brain dead. I come home only to rest, but I go berserk if I stay too long. It suffocates me."

"I felt the same way when I left home. Then I realized that what I was choking on was my own excessive ambition. Once I got what I thought I wanted, it seemed like pure smoke. Smoke and ashes."

"So what do you want now?" Geneva asked, leaning intently

into his gaze, sensing the parallels along which their lives lay.

"Reality. Living a real life and not just an advertisement of one in *Forbes*."

"So what is reality for you, Mr. John Smith, god of fire and iron, visionary, beloved of Christ?"

He dropped his eyes with a smile, then returned her mocking gaze with candor and humility. "Reality is knowing God. It's working with your hands. It's walking the ridges as the sun comes up." He paused, then added quietly, "It's the love of a good woman."

Geneva had partly expected such an answer, but she had not expected the reaction it would cause in her. At his words, she felt as if a thunderbolt had shot across the table, striking her violently in the chest. She experienced a physical pain, followed by bewilderment, for she felt a sudden desire to leap from her chair and run, but she was rooted as surely as the ancient willow oak from which she had swung in the tire as a child. She sat very still and silent, something deep in her heart verifying the truth of John's words.

"I envy Rachel and Wayne," John continued, oblivious of Geneva's apocalypse. "Horses in the stable, dog at the hearth, children in the garden. Even when I was living it up in New Orleans, I never really liked being a bachelor. Freedom isn't all the playboys insist that it is."

Geneva studied him, remembering Howard's "need" for freedom. "So why aren't you already married? I can't believe you haven't had at least forty or fifty offers by now," she said.

He laughed. "I guess I've been unlucky. Back when I was surrounded by possibilities, I had the stupid notion that love could tie you down in ways that I wouldn't like, and now that I've grown up enough to think straight, I can't seem to find a lady who appreciates me enough to put up with all my quirks. You know, this one resents the time I spend around stables, that one says, 'forget children, I'm going to have a career.' One girl I dated for four months and then blew it because I didn't know she's afraid of heights."

"What happened?"

"Took her up to Buttermilk Knob and tried to get her to climb the granite outcroppings. She hasn't spoken to me since."

Geneva smiled, "I know what you mean. I made the mistake of taking my college roommate up there. Thought we'd have to call the National Guard to get her down. But surely there are lots of women around here who like dogs and horses and children—and heights. I could name a dozen of my cousins who would lasso you if they could get close enough."

"Yes? And how many of them have read *War and Peace?* No offense to your cousins, but it seems that all the smart ones leave. The first girl I met here, real pretty, big blue eyes, sweet smile. I took her to see *Hamlet,* and she hated it! Came out of the theatre declaring that Shakespeare wasn't all he was cracked up to be. His plays are full of clichés! You know, 'To thine own self be true,' 'I smell a rat.'"

"'And 'it smells to heaven,'" countered Geneva.

"And what about you?" he queried, abruptly turning to her. "Why hasn't a beautiful, articulate, educated, healthy, outdoorsy woman like you already been snapped up?"

"I guess I've been unlucky, too," began Geneva slowly, unwilling to admit that Howard had thrown her over. A tiny latch slipped into place in her mind as she thought about his abuse of her. She narrowed her eyes and firmly decided that his name would never darken her lips again.

"Ever been close?"

The lie slipped like silk from her mouth, "Heaven's no! I've spent my adult life being disgruntled with men. I guess I'm just too picky."

"Well, aren't we a couple of choosy elitists," smiled John. "Now, I believe we'd better leave if we are to get a good place to sit. We can order our dessert to go, and I'll have this thermos filled with coffee so we can picnic on the lawn before the performance."

They drove out to the botanical gardens perched on a gentle slope at the edge of town. John held Geneva's hand as they strolled to the grassy lawn banked by rhododendrons and mountain laurel. There they spread a quilt on the grass among other picnicking audience members, many of whom glanced their way as they settled themselves.

"We must look like a couple of escapees from the emergency room," remarked John, indicating his cast and Geneva's sling. Geneva did not mind being watched. She knew they were the best looking couple there, handicapped as they were. But she felt a general uneasiness descend upon her each time she looked at John, so handsome, so earnest and attentive. She felt herself sinking down into the quilt upon which she sat, feeling submerged in its dizzying pattern. The game that she had hoped to play was getting out of hand; the country twin was becoming too comfortable, too delighted by everything she saw and heard and felt tonight. As if summoning an incubus, Geneva called to her city twin, willing her to come and save herself. She wracked her brain for a reason to stay aloof, to shield herself, to remember why she needed to go back to Washington.

City Twin came, but she was weak and addled. She babbled something in Geneva's ear about *art and society*, but the wind blew the words away so that Geneva felt only a soft breath, meaningless. She brushed it aside and turned her bright eyes toward John.

A puff of mist appeared in the laurel behind him. Fairies materialized out of the rhododendron blossoms. Surprised, Geneva looked around. Fairies were rising out of the mist all around them, sitting in trees, lounging on the grass, knitting clover chains, chasing one another amid fireflies just beyond the fringe of foliage around the audience. Music began. On-stage, players dressed in Edwardian finery had appeared, dancing in stately procession.

Geneva was immediately impressed. She had not expected the production to be particularly imaginative or technically sophisticated; she wasn't interested enough to even pick up a program. She had merely hoped the players would not butcher the language. But already her eye was delighted, and her ear followed the moment Theseus uttered his first lines:

> *Now, fair Hippolyta, our nuptial hour*
> *Draws on apace. Four happy days bring in*
> *Another moon; but O, methinks, how slow*
> *This old moon wanes! She lingers my desires,*
> *Like to a step-dame, or a dowager,*
> *Long withering out a young man's revenue.*

From there, the play ebbed and flowed like a symphony, binding Geneva in its spell, impressing even the city twin, who slipped quietly by her side as she watched, evaluating, criticizing, admiring.

The production had begun conventionally enough, with the mortals played as genteel ladies and gentlemen, stiffened by layers of clothing, custom, and manners, but when the fairy scenes began, Geneva knew there was a masterful, bold director behind this production. Playing on a darkened stage, the fairies wore headdresses of dimmed neon, and their costumes were painted with glowing paint; Puck wore tiny wings made of fiery sparklers at his shoulders. The magic slowly engulfed and liberated the mortals (and Geneva) until, at last, the final scene erupted with fairy dust and fireworks. It was the most exciting production that Geneva had ever seen.

By the end of the evening, she was tingling, remembering her own short-lived theatrical career and wishing for the first time in a long while that she had not abandoned it. Part of her was alert, actively thirsting for the excitement that theatre offered; the other part drifted along dazedly, feeling as magical and as transfixed as if she lived in the Athenian wood under the influence of Oberon's wondrous potions. The fireworks shooting over her head, challenging the bright, clear stars, seemed to have no purpose but to signify the intensity of Geneva's passion for life, for her need for love, and, perhaps because she needed something or someone to absorb that passion, for the man who sat beside her. So engrossed was she in her own feelings that she could not think any farther than this immediate moment and of how she wanted it to continue. If John had asked her to fly to the moon with him, she unquestioningly would have started flapping her arms.

Then there was the long, winding drive home under the midnight stars scattered like quicksilver across the velvet night and the almost-cold air raising her hair into a thousand tiny, invigorating whips. Geneva felt suspended in time, a blaze of motion, a comet. But when they finally pulled up to Rachel's and Wayne's darkened house in the early hours, Geneva shook herself, bestirred by the reality of the imminent good-bye facing her. She prayed that he would ask her out tomorrow, and the day after, and the day after. She turned to him, smiling languidly.

"I believe I have been enchanted this evening. There seems to be magic all around me."

"If I could have, I would have slipped you some of Oberon's potion."

"You're better off not having any," she laughed. "I feel drunk already."

"It's the air—I've found it intoxicating from the moment I came up to this mountain. Would you like to walk?" John opened the door and helped her out into the velvety night waiting to embrace them. The sky and the earth were larger than ever they could be under the conquering sun. They made Geneva feel dwarfed and frail, as small and insubstantial as the grasses writhing in the soundless wind.

In the silence, John lightly laid his hand on her shoulder and together they walked in their awkward, mismatched gait toward the fence. The horses were bedded in their stalls, but the pasture pulled them, as if they expected to see ghostly forms cantering through the wildflowers.

The moon was gone, long ago stolen behind a shadowy

mountain. Geneva stopped at the fence, shivering in the wind, her body begging John to hold her. He looked at her and gently pushed away the hair that had blown across her face.

"Would you mind if I kissed you?"

Geneva was grateful he had finally thought of it. She felt like she had been holding herself back all night, and now she fled to his arms, propelled by wind and feeling. When she kissed him, she felt herself sinking, or floating, into a soft blackness bordered and spangled with vivid colors. As she sank into this bliss, she suddenly felt a tingling current shoot through her body. It hummed and sparked her senses like nothing she had ever felt before, and every nerve in her body and in her heart told her that this must at last be the love she had always yearned for. She felt it to the very bedrock of her soul.

She began to tremble uncontrollably. She forgot who she was, where she was. She felt bewildered for a moment, trying to register the sensation she was feeling, when suddenly John pulled his lips away from hers and stepped back with an exclamation, jerking Geneva with him. It wasn't until the current stopped that Geneva realized she had been standing in the tall grass resting against the electric fence.

John was laughing. "What a kiss!" he exclaimed. "For a second there, I thought that was you doing that to me!"

Geneva laughed, too, but not as heartily. She was still hoping it was love.

Still laughing, John led Geneva to the house, and despite her reluctance to end the night, she followed docilely. Her lips were burning for another kiss like the last one.

On the porch, John turned to her and pulled her to himself once again. "I'll see you tomorrow," he murmured, his face nestled in her hair.

"Oh yes. Yes. When?" Her heart fluttered at his assertion that they would see each other again so soon.

"About six? Is that when the party starts?"

"Party?"

"For Rachel and Wayne. I've been invited, you know."

"Oh, yes! That party." She felt too good to be embarrassed by her mistake. "I thought you were referring to all this kissing."

He chuckled. "Even without the external electricity, your kisses remind me of Puck's sparklers, but on a grander scale." He looked at her a moment more before she wriggled her arm out of the sling and threw it and its twin around his neck and gave him a series of soft little kisses punctuated by her rapid breath. After a few moments of this, John gently disengaged her arms and cleared his throat. "I'd better be going."

Geneva worked very hard to hide her feeling of being rebuffed. She laughed lightly, "Sorry. Summer nights sometimes do this to me. I'm sure I'll be terribly embarrassed in the morning."

"I hope not. This has been too perfect to regret." He lingered a moment, obviously unwilling to leave. Despite the fact that she had told herself that she would behave more decorously, she fell into his arms again, kissing him with all the passion that sang inside her.

He was delicious. She felt his heart pounding, his hand convulsively entwined in her hair. He kissed her eyes, her mouth, her neck, and she felt him trembling as he caressed her face and throat. Gasping, they gazed at one another. Geneva felt her knees buckle.

"I'd better get out of here," he said, "before I start begging you to marry me tonight."

"And then regret it in the morning?" she teased.

He looked at her squarely, the same look of longing that she had seen that first day came into his eyes and bore deep into her. "I doubt it. Good night."

Geneva had difficulty closing her eyes that night, and when she did find sleep, it was laced with delicious, exciting dreams in which she was running effortlessly across the high ridges gilded with deep, golden grass. *I will never be the same again,* she sang in her dream. But toward morning, she woke, startled, feeling something she could not articulate calling to her. The sun found her sitting bolt upright in bed, whispering Howard's name.

When at last she rose after the fitful morning, Geneva felt torn and sorrowful, aching for something beyond her grasp, something she could not name, which was not even fully formed in her mind. She only knew that she was seized by restlessness and a need for something more.

Rachel, Wayne, and Gaynell tried to tease her about her night out, but she refused to be drawn into a discussion of it. Instead, she took Fairhope out for a long ride up across Jim Gordon Mountain and through the valley beyond. As she rode, she tried to sort out her feelings about Howard and about John Smith—about herself. She compared her two lives. She hated to give any of it up, the splendor all around her in the soft, summer mountain days, the glitter and the hard, smooth feeling she got when she stood back and looked at what she had created when she worked at her craft. She felt a wild impulse to ride Fairhope straight over the mountains, into DC, but she remembered forlornly there was nothing left for her there: no lover, no apartment, and no job. She began to regret her burned bridges.

Then she remembered how the ice glittered on the trees in January and the clean, delighted brook where the wild iris grew. She turned Fairhope's head and broke into a canter toward home. *Howard would never love her. He was too busy loving himself.* She would give this John Smith a chance, and if he could convince her that life here with him would be worth it she would stay.

She returned by four o'clock, in time to see everyone dressed to go to afternoon church services. Gaynell asked her to accompany them but winked at Geneva so that she would volunteer to stay home.

"You go on," said Geneva, catching her cue. I've been wanting to cook some chili, and to do it properly, I need at least three hours. Come back hungry."

"We will," sang out Gaynell as she herded the family out the door. "Back at six thirty."

Geneva was glad to be alone with her thoughts. She fed the livestock, knowing that Wayne might be having too good a time to take care of that chore later in the evening. As she scooped grain from the bins, she fought an impulse to saddle up again and ride over to John's house, to fling herself in his arms and ask him to save her from herself. *No, better let him come to her. And he would, too,* she smiled to herself. He would come to her soon enough, as surely as the whippoorwill finds his mate. She hummed as she ran the vacuum and laid out plates and silverware and went through the music for the party. She wanted everything to be perfect, but frankly felt that it could be nothing but. The smile never left her face as she bathed and picked out a loose skirt and soft blouse. The magic would continue; she could hear it laughing on the mountaintops.

Four

Geneva decided not to wear her sling that evening. Her elbow really did not hurt, and besides, she had no desire to hear the story about her trip through the blackberries. That one usually led to several others concerning her adolescent awkwardness. Yes, she was done with that sling. No need to expose herself to anyone's misplaced amusement.

The revelers began arriving early, and the moment they passed the threshold, Geneva felt herself becoming wrapped in the comfortable cocoon of family: aunts, uncles, cousins at various stages of removal. Without becoming aware of it, she slipped into her old, familiar West Virginian idiom. Within five minutes, she had slapped her thigh twice and had dug her elbow into her cousin Jackson's ribs over a remembered family anecdote.

Mam-ma Turner, frail and transparent-looking, but straight of back and radiant as ever, arrived bearing several pans of gingerbread and fresh apple pies. Geneva hugged her lightly, holding herself back for fear she would crush her fragile body.

"Law, honey, what kind of hug is that yer agivin' me?" exclaimed

Mam-ma. "And that little old peck on the cheek? You come here and give me a right proper hug and kiss!" As she put her pans down and wrapped her arms around Geneva, her frailty gave way to something strong and maternal. Geneva fleetingly hoped she would live forever.

The crowd grew quickly, laden with food, drinks, crepe-paper streamers, and baby gifts; all busied themselves preparing for the party and making plans to hide and jump out to surprise Wayne and Rachel. Geneva was in the kitchen when John arrived. When he came and told her how much he had enjoyed the evening before, she found that she was torn between uncharacteristic shyness and disappointment that he did not sweep her up into his arms like he had last night. They merely smiled awkwardly at one another, not quite knowing what to say with so many of Geneva's relatives within earshot. She peered at him through her lashes until her least favorite cousin Lilly, who was at least as idiotic as she was beautiful, came in to ask John to help with the decorating.

The next sight Geneva caught of them, Lilly was standing on a ladder in her stiletto heels and miniskirt, the backs of her perfect knees three inches from John's eyeballs. Geneva was profoundly irritated by the way Lilly kept shaking her head and flinging back the river of her shimmering pale hair and running her fingers through it so that it would lift and catch the light. She personally felt it was tacky to wear hair that long, all the way down to her fanny. It was obvious that she wore it that length deliberately to show it off and to pull the eye down to her tight little ass. Geneva had beautiful hair and a cute little ass, too, but she didn't advertise it to the world, did she? *What a little hussy Lilly could be!*

Geneva glared at her first-cousin-once-removed for a moment, contemplating her little, darting eyes and the way she always painted them up to make them look bigger. *Ferret Face*, Geneva thought, recalling her favorite nickname for Lilly, then she turned with her nose slightly elevated and walked back into the kitchen. She was above competing for John's attention and would wait for him to seek her out, once he had enough of looking up Lilly's skirt.

"Here they come!" someone called out, and the unwieldy crowd rushed into the back yard or huddled together behind furniture. Geneva dashed out the front door, crying loudly, "Hello! Welcome home!" then she ushered the group into the living room, which erupted with live bodies and shouts. Rachel and Wayne burst into laughter, and the party began.

Geneva discreetly sought out John with her eyes, but every time she saw him, he was surrounded by women, and she was determined to show that she was having fun without him. Once she caught him heading in her direction, but someone intercepted him, and then she was suddenly cornered by Lilly's sister, Sally Beth, equally blond and shapely, but if possible, even dumber than Lilly. She wearied Geneva with her habit of talking in exclamations, as if it might help enliven her excruciatingly boring and one-sided conversations.

"*Geneva!* Yew are here! Somebody told me yew came home! That's *great*! We'll have to get together *soon*!

"Yes," replied Geneva, her smile already feeling weary. "I understand you are to be congratulated."

"Oh, *yes!* I passed my *cosmetology* exam!" she said with a little exhalation of the breath as if she had climbed to the top of a very high mountain. "*Finally!* Yew know that was really *hard!* Yew just wouldn't *believe!* Yew know, they ask questions about *chemistry!*

"Really? How—"

"Oh, *yes!* I mean, I was really *shocked* the first time I took it. I jist looked at it and thought I would *die!* I barely got through the *first page!* But I decided that maybe I should really study for the second time? Yew know, maybe take it really seriously? And I did! *I really did!* Yew wouldn't *believe* how hard I studied! And then when I took it again, it was *so much harder!* I mean, I don't think they got those questions from the textbook I studied!

"But this time, I was really prepared. I mean, I read *two* books this time, and then I got hold of an old test and studied that, too? I was so *proud* of myself, I was so good! And then, this last test wasn't nearly so scary—yew know, it's amazing how yew get more confident when you go through something a few times!"

"I know what—"

"But I *really* and truly *did* pass it this time! And I'm so looking *forward* to starting work! There's this sweet little place over in Tucker? It's opened up, and I have a job there *right off!* I get to start off as a stylist, and I am so excited! Geneva, yew *must* let me do your hair!" she gushed, then raised a hot pink fingernail and delicately fluffed her own coiffure, which was something to behold. Sally Beth's hair had always been baby fine and flyaway, but somehow she had figured out a way to elevate it to astonishing heights. The masses of stiff, blonde curls were adorned with a hot pink bow that exactly matched her lips, her fingernails, and her toenails, which peeked out from her open sandals bedecked with large imitation jewels (a trademark of hers since junior high). Sally Beth was a vision of working class pulchritude.

"That would be great, Sally Beth," replied Geneva. But Sally Beth's attention had turned to the room around her.

"Say, yew did such a *good job* with this party! You know, it reminds me of the shower that Leslie Ann and Jeannie Marie gave for Ruth Leigh last summer? Oh, yew missed that one, up there in Washington! How is Washington? Isn't it just *awful?!* I heard there's lots of *crime* there, all those drug addicts *mugging* people?"

"Well, actually—"

"Oh! I cain't *imagine!* I hope yew aren't going back! But it's *too bad* yew missed this shower! Yew jist wouldn't *believe* the way they did it! It was a surprise shower, and you know how Ruth Leigh loves yella?! *Well!!* They did it so *everything* was all yella, and everything was a *surprise!* They had all these yella balloons everywhere? And they had these *little bitty* surprises in them all? And we all went around like crazy stomping on these balloons, and there were gift certificates for Ruth Leigh, printed on yella paper, or little yella trinkets inside! And, *oh!* Jeannie Marie's mother baked this *yummy* yella cake, and yew just won't believe this—it was all *chocolate!*"

"No! You don't mean it!" exclaimed Geneva, searching the crowd behind Sally Beth for means of escape. She was growing desperate.

"I do!" crowed Sally Beth. "Chocolate with *chocolate icing!* She had used white chocolate and had colored it all with bright yella food coloring, and it was all such a *surprise* when we tasted it! And, *oh!* There was this punch? Which was yella, and of course, we expected it to be *lemon* or something, but it was *grape*! I mean, it was the most surprising thing! And they made this big yella ball, like a piñata? And made Ruth Leigh whack at it with this big yella bat, and inside was the most *gorgeous* yella gown and robe—you know how good Ruth Lee looks in yella, with that hair! And of course, there were yella streamers everywhere! I jist felt like I was in the *sunshiniest* place ever!"

"Sounds wonderful!" gasped Geneva. "I am so sorry I missed it! Oh, golly! Is that Dianne out on the porch? I thought she was in New York!"

"Oh *no!* She came home *ages* ago! A year, at least! But she missed that shower, too! I don't know where they found them, but they had put these really bright *jonquils* everywhere! Imagine! In *July!*"

"How surprising! Excuse me! I must go say hello to Dianne!! I had *no idea* she was home! Sally Beth! It is so good to see you again! We will have to get together *soon!*" and she fled outside as Sally Beth sang out, *"Really!"*

Dr. Zhivago came running up as soon as she stepped onto the porch, rubbing against her legs and meowing as if he had missed her. She picked him up as she moved over to the swing where Dianne stood talking to yet another of her female cousins, Janet.

"Geneva! You really are here!" exclaimed Dianne. Geneva winced.

"Just barely! I've been cornered by Silly Beth for the last *three hours,* at least!" she gasped, using the nickname the cousins had given Sally Beth years ago.

"Oh, sorry," smiled Dianne. I'll speak totally without inflection for the rest of the evening so you can even out. How long have you been home?"

"A few weeks. But I didn't know you were home. Silly Beth said you've been down for a year. What's going on? You were doing beautifully when I was up to see *School for Scandal*. Did it close? I thought it might even still be running."

"Oh, it ran until this past May. But we turned it over to someone else and moved here early last summer. Charlie's bought a hardware store."

"What!?"

"Yes, believe it or not, it was all Charlie's idea. Oh, I really wanted to come, too, ever since the boys were born, but I never thought we would. You know, we always want to give our children the same kind of magical childhood we had."

"I suppose so," began Geneva slowly.

Janet broke in, "Gosh. I can't imagine a more magical place than New York City, especially since you work in the theatre."

"Well, yes. It is magical, in its way, but isn't the same—all artificial—not like this," she swept her hand toward the mountains shimmering in the late sunlight and continued, "I never figured that Charlie would ever want to move here. You know, he grew up in Manhattan, and his idea of getting back to nature is a jog through Central Park loaded down with a mace canister and a police whistle."

"You're exaggerating," accused Janet.

"You tell me," countered Dianne. "A couple of years ago, Charlie was on the Brooklyn Bridge on his motorcycle, and he was in heavy traffic. He tried to zip around a few cars—he can be a real smart ass when he's on that motorcycle. But this guy saw him coming and deliberately bumped him. He fell over and slid for about ten yards, between his bike and the pavement, and smacked his head against the curb. And then, while he was lying there, bleeding, all skinned up from cheek to toe, practically in a coma, all these cars start honking at him and people are yelling and cussing at him to get out of the way. So he drags himself to his feet and he tries to push his bike over, but he keeps stumbling around and vomiting from a concussion. Well then this mounted policeman comes up. Old Charlie thinks he's coming to rescue him, but all he does is look at Charlie like he's bored to death, and he says, 'Hey, Buddy, move it. You can't park this piece of junk on the bridge. Get outta here!'

"So poor Charlie pushes his bike all the way across the bridge, stopping to throw up every couple of minutes, and everybody's honking and swearing at him, and as he's walking, the whole time he's muttering to himself, 'I'm outta here.' So as soon as he finished designing the show he was working on, we packed up and came here."

"What are you doing?" asked Geneva, incredulous.

"We took over the outdoor theatre in Tucker. I mostly run it and direct shows, and Charlie still does technical design, but it doesn't make enough to support us both—yet, anyway, so Charlie is running this hardware store. We sold our apartment in Manhattan for a fortune and bought the store and this charming little house out in January Falls. The kids love it, Charlie loves it, and I feel like the heavens have opened up and given me my heart's desire. You'd have to dynamite me out of here."

Geneva brightened. "Are you telling me you directed that production of *Dream* I saw last night?"

"You saw it? What did you think? Charlie did all the tech work on that. We had to get all kinds of permits to do the fireworks, but I think they were worth it."

"Dianne, it was wonderful. It made me want to get back into theatre."

"When did you drop out? Last I heard you were going for the MFA. Set design?"

"And lighting, but I never finished. I got sidetracked into doing retail design full time and never got back to it. I meant to, though, and I sure miss it."

"Really?" asked Dianne, interested. "Are you doing anything now? You know, community theatre, that sort of thing?"

"No, but I have been thinking about it ever since last night."

"Well, what luck that you're here. Charlie has his hands full with the hardware store. You wouldn't believe how macho he's gotten since he got that thing. He even bought himself a '68 Chevy truck with a gun rack, and he keeps insisting that we've got to get a hound. Can you imagine an old hound around our little Tybalt?

"Anyway, now that Charlie's busy being a redneck and running this store, we need someone with a broad background... hey, you could even perform sometimes, provided we could keep you from falling all over you own feet on stage."

Geneva winced, hoping that the blackberry thicket incident would not come up. She resented Dianne's implication that she might still be clumsy, but she chose to let the remark pass.

"Do you think you might be interested? We start work on the next season in February. Of course, we can't pay much, but you can survive. We all have part-time jobs on the side. Nobody around here cares about lifestyles of the rich and famous, anyway."

Janet broke in, "I can't believe you two are standing there talking about moving back. Here I've been dying to get out of this little hole, and you both had great lives in beautiful cities and are giving it up. As soon as Daddy gets better, I'm taking my little MBA and hitting the corporate life."

"Shut up, Janet," laughed Dianne. "Take your MBA and become an accountant in Tucker, if you know what's good for you. What do you say, Geneva?"

"An *accountant?* In *Tucker?*" sputtered Janet.

"Ouch, watch the exclamations, Janet. I'm still being reconditioned through uninflected vocalizations, remember," teased Geneva.

"Go ahead, throw you brains away. You'll both be begging to come live with me when I'm living it up in Los Angeles." She sauntered off.

"Watch out for earthquakes," called Dianne after her. "Well, Geneva, do you need time to think it over? I've seen some of your work, and I know you'd do beautifully. I guess I don't need to tell you there aren't many qualified people around here, and I do hate to go through the interview process with new graduates. Too much travel, and besides, there's nothing like a little nepotism to keep things interesting."

Geneva did not need much time to think. The vision of what she could do with this opportunity had already taken shape in her quick mind. Since her ride this afternoon, DC had begun to seem decadent and sordid to her here among her clean, windy mountains. And there was John. He might be a reason to stay here for a while, perhaps forever. Tickled with the possibilities, Geneva smiled at Dianne. Already she was imagining John and herself playing Romeo and Juliet... *no, maybe Anthony and Cleopatra. That was a more interesting relationship. Maybe he could be persuaded to give some time from his busy practice and get back on stage.* She positively tingled with the thought. "I just might be interested. Let's get together and talk it over," she said, stroking Dr. Zhivago.

"Okay, there's time. Nice cat. Is he yours?"

"Yes," replied Geneva. "He gave me a bit of a scare this week. Had a bout with high blood pressure."

"High blood pressure?" asked Dianne incredulously. "Nah. Cats don't get high blood pressure. They're too lazy!"

"Well, this one did. John Smith, the vet in there checked it himself." She indicated John through the open door.

Dianne laughed. "That crazy John. What a liar. Why, he's been pulling your leg!" Geneva stiffened, but Dianne laughed harder. "Last summer he convinced Charlie that skunks won't spray their perfume during the night of the summer solstice. And then told him that people would pay five hundred dollars for young skunks for pets. That seemed reasonable for Charlie. He's from New York! The idiot went out all night looking for them. I was out of town that week and so didn't know a thing about it until I got home and found that he'd shaved his head. He'd found a whole nest of them and just about didn't make it out alive. I'm just glad he didn't take the boys with him!" She shook her head, laughing for a full half minute at the memory. "But we got John back. Sent him on a day-long hike with Sally Beth and Lilly together! And we're cooking up another good one. We'll spring it on him one day when he's not suspecting it. But Charlie's easy to dupe, being a city boy. I'd think that you would know better!" She sputtered a laugh again. "High blood pressure!"

Geneva pasted a polite smile on her face and excused herself, mumbling something about replenishing the carrot sticks, then headed straight for John, who was enjoying the company of four women who looked as if they might be on leave from their jobs as playmates of the month. Lilly was one of them, leaning toward him, her ample breast nestled against his arm. Geneva approached them from behind to get a closer look. The women were doodling on his cast with felt tip pens.

"Come on, John," one of them laughed. "Tell us how you really broke it."

"Well, I really was helping to fight a wildfire at an oil well in Houston. It blew up and knocked me for a loop. When I came to about three days later, I was in this cast. Severe concussion. Couldn't remember a thing for week or two. Burned off all my eyelashes and eyebrows, too."

The four women collapsed with laughter, shrieking and punching him. One of them began to sketch a picture of an explosion and a figure wearing an elaborate cowboy hat doing loops through the air, right beside one of a king tumbling off his throne. Geneva whirled and marched into the kitchen, where Rachel sat talking with Ray and three relatives.

"Do you know what I just heard?" demanded Geneva. "John is out there telling people that he broke his leg fighting a wildfire in Texas. And cats don't get high blood pressure!"

Aunt Hattie laughed, "He told me he was water-skiing in the Mediterranean, and Buck got the story that he was parachuting."

"Mine's better," drawled Uncle Henry. "He told me he was hang gliding in the Alps."

"Bungee jumping," corrected Ray. There was a general burst of laughter, but Geneva did not participate.

"What a liar!" exclaimed Aunt Hattie. She turned to Geneva. "What did he tell you?"

Geneva smiled through gritted teeth. "He was rescuing a woman on a runaway horse."

Everyone except Geneva looked delighted. Uncle Henry slapped his knees several times. "That's the best one!" they crowed. Geneva was thinking of a different adjective, but she said nothing while she glared at her sister. Rachel pulled her into the chair beside her, explaining with a smile, "John's a bit of a tease, Geneva, and he loves to keep people off balance. He makes up outrageous stories and tells everyone a different one so that we're all kept guessing. It's sort of a game with him. I doubt if he's told anyone the real truth." Rachel looked at her anxiously. "I hope you aren't mad at him. He's just having fun."

Geneva flared her nostrils. *Another lying man! And she almost fell for him!* Icily, she threw back her head and smirked at Rachel. "Oh, no, I'm not mad. I'm used to hearing men's lies. I find them rather entertaining. Excuse me. I think the air is getting stuffy in here." She flounced through the living room, then strode outside, glaring at John on the way out. There was some satisfaction to be derived from seeing the surprised look on his face.

She headed for the creek, then struck up the hillside toward the heath bald half a mile from Rachel's house. The late sunset had alighted the west, flooding the face of the mountains with its glow, but amplifying Geneva's sorrow. She shuddered with angry sobs as she looked at it, but she was too mad to really cry. Mostly she gritted her teeth and spat out pejoratives, wishing she had something worth throwing. All she had were stones and pinecones, which were terribly unsatisfactory because they did not break.

"I am through with men. Absolutely, undeniably, no holds barred, through," she muttered in the softening light. As she stormed, a satisfying scene began to fill her head. *She would become a hermit, a sinewy old mountain woman, hard as ivory and prickly as cactus. No, wait. That wouldn't do. She would stay beautiful, and men would risk their lives to come for a glimpse of her. She would keep a shotgun and run them off if they dared to venture up into her citadel. But when they caught sight of her face, they would be inflamed with desire, and they would yearn and pine, then ultimately die with unrequited love. She would become legendary, known as far as Maine and Georgia as the misanthropic beauty who trained her cats to scratch out the eyes of any male old enough to shave.*

Her mind began to stray into another line. *There would be a particularly handsome man, named... Lord... Ruston. He would ride up every single day on a big Appaloosa stallion because he pined for her so, but she would refuse to see him, and her mountain lions would...*

But then, the memory of John's green eyes flashed before her, and she felt Howard's touch, and the fight went out of her. As the misery engulfed her soul, she began to cry in earnest. She tried to tell herself to stop, that she was making her eyes all red and swollen, but to no avail. *Why were men so awful? Howard had left that terrible hole in her heart, and now John had filled it with salt. She hated men! She would kill them all if she could.*

She grieved well past nightfall, then made her way sorrowfully down the mountain. The party was still going on, so she climbed in her bedroom window and collapsed on the bed, exhausted, but certain that she would not sleep.

She did sleep, immediately, deeply, and dreamlessly, as if her mind were trying to avoid contact with the wound. But several hours later she woke, thirsty from her earlier tears. Walking through the dark, silent house, she felt her way into the kitchen. She heard voices on the back porch. One of them was John's, speaking her name. Breathlessly, she flattened herself against the wall, then crept to the open door and settled herself on the floor to listen. Rachel was there, too, and so was Wayne, but she could not hear what they were saying. Sammy, the Irish setter snored softly.

Carefully, favoring her sprained elbow, she crawled on her hands and knees to the dining room, then tiptoed out the front door and around to the back. When she rounded the side of the house, she crawled again, stealthily, hardly daring to breathe. She heard Sammy growl once, then as he caught her scent, he thumped his tail on the floor and grew quiet again. Geneva let her breath out, then continued her journey behind the dahlias until she reached the back steps where she could hear clearly the conversation just three feet way. For the second time in as many weeks, she sat on the bare ground and settled herself behind the bushes to eavesdrop on the man she might be able to love and/or hate. She hadn't quite made up her mind yet.

Rachel was speaking. "John, I'm sorry. There may not be much hope. She's incredibly fickle, and you know she's real sensitive about men who lie to her. She'll think she is in love one minute, and the poor shleck will do to something to irritate her, and that's the end of that romance. The last guy she got really serious about may yet be picking glass shards from his scalp." Geneva cringed, remembering her conversation with John about her lack of attachments. *Damn it Rachel, can't you keep a secret?* She held her breath and swore that if Rachel told him that Howard had jilted her, she would personally see to it that her sister never slept through a peaceful night again.

Wayne broke in with a laugh. "She's almost as big a liar as you, John, only she doesn't see it as lying, exactly. She just rearranges the facts to suit her."

This was her favorite brother-in-law speaking? Geneva felt a growl beginning deep in her throat. Sammy moved suddenly and returned it, low and menacing. Geneva forced herself to be quiet.

"Yes," laughed Rachel. "You two really are perfect for each other. I've never seen two bigger romantics in my life—and both of you will plot and scheme and lie like hell to make things turn out like you want them."

"I'm not the plotter," countered John. "You're the one who told me I had to sweep her off her feet before she'd stay interested in me for more than five minutes. And you know I'm all the time telling tall tales just for fun. I thought she'd like to hear a romantic tale about rescuing a maiden."

"Oh, she loved it!" giggled Rachel. "But she took it seriously, and it sure backfired. I'm just glad you didn't tell her about your Congressional Medal of Honor."

"Or your Olympic gold," said Wayne. They all laughed.

"I just about did," said John, "but somehow I was afraid she'd believe me. She's gullible, isn't she? You know, I really do like her, and I don't want to tease her too much." He paused, then spoke again. "Do you think she'll forgive me?"

"It will take some work." There was a pause. "Ever heard of Jacob's Mountain?"

"No. Where is it?"

"You climb up to the laurel bald behind the house, then follow the ridge west for about two miles. It's where I caught Wayne. Didn't I, honey?"

"You little fool. It's where I caught you."

"That's what you think. Geneva and I plotted for weeks to get you up there—the magic is better when the moon is full."

Wayne sat silently for a moment. "I guess you're right. I was too scared to look at you before that day, even though I sure spent many a sleepless night thinking about you—." He snorted. "World's biggest geek falls in love with Miss America. And when you came riding up, the wind blowing the grass all around you, I felt like I could sweep you up and carry you off."

"Uh-huh. Witchcraft," said Rachel.

"In your eyes," replied her husband.

"Fairy potions," said John. "Do you happen to have the recipe?"

"Aw, you don't need it," came Rachel's voice. "You're cute enough without it. Besides, Geneva will come around, once she realizes how much fun you are."

"Do you think I'll have to give up my tall tales?"

"Not until Geneva gives up hers. Two weeks after hell freezes over. Give her enough time, and she'll come to love them. You'll never bore her."

"I hope so," sighed John. "She sure is pretty. And fun. I like her spunk."

"Yeah, well, believe it or not, I really think you're outclassed," laughed Rachel.

"What do you mean?"

"Oh, just that you don't always get away with your lies and maneuverings."

Geneva sat very still, not daring to breathe, yet almost suffocating from excitement and rage. She would have panted, shouted, shrieked, but she did not know for which reason. Clearly her sister and Wayne were conspiring with John behind her back, which infuriated her. And those awful things they were saying about her! But on the other hand, it was clear that John really, really liked her!

From the corner of the house came a dark, feline form. It was Petrarch, who caught her scent as soon as he made it past the wellhead. Delighted to find his mistress during his nocturnal prowl, he streaked to Geneva, rubbing against her and mewing loudly. Geneva held her breath, stroking him, trying to silence his excitement. Presently, they were joined by Esmeralda, then Evangeline and her two kittens. Geneva frantically tried to pet them all as they ecstatically climbed over her, meowing and creating such a racket that Sammy scrambled up, barking hysterically.

Wayne's voice rose above the noise. "Cut it out, Sammy. It's just those stupid cats. You don't need to go terrorizing them tonight. You might give them high blood pressure."

Geneva gritted her teeth against their laughter. *Everybody's such a comedian.*

Sammy was determined to be let out. Geneva had always thought that Rachel should teach that dumb dog better manners, and now the fool idiot was about to flush her out of her hiding place.

Quickly, lest someone open the door for Sammy and discover her, she hastily began crawling back through the border flowers along her entry route. The cats, ignoring Sammy's barks, followed her, rubbing their heads against her face and getting fur in her mouth.

Suddenly she stopped cold. The light from the porch fell dimly across her path, and there, coiled on a rock smack in the dahlias, lay a copperhead, at least three feet long, grinning its venomous grin and daring her to come closer. The cats caught sight of it about fifteen seconds after Geneva did, and their backs went up, accompanied with hisses and growls. But after this one brief show of bravado, they abandoned Geneva, who took a couple of shallow breaths and began to crawl backwards. About that time somebody finally freed Sammy, who took out after the cats, and when they eluded him, he frisked over to Geneva, tongue lolling.

You stupid dog, she thought, as she pushed him away. *Don't you realize there's a copperhead not four feet from here? Get out of my face!* She shoved him several times before Sammy caught the hint and gave up his slobbering caresses. He lumbered back up the porch steps, and the moment he began whining to be let in, Geneva again retreated from the porch door, straining her eyes in the darkness for sight of the snake. She wanted to pray, but somehow felt unworthy, and besides, it was difficult to beg for mercy while she was thinking murderous thoughts about her sister and brother-in-law. A glance behind her let her know that the copperhead had disappeared from its rock. Still, she sat silent, hoping earnestly that it was not seeking out her body heat, which by this time was getting pretty high.

She swallowed hard, shut her eyes for a moment to improve her night vision, then opened them wide, all the while trying to make herself small and invisible against the porch columns. Yes, there it was, slowly making its way in her direction. John was saying, "Tell me more about this Jacob's Mountain. What makes it so magical?"

Rachel's voice floated through the darkness, "Only the fact that Geneva thinks it is. If you can get her to agree to go with you, she'll probably be convinced that she'll love you forever, you poor man."

The snake had momentarily stopped, its tongue flicking out, tasting the air. Between it and Geneva lay a short, sturdy stick with a forked end. Very slowly and gently, she reached for it, her eyes locked onto the copperhead's, her hand inching forward almost imperceptibly. The snake glared at her with its beady, malevolent eyes, daring her to come closer, flicking its tongue steadily, communicating to Geneva that one of them would die tonight.

Playing chicken with a copperhead big enough to swallow me whole, she thought grimly. *How do I get into these messes?* But she was sure she would die right there in the dahlias before she allowed herself to be discovered. It was, to provide an understatement, a very tense moment.

Wayne entered the conversation. "Actually, I think that she'll make a pretty good wife once she's convinced that she wants to settle down. She's almost as much fun as you are, Rachel."

"She's certainly fun loving," returned Rachel. "But John," she continued in a warning tone. "Don't lead her on. I don't want my sister hurt."

"Yes ma'am. I've already made up my mind on that one. Strictly honorable and all that."

Geneva thought scornfully, *I'm about to be eaten alive by a poisonous snake, and you're worried about some man hurting me. I'll show you how tough I can be!* She lifted the forked stick and shoved it at the copperhead, pinning its wide, flat head against a mound of soft dirt. Although she pressed with all her strength, she could do no more than imprison it, and she was forced to hold her hand closer than she cared as the snake writhed and flailed at the air around it. Geneva gritted her teeth, sweating, and held on.

Somebody let Sammy back onto the porch. He flopped down noisily, panting, pleased with himself. Now Geneva was free from the threat of discovery via Sammy, but she could not release the snake. She dug in her heels and pressed against the stick, but the copperhead slowly began to squeeze itself forward. Geneva pressed harder, rotating the stick slightly. She prayed it would not break.

Just when she was sure her arm would drop off from fatigue, John commented on the lateness of the hour. On the porch, the trio rose in unison; Sammy thumped his tail, clamoring for a caress. As John said goodnight to his host and hostess, opening the back door and lumbering down the steps, Geneva could have touched the caricature of the cartwheeling cowboy on John's cast from where she sat. She pressed her head against the porch supports, holding onto the stick desperately as the strength fled from her arm. Silently, she waited until Rachel and Wayne had gone indoors and John had started his Jeep, then she eased sideways until she was able to place the fingertips of her left hand on a sizable stone. Slowly, agonizingly, she reached until the fingers slid over the top of the stone and pulled it toward her. The stick felt slippery in her hand; the snake flipped and lashed out, inching forward. Any moment now its head would be clear enough to reach her.

The sound of John's engine faded away. Not trusting the strength in her right arm any longer, Geneva bolted from her position, jerked up the rock, and before the snake realized that it had been freed, slammed it squarely on the poisonous head. Trembling, she lifted herself from the flowers, scooted around the side of the house, and hoisted herself into her bedroom for the second time that evening. Then she stripped out of her dirty clothes and fell into bed.

When she awoke, Geneva's first thought was to find a way to confront Rachel and Wayne about their slander of the night before. It wouldn't do to upset Rachel this late into her pregnancy, yet she felt she couldn't wait long before she at least let her know she did not appreciate her underhanded schemes. *Some people,* thought Geneva, *are positively diabolical. Imagine Rachel plotting against her own sister!* Because Rachel had been helping John to woo her, Geneva felt a little less piqued than she might have under different circumstances, but what if Rachel tried something like that with someone Geneva did not particularly like? What right had she to help someone trick her into going up to Jacob's Mountain? Geneva felt the righteous indignation rise up inside her. *She would never stoop to such tactics!* Irritated with everyone, she rose and went to breakfast.

Over cantaloupe, Rachel asked her if she were still angry with John, but Geneva brushed the question aside.

"You really worried us last night," Gaynell chided, "and John and several others went off looking for you. It was lucky Rachel found you sleeping in the bed before they got too far."

"Sorry," said Geneva, not especially contrite. "I just wanted to be alone for a while, think things over."

"That's okay, honey," said Rachel softly, then changed the subject. "I have a checkup this morning, so I thought I'd ride in with Wayne. If you're not too busy, maybe you could come into town later on and pick me up. We need some groceries."

A nice little plan stepped neatly into Geneva's head. *She would get Rachel off alone, away from Wayne, and away from Gaynell, too, who would no doubt stick up for Rachel. Today might just be the perfect day for a drive up the mountain with her loving big sister. After all, it had been a while since they'd had a heart to heart...*

"That's fine," she said sweetly. "As a matter of fact, I wanted to head over to Hickory Holler today, so we could just go on from there."

"Why do you want to go to Hickory Holler, Geneva?" asked Wayne.

"Well, you may have noticed I didn't give you a baby gift last night. I want to go over to that old woman who tats—what's her name, Mama?"

"Mrs. Wheater?" offered Gaynell.

"Lives in that old house on stilts? Big spring in the back yard?"

"That's her."

"I want to commission her to make a pair of christening caps. What do you think?"

"Why, Geneva, what a lovely thought," said Rachel.

"Oh, I don't think you should go," cautioned Gaynell. "There's a full moon tonight, and I don't think you should get too far from the hospital. You might just decide to have those babies tonight."

Rachel laughed. "Mama, you don't really believe that, do you? I still have four weeks to go, and I don't feel a bit ready. Just some Braxton-Hicks contractions now and then."

Wayne countered, "Yes, but you're awfully big. I don't think it's a good idea to travel all the way over to Hickory Holler."

"Wayne, it's not that far!" insisted Rachel, "And it's going to be a beautiful day. I tell you what. I'll ask Jackie if I can go, and if she says okay, I'll let you know. We'll take it easy, maybe take a picnic and be back around dark. I think it will be great fun. Besides, I'm getting a bad case of cabin fever. Riding around can't be worse than walking."

"Okay," sighed Wayne. "But if you feel anything, you turn back. You don't want to go into early labor back up in the high country."

"I don't like it," insisted Gaynell. "I know what full moons can do. I had both of you at a full moon."

"Yes, but there aren't that many premature births during a full moon," said Wayne. "I think they'll be all right."

"Great," said Rachel happily. Geneva felt a little guilty and decided she would not be too hard on her about the things she had said last night. And she would be getting heirloom lace christening caps for the babies. That, of course, was the real reason for the trip. Geneva finished her breakfast quietly, and after Rachel and Wayne left, she washed the dishes and packed a generous picnic.

"You may need some supper," worried Gaynell, "so take some extra sandwiches and these bananas and apples."

"Mom, we'll be fine," sighed Geneva, rolling her eyes. "Why is it that mothers are so overprotective?"

By nine thirty, Geneva was off in her little Mazda, quite looking forward to the trip into the high country where the rhododendrons and mountain laurel would still be in bloom. She met Rachel at the clinic, and after Rachel called Wayne and her mother to verify that Dr. Samson had declared her weeks away from delivery, the sisters were off for the drive to Hickory Holler.

If one were in a hurry, one could make the round trip in four hours, but Geneva and Rachel planned to take their time, stopping at every vista view and waterfall and chipmunk burrow. Before they got out of Tucker, they discovered a flea market and stopped for two hours, then Rachel, always hungry, insisted on eating lunch before they began the trip in earnest. It was well after noon before they began their ascent into the high mountains, and some time after that before Geneva could summon up enough remembered anger to discuss the incident of the night before.

"Oh, for heaven's sake, Geneva," groaned Rachel after Geneva had finished with her account of what she had heard and how she felt about it. "That's exactly what we were talking about. You're all the time doing things like hiding in the bushes and climbing in windows and telling men you like that you've never been serious about anyone, and then you get in an uproar when somebody tells a joke and you don't get it. You're one of the biggest liars I ever knew, but you'd sooner die than admit it. It's like you're in some crazy story of your own making, where you're the heroine, and you keep coming up with more and more bizarre situations just because you can. Don't you dare accuse me of slandering you. If that snake had bitten you, you would have had some explaining to do."

"Rachel, that's not fair. Wouldn't you try to find out what people were saying if you knew they were talking about you?"

"Of course, but I wouldn't get mad at somebody else for pulling the same stunt. Sheesh. What a hypocrite."

"Well, what about your conspiring behind my back with John? You're supposed to be on my side."

"I am on your side. But I'm also on his. The two of you are exactly alike, and you belong together. If I have to connive to keep you from blowing the best thing that ever happened to you, I will."

"What makes you think we're alike?"

Rachel hooted. "You both are about the most moony-eyed idiots I ever saw. Who else but you would name her stupid cats after great lovers, and who but John would find a way to make his name sound like he was descended from royalty? And speaking of names, Ms. *Le Noir*, don't you think it's a bit much to try to improve on your own father's name?'

Geneva felt outmaneuvered. "Oh, let's drop it, Rachel. I forgive you. Now shut up."

"Oh, thank you! I am forever grateful for your more than generous mercy! Now, are you going to go out with John again or what?"

Geneva tried to pout, but she couldn't help smiling. It was kind of nice to know that John really was concerned about her. *He had gone looking for her last night...*

"Wanna place bets on which one of you will get the other up to Jacob's Mountain?"

"Rachel, I have no intentions of taking John or anyone else up there. Really! The man lied to me!"

Rachel ignored her remark. "That poor man," she said, shaking her head. "John doesn't have any idea of what he's up against. I'd bet on you any day, and I bet you will do it in a way that no one can imagine. Probably make John think he's luring you up there and he'll feel guilty about it for years. And you'll help him perpetrate the myth!"

They both laughed. Geneva knew her sister might be right about that, for she had already begun toying with such an idea herself. Not seriously, of course, just as sort of an academic exercise.

Suddenly Rachel squealed, "Oh, Geneva! Look! *Look!*"

"Where?" Geneva craned her neck around.

"Pull over! Quick! Oh, go back, there was a pull-out back there. Oh, Geneva! I've never seen anything like it! *Hurry!*"

Geneva nearly tore the transmission out getting her car into reverse while it was still moving. Rachel had already jumped out, leaving the door open, and continued to scream loud shrieks of joy. Geneva jumped out of the car, looking back across the pass they had just crossed. Ahead of them the sun was shining; behind them the clouds had rolled darkly across the pass. But above them, glimmering in the afternoon light and vivid beyond imagination, was a double rainbow, with both arcs complete, straddling the sky from mountaintop to mountaintop. Geneva's soul soared up to those rainbows, which seemed to be made of grace—a gift straight from the hand of God. She wanted to climb on top of her car, to run back and clamber up the taller mountain, anything to reach that wondrous picture they saw there in the roiling, magnificent sky. Rachel was still screaming and laughing, pointing as if crowds of people were asking what she found so interesting, and Geneva couldn't stop shouting, "Oh, look! Look!" and clapping her hands. And then they both stood rapt and silent, alone in the chilly air, grateful for their own eyes, yet wishing they could share it with everyone whose lives touched their own. Rachel walked over to her sister and put her arms around her waist, and together they watched until the clouds rolled over and around the vision and left them alone. They stood silently for a while longer, filled with gratitude that some moments in life could be so sweet.

It was much later before they could bring themselves to leave the spot, hoping for a reoccurrence. They got the blankets out and lay on the hood of the car, always keeping their eyes upward, scanning for the treasure that only shortly before had been laid before them. But at last it began to rain, so they took cover in the car and made their way slowly up the mountain. It rained torrents, fountains, so hard that a few times Geneva was forced to pull over to wait for it to slack off before she could continue. With the rain came angry lightning, slashing all around them, more like mythical bolts from Zeus than merely earthly lightning bolts. The thunder was so loud and the flashes so close and bright that the women began to feel under siege, as if perhaps they had seen the rainbows illegally and had displeased their owner. Rachel shivered and commented nervously,

"Gee, I'm glad we aren't afraid of thunderstorms!" They laughed, and then crested the ridge. As suddenly as the rain had started, the sky turned blue again. The road there was dry, and the wind no stronger than the breath of one of Evangeline's kittens. Geneva and Rachel felt more thankful than they cared to let on.

They arrived at Mrs. Wheater's rickety old house much later than they had expected to. The place looked the same as Geneva had remembered it. Built of unpainted clapboard, it was perched upon a slope so steep that the front porch was built high on stilts. The whole rickety structure looked as if it would tumble down in the next strong wind. Back off to the left of the house gushed an exuberant spring, which emptied into a deep pool ringed by beech trees, then tumbled on down the mountain in a breathless, foamy rush. There were no signs of electricity or telephones; indeed, there were ample indications of no indoor plumbing. An outhouse sat off to the right; in the front yard a big cook-pot hung above a fire between forked sticks. Mrs. Wheater, bathed in a golden afternoon sunray, stood boiling clothes in the pot, adding handfuls of homemade lye soap shavings. Clothes hung about on clotheslines supported by leaning beech poles while Mrs. Wheater jabbed at the frothing pot with a paddle and smiled at her approaching company. The sisters felt as they always did here—that they could have been stepping back two hundred years in time.

There was a serenity about the ancient face as the old woman shaded her eyes and greeted them.

"Howdy."

"Hello, Mrs. Wheater. Do you remember us? Geneva and Rachel Lenoir," said Rachel.

"From the looks of ye, ye ain't no Lenoir now," said Mrs. Wheater soberly. "I surely hope ye got a husband, child."

Rachel laughed. "Yes, indeed, ma'am. And my condition is what brings us here. Do you still tat?"

"Yes, child, I do, though not as much as I useter. I turned ninety-four last month, and I don't see so well now."

Geneva looked at her eyes, which were as blue and clear as those of Rachel's small daughters. "Well, ma'am. I want to ask you if you would tat two christening caps for my sister's twins who will be born next month sometime. They will be my gift to them."

A smile beamed from the old face. "I will. Proudly. Twins is a blessing. I had two sets myself, and never were babies sweeter. They'll be girl twins, I reckon."

"I wouldn't be surprised, " said Rachel. "Boys are about as rare as bluebirds in January on both sides of our family. But what makes you think so?"

"Yer carryin' them right wide, like they's alayin' side by side. Ifn you kin tell yer expectin' from behind, they's girls. But ye shouldn't be up here this close to time. They's a full moon tonight, and they's asittin' real low. Likely they'll come soon. Mebe tonight."

The sisters smiled at Mrs. Wheater's lore. "All right," said Rachel. "If we can get a drink from your spring, we'll be off home right away. When do you think you can have the caps ready?"

"Ye come back one month from now. I awready got me some fine pieces goin', and I'll work ever chancet I git. But don't run off yit. I got some raspberry leaf tea for ye to take with ye. Ease your time." She moved slowly into the house and returned with the tea tied up in a cloth. Then she took a dipper, and walking around the house to the shimmering, clear pool, she dipped out a drink for each of them, and then another and another. They drank thirstily, knowing the water came from the very heart of the earth, cleaner and sweeter than water they could drink from anywhere else.

"Thank you," they said solemnly, feeling strangely reverent around the frail, bent woman, whom they knew to be stronger than either of them. She had raised a dozen children of her own and several others as well, and she embraced her rough life with a joy that neither Rachel nor Geneva could begin to fathom.

"Just a minute," said Rachel, moving toward the car. She returned carrying a loosely woven shawl in a soft red and handed it to Mrs. Wheater. "Here, I wove this from the wool of my sheep. I'd like for you to have it."

Mrs. Wheater stroked it, possessing it with her ancient, spotted hands, the fingers bent and carbuncled. But her touch was like a living thing, sparked with something like the desire of youth. "Did ye dye it with sassafras bark?"

"No," replied Rachel a little regretfully. "Just regular dye. Does sassafras come out this color?"

"Yes, indeed, and sourwood and sweetgum are red, too. Horsechestnut and hickory are yeller. Shingleoak comes out right purple."

"I'll remember that and try them next time around," said Rachel, looking at her intently, as if she wanted to memorize the lines crowning the woman's face, as well as her lore.

"Thank yew, girls, fer comin' ter see me. And thank yew for the perty shawl. It'll be a comfort, come cold weather. Now git on back down this mountain. I expect it'll be dark afore yew make it past Horse Creek. I got my warshin' to finish here afore I lose the sun." She shaded her eyes against the falling sun. "Looks like it's mebe too late, though. We had us a good rain early on this evenin'."

They turned to leave, but as they reached the car, Rachel called out, "Mrs. Wheater?"

"Yes, girl?"

"Does a double rainbow mean anything special?"

"Yew seen a double rainbow and you expectin' twins?" She scratched the back of her neck with a long, slow stroke. "Was they whole?"

"Yes."

"Was one of 'em brighter the othern?"

"A little."

Mrs. Wheater stood still for a moment, squinting down the long tunnel of her memory. Finally she spoke slowly, "I ain't fer certain it's true, but I've heered tell it means one will be a beauty, and real feisty. The othern will be sweet and easy. And one will be right handed, the other left."

"Thanks, Ma'am."

"Good-bye. Don't fergit ta drank yer tea."

Five

Mrs. Wheater had been right. It was already twilight by the time Geneva and Rachel crossed the creek that bounded Hickory Holler on the west, and the moon sat low in the east, full and round, bigger and more silvery than Geneva had seen it since childhood. Rachel leaned out of the window, looking at the moon behind them as they drove over the rickety bridge.

Watching swirling waters lapping at the high creek bank, she commented, "I guess this is Horse Creek. Golly, the water is up since we came in here. I'm glad we were able to get out before— Oh!" The exclamation broke Rachel's sentence off sharply. Geneva pulled her own eyes from the rabid creek to glance at her.

"What is it, honey?"

"I just felt a contraction. A hard one," replied Rachel, sounding surprised.

"Rachel, don't you dare tell me you're going into labor," warned Geneva.

"It's probably nothing. I've been having Braxton-Hicks contractions for a few days now. That just may have been a strong one. It surprised me, that's all."

Fifteen minutes later, Rachel drew in her breath sharply and put her hand low on her belly. Geneva pulled over to the shoulder of the road and stopped the car.

"I think we'd better not take the scenic route back. Surely there's another, quicker way off this mountain. Hand me the map in the glove compartment."

Rachel searched through the compartment, producing a ragged map that came apart in her hands as she opened it.

"How old is this map, Geneva? Is this the only one you have? It covers Virginia, too. Don't you have one that covers just West Virginia?"

"This will do," said Geneva, wishing she had one of Howard's slick, detailed road atlases that mapped out every byroad and trail. "Oh, here we are. This road we're on is somewhere up above highway one forty. When we hit it we can go back the way we came, but see, if we head east on one forty instead of west that will take us up the mountain instead of down for a way, but here we can cut over on this little road—is that one sixty-eight? One eighty-eight? Oh, well, we can find it, and that will take us over here to twelve-twenty, and straight into Tucker, sort of. We can find our way once we get off the mountain. This will put us out above Cleland anyway, doesn't it? And if you're in real bad shape, we can stop at the hospital there. It's a whole lot closer than Tucker."

"I don't know, Geneva. This one sixty-eight or whatever it is looks pretty iffy to me. See, it looks like it doesn't connect all the way over to twelve-twenty."

"That's just because the map's torn. Surely the road goes somewhere, and it travels straight toward twelve-twenty. And look, Rachel, it really is shorter, even with all the curves. I bet once we get to twelve-twenty, it'll be straight downhill."

"Okay," sighed Rachel, "but it's your neck if we get lost. What am I saying? I'm the one with my neck in the noose. Let's get out of here. I feel another contraction coming on."

Geneva turned uphill into the bright, lazy moon resting on the top of the mountain above them. Half an hour later, she pulled the car over and picked up the map beside her. She switched on the light, intently examining the faded streaks of colors and lines inked into the ragged paper.

"What are you after?" asked Rachel, her voice tight and worried.

"I'm not sure. It seems like we should have reached the turnoff by now, but it's so dark, I can't see anything." This was a lie, for the moon still shone huge and bright in the cloudless sky. "Did you catch the number of that road back there?"

"Geneva, are you lost?" demanded Rachel, then she added, "Oh, no here comes another one. It's been only fifteen minutes. Geneva, I really am in labor now."

Geneva felt the panic sear through her, but she forced herself to breathe slowly and sound calm. It wouldn't do to let Rachel go into hysterics now.

"No, I'm not lost. I just think I missed a turn. I'm going to turn around and look at that road we just passed." She turned the car around and roared back down the mountain to the intersection. A rutted road lay off to their right. There was no roadsign.

"That's not anything," said Geneva, still fighting to sound calm. "We'll just keep going in the direction we were. We'll have to find the turnoff pretty soon. It shows it right here on the map."

After another half hour, Geneva knew she was lost, but she kept silent, hoping to hide that fact for a while longer from Rachel, who was obviously seriously in labor.

Rachel sensed her desperation. "I don't know if you know this, little sister, but I happen to have quick labors. I hope you are prepared to deal with another double rainbow tonight." She began gasping.

Suddenly Geneva caught sight of something wonderful. A ramshackle settlement appeared dimly ahead of them. It was completely dark, but at least she thought she might find somebody who could tell them where they were. But just as she began to let the tension ebb from her shoulder, the Mazda's engine backfired twice, then clanged, sputtered, and died. Geneva pulled over to the shoulder.

"Oh, God, please help," moaned Rachel.

"Look," pointed Geneva. "There's something that might be a filling station ahead. We're headed sort of downhill, so I bet I can coast into it." She put the car in neutral, then opened her door and stepped into the road, pushing the Mazda back onto the pavement, where it began to roll briskly. In a moment they had pulled into a closed service station. Two men stood darkly beside a pickup truck, holding flashlights and peering into the depths of its engine. They did not hear the Mazda's silent approach.

"Oh, great," wailed Geneva. "Looks like two professional rednecks here to come to our rescue."

"Geneva, this is not the time to be a snob." Rachel paused, breathing carefully for a long contraction. "You'd better get out there and get those guys to help, and I mean it!"

Geneva jumped out of the car and moved toward the men, who by this time had looked up and were studying her intently. One was tall, slim, and dark, with acute good looks marred by an obviously hard life. He could not have been thirty, but he looked gaunt and worn, although he stood straight as a post in his faded shirt and greasy jeans. He did not move when he caught sight of her, but stood quietly, his hands hanging loosely at his thighs. *There was something menacing about him*, thought Geneva.

The other man looked a little younger. He was blonde and thin, typical of the Anglo-Saxon folk who peopled these hills, with a long, narrow nose and slender face. He had turned more slowly with an awkward, forward head slouch, hands seeking his hipbones. As Geneva approached, he removed the cigarette that dangled between his lips, dropping it to the ground and stepping on it casually. She was not exactly afraid of them, as she would have been afraid of similar looking characters on a dark night in DC, but something about the situation and the fact that she had just spent the last two years in a violent city made her wary.

Geneva mentally shook herself. There were merely the harmless, common hillbillies who lived here, daily eking out a living from the rocky slopes. If they weren't drunk, they probably were safe enough. She knew their kind well enough to know that there was still a fairly rigid code of honor among them: they would not hurt women in need of help. *But it would not be a pleasant night with them*, she thought. From the looks of them, they probably had a few old refrigerators and rusty cars resting in their front yards, and there would be absolutely nothing to talk about all the way to town if they drove them to Tucker. It was difficult to take Rachel's advice and not appear snobbish.

"Hello," she began politely.

The dark one gazed at her soberly, but when she stepped into the light, a sudden grin split his hard, dark face. "Hi, Red," he said.

"Look out," guffawed the other one. "He likes redheads. Hell, he's been marrit to two of 'em."

Geneva was a little taken aback. She had not expected anything but humble politeness from them, and she did not like the intensity of the dark one's countenance. She continued, "My car's broken, and I need to get my sister down off the mountain…" She trailed off, looking hopelessly away from the stare of the dark man who glanced briefly at her car, then returned his slow, steady gaze to her.

"I kin fix yer car fer ye, if ye gimmie a date," said the pale man. He was looking at her with obvious appreciation, his narrow shoulders hunched forward, a grin which sat somewhere between a leer and a mark of idiocy alighting his face.

Geneva swallowed hard. "I really don't think—"

Rachel's voice interrupted her. "For heaven's sakes, I know you. Your daddy sold us the farm up on Raven Creek. I went to school with you. I'm Rachel, Rachel Lenoir. My husband is Wayne Hillard."

Geneva forgot to wince at Rachel's mispronunciation of the family name. She was too busy trying to decide if she could trust these rubes to take them to the hospital. Maybe it would be better to find a phone.

"Is there a phone around here?" she asked, but no one heard her. The dark man was walking swiftly toward her, his face intent.

"Rachel Lenoir?" His pronunciation was even worse than Rachel's. Suddenly he dropped the stony façade to smile sincerely at Rachel. "Lordy, girl, I ain't seen you since the ninth grade. Was that you bought that Raven Creek place?"

"Yes, and that's Geneva—" began Rachel.

"Little Geneva?!" he exclaimed in his rapid Appalachian speech, turning to her, "Well, if you ain't growed up!" He turned to his companion excitedly, "You won't believe it, but this here was the scrawniest little old thing you ever did see. And just look at her now!" He laughed. "I'm Hard. Hard Knight," Geneva heard him say as he bobbed his head at her.

Geneva fought for meaning through the dialect. A faint, familiar bell tinkled deep in her mind at the sound of the first name. She didn't remember this man, but the name struck her. "Haa-waard Kni-eght?" she articulated primly, making the first name two syllables and placing the diphthong in the second, willing him to be schooled in the proper pronunciation of his own name.

"Yeah, Hard," came the eager, smiling reply. "This here's my cousin, Jimmy Lee."

Jimmy Lee grinned at her. "Jimmy Lee Land. Hidy," he said, giving her a little, cringing bow. Before she could respond, Jimmy Lee jerked his head sideways at the sound of a low growl coming from the darkness. Geneva turned her head toward it, too, in time to see a rangy dog, part hound, part who-knows-what, slinking low and menacing around the corner of the service station building. The growl deepened in intensity.

"Lamentations!" cried Jimmy Lee sharply. The growl grew louder.

"Lamentations!" cried Jimmy Lee again, louder. "Calm down! Don't git yersef all worked up, now. Jist shut up! Don't mind him, ma'am," he apologized to Geneva, looking very embarrassed. His eyes darted back to the dog. *Lamintaaashuuuuuuns!* Don't yew start!" His voice held a desperate warning.

But the dog was still inching forward, his growls growing louder and meaner. He began to bark in a strange, snarling way that nearly terrified Geneva. She took a step back. Lamentations looked back over his shoulder with wide, rolling eyes, growling louder, then snarling and barking. Suddenly, he gave a mighty leap backward and started chasing his tail in a frenzied display of hysterical anger, snapping and thrashing, yelping and barking. Jimmy Lee cringed with embarrassment, while Howard Knight dropped his eyes and raised a hand to his mouth. Geneva thought he looked like he was hiding a grin.

At last, Jimmy Lee sprang into action. "Lamentations!" he shrieked, picking up a newly downed leafy branch that lay near the truck and striding resolutely over to the frenzied dog. "Igod, yew stop that! *Now!*" He proceeded to flail at the dog with the branch, which was so large and full of leaves that it did not serve as a proper beating stick. It merely looked like he was waving it gently through the air around Lamentation's head, brushing the animal with the leaves. Geneva stared, astonished. Howard Knight was wiping his mouth with his hand and his shoulders moved convulsively. Jimmy Lee shouted louder, redoubling his efforts to control the waving tree limb.

The dog finally slowed down, then gradually stopped his circling. He made one last snap at his tail, which, Geneva noticed, was bent in several places and lacked big patches of hair along its length. Jimmy Lee dropped the branch, then turned to Geneva apologetically. "Don't mind him, ma'am. An eagle tried to carry him off when he wuz a pup and dropped him on his head. He ain't been right since. Good dog, though," he added lamely.

"Howard, I'm sorry, but we've got a real problem here," broke in Rachel. "I'm having a baby—two of them actually, and we've got to get to town right now. We're lost, and don't even know how far we are from a hospital. Are we anywhere near Tucker?"

"About three hours, I reckon, but you're on the wrong road, and you're goin' the wrong way. Ye kin cut over on Tab Cat Road about a mile up ahead to git over to the highway, then turn south. Yew stay on this road, ye end up in Kentucky."

Geneva was quiet, thinking desperate thoughts. She remembered the times Howard, the boyfriend back in DC had scolded her for getting them lost in the city. She had thought she could do better out in the open, on her own turf.

"Can you take us?" Rachel looked at him despairingly, then closed her eyes while she breathed very deliberately for a full minute.

Howard Knight's expression changed abruptly. He whirled, slamming down the hood of the pickup truck. "Jimmy Lee," he directed the young man beside him, "yew jump in the back. We cain't waste no time." Striding to Geneva's car on his long legs, he gently helped Rachel out, then nudged her toward his truck. "You git in first," he instructed Geneva. "I got a stick shift, and she ain't gonna fit."

Geneva obliged. Jimmy Lee was already perched in the bed of the pickup truck, looking pale and worried. He held Lamentations closely in his arms. Howard virtually lifted Rachel into the truck, then sprang around to the driver's side.

The truck jerked forward, spinning gravel into the two ancient gas pumps, then laid rubber on the blacktop as Howard Knight attacked the mountain road. Geneva closed her eyes and fought the urge to wrestle the wheel away from this crazy man who drove as if the road were white hot. She felt like she might be on a wild amusement park ride, but a moment later, when he turned off the highway onto a dirt road marked with a one-way sign, the amusement park image gave way to something far more sinister.

Oh God. Oh God. Oh God! Geneva peered into the darkness beside the window and wondered, nearly aloud, where he was taking them. Her ideas about the hillbilly code of honor dissipated before images planted by horror movies which told of backwoodsmen kidnapping helpless women and holding them in filthy cabins, maybe even in caves deep in some mountain ravine, foiling all attempts of their loved ones to find them. *It would not be difficult to dispose of her car. She and her sister and those approaching babies might never see civilization again. Oh God. Even dogs would not be able to track them. They would disappear off the face of the earth...*

It was an incredibly bad road, so bad that Geneva wondered if it were a road at all, or simply an old riverbed, so filled it was with rocks and ruts. Howard was forced to slow down, but not enough, as far as Geneva was concerned. She already felt she might be suffering from a whiplash injury. Rachel moaned once, then cried out aloud. Howard glanced over Geneva's head at Rachel and slowed to a crawl.

"Sorry about the road," he said, "but we won't be on it long, and it takes a big piece out of the trip. He looked again at Rachel's face, white and frightened in the moonlight pouring over her, lighting up her golden hair and giving her an ethereal glow. "We're gonna make it, girlie," he continued reassuringly. "This here road's as sweet as a lady once yew git past this part that got warshed out last spring. She'll take us right on over to the main highway, and then we kin git you offa this mountain."

Sure enough, the road evened out shortly, becoming less of a washboard and more of a real road laid over with gravel. Geneva's more spectacular fears of the strangers diminished with the dark man's gentle tone. Still, she watched him with suspicion as he drove. His jaw was hard, the muscles clenched in the clean chin, and his dark eyes held a quick, desperate look as he maneuvered the truck around the rocks and switchbacks. He kept glancing at Rachel. Geneva noticed that he seemed to relax as five, then seven, then eight minutes passed without a contraction.

Geneva felt desperately helpless, bouncing between the hillbilly and her huge, laboring sister, and she wished fervently that somebody would say something to ease the clawing tension. She cleared her throat and said inanely, "So, Howard, I don't remember you. Did you go to Tucker High?"

Howard steered the truck halfway up an embankment to avoid a boulder in the road, then bounced back into the smoother ruts. "Haw, no. I quit after the ninth grade. Didn't see no sense in it."

"Oh," Geneva said quietly. Her fear subsided enough to allow her to be aware of the ugly head of elitism rearing up in her brain.

She felt her head go back, her nostrils flare; the city twin sat in a huff, but the country twin tried to be cordial.

"So, do you farm up here?" It was all she could think of to say.

Howard glanced at her briefly, the first time he had looked at her since he had seen Rachel's predicament. She saw his face harden, his eyes narrow, then he turned his eyes back to the road. After a moment, he spoke.

"I got me a little cash crop back up in one of the hollers." He grinned slyly, keeping his eyes straight ahead. Geneva sensed that he was taunting her.

"Tobacco?' she asked brightly.

"Naw," he guffawed. "Hemp. But don't tell nobody. Them revenuers has been snoopin' around, actin' suspicious. Can't nobody find my patch, though."

"Hemp?" asked Geneva. "You mean what they make rope out of?"

"Marijuana, Geneva," said Rachel gently. "A lot of the farmers up here need a good cash crop just to hang on to their land, and it's one of the most lucrative."

"Oh," said Geneva again, then fell silent for several more minutes. She listened to Rachel breathe.

She thought about Howard's cash crop. At one time in her life, she had smoked quite a lot of grass, and she remembered that it had drastically altered her life for a short while. In fact, she credited several interesting decisions to it: her choice of a major, her way of looking at the world; it had even played a large role in the loss of her virginity. Looking back, she remembered how much she might have regretted that last event if she hadn't enjoyed it so much. Now the only thing she regretted was the young man with whom she had been involved.

He had been an actor, an MFA student from New Jersey, and he had been one of the most beautiful, most talented people she had ever met. She had been a freshman straight from the hills, straight from the Puritan values of her home nest and of the First Congregational Church of Tucker. Because of Jerry, she had changed her major from education to theatre, finding in him a mentor and an inspiration. She adored him and took every opportunity to be near him, hoping he would notice her and ask her out.

One night he invited her to his apartment, offered her a toke, and then seduced her. She had loved it. She had loved him, too, she thought, and, forgetting everything her mother had ever told her about Yankee men, and an agnostic to boot, she had moved in with him, feeling beautiful and important and reckless. She and Jerry had smoked a lot of dope, and they had always made love while they were high. For three weeks, she believed she had discovered the meaning of life.

Then one night, Jerry had laughed while he was rolling a joint, saying, "I love it when you get high. You're such a slut. The worst I've ever seen. A hillbilly slut." He threw back his head and laughed for a long time, then reached over and pinched her bare nipple, hard, through her T-shirt. Still laughing, he told her how he always enjoyed making it with sluts. Then he threw himself at her, pinning her under him, kissing her and fondling her. Geneva had lain stock still under his weight, too stunned to move, hearing her mother's voice, her father's voice, her grandmother's voice, even the voice of Miss Lacy, her Sunday School teacher, all warning her, all telling her to *run, run, run, to get away, or she would be lost, drugged, damned, dragged off into a gutter, surrounded by leering men who would laugh at her and hurt her.* Responding reflexively, she had brought her knee up sharply into Jerry's groin, then she shoved him off and walked out. She had never spoken another word to Jerry again except once, when they were in a play together, and then it was only the lines she had to deliver. Nor had she ever touched illegal drugs again.

Suddenly Rachel gasped, "Oh, Howard," she said breathlessly, "I've messed up your truck bad."

"How, darlin'?"

"My water just broke all over the place. Oh, gosh, what a mess."

"Hey, don't you worry about a little mess in my truck. Just last week Jimmy Lee got drunk on somma his no good moonshine and puked all over the place. A year or two back, my cousin Billy Ray got in a knife fight and bled to death all over the front seat here. Don't you worry about no mess."

"He died right here in this truck?" gasped Geneva.

"Yep. We tried to make it to the hospital, but we only got as far as Bearhead Creek."

"I'm sorry," began Geneva, then her words died. The night was beginning to seem too unreal.

"Oh, that's awright," said Howard with a grim laugh. "He was a mean sonnava bitch anyway. He deserved everthang he got."

Without warning, Howard slammed on the brakes, turning the steering wheel sharply to the right. The truck skidded, then spun around and crashed down an embankment. Geneva felt a clean, sharp hurt in her left temple, and for the next few moments, she felt dreamy, watching everyone moving silently through milky clouds. She shook her head. Her ears filled with sound—raging, thundering, oceans of sound, somehow connected with pain. She looked at Howard in confusion, expecting him to explain the roar.

He seemed much too close. She tried to move away from him, but movement required an enormous effort. There was a terrible weight upon her. After a moment of struggling, she gave up and looked at Howard again. He was holding his hand to his head, and as Geneva watched, still wondering about the roaring, he began to delicately prod his forehead that had bloomed red with blood. As he turned his head, he caught Geneva's eye, then stared straight at her for what seemed like a long time. Slowly, as if he were moving under the sea, he moved his hand from his own face, reaching out to Geneva's. She watched him without curiosity, expecting the touch, wondering if she would feel it. But just as his fingers closed the distance between them, he startled and drew back his hand. Somewhere a woman had begun screaming. A vague pain settled in Geneva's right ear.

Howard swung his head to his left, peered into the darkness, then looked quickly toward Geneva, then past her. There was a click, as if something mechanically shifted into focus, and Geneva became more aware of what was happening. Looking out Howard's window, she saw black water at eye level less than three feet away, swirling angrily past newly overturned trees. The truck they were in was upright on its wheels, but resting on so steep an embankment that at first Geneva perceived that it was lying on its side. The roaring sound came from a waterfall ten feet away from their heads; the screaming came from Rachel, who was lying against Geneva's right side, her open, screaming mouth pressed against Geneva's ear. Geneva, in turn, was lying against Howard.

"What is it?' Geneva asked. Her voice sounded oddly calm.

"Bridge out," returned Howard grimly. "Musta been a flash flood from the storm."

Rachel, screaming and gasping, grabbed Geneva's hand and stared at her, her eyes wild and unfocused. Howard reached across Geneva to hold Rachel by the shoulder. "Don't go off on me now, honey," he said, looking fiercely at her and squeezing her arm. Waiting until the contraction ended, he asked, "Did ye git hurt?"

Rachel focused on him, panting. She shook her head, no. Geneva suddenly felt irrationally annoyed. Here she was, wedged between this forward man and an incredibly fat woman, as smashed as a banana sandwich, and nobody was paying one bit of attention to her plight. Howard and Rachel were talking around and through her as if she did not exist.

"Yer doin' jist fine and we're goin' to git ye out of here so ye kin have them little babies in a nice, clean, hospital," he said gently, patting and stroking Rachel's head.

"I don't think so," whimpered Rachel. "I think I'm close to transition." Geneva's hurt brain registered a new level of understanding. *Something was happening to Rachel! Something bad!* As if to confirm her thoughts, Rachel vomited into her sister's lap. Piqued, Geneva merely sat there, which she would have done even if she could have moved. There was nothing else to do. The world was conspiring against her.

"Jist hang on," commanded Howard. "I know what to do." He

squirmed out of the open truck window and began making his way up the bank toward the passenger side. As soon as he had vacated his seat, Geneva slid helplessly against the door, pushed by Rachel's considerable weight. After another moment of muddling through her confusion, Geneva squeezed herself out of the window and followed Howard. She did not know what else to do. Clambering up the embankment, Howard suddenly stopped and wheeled, fairly tumbling into the stream.

"What are you doing?" screamed Geneva above the roar.

Howard turned briefly, then pointed downstream at a dark lump huddled on a sandbar. It was Lamentations, worrying with another, smaller lump protruding out of the water.

"That's Jimmy Lee," he said, stepping into the waist-deep, swirling blackness, fighting his way, falling down and fighting his way back up again. The water was pulling at the motionless form. Lamentations had caught Jimmy Lee's shirt collar in his teeth, and bracing feet into the soft sand, strained to hold the man's head out of the rushing water. The current caught Jimmy Lee's body in an eddy and began moving it downstream. Slowly, an inch at a time, the water gained against Lamentations, until the dog, too, was submerged in the angry water.

The fog in Geneva's brain lifted, and everything fell into sharp focus. She did not wait for Howard's cry for help, but flew into the swollen creek. The moment her feet hit the mossy rocks she slipped, plunging into the icy, unbelievably strong current. Caught in its frenzied embrace, Geneva struggled to keep her head above water as it washed her downstream, buffeting her, bruising her whole freezing body against rocks and logs. Despite her desperation, her mind cleared enough to react. She crouched down into the wild torrent to keep her center of gravity low, and she fought the current, grabbing the rocks, shoving with her feet, half swimming, half scrambling her way toward the drowning, perhaps already drowned man.

Howard was already there; Lamentations had disappeared, but Howard had turned Jimmy Lee's face up out of the water and was pulling at him with all the strength in his powerful arms and legs. Slipping on the glassy rocks, he fell down repeatedly before Geneva reached them. Keeping low in the water, sometimes on her knees, Geneva helped him inch Jimmy Lee, a limp, dead weight, toward the bank.

"Oh Lord God," moaned Geneva as they shoved their burden toward safety, now several yards downstream from where they had begun. "I can't take any more of this."

"Yes yew kin. Git up there and pull. We hafta haul him up on high ground and see if he's still alive."

Geneva forced herself out of the water and up the bank, holding Jimmy Lee's arm so the current could not pull him away from Howard. Together, she and the dark man dragged the unconscious form up the river bank to a safe place, then Howard dropped to his knees and put his head to his cousin's chest. Rolling him over, he began working furiously to pump water from the drowning man's lungs. Rachel screamed from the truck. Geneva felt like wailing herself, but suddenly, Jimmy Lee began coughing and struggling, and Howard stood up abruptly. "He's awright. Stay here. I'll be back direckly. I got kin lives just up this holler."

He ran, disappearing into the dark, swallowed by the huge, roaring, black forest around her.

Geneva had never felt so alone in her life. She looked in the direction he had run for several seconds, lost in helpless despair and panic. But just when she thought she might run after Howard, now her only hope, her only link to safety, Rachel's screams snapped her back into focus. She scurried down the bank to peer into the window at her sister.

"What's happening? Where's Wayne?" cried Rachel, bathed in sweat. "Oh, I can't stand this!"

Geneva gritted her teeth and said resolutely, "Listen, honey. You gotta get in control. We've had a wreck, and Jimmy Lee's been hurt, and Howard's gone for help. Now breathe. No, don't thrash around. Breathe. Concentrate. Look at my face. That's it, *breathe*. That's good." She reached into the truck and pulled Rachel toward her, stretching her out on the seat so that she reclined at a fifty degree angle, practically standing upon the door of the truck. Rachel grew quieter.

"That's good. You're doing great. Try to take the next one on your own. I gotta go see if Jimmy Lee's all right."

Geneva ran back to the injured man. He was still lying beside the surging creek, but his eyes were open and he looked at Geneva dazedly.

"Am I daid?" he asked simply.

"No. I think you're fine. Can you sit up?"

"No." He said it without emotion. Then he closed his eyes again. Geneva ran her fingers over his head. Behind his left ear was a gash, and her fingers came away from his head feeling sticky and warm. She wished she could faint, or better, wake up and find herself in the downy four poster back at Rachel's house. Where was this Howard?

She ran a short distance up the slope in the direction he had taken, but something told her she was behaving irrationally, so she turned back to the truck, hoping with all her considerable will that Rachel's labor would slow down. Back in the truck, Rachel was deep in concentration, allowing her brain and body to work together through the intense contraction which had taken hold of her. She was breathing deeply and deliberately, her eyes focused on the rabbit's foot hanging from the rear view mirror.

"Oh, *good girl!*" Geneva said, almost sobbing. She had never seen anyone in labor before, but she knew Rachel had regained some control over her pain. She stroked her sister's head until Rachel growled though gritted teeth,

"Don't touch me. I'm going to do this all by myself, and then I'm going to kill Wayne, and you, too."

Bewildered, Geneva made her way back to Jimmy Lee, who was breathing steadily, his eyes still closed. "Jimmy Lee. I don't know you, but I sure hope you don't die on me. *Oh, God, please don't let him die!*" she sobbed. "Howard! Howard, where are you?" She suddenly remembered that she had been calling the name of her former lover without even recalling his face, and she laughed hysterically at how she had repeated that very name in grief and heartache only the day before. *Oh, God,* she began again. *Please let me grow up before I make any more wedding plans.* Then she put her head to Jimmy Lee's chest and listened to the faint, but regular, heartbeat.

It came to her that she was cold, very cold, so cold that she had been shivering ever since she had fallen into the water to rescue Jimmy Lee. And if she was cold, Jimmy Lee could be in real danger. She remembered something about keeping shock victims warm. Again, she ran back to the truck to look for blankets or something with which to cover him. Rachel was quiet, but she gave Geneva a murderous look as she passed by. Geneva knew there was nothing in the cab, but she thought there might be something in the back, so she hauled herself upon the tire to peer in. Nothing. Just some tools and a few greasy rags. Not enough to do any good at all. In despair, she looked around, racking her brain for some solution. *How do you save a man from hypothermia?* Then she noticed the shovel, a big, heavy garden shovel a few yards from the truck. It could do some serious digging in the right circumstances. She grabbed it, and returning to Jimmy Lee, began to dig a shallow trench the size of a man, working quickly in the soft humus. When she finished the trench, she rolled Jimmy Lee into it and covered all but his head with the dirt, still warm from the earlier sun.

This is all my fault, Geneva mumbled as she worked. *Here I am, dragging my pregnant sister up to the top of a mountain where there are no phones, no ambulances, not even any bridges. And why? Because I'm stupid, self-centered, and full of crazy notions. I could have gone up by myself to see Mrs. Wheater. But no, I had to drag Rachel along just so I could yell at her for telling the truth about me.* Her voice grew louder. *Oh, God. I promise I won't go hiding in any more bushes. Let Jimmy Lee live. Let Rachel and the babies be all right. Oh, God, I'm so sorry!*

Jimmy Lee moaned, pulling her attention back to him and his wounds. The moon had set, and the dawn was still hours from offering its promise of light, but Geneva tried to peer at Jimmy Lee's head as she probed gently with her fingers over his bloody scalp. She hoped the skull was intact. Perhaps the gash behind his ear was superficial and he was only unconscious, not in a coma or dying. Because she did not know what else to do, she gnawed at the hem of her skirt until she had started a tear, then ripped off the circumference and carefully wrapped it around Jimmy Lee's head. Somewhat calmed by the sense that she had been productive, she slowly made her way back to Rachel to hold her hand and stroke her forehead until the laboring woman began another contraction and demanded to be left alone.

After what seemed like long hours of running back and forth between Rachel and Jimmy Lee, Geneva heard loud noises in the thicket. Enormous shapes loomed up from the shadows, causing Geneva a moment of terror before she realized that the shapes were only a team of Percherons. Howard Knight was holding the lead, and behind the horses trailed a buckboard wagon.

"Oh, Lord God, he's dead awready," moaned Howard the moment he saw the mound of dirt over Jimmy Lee's body. "She's done gone to burying him. Oh, Pappy, Mam-maw, I'm sorry!" Confused, Geneva peered into the darkness. After a moment, she saw an old man sitting in the buckboard, his head in his hands, his body shaking with grief. An equally old woman peered out from underneath a shapeless hat and wrung her hands.

It took another moment for Howard's words to register, but the instant they did, Geneva jumped up, shrieking, "No!" Running to the buckboard in her sudden fear that Howard might complete the burial before she could stop him, and desperate to end the grieving of the old people who had come to her rescue, she hurriedly explained, "I just covered him up to keep him warm. He's fine, really. Just cold." She was having trouble keeping her own teeth from chattering.

The old man's tears stopped abruptly, and he lifted his eyes to hers. "Ye say he ain't daid, honey?"

"No sir," returned Geneva. "I'm sorry I scared you. I didn't know how else to keep him warm."

"Praise Jesus!" shouted the old man. He leaped out of the buckboard and flung himself across the would-be grave, wailing a long, loud prayer of gratitude.

The old woman, tiny as a child, climbed down from the wagon and addressed Howard. "Chap, Look Jimmy Lee over and if ye think it's awright to move 'im, git Pappy to hep ye lift him in the buckboard. Where's that woman?" She straightened her back and looked around her.

"Mam-maw, Miss Rachel's still in the truck, I reckon. This here's Miss Geneva. Geneva, these here is my folks, my Grammaw and Pappaw. They've come to hep ye."

The old woman glanced at Geneva and nodded, then hurried to the river bank, slipping toward the truck, surprising Geneva with her quickness. After a second's hesitation in which she worried about the buried Jimmy Lee, Geneva hurried after her.

"How often are yer pains acomin', child?" Howard's grandmother asked Rachel.

"Often," was all Rachel could say, between pants. I gotta *puuush!*" She ended the sentence with a deep groan. Geneva did not know anything about these matters, but it appeared to her that Rachel was already pushing.

"Not yit, honey. We're gonna git yew outta this here truck and up on flat ground, then ye kin push away." The old woman never took her eyes off Rachel, but called over her shoulder, "I need me somebody over here to hep me lift her. She ain't walkin' nowheres." She addressed Rachel again, and her voice gentled, "Now don't ye push yit, honey. Jist another minit. Kin ye hold back a minit?"

Rachel, her eyes bright and wide, nodded silently, and closed her eyes, breathing slowly, deliberately. Howard left Jimmy Lee and his grandfather, who was still shouting his praise to heaven, and ran crablike across the steep slope toward his grandmother. Geneva helped them ease Rachel downhill, out of the truck. Even as they worked, another contraction took hold of Rachel. She began a series of short, puffing breaths. He face paled; she willed her body to relax, despite the enormous desire to push that thundered over her, engulfing her.

"Tell that old fool to shut up and git somethin' to lay her on," ordered the grandmother. Howard glanced toward his grandfather, then back at the old woman, but he did not move. With a snort, Mam-maw marched up the bank toward the old man, took off her hat, and began thrashing him with it, shouting, "Yew idiot!" Cain't yew see this ain't no time to be aprayin'? Git up offa there and act like a growed man!" The old man merely prayed louder, burying his face in the soft dirt over Jimmy Lee's chest, wailing in a strange, unintelligible voice. Mam-maw thrashed harder, but the old man would not stop his devotions. He lifted his hands up, shouting, "Thank ye, Lord, for deliverin' my boy from the jaws of death. Thank ye Jesus! Save this boy! Take care of these little babies acomin' into this world. Lay yer healin' hand on this laborin' woman and ease her pains! Touch Jimmy Lee, too, Lord. Open his eyes. Anoint his head with your healin' touch, Oh, Lord God, oh, Jesus!" and again he broke into another language which Geneva could not decipher.

For a little while longer, the woman continued to thrash and utter her own commandments for the man to cease, but shortly, she seemed to lose interest, for the blows turned into little pats, then to a futile fanning over the old, white head. The action reminded Geneva so much of Jimmy Lee's impotent attempts to stop Lamentations' tail-chasing with a leafy switch that she wondered if it was a family trait to discipline people and pets by beating them with soft objects. As the blows lessened, Geneva turned, searching the darkness for the poor dog that had helped to save Jimmy Lee's life.

Lamentations was nowhere to be seen, but Howard came into view, dragging a sheet of plywood from the wagon.

"I got, it Mam-maw. Ye kin quit ahittin' on 'im and come on back. I got it."

Abruptly the old woman dropped her hat and scurried back down the embankment, muttering, while Howard laid the plywood beside the truck. Together, Geneva, the old woman, and Howard eased Rachel onto it. Geneva looked into her sister's face, frightened and astonished by what she saw there. Rachel's eyes were glazed, and she wore a fierce expression that did not fit her gentle face. Geneva turned in her fear.

The old woman suddenly lost her pique and turned her attention to Rachel. "Awright, now we're gonna pull ye up this here bank. It'll be rough, but jist hold on a little bitty minute. Git on that side, Chap. Little Miss, ye reckon ye kin push from the bottom?"

"Yes, of course," said Geneva, slipping down the bank to within inches of the roiling water but glad to be able to offer something other than her panic.

They all pushed and strained, including Rachel, who by now had given up all pretense of slowing the birth of her babies and was laboring to push the life from her womb, rising to her calling as women have done since the beginning of human time. By the time they had reached the top of the bank, Rachel was oblivious to all that was around her—so concentrated she was on her laboring. Geneva stood aside.

"Lordamercy, she's apushin' fer real now. Yew there, git her drawers offen her," the woman instructed Geneva. "Chap, git my bag and some quilts offen the buckboard. We gonna have us a coupla babies here in a minit."

Geneva lifted Rachel's dress and tried to slide her panties off, but Rachel's legs were splayed wide, knees up. Seeing Geneva's helplessness, the old woman shouldered her aside and cut them off with a pocket knife, then she circled around behind Rachel and gently but firmly pushed her forward until she was sitting nearly upright.

"Okay, honey. I'm gonna put this quilt under you sos yer little babies will have somethin' soft to land on. Kin ye set up a little more? Put yer feet up under ye and kindly squat like, but not too much." Rachel did not comply. Her eyes were closed, deep groans came from somewhere in her bowels, for she was pushing hard, hard. Geneva had never seen anything so intense.

Golly, no wonder they call it labor, she thought to herself.

Together she and the woman propped Rachel up and rolled the quilt underneath her. Rachel pushed again, the groans leaping from her lips like wild animals. Then the old man suddenly shouted, "Amen, Lord! Thanky Lord!" then he sprang up, busying himself with raking the dirt off Jimmy Lee.

"Chap!" he shouted, "Git over here and hep me git Jimmy Lee in the wagon. We ain't got all night."

Howard, no longer needed with the women, sprang to his side. Rachel pushed and groaned louder and louder so that Geneva felt inundated with the sound. She shook her head to try to focus on something other than Rachel's apparent agony.

The old woman spoke calmly. "That's real good, honey, yer doin' jist fine. Here, hold this here light fer me, girlie." She gave a short, delighted laugh. It sounded like a child's laughter. "I see me a little head acomin', and I need both hands to catch it." Handing the flashlight to Geneva, she uncorked a jug of clear liquid which she poured over her hands. Recognizing the smell of corn liquor, Geneva hoped it really would serve as a proper antiseptic. But she did not worry about dirt for long. Her attention was pulled to the scene before her, her eyes soaking up the miracle. A tiny head was crowning. With the next push, Geneva could see the face of the child who would carry the genes, the life that had sustained her sister, herself, her parents, each of her ancestors who had worked the soil and worshiped and borne children and had looked at the startling sky and had been glad to be alive.

The child was suddenly out, wet, glistening, and screaming. Geneva stood rooted, speechlessly watching the babe and the old woman until she had wrapped her in a soft quilt and handed her to Geneva.

"Keep up with that light, girlie, we got us anothern' acomin' right now!" She bent again in time to catch another tiny head as it pushed its way into the cold, starry night.

Geneva held her baby niece and laughed and sobbed and looked into the little face, which suddenly calmed and peered back at her. Geneva sought the eyes, which seemed rooted in the depth of all life and wisdom, and she felt herself falling in love.

Half an hour later, Geneva sat wrapped in blankets in the back of the buckboard. She was still holding her niece, had, in fact, refused to give her up long enough for Rachel to hold her, but had simply held her next to Rachel's head so the new mother could see her and touch her. Rachel lay next to Geneva, holding the second twin and occasionally reaching up to put a hand on her other daughter. The old woman sat at Rachel's right side, stroking the proud mother's forehead and frequently lifting the corners of the quilts to peer in and grin a semi-toothless grin at the two newcomers into the world.

Jimmy Lee, still unconscious, lay at their feet, a silent reminder that all was not well. Howard led the team of mighty horses back up the hill; the old man sat on the forward seat and held the reins. They were bouncing slowly uphill under a high canopy of trees into the cold darkness of night, but Geneva felt light and warm. She had just experienced a miracle. She felt that her sister, so recently brushing shoulders with death, now laughing and singing, should be canonized.

"Oh, law," said the old woman, "I ain't had me a night like this since December the sixth, nineteen forty-one, the night of Pearl Harbor. Lordy, that's more'n thirty-five years ago. I had to deliver a youngin in a blizzard and the baby was laid wrong so's I had to turn him around, and I didn't have no hep cause the daddy had done passed out the minit I got there."

"Did everything turn out all right?" asked Rachel, sympathetic for the woman laboring under conditions worse than her own.

"No, the baby was real purty, but they wuz somethin' wrong with him, and he didn't grow up with good sense. I don't know iffn it was because of being laid wrong or if they was somethin' else wrong with him. But he was a purty one—real blue black hair and skin as white and pink as a dogwood blossom. And he was real sweet, too. He had him a passel of brothers, and all of them was smart as whipsnakes, but none was no sweeter. Birds would come and light on his shoulder, and he could walk right up to a beehive and the bees would crawl all over him and not sting him. I never seed nothin' like it."

"What happened to him?" asked Geneva.

"He liked to go off by hisself sometimes, and when he did that, he'd tarry for days, roamin' the woods til he either come on back by hisself or somebody found him. He disappeared one day in the fall, and they didn't find him atall, searched all fall and winter. But in the spring, they found some of his gear warshed up on a creek bank down below a high lookout. Most folks think he fell off the mountain and got et up."

Rachel pulled her child closer to her. The three women fell silent for a while. Then the old woman sighed and said, "Whatcher gonna name 'em, honey?"

"I had some names picked out," said Rachel, "But somehow they don't seem right now. What's your name, ma'am?"

"Lenora's the name my mama give me. I go by Sissy."

"Lenora, that's a pretty name. A lot like our family name, Lenoir," smiled Rachel. She looked down at the small face so close to her own. "I think I'd like to name this one after you, Lenora."

"They, howdy!" crowed Lenora. I ain't never had no child named after me, as many as I've brung into the world. I thank ye, honey."

Rachel looked up at Geneva, who was smiling at her new niece. "And I think that one should be named for you, Geneva. We can call her Genny so we won't get you mixed up. What do you think?"

"I think you do me too great an honor, big sister," said Geneva, feeling the tears well up. "Especially considering that because of me you had these babies practically on top of a mountain in the middle of the night with no doctor."

"I'm glad they were born here," smiled Rachel, looking around.

"This is where they belong, here in this wild, beautiful place. From the beginning, everything about their lives will be special." She leaned her head back against the quilt and snuggled down, sighing deeply, then she opened her eyes and brightened.

"What time is it?" she asked.

"A little after midnight, maybe one o'clock." replied Lenora. "I cain't see the stars through the trees, but I reckon we got a few hours afore the sun comes up."

Rachel grinned. "These babies' birthday is July seventh. What about that! Seven, seven, seventy-seven! Is that a sign of good luck, or what? After that double rainbow, on this mountain."

"Boy howdy! They'll sure have a tale to tell!" agreed Lenora.

Rachel sighed again and settled back down into the quilts. Presently, it grew silent except for the soft breathing of the horses and the creaking of the wagon.

"Twins is special," mused Lenora after a lull. "I was a twin, and I know that twins is closer than anybody, sometimes even closer than mamas and their younguns." She grew quiet, looking up at the canopy of leaves and sighed a long, shaky breath before her gaze dropped and she peered into the darkness before her. "These two shared the afterbirth. They'll be as alike a two sips of water," she said at last.

"You were a twin?' asked Geneva.

"Law, yes." She looked a Geneva suddenly. "You say your name is Lenoir?"

Geneva nodded, silently accepting the old woman's pronunciation.

Yer granddaddy Clayton?"

"Why, yes. My dad is Ray."

Lenora nodded. I knowed your granddaddy. Good man, but he was the cause of my sister adyin'."

"What?"

"Yessir. I had me a twin sister 'til I was fifteen year old. Purty little thing, but didn't have no more sense than a fuzzy little chick—looked about like one, too. Light hair, all curly on end, stood out from her head like a halo

"But what happened to her?"

"She loved yer granddaddy, that's what happened to her." Lenora looked at Geneva and dropped an ancient, spotted hand on Rachel's head, bright in the shafts of starlight filtering through the trees.

"You don't know me, child, but oncet our families was close, like neighbors, almost like kin. Yer granddaddy and my daddy and brothers use to hunt together. He'd thunder up this mountain on his big, fine bay horse, jist alaughin', and he'd bring me and Laurel things, ye know, like a handful of huckleberries or a jar of sourwood honey. He'd come on up to the house and rear up his horse and make it thrash its front feet like he was gonna tear right on up the front steps and through the house, and he'd holler, 'Laurel! Sissy! Come out here and see what I brung ye!' And law, we'd drop whatever we wuz adoin' and come arunnin'.

"One time he had us a bear cub. Its mother had been shot through the lung and had run off and died, and its brother had died a starvation. He found this little baby bear acryin' and whimperin' by its dead mother and brother, and he jist caught it up and brung it on up the mountain. And when he come up th' mountain that mornin', it wuz spring, and everthang was all green and wet. The sky wuz jist a blue as a robin's egg, and the sun wuz astreamin' down like it wuz rainin' silver. He wuz singin' a song about acomin' to meet his love in this big, happy voice he had, and Laurel come out of the thicket and stopped dead in her tracks. From that day on, she loved him.

"She wuz twelve year old, and yer granddaddy wuz twenty, and thought of her as jist a little bit of a thing, but she loved him like a growed woman would love a man. He reached over and give us that little bear cub and said, 'Ladies, here's one hungry little baby. Yew feed it some fresh sweet milk and let it foller ye around, and when I come back, I bet I see it athinkin' yew two is its mother.' And then he galloped on up the mountain into that silver light, alookin' for my brothers, and Laurel jist stood there, lookin' after him, holdin' that bear cub, and she said, 'Sissy, that there's the man I'm agonna marry.'"

"Did my grandfather know she loved him?"

"I reckon he had to of. Ever time he come up the mountain after that, she wuz amoonin' over him. She raised that bear til it was old enough to take off on its own, and ever time Clay come by, she'd try to put it in his arms and say, 'Clay, this here's mine and your baby. I'm agonna take care of this baby fer ye, and someday, I'm agonna take care of the real babies we have together.' And she kept badgerin' him about a perty little farm she wanted him to buy her down by Raven Creek. She'd seen it once and had plumb decided that wuz where she and Clay would live together.

"Well, I kin tell yew, she jist about plagued Clay to death, agoin' on like that, 'til finely he quit comin' up. He'd jist meet my brothers in the woods to go hunt. But Laurel didn't quit for a minit. She got to where she'd hide in the woods and look fer him when she knew they wuz huntin', and one time she follered 'em and near got shot fer them thinkin' she wuz a deer."

"What happened then?" Geneva felt a tearing in her heart, knowing the yearning the child must have felt.

"Well, Daddy nearly whipped her over that, but Daddy never whipped none of us. Never. He jist threatened to, then he cried and tole her he'd die if innything happened to his baby girls, and she swore she'd quit follerin' Clay around when he was huntin', but then she took to goin' over the mountain to his house. It wuz a six mile walk, but she'd run over there ever chance she got, and she'd hide out, awaitin' for a glimpse of 'im. I don't think he ever saw her then, but I knew when she'd go. She'd come back with a funny smile all over her, and she'd jist shake, not like she wuz skeert, more like she was so fulla life she couldn't hold it all in her, she was so little bitty. It seemed like the light wuz jist astreamin' out of her, and she'd come skippin' through the trees like a little fairy or somethin'."

Rachel was quiet. Geneva thought she might be asleep, and she felt privileged to hear such a story in the still, starry night. She looked greedily at Lenora, waiting for her to continue.

"Yer granddaddy wuz a handsome feller, and he wuz real happy-like, and he had a gentle way with girls, so hits no wonder he had his pick. Afore long, he took to courtin' Neecy McFarlan—that 'ud be yer granny—and when she found out that they wuz agittin' married, Laurel like to have died. She didn't eat for nuthin' the whole month afore the wedding, and then, afterwards, she took it in her head that she wuz agonna have a baby by Clay even if she couldn't have him.

"She made up this big plan. Neecy went back to her mama's house about once ever two or three months fer a week at a time, and so Laurel decided she'd go to Clay and bed with him the minit Neecy got out of the house. She tole me what she was aplannin', and I pitched a fit. Most of the time I did everthing she tole me to, but this time I told her she was plumb crazy. To tell ye the truth, I wuz a little skeert of her—or not skeert—I jist looked up to her. She had a way of makin' me think I wuzn't a smart as she wuz, and she wuz so perty and so fulla this light all the time, ashakin' and apourin' out light. It wuz like she wuz more than a ordinary person."

"But this time, I knowed what she wanted wuz plain wrong, and I told her so. And she backed right down and said awright, she wouldn't do it, but the very next week, when Neecy went home to her mama, Laurel lit off down that mountain, hell bent on beddin' with Clay."

"Poor child," murmured Geneva, stroking Genny's tiny head.

"Well, when she got to Clay's house, he wuz gone, so she got right in the bed and waited fer him. He got home late at night and when he found Laurel in the bed, he jist turned and walked right outta the house. Far as I know he didn't say a word to her. Jist walked out like he never saw her."

"How awful!" Geneva exclaimed. "Why did he do that? She was just a child!"

"Yes, she wuz a child, but by this time she looked like a growed woman, and she wuz about the pertiest thing yew ever looked at.

After she died, I heered Clay atellin' Daddy that when he saw her, she looked like a angel, sittin' in that big bed with the white sheets around her spread out like wings, her hair like a crown, or a halo. And all of a sudden, he felt like she wuz stronger than he wuz, like if he come in that room and spoke to her, she'd reach out and she'd have him, and he wuz too skeert to talk. He said all this to Daddy, and they wuz both acryin', but all of a sudden, Daddy quit cryin', and said, and I'll never fergit this, 'cause when he said it, I knew he wuz aspeakin' God's pure truth. He said, 'Clay, I know what yew mean. Sometimes she skeert me. I know what ye mean. They wuz somethin' about her that could make a body feel puny as ghost piss, and there ain't nobody who could stand up to her.' And then, he got real quiet like, and I could swear I heered him say—at the time, I didn't believe he could of, because she wuz always his best darlin', but now, lookin' back, I think he said, 'It's best she's gone. They wuz jist too much wildness in her.'"

"But how did she die?" Geneva wondered.

"When Clay left, she up and took off fer home, and she slipped in the creek and broke her leg real bad. The bone come right out through the skin, and she laid there fer a day or more afore we found her. Doc come up and had to cut off her leg jist below the knee, but blood poisonin' set in and she died three weeks later."

"What a tragic story," said Geneva, truly appreciating the pathos of it. "I'm sorry it had to end in such an awful way."

"That ain't the end of it," mused Lenora. Yer granddaddy felt so bad about her alosin' her leg, he come up and begged Laurel to fergive him. He thought it wuz his fault she'd fell. Hit wuz a Sunday, and nobody knew Laurel had blood poisonin' and everbody but me had gone to church. They'd left me there to take care of her. I wuz the only one she could tolerate at that time. Right after they left, I noticed these red steaks arunnin' up her leg, and she started thrashin' around with fever. Clay come up right then, and he come right into the room where she laid, and he jist set there by her pallet, aweepin' and apromisin' her the moon if she'd jist fergive him and take this weight offen him. And then Laurel, she tole me to go pick her some watercress, but I didn't go. I jist hid out by the house and peeked in the winder so's I could hear ever word they said.

"And then Laurel said, she said, 'I cain't have no babies cause I'll be daid this time next month, but afore I die, I'll have a piece of you, Clayton Lenoir, yes, and I'll make you grieve for not lovin' me in time. And then, right there, missy, Laurel opened up the kivers and pulled poor old Clay into the bed with her, and the next thing I knowed they wuz kissin' each other and weepin', and they wuz holdin' each other like they wuz afightin' off Death hisself. It wuz all I could do ta keep from cryin' out myself. But I jist stood there and watched them all tangled up together, both of 'em in fever, both of them awishin' they had it all to do over agin, but tryin' to make up for what went wrong.

"I left then and went for the watercress, and when I got back, Clayton wuz gone. Laurel wuz white and grievin'. She fell off real quick after that. Clay never come back til after she died, but the next week he sent up a deed to the Raven Creek place—he had done bought it and put her name on the deed, like she always wanted. After Laurel died, Daddy tried to git him to take it back, but he said to give it to me.

"I married Ike the next summer—that was the year nineteen and fifteen. I cain't believe that was sixty-two years ago, come next month! I wuz sixteen year old, and I remember it like it wuz no time atall. We farmed that place fer awhile, but even though it wuz, I guess, the pertiest piece of land in the county, I never felt right livin' there, knowin' it wuz really kind of like Laurel's grave. Ike got called up in the Great War, and I moved back up here where he had been farmin' afore, and we just stayed on. I give it to my boy Jesse, Chap's daddy, when he got married. Chap, that's what we've called Hard ever since the year he wuz borned. Uster call him Little Chap, then jist Chap. He don't like it much, though, and so goes by Hard whenever he kin," she smiled, and continued, "ain't it funny how these things come around though. That wuz the very piece of land that Jesse sold to yer sister and her husband not three year ago."

Geneva sat quietly, grieving over something more than just the child who had loved and conquered her ancestor. She grieved for herself and her soul, which she knew was diluted and tamed, like a candle that has glimpsed an inferno. She wondered if hearing this story would cause her to be changed as much tomorrow, next week, next year, as it made her feel changed now, and then she grieved more because she knew it would not. This night would stand alone as a beacon in a long life of ordinariness. She would never be as intensely involved with living, with the essence of being as she was now. How contemptuously she regarded her heartache over Howard Graves now! The glittering promises he had given her were nothing compared to the naked sorrow, the quintessential love that the child and the man had given to one another in her last few hours.

She thought about the farm where Rachel and Wayne had conceived these children, in a room very much, perhaps, like the one where Laurel lay and waited to claim Clay for a night. Now, the child Laurel had wanted would never be more than a dream, dead to all but herself and this old woman. She thought about the treachery of love, and the cleansing wind as it coupled with the trees. She wondered why Howard Knight or his brothers or sisters had not become heir to the lovely farm that had come back to her family.

"Why did he sell the farm, Lenora? Did he need the money? Did he hate to give it up?"

"No, dearie, he wuz glad to be shed of it. Chap lived there for a while, but he had some hard times there, and we began to feel like it wuz a curse to us."

"What do you mean?"

"Chap lived there with his first wife til she died. She wuz a fine, big, healthy girl, with a headful of bright red hair. To look at her would scare ye to death. She looked like she could chew ye up and spit ye out without a thought, but she wuz real gentle, and didn't have no temper atal. I knew fer sure she'd raise a passel of strappin' younguns. She wuz built jist right fer childbearin'. But she died right after the first one got started. Somethin' just broke inside and she bled to death afore anybody knew anything wuz wrong."

"I'm sorry," said Geneva. The words felt impotent, silly, in her mouth.

"I know. Chap took it real bad. Then he up and married a silly little piece of nuthin' jist a few months later. Didn't hardly know her, but he said she had to be a good-un because she had red hair, too. Dang fool boy. I could see right off there wuzn't nuthin' to her. She took up with one of them longhaired rock and roll boys who thought he'd make it big, and she run off to Nashville with him after she hadn't been married to Chap no time."

The wagon jolted to a stop. Jimmy Lee sat up suddenly, gingerly rubbing the back of his head. "What in the hell is agoin' on here?" he demanded. "How did I git all wet?"

Six

The night was waning when Lenora led Geneva and Rachel into the small frame house she and Ike called home. Geneva found the place modest but surprisingly well appointed and tidy, and she and Rachel were especially relieved to find a telephone. When Rachel called home, Wayne insisted on coming immediately, although his wife begged to be allowed to sleep for a few hours first.

"You can sleep til I get there," he insisted. "Just put somebody on who can give me directions." Rachel sighed, surrendering the telephone to Ike. Lenora bustled the women and babies off to the bedroom for their brief rest.

Rachel dropped off to sleep immediately, but despite exhaustion and a warm bath, Geneva lay tense and excited, the events of the evening churning in her mind. She gazed out into the pulsating night, textured with living sounds and the bright wash of the Milky Way streaming across the vast, black sky. She felt strangely powerful, as if she had just vanquished something formidable, but rather than finding contentment in that, she grew more restless. In addition, the cut on her head she had suffered in the accident hurt just enough to bother her when she tried to close her eyes. Finally, after tossing and turning for nearly an hour, she climbed out of the bed she shared with Rachel and tiptoed past baby Lenora sleeping on a pallet on the floor. The other infant, Geneva knew, was still being rocked by Lenora in the other room.

She entered the front room to find Lenora humming softly to Genny. The old woman smiled at Geneva. "It ain't been too long since I last rocked a baby. I got me nine grandchildern, and fourteen great-grandchildern. They'll be another one soon, I expect. Ever one of 'em that was borned has lived. That's more'n I kin say fer the way things wuz back when I wuz ahavin' 'em. I had me eight babies, but only six of 'em made it past they fifth year."

"I never thought about how much courage it must have taken just to live up here in these mountains back when you were raising your children," mused Geneva.

"It still takes courage, child. A high mountain is about the pertiest thing on God's earth, but it's a hard thing to live on, too. Ye gotta make plenty of sacrifices to do it, but I ain't complainin'. I'd rather see me a perty spring rain or a stand o' dogwoods in bloom than a shoppin' mall any day. If ye ask me, it takes a lack of good sense to live down in a town somewheres." After she had rocked silently for a while, she glanced back up at Geneva.

"What are yew adon' up? Ye'd better git ye some sleep. Yer folks will be here afore long, and ye'll be plumb beat afore ye git home. Why don't ye git on back to bed."

"I can't sleep," Geneva sighed. "I suppose I could, though, if I could shake this headache. Do you have any aspirin?"

"No, I ain't got no aspirin, but I kin make ye some tea that'll put ye right down. I give it to Ike when his teeth get to hurtin' 'im, and he says it does make a world o' difference."

She rose slowly, handing the baby to Geneva, and moved into the kitchen off the main room. Soon she returned, handing Geneva a steaming cup. "Well, I'm plumb out 'o willerbark tea. Chap cleaned me out of most of my herbs and took 'em up to his cabin.

But here's somethin' that might make ye sleepy. At least ye won't mind yer hurt so much. Now, I'm jist gonna put this here child down," she said, taking Genny back into her arms. "I reckon she'll let her mama git some sleep afore she starts hollerin' fer her titty." She paused to stroke the down on the child's head and chuckled silently. "I kin tell thisun's gonna be a feisty one. She'll have a mind of her own, that's fer sure." Bending her head, she brushed her withered cheek against the soft baby flesh, then she straightened and smiled at Geneva. "Good night, honey. I'm gonna git me some shut-eye, too."

Alone, Geneva sipped her tea. It was sweet and minty and it held another flavor she could not quite place: faintly familiar, yet odd. But as she sipped, the cup cradled in her hands and warming her, she felt herself relaxing. She rocked and hummed to herself and thought about babies, the miracle of the whole process. She wondered how long it would be before motherhood overtook her with that supreme intensity she had seen in Rachel tonight. It was both awful and wonderful, how Rachel had been overwhelmed by this force of Life, how she had both succumbed to it and had worked with it to bring new, separate human beings into the world. It was bigger than anything, bigger than Love, even. It gave her pause.

Before long she began to feel a little dizzy, and although Lenora had promised her sleep, she felt herself growing more awake and just a little excited, definitely giddy. She rose, shaking her head, and moved out onto the porch. Although the coolness prickled her flesh through the threadbare, once-flannel nightgown, she felt no desire to return to the warmth and safety of the house; she felt more like running into the forest to find something to challenge.

A light shone from the barn. Geneva imagined her body softening, rising, transforming into something like a luna moth, compelled to the light that split the black night and gilded the ground at her feet. She drifted toward it, singing a little song, sometimes skipping a little as she walked. When she reached the open door, she stopped, watching wide-eyed at the beautiful scene before her.

Howard Knight was grooming the horses, talking in a sweet murmur to them, rubbing and brushing their coats to a high gloss. He had stripped to the waist, but he still wore the jeans he had doused while saving Jimmy Lee. As Geneva watched, she saw the smooth muscles ripple in his back and arms. His coppery skin glowed like reflected fire; his black hair caught the playful light, absorbed it, then threw it back in iridescent detail, as coal sets free the shimmering rainbow. Geneva clutched the door and stared unabashedly.

"*Ooooh,*" she said.

Howard turned, smiling at her without missing a stroke of the rhythmic brushing. "Howdy. I expected yew to be asleep by now. Them babies all right?"

"They are *fine*," Geneva replied emphatically, watching the muscles in the horses shoulders, the rippling in Howard's. Suddenly, she wanted to touch them, to see if the skin was as smooth as it looked, the muscles as hard. Like one sleepwalking, she glided toward him, her hand outstretched. His back was turned. She touched his shoulder, then ran her hand down the long arm, her fingertips tingling from the contact of flesh. Howard froze in midstroke. Geneva placed her other hand on the other shoulder and began the same long, slow caress. She began humming.

Howard dropped his brush, standing tense and solid, like the hart that senses danger, then he turned to face her, so puzzled in expression that Geneva had to giggle. She loved the naughty, shapeless thoughts tangling her brain, and then, as if to feed those thoughts, to give them body and shape, she placed all ten fingertips on his pectoral muscles and began another slow, downward stroke. His chest was completely smooth and hairless. It smelled of horse and hay and looked like fine leather. Geneva had never been so fascinated with skin before. She couldn't stop touching it.

"You don't have any hair on your chest," she marveled.

"My mama was a Cherokee," he replied, his breath coming in a single, short gasp as Geneva leaned forward and nibbled at his nipple. The impulse to kiss him washed over her like a warm rain, and the world slowed, then stopped while she delighted in the complete, absorbing logic of this moment. She surely would kiss him. Indeed, there was nothing more important to do in the world but kiss him. She turned her face to his and moved in, sliding her arms around his broad, smooth, brown back, gazing up into his eyes. Howard's face had altered; the countenance of the tall, fierce man who had faced her earlier that evening had blurred into a soft boyishness, his eyes had become full of wonder, confusion, and—*oh, yes!*—delight. Geneva felt his vulnerability and found it particularly attractive. She kissed him once and sighed, then, with half-closed eyes, she licked his lips and began to nibble each one between her teeth and the tip of her tongue. He swallowed hard, then suddenly stiffened again. Taking her shoulders in his hands, he looked closely into her face.

"Miss Geneva, did my grammaw give yew anything to drink by any chance?"

"Just some tea, you beautiful, tan, smooth, man. She was straining forward, trying to kiss him again. The barn smelled warm and horsy. Pleasure was oozing from every pore, every follicle. She rolled her head around and looked at Howard coyly, drunkenly.

His eyes lost their softness and began shifting around, as if he were looking for some means of escape. He licked his lips nervously. "Oh, Miss Geneva, I think you'd maybe better git on back to the house. I got me a feelin' that in the mornin' yew may think twice about what you're adon' right now."

"Don't be silly, Howard," she laughed. "I mean, Hard. Zat your name? Hard? Well, are you?" She threw back her head, delighted, and laughed a long time at the pun. *Shakespeare would have loved it!* "Are you, huh, huh? Can I see?"

With the speed of a striking cobra, she grabbed the waistband of his jeans, yanked him toward her, and before he could comprehend the meaning of her actions, had flipped open the snap. Howard took a faltering step backward, hands clamped over his belly button, but Geneva was too quick for him. Leaping again, she yanked a hand aside, and had unzipped his pants before he, in his confused state, could jerk away from her.

He gave up trying to fend her off and turned to run. Geneva was after him, by this time howling with laughter. "Are you, Hard, are you? Let me see! I won't hurt you! Just let me see!"

Around the barn they went, Howard trying to talk sensibly, Geneva in hot pursuit and laughing so hard she kept falling down. But each time she fell, she lunged for him, and would have caught him if he had not managed to sidestep her. Finally, he scrambled up the ladder into the hayloft. She didn't waste a second before she was up behind him, but she hesitated when he, grabbing the ladder, pushed it forward so that Geneva hung suspended halfway up, balanced only by the strength of the desperate man's arm.

"Aw, Haaaarrrrd," she whined. "Let me up. I'll be good, I promise. I was just foolin' around. You can trust me."

"Miss Geneva, I want ye to git back down this here ladder. You don't know whatcher doin'. You've done got aholt of somma Mammaw's hemp tea, and it's made yew dizzier'n a June bug on a string. Not to mention crazy. Now git on back down."

Geneva was climbing up. "Whatcha gonna do, Hard? Beat me off with a handful of hay?"

"Git *down*, I said. Miss Geneva, please don't come up here. Please ma'am," he pleaded. "I like ye a lot, but yer askeerin' the shit outta me. I don't know what ta do with ye."

"You don't have to do a thing with me, Hard. I just want you to take your pants off and let me look at you. Are you this smooth all over? You got nice, warm, brown skin like this all over? Are you hard? I just wanna see."

"Oh, Lord God, Miss Geneva. Don't ye take another step. Oh, shiiiiutt." She had topped the ladder and leaped at him, just a millisecond before he released the ladder and dodged her. He turned to run, but she tackled him as smoothly as if she had practiced the move on a professional field, flying low and grabbing him around the knees. He was bigger and considerably stronger than she was, but he was able to break away only enough to trip himself up again, and down he went, over the side of the loft, onto the floor below.

Geneva rode him down, thrilled by the short flight with her arms wrapped around his warm, wet body. But when they landed, she recoiled momentarily as she felt a hard, sharp pain shoot up her arm from her recently injured elbow.

She caught her breath, writhing for a moment before she managed to force the pain aside and pull a cloak of dignity around her shoulders. She sat up as regally as she possibly could. Howard was out cold, lying spread-eagle on his back, his eyes half closed and rolled back into his head.

"Good grief, Howard," she sniffed. "I never saw anybody so prissy in my life. I just wanted to take a look at you. You think I'm trying to rape you or something?" She felt like scolding him. "Besides, don't you know that a gentleman always complies with a lady's request?" This thought struck her as funny somehow, but she masked her giggles with the sternest expression she could muster. "Now I have to do this myself!"

Panting with the effort, Geneva yanked at his sodden jeans until she had partially relieved him of them. Standing slowly, cradling her hurting arm, she looked down at him and shook her head seriously. "Nope. Not hard. But not bad." She turned, walked back to the house, and climbed into bed.

She awoke a few hours later with the morning mist wafting into her consciousness. Coming from somewhere nearby was an irritating sound—insistent, repetitive, "Whaaa, whaa, whaa, whaaa, whaaa, whaaa, whaaa." And then there was a second voice added to the first so that there was a chorus of "whaa whaaas." Geneva rolled over and caught her breath sharply, grimacing as she became aware of a searing pain radiating from her elbow.

Rachel and Wayne were on their knees in the floor, picking up two little bundles. After a moment of a dazed searching through her fogged brain, Geneva remembered…

Everything.

Especially the part about how she hurt her elbow. A white-hot, urgent need to disappear engulfed her. Her first impulse was to grab her clothes and flee on foot down the mountain. If she started immediately, she could reach a road before night and hitch a ride into town. Rachel and Wayne could stay until they were ready to drive back home, but Geneva needed out *now*. She hoped to make it back to the farm, but if she got lost in the woods and was eaten by a bear, that would be an okay alternative. Anything other than face Howard Knight this morning.

"Good morning, Geneva," came Rachel's voice, sunny with happiness. "Can you believe it? We made it through the night with no major mishaps." Geneva suppressed a groan.

"Wayne has declared all three of us perfectly fine, and now he's ready to look you over. We thought we'd let you sleep as long as you could. Want him to check out that cut on your head now?"

The groan surfaced loudly.

"Oh, darling, does it hurt? Wayne didn't want to take off the bandage until you were awake. Of course, I never really noticed it, but Lenora says you'll probably need stitches." She smiled as if she suddenly remembered a delightful secret and climbed back into bed. "I feel pretty good, considering, and the babies have all ten toes and fingers." She stopped to beam at the baby in her arms before she added, "and it's clear they're both geniuses. That Lenora ain't a bad midwife." Geneva narrowed her eyes at the genius child sucking at Rachel's full, round breast. Rachel, pleased beyond definition, turned to her husband with a look radiant with love. Wayne sat beside her and held the second baby to the other breast so that the two could suckle simultaneously.

The whole scene was disgusting. Rachel was unabashedly baring her whole torso to everybody in the room without an ounce of modesty, looking like a love-sick calf at the very man she had vowed to kill just hours ago. Geneva quietly wondered how long postpartum insanity generally lasted.

Rachel turned to her sister, "Oh, Geneva, I forgot to get water.

Hurry and get me some. Nursing makes me as dry as sand."

Not moving, Geneva glared at her. Why can't Wayne get it? He's already up."

"Silly, he can't let go of little Lenora. It would be cruel to make the poor thing break away now, and I haven't figured out how to do this with both of them. Now hurry. I'm dying!"

"I'm going," Geneva muttered, easing her sore body out of the bed, then scurrying, once her bare feet hit the cold pine boards. Lenora stood in the kitchen, frying ham in an enormous iron skillet. Geneva grabbed a glass, explaining her errand. Lenora nodded.

"Breakfast'll be ready in a minit. I got ye some clothes laid out on the cheer in thar. Yew got vomit, river mud, blood, an' everthang else on the clothes yew had on. Yew an' yer sister kin jist wear 'em on home. Now hurry. This ham's about done."

Geneva thanked her, feeling suddenly starved in the ham-scented atmosphere, and remembering that she had not eaten since lunch yesterday, she decided she could at least stay for breakfast. But her determination wavered as she passed the window and glimpsed Howard out in the yard. She ducked her head and hurried to the bedroom.

"Breakfast is about ready, so I'll bring you a plate in here, and I'll eat with you so you won't get lonesome," she said as she handed Rachel the water.

"Oh, I can get up. I'm starved, and I'm looking forward to breakfast with these good people. Aren't they wonderful the way they came to our rescue last night? I owe them plenty. And Geneva," she warned, "I hope you can get down off your high horse and be a little nicer to Howard than you were last night. You are not too good to show him the same friendliness he showed us."

Geneva smiled weakly. "I got a lot friendlier later on," she said, glancing out the window again. Howard was wearing a shirt this morning, she noticed. And a belt.

"Well, I hope so. Now at breakfast, be sure to be nice to him. It's obvious he likes you. Don't be a snob."

After the babies finished their breakfast, Wayne left them alone so they could dress. Gaynell had had the foresight to send some clothing, so they did not have to take further advantage of Lenora's generosity. By the time their hostess had called them to breakfast, Geneva was feeling somewhat less hungry than she had earlier, possibly because she had eaten most of her fingernails between then and now. Nevertheless, she meekly found a place at the table and sat down as the men came into the house.

Throughout the meal, Rachel, Wayne, Ike, Jimmy Lee, and Lenora chatted like old friends, but Geneva and Howard each kept their heads down, mechanically forking food into their mouths. Geneva's cheeks were flaming, but once she glanced discreetly at Howard and saw that his face looked as hot as hers. She felt so sorry for him that she looked more directly at him and smiled tentatively. He smiled back, then after a moment, looked down again, hiding his mouth with his hand.

Without warning, a tickle rose up from the pit of Geneva's stomach, now warmed and comforted by the ham and biscuits, and when the tickle reached her throat, she coughed and squirmed in her chair. Howard glanced at her, then away again, rubbing his mouth vigorously. His face flushed again; his shoulders shook while Geneva battled with the sure feeling that she could not conquer the giggles rising like bright balloons from her belly. Suddenly, Howard pushed back his chair and hurried out of the room while Geneva fought for control by placing a slab of butter on her biscuit. She wanted to run, too, to rush out into the cool morning and throw her head back and laugh into the trees until the tears streamed down her cheeks, but she breathed deeply and focused on controlling the rising, bubbling tickle and found contentment in the knowledge that she would be able to get through the day.

Immediately after breakfast, Wayne insisted on checking Geneva's head injury, but when he discovered that Jimmy Lee had been knocked unconscious for a time, he thought he'd better see to his scalp first.

"It's not too bad, Jimmy Lee. Not deep, but you might want

some stitches so it will heal faster. You've got a big bump here that probably caused you to pass out. You breathing okay now? Any dizziness?"

Jimmy Lee shook his head vigorously. "I don't reckon I need no sewin' up," he insisted. I been cut worsern' this before." He gave Geneva a strange, shy look. "This here lady saved my life. I'd be pleased if ye'd quit fussin' over me and take kere 'o her."

"Good Lord, Geneva," commented Wayne when he took off the bandage that Lenora had put on Geneva's forehead the night before. This really is a nasty cut. There's no doubt that you'll have to have stitches. If you don't, you'll have an ugly scar."

"Yeah, well, Wayne, what really hurts is my elbow," said Geneva, by now acutely aware of the discomfort it caused her.

"Yew hurt yer elbow, too?" asked Jimmy Lee, surprised.

"Geneva, you didn't tell me you hurt your elbow!" exclaimed Rachel.

"And ye did all that diggin'!" added Lenora.

Wayne rolled up Geneva's sleeve to examine her arm, and the moment he caught sight of her elbow, he gave a long, low whistle. Geneva craned her neck to look at it, gasping in surprise. No wonder it hurt so much! She wondered why she hadn't noticed it while she dressed. It was twice its normal size, red, and angry. When she touched it, it felt hugely hot. The way it throbbed, Geneva wondered if she might have done something serious to it.

Everyone crowded around, looking at Geneva's wounds, marveling at how strong she had been, how she must have suffered as she braved the rapids and wielded the heavy shovel to save Jimmy Lee's life. Geneva felt intensely embarrassed, knowing how the elbow had really been injured, and more so knowing that Howard probably suspected the truth. She looked up, catching his eye as he leaned against the door frame, and blushed to the roots of her hair. Howard looked at his shoes and pressed his lips together.

"Geneva, are you all right?" asked Wayne, concern in his voice. "You just flushed. Do you feel hot?"

"Never mind. I guess we'll just have to get to the hospital to get this taken care of. But I know Howard was hurt, too. Did you check him?"

"Yes. He's all right. Cuts and bruises and a bit of a headache this morning. He somehow managed to bang up both the front and back of his head, though I'll be damned if I can figure how. But you're the one I'm worried about. Let me give you something for the pain here." He turned to rummage in his bag.

"I'm fine," she insisted irritably. "Just wrap it up and let's get going."

Wayne wrapped her elbow and gave her some aspirin, then he joined Ike and Howard outside to load the car. Rachel carried baby Lenora into the kitchen to sit while the older woman washed dishes and entertained her guest with midwifery stories. Geneva sat alone in the living room, rocking Genny, listening to the voices drifting in to her, pondering her embarrassment but chuckling, too, and wondering if she should tell Rachel about the events of the night before.

After a while, she became aware of another presence in the room. She turned to see Jimmy Lee standing in the doorway, looking pale and timid, smiling tentatively. When she caught his eye, he flushed violently and attempted to speak, but he choked on his words, Yet, his eyes were locked directly on hers, and when he found his voice, he spoke earnestly.

"Miss Geneva, I aim ta thank ye," he began. She started to protest, but he shook his head and plunged on. "Yew saved my life last night, and I'm beholden to ye. And ye done it with a busted up arm, and I know ye suffered fer my sake." Geneva lowered her eyes and tried to regulate her heartbeat. This was an awful mess.

He continued, "Yer like a angel to me, Miss Geneva. I know I ain't good enough fer ye, but I want ye to know that I have feelin's fer ye."

Geneva's head snapped up. What was he saying? *Oh, Lord, he was declaring himself!* She glanced around the room, hoping Wayne or Rachel would come in before he said another word.

Jimmy Lee advanced toward her, his face shining with

earnestness, and—*oh dear*—infatuation. He continued, "There ain't nuthin' I wouldn't do fer ye. I wish ye'd give me a chance to prove mysef. I…"

Geneva jumped up. "Jimmy Lee, you are too kind. You would have done the same for me, or anybody, I'm sure, and my elbow was not hurt as badly as you think. Please, I—" she groped for words which were both kind and firm but discovered that she was completely inept in the situation.

Mercifully, Wayne, Ike, and Howard walked in. Geneva startled; Jimmy Lee hastened back across the room, his face scarlet. Geneva knew she looked guilty, too. There was an awkward silence, then Ike cleared his throat and said gently, "I reckon yer set to leave, and I'd like to pray over ye afore ye go."

"Of course," replied Wayne. He called Rachel and Lenora from the kitchen, and everyone went outside to stand in a silent circle, looking expectantly at Ike.

Geneva had not yet had a good look at him, but this morning, under the soft blue sky, she turned her eyes fully upon his kindly face, wrinkled as a cauliflower, but glowing with serenity and life. His eyes were as clear and blue as bright sapphires beneath bushy white eyebrows that jutted out like wild brambles. To Geneva, he looked like a very old person with very young eyes and an even younger soul, a soul milk-fed by the hand of goodness. Geneva felt her tiredness and anxiety melt from her as she looked into this ruined, radiant face. Ike gazed at each of them briefly, then he lifted his head and called on the name of the Lord.

The morning was a fine one. The sun was full up, a golden disk in the azure sky, but mist still clung in the low places and dew bejeweled the grass and the lacy spider webs. Below them, wet and shimmering, lay the forest through which they had come the night before. It was a wild, uncompromising place, alive with light and shadows. Huge trees and boulders towered over a tangle of rhododendrons whose blossoms dropped upon the surface of the creek and hurried away toward the mother river. The creek itself roared and foamed, crying out its own fecund song, which lifted to the treetops and into Geneva's soul. Ike's fine voice floated above the sound so that no one had to strain to hear him.

As if in response to the prayer, the air turned golden all around them and warmed them as they stood there, listening to Ike pray for their safety and give thanks for the two healthy newborns. Geneva felt a Presence, as if the place had become holy, and God had ventured here to find them and bless them. Her spirit quieted, and Peace flowed in her and all around her.

When he had finished, Wayne, Rachel, and Geneva shook his hand warmly, then Wayne turned to thank Howard. "The creek should go down soon," he remarked. "You just leave the truck where it is and I'll come back tomorrow and help you pull it out. I'd consider it a privilege to work on it with you."

"Yessir," said Howard gravely. "That old truck kin set there awhile, and if you cain't git up here, don't you worry none. I got plenty of kin to help me with her. No, don't you worry none about that old truck."

He turned to Geneva. Directing his gaze somewhere in the vicinity of her knees, he spoke in a low voice. "Miss Geneva, I'd be glad to take care 'o yer car fer ye. I reckon I kin fix most anything wrong with it."

Wayne started to protest that he needn't bother, that he would retrieve the Mazda, but Geneva cut him short.

"Thank you, Howard. I think that's very gallant of you." She smiled timidly, caring very much that he should not think her ungrateful. Hesitating, she continued, "We've… been through a lot together, and I hope we can be friends."

Catching the import of her words, Howard recognized there not only the gratitude and the amusement, but also the humility. He looked her full in the eyes; his own were warmed by his open smile.

Seven

Geneva was half dozing in the porch swing when John strolled into her line of vision. For a moment she sat a little confused, trying to remember if she had decided whether or not she was going to be angry at him. She was sure she had made up her mind one way or the other, but when she saw him standing there, bathed in the rays of the afternoon sun so that he seemed nearly transparent, she could not make her brain function well enough to remember her decision. She wisely kept silent until he spoke.

"Hi, beautiful. I see you've been tangling with mountain lions again," he said. His tone was a shade too casual.

"Why, whoever told you that outrageous lie? I got the bullet in the head when I was leading a Chinese demonstration for democracy and broke the arm when I fell out of the helicopter. I was helping James Bond escape from the scene. When did you get your cast off?"

"Yesterday, when you were getting stitched up. I managed to sneak up to see Rachel and the babies, but they wouldn't let me in to see you. I understand you've had an interesting couple of days."

"Not bad. I try to stay busy."

"So I heard. You feel like walking?"

She did. She was surprised at how much she felt like walking next to John, especially now that his cumbersome cast was gone. She matched her stride perfectly to his as they strolled into the field.

"How are the Three Stooges doing?" she asked, shyly, half afraid to bring up the subject of cats.

"Fine. Moe had a touch of hypertension when he found out you were missing, but he's fine now that you're back. Would you like to see them?"

"Yes, I would," she smiled. No doubt they had grown since she had last seen them, and she found herself surprised by the fact that she missed them. Besides, the field looked so inviting, she thought it would be nice to stroll over to John's place with him. Geneva looked up to smile at the sun. It seemed to her like a huge target, and she felt like an arrow destined to fly into the very heart of that sun, so glad she was to be alive and reasonably intact on such a day as this. The wildflowers turned their merry little faces toward her as they passed, and it seemed perfectly right that John would take her hand while they strolled through the avenue of color.

The kittens were rambunctious—more wild than ever. They allowed Geneva to scratch their heads but would not let her pick them up. After only a moment of violent play, they disappeared around the side of the house.

"Let's go inside and get something to drink," suggested John. "Maybe you'd like to see my Congressional Medal of Honor."

Geneva smiled. She liked the game they were playing, now that she knew how to play it. Their conversation seemed to be effortlessly crafted, but perfectly matched, like a string of apt metaphors, like rhymed couplets. "Okay," she said, mounting the steps to the porch. "I happen to know medals of honor pretty well. I have dozens of them myself."

She paused to glance down at the nail upon which she had torn her shirt not three weeks earlier. Since then her life had become amazingly eventful, but Geneva did not mind. It was nice to stay busy. John stood beside her, leaning on the rail, looking out over the next field. There was a long, comfortable silence, then John stirred and dropped his eyes. When he spoke, his voice was low but solid, nearly palpable in that transparent air.

"I'm sorry I misled you with all those stories I told you," he said. "I don't suppose it would help if I said that I didn't mean for you to really believe them." He smiled a little sheepishly. "I tend to do stupid things like that. You know, make up tales just for fun." His smile broadened. "I should have been a professional storyteller. Maybe I'd get it all out of my system."

"I understand," she replied simply, tossing her red-gold mane and letting her lips curve into an arch little smirk. *Pay-back time,* she thought, and said aloud, "Some people are just born liars. You have to make accommodations for them." She couldn't help but add with a twist of lemon in her voice, "I happen to be someone who loves the truth."

John's shoulders sagged. He turned his gaze back to the ground. Geneva could feel his wretchedness oozing from him in little waves. His brow furrowed, he moved restlessly, then he spoke again, more slowly, his voice no longer strong. "I suppose we ought to really come clean, and this is the perfect spot to do it, considering as how that little nail down there was what started a whole series of lies." He pointed to the fateful nail.

Geneva's stomach dropped to her knees, but immediately afterward she suddenly felt wronged by the turn of events. Anger welled up. *Rachel had betrayed her! But when?* Geneva sifted through the sequence of events since the night of the copperhead, searching for a moment when her sister might have told John about her encounter with that nail.

John laughed ruefully, "Isn't it awful how one little incident can snowball into a whole series of lies? I mean, you think you can get by with one little indiscretion. Nothing, really, just one little thing you'd rather everyone didn't know about, and the next thing you know, you've told some whoppers all over the place. Then you can't get out of them. What a mess."

Geneva's skin prickled with the alarming realization that he was being vindictive! *How dare he choose this particular time, just when she was pretending to get on her soapbox for truth and honesty to let her know that he knew!* Her eyes froze on the nail and she chewed her lip. *What would he say to her next? Would he laugh at her, chastise her, call her a hypocrite?* The thought made her angry, and the more she thought, the more the anger filled her, tart and hot in her mouth. Her heart pounded with it; the overflow blazed from her eyes. *What a malicious soul to trap her like this, to confront her with the evidence in such an oblique way!*

But she would not allow him to lord it over her! *Sneaking, conniving coward. This beat all!* She drew herself up tall, facing him, declaring silently that she would not meekly apologize to him for peeking in his window! She had done no harm, and besides, he should have been home when she came to see him that day! *Really!* She gave him her haughtiest expression.

"Whoa," he said, taken aback by her fiery eyes. "There's no need to get your back up. I really don't think it was that bad."

"You don't?" she asked, softening.

"Well, no. It's just that I didn't want to tell anybody I did anything so foolish as fall off my own front porch. Everybody else loved my stories."

Geneva felt distinctly confused. Something told her she was not quite grasping his meaning. She waited.

He pointed to the nail. "You see that nail?" he asked.

She cleared her throat, cautious. "Yes."

"I had to replace that piece of siding; carpenter bees had started in on it, and it was muddy down there, so I tried to do it from up here." He laughed. "You should have seen me hanging off this porch rail, upside down, trying to hammer that thing on. I got the first nail in all right, but I just got that one set, then I slipped and fell off the porch. That's how I really broke my leg." He chuckled. "Now don't you wish you had let me stick to the damsel in distress story? So much more entertaining."

Relief rushed in to fill the vacuum that the retreating anger had left, and a little breathless, Geneva turned her dazed face away from John toward the green field and the silvery sunlight laughing through the grass. No damsel had ever been more timely rescued than she was at that moment! After a long pause in which she composed herself, she smiled at John, eyes full of forgiveness. "John," she said, using her silkiest voice. "Would you like to go riding with me tomorrow?"

He could not go tomorrow, but he could go the following week, and so they did, and nearly every day thereafter. Long, exhilarating rides in the evening dusk took them over mountains and through fields, splashing through streams and jumping over crevasses, and Geneva felt full of power and life. Her good arm grew strong, the hand callused from caressing the reins, and the injured arm mended along with her soul as she laughed and galloped and played in the dying sunlight and long shadows. It was a friendly time; John did not kiss her or even act as if he thought about it, but Geneva found a comfortable goodness growing between them. It surprised her how much she enjoyed just being with him. The subject of lies never came up again.

Life at the farm also became serene and idyllic once again. The babies were already growing fat, and Rachel moved about the house with dignified grace, reveling in her ability to bring forth life and nurture it so effortlessly. Geneva was awed, even intimidated by her huge breasts, so abundant with milk that they often, and without warning, erupted like fountains, soaking the front of her blouse.

Geneva renewed her friendship with her relatives and old friends who came to admire the newborns and found herself sliding, at first inch by inch, and then in a mind-numbing rush, toward the feeling of complete security and harmony among her home folk. She was so content that she did not even mind when Evangeline turned up after a long absence with nine kittens trotting after her. She just laughed and gave them away to whichever cousin happened to be visiting.

The weeks evaporated, and August rained gold sunshine upon them, making them all feel like children again, happy in the knowledge that joy is the purpose of life. The city twin went into deep hibernation while the country twin grew strong and sassy and became increasingly interested in John, although his interest in her still did not seem to grow. He was friendly and funny, and he always seemed to be around, but he never looked into her eyes, nor did he gaze with longing whenever he thought she was not looking, although Geneva gave him plenty of opportunity to do so. It was the only flaw in this idyllic time, for it made her anxious. He was the first man she had ever found attractive who seemed to have no attraction to her. At first she found this merely annoying, but soon she began to be obsessed with the idea of making him want her. She found herself reliving those first kisses they had shared and watching his every move as he reined in Redneck, the fine, red gelding, or rode him hell for leather across the watercolor meadow.

The thought of Howard Graves slept dreamlessly beside the city twin; in fact, Geneva never thought of him anymore. Instead, without realizing it, she resurrected her restructured Master Plan, the idle indulgence that had landed her behind John's holly bushes. After allowing it to ferment, mulling and churning it in her mind, she began to find the idea of marrying John and taking the job that Dianne had offered more and more satisfying. At last, she made up her mind that was what she wanted, and so set about seriously working out the practical matters, such as would they have time to get married, have the honeymoon, and get back by February so she could begin the season? And there was the trickier chore of making John fall in love with her and getting him to propose (and in a hurry) without making him feel like it was her idea.

She finally came to the reluctant decision that there would not be time to do the wedding right and still start work in February. She wanted to enjoy a longish engagement to give everyone enough time to be properly jealous, and then at least a month in… *Paris?*

Not in winter… Barbados? Skiing in Vancouver? Maybe they could hire a yacht and sail around the Greek Islands…

Then there was the matter of John's house. *The bathroom was too small, so they would have to add on, and she really wanted to redecorate. She would keep her apartment in DC as an investment…*

She planned. She worried through each consideration carefully. She prioritized her goals the way she had been taught in the self-actualization course she had taken the year before, and at last, late one night, tossing in her cool bed, she determined that the first task she must complete would be to become engaged. Of course, the event would have to be planned carefully so that it would be beautiful and exciting enough to satisfy her need for romance. One doesn't become engaged very often, and the memory should be enough to raise the goose flesh for the rest of her life.

Howard's proposal, she remembered, had been so disappointing she was barely able to reconstruct it in her mind. There was something to do with a silly argument over who loved whom the most, then some tears on her part. The actual moment of "Will you?" (or was it, "Oh, all right!") and "Yes," was rather anti-climactic.

She decided that the best and quickest way to achieve her goals would be to seduce John in a perfectly perfect setting. And it had to be now. If she waited too long, it would be too cold to loll naked in the sunshine, and that's where the romance was. Waiting for long winter evenings and firelight would be okay, perhaps, but summer somehow seemed sexier to her. *He should pick her up and carry her into the dappled shade by a murmuring brook. And the sun would rain down gold, and they would breathe the honeysuckle and hear the wind and the sounds of the wilderness around them.*

She gave a happy little sigh thinking about how she would yield to him gently, tenderly. Or would it be passionately? *They would thunder on the horses on top of a high mountain, and he would sweep her into his arms, and fire would leap up between them*—she remembered the electric fence—*and they would cling desperately to each other, yearning, panting…* She gave another happy sigh and shivered and began another possible scenario.

Actually, Geneva had very little experience in accomplishing a seduction. Both Jerry and Howard had taken the initiative, though Jerry had certainly had an easier time—actually, effortless time. He had merely handed her a joint and after two tokes she had ripped his clothes off. Poor old Howard had to beg for months and was finally forced to come up with a nice little emerald and diamond engagement ring before she finally yielded. As she remembered each incident, she realized that both men had fallen short in her ideas of what a good seduction should entail. In fact, if it hadn't been for the aphrodisiacal qualities of marijuana, her affair with Jerry would have been a total disappointment, and Howard had always seemed to be awfully businesslike or in a hurry somehow, perhaps because he always played Vivaldi when they made love. But his satin sheets had been nice, and afterward, they always went out to dinner at the Watergate or watched classic movies. Oh, well, she knew enough to show John how to do it right. She lay very still beneath the white sheet and visualized it. *Maybe get him up to Jacob's Mountain and lie in the long, silken grass and watch the blue sky deepen both above and below them?* The image made her head swim, but she rolled over into the arms of sleep, knowing he didn't stand a chance.

Saturday, she was ready for him. Today, she would begin. The actual event would not happen today. No, she would just make him very aware of how desirable she was, make him wonder what it might be like to taste her sweet, young flesh. Today would be for awakening his desires. She would make him wait another… oh… six weeks? before it got too cold up on the mountain. Besides, she had more practical details to work out, like who would be responsible for protection. If she made him think he was seducing her, he would have to bear that responsibility, and it would make her seem the innocent party. *Yes. Make him think he is the one orchestrating the affair.*

She bathed and perfumed and dusted and stroked herself into a picture of sleek desirability. She even put on makeup, which she rarely did these days; it seemed so silly here among the horses and rocky trails. But she wanted to be stunning, so she stroked on mascara, then packed a picnic into her saddlebags, tucking in a bottle of wine with a giddy little pat. It would not be Jacob's Mountain at this point, unless he mentioned it. She knew that he knew that she knew the power of the place, but he did not know that she knew that he knew, so she had the advantage there. The only problem was that where he thought he could suggest it "innocently," or guide them there without suspicion, she knew she could not. But there was no need to worry about that at this point. He would surely suggest it in time.

They took a high trail, one that John suggested and Geneva remembered from her childhood. She had loved it then, and today it welcomed her like a child again, teasing her through hardwood forests, cool and deep with shade, opening now and then to sunshine and laurel thickets. At one point, the trail narrowed around a rocky outcropping, then widened again into a glen thick with ferns. Ahead of Geneva, John pulled Redneck up without warning.

Fairhope had to sidestep to miss him, and Geneva's foot brushed against Redneck's haunch. The horses danced and sidestepped until they both stopped side by side. Twenty feet ahead of them stood a strange, shining figure, dressed in rags, barefoot, but proud and solid. His head and chest were entirely engulfed by a cloud of the white, fluffy hair of his head and beard. He was short and small-boned with the face of an elf or a gnome. Ruddy, blue-eyed, he wore a constant, genetically formed smile upon his gladsome countenance.

"Holy Miracle," Geneva breathed.

"Well, I wouldn't go so far as that," said John under his breath. "An apparition, maybe."

"No, it's Holy Miracle Jones. I haven't seen him for years. He's grown older," she said, thinking of long summers past.

The figure, which had not moved, spoke, or rather shouted at Geneva and John with a rusty, high-pitched, nasal brogue, "HAVE

YE GOT ANY TERBACCY?"

Geneva gathered her wits quickly. "No. But we've got food. Cheese and bread, and some fruit. And some wine. Do you want wine?"

"NO," hollered the little man. "NO WINE TO POLLUTE THE TEMPLE. KEEP AWAY FROM STRONG DRINK, THE LORD SAYS. I'LL SAVE THE WINE FER THE NEXT COMIN'." He pointed to a boulder off the trail. "LEAVE IT THERE. THEM HICK'RY NUTS IS YOURN, AND THE HONEY."

John did not move but looked curiously from the man to Geneva while she dismounted and emptied her saddlebags of the food. "Give me your shirt," she said in a low voice.

"What?"

"Your shirt. Take it off. I'll buy you another one. Just take it off and give it to me."

Without speaking, John peeled off his shirt and handed it to Geneva. Quickly, she rolled it up and placed it and the food on the boulder. She picked up a burlap sack lying there, and without looking in it, she called out, "Thank you, Holy Miracle. I will share these with Rachel. She just had two more little babies."

"I'M GLAD TO KNOW IT. GOD BLESS THE GIRL AND THE LITTLE ONES, BACH. AND GOD BLESS YE, TOO, GIRLIE. I SEE YE NEED HIS BLESSING, YE GOT A THISTLE IN YER SOUL."

"I'm sorry. What?" returned Geneva.

"A THISTLE!" came the shouted reply. "A THISTLE, IN YER SOUL. AH, IT HURTS, BUT IT'S SUCH A PRETTY HURT, SO YE ALMOST LOVE IT. BETTER WATCH OUT, BOY!" he shouted to John, "THEM PRETTY HURTS IS SLOW TO HEAL, AND THEM THISTLES CAN PRICK YE, TOO. I THANK YE FER THE VITTLES. GOD MEND YER SOUL AND GIVE YE BOTH YER HEART'S DESIRE." He stepped off the trail and disappeared.

"What on earth..." began John.

"Don't say anything, just go on," interrupted Geneva in a low voice. "I'll tell you about him on up the trail. Go on," she urged again.

They rode perhaps a half-mile in silence before John pulled in the reins and dropped back beside Geneva. She was lost in her memory, so he did not press until she was ready to speak.

"Sorry about your shirt," said Geneva. "I will buy you another one. It just looked like he needed it. His rags looked as thin as air."

"Forget it," replied John. "I was glad to give it to him. I'm just sorry I didn't think of it. Who is he?"

"Holy Miracle Jones," she said slowly, feeling very small and far away. "He lives here in the woods. We used to see him quite often when we were children. His father, too. They were both very special, like the pride of these mountains, and we've always felt responsible for taking care of them."

"You've known him a long time?"

"Forever. I think one of my earliest memories may be of him and his father. They are… were…" she searched for the right word, "mystics, I guess. I used to think of them as fairies or elves but that was just a childhood fantasy. There is a kind of holiness, or mystery about them, though, and everybody who ever met them thinks so, too. I always associated them with flowers and good, pure things. They had the ability to heal sick animals. Whenever Rachel or I would find a baby bird or a sick squirrel—anything, we'd come up the trail to Jacob's Mountain and yell for him. That's where they lived, and most of the time, either he or his father would just appear out of nowhere. Both of them were very shy, and they would stay twenty or thirty feet away, and yell at us, like he did today. We'd put the animal down, and usually some food or clothes, then we'd leave. If we came back later, the animal and the food would be gone, and then, a few days or weeks later, we'd find it on our back porch—the animal, that is—in a beautiful basket made of willow or honeysuckle vine, with the honeysuckle blossoms still fresh on it. It would be all well again, usually sleeping soundly. When it woke up, we'd let it go."

"Why do you suppose he'd bring it back to you?"

"I'm not sure," replied Geneva. "I think just to give us the pleasure of seeing it scamper or fly away. And it always did give us such pleasure." She felt dreamy, remembering those bright moments when she could feel the beating heart of a meadowlark in her hands and the way her own heart lifted with the wings of the creature as it took flight.

"I never got close enough to get a really good look at them," she said, regretfully, "but once when we were out, up on the ridge near Jacob's Mountain, Rachel fell off a cliff. She slid and dropped probably a total of thirty or forty feet and was knocked out cold. I couldn't get to her, so I ran all the way home. When I got there, Mama and Daddy decided to get ropes and a litter before they went after her. You know, they didn't want to waste time running back and forth unprepared. It took us maybe twenty or thirty minutes to call people and prepare for the rescue, and then, when we stepped out in the back yard, there was Rachel, lying peacefully in the rope hammock, a crown of daisies on her head, and more flowers in her hands, and her arm tied up close to her chest. It was broken, but she said it hardly hurt at all while we were getting her to the hospital.

"Did she know who had brought her home?"

"She said she remembered being lifted up and delicious smells, like violets, but nothing else until we woke her there in the hammock. We're all pretty sure it was Holy Miracle and his dad.

"What a good story. Who are they? Where did they come from?"

"I don't know the whole tale, nor how true it is, but years ago my grandfather told me that Holy Miracle's father was Welsh, his mother English, and their families were bitter enemies. Apparently, his father's father had been instrumental in a rebellion against the English and had killed someone close to the throne. At any rate, he was caught and executed, and his family, most of them involved in the rebellion, too, either went to prison or escaped the country. Holy Miracle Jones' father—his name was Pwyll. I'm not sure I'm pronouncing that right—was just a child when he came here with his family, but his parents and his older brothers harbored a hatred for the English because they had grown up in this family that had been always at war with them. They were like the last of the true Celts that had chafed under English rule.

"Anyway, the story goes that Pwyll grew up and fell in love with a girl from an English family. And she was related to a family who had been responsible for some supposed wrongs to the Joneses. Pwyll's father and brothers all hated her from the get-go, accused her of being an English witch and stealing the youngest son for some vile purpose, and they vowed that Pwyll would never marry her.

"And then, of course, her family got all mad about it, too, and vowed that she would never marry him. But they did marry, in spite of all the animosity. They eloped and came to live on top of a mountain near here, Jacob's Mountain, and people say that their love was so powerful that when the families came up, all prepared to do battle, they took one look at them and forgot their anger. They gave them their blessings and left in peace."

Geneva fell silent as she let the memory of this remarkable and almost forgotten family warm her like a live ember. It had been so long since she had seen that joyful face, and there was something stirring deep within her that caused her to yearn very much for those magical summers when she saw broken wings mended and soaring.

"So what happened then?" John interrupted.

"I don't know how long they lived together, but Holy Miracle was their only child, as far as I know. The mother was injured somehow and delivered the baby prematurely, just before she died. They say that with her last breath, she named the baby Holy Miracle, because he was the result of their miraculous love. And then, they say, Pwyll went kind of crazy. Before, he had been a regular social kind of fellow, but after his wife died, he became very reclusive and wouldn't allow anyone to see his baby, even though his family and hers came and begged him to bring him in to live with them. They lived in their cabin for a few years, until Holy Miracle was around nine or ten, and then one day, they burned the cabin to the ground and lived in the woods from then on. I don't know how they survived the winters, but they always seemed pretty hale whenever we saw them. My guess is they found a good cave with a hot spring in it. Did you notice how clean he looked? He's like that every time we see him, dressed in rags but shining clean." She smiled at the picture of Holy Miracle standing in a shaft of sunlight on the trail. *It had been so good to see him again.* She went on. "It's pretty much certain that Pwyll is dead. I haven't seen him since Rachel's accident, and, goodness, Holy Miracle looks ancient, doesn't he?"

"I've heard of Jacob's Mountain," mused John. "They say it has magical powers."

Geneva hesitated. She had no choice but to get it out in the open. "Yes. Legend has it that the spirit of Love lives there and that it will inhabit anyone who goes there. Enemies have been known to make peace, and virtual strangers have fallen in love at first sight. That's where Rachel and Wayne first decided they cared for each other."

"I heard that story," replied John. "I think it's a beautiful legend. Do you believe it?"

She sighed. No, when she really thought about it, she did not believe it, although she wanted to with all her heart. *It would be wonderful if Love were a living thing, could really be pure and simple, would heal all hurts and make the tattered soul whole again.* "I don't suppose I really do," she said sadly. "The mountain heart loves legends and romance. It would be easy to keep a story like that alive."

"What did he say to you? That you had a thistle in your soul? What did he mean by that?"

"I have no idea," returned Geneva. "He often says cryptic things like that. I don't know what he thinks he sees." But her heart felt profoundly sad that Holy Miracle had seen something amiss with her. His words brought home her long unhappiness and her futile searching for—What? She only wished she knew. *Could the old mystic really see her soul? Could he help her heal it?* She shook off the thought. *Old mountain hermits could not possibly know the longings of her heart.*

They traveled in silence until the forest gave way to grass and sunshine. Before the sun had a chance to crest, Geneva and John found themselves gliding across the grassy bald, opulent with the scent of summer jasmine. Softly, the wind blew away Geneva's sorrow; she felt her heart lift and brighten, and in response to the new joy overtaking her, she spurred Fairhope to a dead run through the long, soft grass, challenging John with one short whoop. He was right behind her, a war cry in his throat. She beat him to the crest of the mountain, then dismounted while Fairhope was still in motion, feeling drunk with power and purpose. She flung her arms out and spun around in the merciful light, then ran and, laughing, leaped into John's bare arms the moment he had dismounted. *It was a perfect day to begin his seduction.* She hoped he would do it right.

They had no food except the hickory nuts, which they dipped in honey and ate with their fingers, and they drank Geneva's wine and talked about how they felt like gods up here above the world, feasting on wine and honey. When the bottle was emptied, Geneva lay back into the grass, feeling languid and full of warm sunlight. He was beautiful, sitting there in long, waving grass, lightly tanned, the light hair on his bare chest glinting gold in the thin, pure light. He was powerfully built, wedge-shaped, made to work with large animals. But his hands were sensitive looking, long fingered and tapered, though callused and work-rough. His hair, curly, longish, and ruffled by the wind, looked very touchable. She remembered it as being soft and smooth in her fingers. She yearned to touch him, but decided to tread very carefully. She would not make the first move. Giving him her best, come-hither smile, she teased, "John, do you work all the time? Don't you ever go on vacations?" She willed him to say that he had always dreamed of sailing to the Greek islands.

"Oh, sure. The last time I went abroad I went to Serbia. I guess I stayed there for a couple of months."

"Serbia?"

"In Yugoslavia. You remember back when they had the big earthquake?"

"Why did you go to Serbia of all places?"

"To help the victims. You know the Red Cross needed volunteers, so I went. There are a lot of farming communities that were devastated, and the livestock was in pretty bad shape."

"Oh." There was a long pause while Geneva considered a way to redirect the conversation. "You like to travel, don't you?"

"Sure. I've been to all the great places. Honduras, Somalia, Kenya. Fascinating people. It's amazing how much spirit people have. Grinding poverty, and yet they're happy and industrious. Sometimes they don't even have the bare necessities, but they feel lucky and grateful if they have enough to eat. I've seen people eat bugs for heaven's sake, and drink putrid water, and yet they'd kill their last chicken to give us a feast just because we'd helped them in an extremely small way."

"How interesting." Geneva shuddered at the thought of being so far from civilization. She wanted Paris. "I'd like to do some traveling," she said after a pause.

"Oh, yes, you'd love it," John smiled earnestly. "I wish you could see how fine most of the people I've met are. Really genuine, good people. Very different on the surface, but once you make the effort to understand and adapt to them and their customs, and if you respect them, there's nothing they wouldn't do for you." He paused for a moment, and his voice softened.

"Someday, I'd like to go back, you know, spend some time really making a difference." He warmed to his topic. "Geneva, wouldn't you just love to go to a place like that and do something that would improve the quality of people's lives a thousand percent?"

The *Absolutely not,* leaped into Geneva's mouth, but she managed to swallow it before it made its way to her lips.

"I bet you'd be wonderful there," he continued, his eyes alight with enthusiasm. "You're so strong and vital. You've got so much to give. You'd be amazed at what you could do." His eyes brimmed with passion.

"As a matter of fact, I wish you'd go with me next week. I'm going to New Orleans. But then that wouldn't be the same. Not much you could do there."

Her ears pricked up. "New Orleans?" *Of course! There was plenty she could do there! There was this darling little jewelry store on Royal Street that had the most exquisite estate jewelry.* "Why are you going to New Orleans?"

"There's a conference there on world hunger, and I'm serving on a panel. Ways to increase the productivity of milk cows in drought stricken areas. That sort of thing." He leaned back, hands laced behind his head. "I'm working with a breeding program; we've done some experiments and have been able to increase milk production by as much as half a percent by breeding cows that can use all the available moisture in what most people would consider dry grass. That may not sound like much, but when you multiply that over hundreds of thousands of cattle that's pretty significant."

This conversation had degraded substantially since she had initiated it, and Geneva wondered when, or if, she could turn it back toward, say… Switzerland and luxury ski resorts where they might loll around naked on bearskin rugs in front of a marble fireplace. The idea of honeymoons seemed far from John's mind, but in spite of her disappointment, she found herself admiring his altruism and his enthusiasm.

"You're a pretty special guy yourself," she said softly, and in her mind she added, *I wish you would kiss me.* His mouth seemed so ripe for kissing, she thought as she looked at his lips hungrily. After a very still moment, he took the hint. Leaning over carefully, his body inches from her, he kissed her softly, then let it linger. *Okay, he had made the first move. My turn.* She wrapped her arms around him and pulled him in close, feeling his hesitation, then his surrender. Warmth spread through her, and as with their first kiss so many weeks ago, she felt herself floating in a dizzy spiral. She was falling into the sun, warm, melting. She let the palm of her hand wander softly over his chest and tasted his mouth. Yes, she hadn't imagined it earlier. *He was delicious. And he was hers.*

She felt his sigh, deep, and painful-sounding as he drew his face far enough away to look at her. There it was, that look of longing. It made her want to kiss his eyes and tell him that she would give him all the love he ever needed. But, sighing again, he averted his face, and when he returned his eyes to hers, they were altered, gentled in a way she had not seen before, and yet troubled.

Her heart was pounding. She was surprised at the intensity of her feeling for him, at how much she wanted him, at her powerful desire to yield herself completely to him, and the words were out of her mouth before she realized their meaning. "Would you like to make love with me?"

Damn! Not now, you dummy she silently cried to herself. *You weren't supposed to say that! That's for next month!* But she was shaking inside, and she wanted very much for him to say "yes." She flushed and lowered her eyes.

He looked up and exhaled quickly with a little chuckle that sounded like a sob. Geneva waited, hurting in the knowledge that everything was at stake. Taking her face in his hands, he looked deep into her eyes, and once again, the longing was there. It made her feel like a puddle of warm, gold liquid, as if she had just drunk a stiff shot of scotch. She felt shy, but nevertheless willed herself to return his gaze steadily. At last he spoke with quiet intensity.

"Yes. I would like to make love with you. I would love to make love with you. I could bury myself in you and stay there forever, and I want to make you love me." He kissed each of her eyes, the palm of her hand, the hollow in her throat. "I want to make you quiver." he said, his voice low and husky, resonant with desire. He lifted his hands and looked at them intently. "With these hands I want to cherish you. With these arms, I want to hold you and protect you." His eyes burned into hers. He seemed to be transported into a different sphere. I want to give you pleasure like you've never known or dreamed of." He rolled on top of her, gathering her close in his arms beneath him, and kissed her eyes again, her lips, her throat, and he murmured, "With this body I want to worship you."

Geneva had never heard such pretty talk before, and it did things to her insides that felt unbearably sweet, a sweetness mingled with yearning, like the heartbreaking scent of jasmine. And with the words that washed over her like stunning white water, she felt the strength in his arms, the essential maleness traversing the length of his body. Just in time, she caught herself drooling. Already she was quivering, her breath coming in quick gasps, and then she felt herself spiraling downward again, as she had at their first kiss, as she felt the fabric of her shirt and flimsy bra somehow melt away, and John's warm hand was on her breast. She closed her eyes and opened her mouth for his next kiss.

It did not come. Dimly, she perceived that his warmth had detached itself from her. She tried to nuzzle closer, but her grasp fell to empty air. Not until she opened her eyes did she discover that he had moved several inches away, and was leaning on his elbow, smiling at her. His face was unreadable.

"What is it?" she asked, dizzy and disoriented. "What's the matter?"

John's smile remained, but his eyes looked sad. "I'm sorry," he said. "I didn't mean to seduce you. I had promised myself I would behave." His eyes dropped to her bare breasts, lingered, then looked away. "It isn't exactly the honorable thing to do, get you up here and ply you with wine on an empty stomach. I guess I drank a little too much, too."

Geneva felt even more confused. *How could he possibly think he was misbehaving when he was doing exactly what she wanted? Okay, so things were happening a little fast.* But she could deal with that. What a time for him to suddenly decide to be a gentleman! *Damn it all! This man was not playing fair!*

"It's okay, John," she said softly, wishing he would kiss her eyes again, wishing he would tear off her clothes and bury his face in her willing flesh.

"No," he shook his head. "Geneva, I've told you I want something permanent. I don't want anything to do with casual love. I want marriage and children, and real…" he groped for the word, "terminal love." He looked at her pleadingly for a long moment, then pulled his eyes away from hers. Very carefully, he said, "I'm hoping you'll love me like that, but I'm not going to rush you or do anything that might make you resent me." He spoke softly to the bumblebees droning lazily among the myrtle. "I know you may find it hard to trust me, considering what's happened between us, and I understand that you don't really know me well enough to accept me like I want you to. But you will. I hope you will. I certainly intend to do whatever it takes to win you." He shook his head again. "I'm sorry, Geneva. I lost sight of how vulnerable you are." Laughing ruefully, he pulled his eyes back to hers. "I guess I thought you'd slap my face. I promise to behave myself from now on."

Geneva felt as though she was the one who had been slapped. This was not going at all the way she wanted. Yet, somewhere inside her, a small part of herself was pleased, although most of her was miserably disappointed at the rejection. Honor had its place, but at the moment it didn't warm her insides and ease the yearning she felt. Besides, if he was telling her he loved her, then why the hell didn't he get down on his knees and ask her to marry him? *Damn!* She looked up at him, her forehead furrowed with confusion and frustration, and suddenly she was embarrassed at her dishevelment.

She had thrown herself at him! She had begged him to love her and not only had he rejected her, but, in his way, had chastised her for her forwardness. Did he really think she should have slapped him? She hooked her bra together and buttoned her shirt with trembling hands.

He became cool, almost a stranger. "Come on," he said, standing up, offering her his hand. "It's starting to cloud up, and I don't think I should keep you out if it's going to rain." Stung, Geneva did not care if it rained torrents, and she resented more than a little his macho, protective attitude. She stood in a huff, running her hand through her hair, and ignoring John's offer of help, clambered up on Fairhope, determined to show him that she was not a dandified toy, something to "win" as he had so ungenerously put it.

The tension between them grew and thickened until they had reached the meadow by Raven Creek. Geneva had managed to keep slightly ahead of him on the mountain trail, but as the woodland fell away and the land opened up onto the pasture, John drew up beside her, pulled at Fairhope's reins, and forced her to a stop. She turned to him, but her eyes hugged the ground.

"I'm sorry," he said. "I don't know how to do this, and I know I've behaved like a fool." He reached across to her face and, taking her chin in his hand, said, "Geneva, look at me." He said it softly but with authority. Geneva looked at him, face burning. "You're a beautiful, very desirable woman, Geneva. I love everything about you, the gold in your skin and hair, I love the way your eyes light up when you see something beautiful. I love the way you look at my mouth and the way you glow when I touch you. I love your eyes, your lips, your graceful neck. I even love your teeth! And the way you hold the reins, and the way you seem to be in love with everything you see. You don't know how many times I have dreamed about making love to you, but I want to be very careful." He smiled. "I don't know whether to kick myself around the block for missing a golden opportunity or congratulate myself on my superhuman restraint. It all depends on how you feel about it."

Despite her lingering embarrassment, Geneva had to smile, lifting her eyes and letting the good words burn into her very center. This was working out all right after all, *Let him woo me*, she decided. This could turn out to be very nice, even nicer, perhaps, than she had expected.

Fighting the urge to leap off Fairhope and into John's arms, she kicked her mare and tore off through the meadow toward the house. She could hear the thunder of Redneck's hooves behind her, and she knew and hoped that John would soon catch her. But for the moment she was content to let the wind whip her face and hair and to let his words resound in her heart. She felt beautiful, and so full of vitality, so ready to embrace whatever life would hand her that she almost forgot her plans. Still, she had not forgotten Paris.

They crossed the pasture at a dead run, neck and neck, but checked their horses' speed simultaneously so they could approach the barn at an easy canter. Then, because they had run the horses so hard for the last mile, they slowed to a cooling walk. As they neared the house, Geneva noticed two vehicles that did not belong to the family. One she recognized as Howard Knight's beat-up old pickup truck; the other was a brand new blue Jaguar convertible she had never seen before. Curious, she pulled Fairhope up and draped the reins loosely around the gatepost.

She dreaded seeing Howard Knight again, remembering her drug-induced behavior, but she trusted him not to make an issue of it. He had called her twice since the night of the accident to report on the status of her car repair and to inform her that he was waiting for parts to arrive, and had never once mentioned her foolish behavior or had said anything to indicate that he even remembered it. So she straightened her back and strode to the house. Turning the corner, her strong legs suddenly faltered, and she would have staggered, except that her momentum had already carried her to the steps where she was able to grasp the porch railing. There, sitting in rocking chairs arranged at perfectly spaced intervals, sat Wayne, Howard Knight, and Howard Whittaker Graves, III, the lover who had callously rejected her.

"Howard!" she gasped. Both Howards turned their faces toward her and smiled. Howard Knight stood slowly, but Howard Graves leaped out of his chair and bounded down the steps, grabbing her up into a hug that took her breath away. When he let her go, she was trembling so violently she had to sit down.

"Howard, what are you doing here?" she asked weakly. Glancing off to her left, she saw John standing quietly, his face closed and inscrutable. Howard Knight smiled down at her, and even at the distance of eight feet she could see the sympathy in Wayne's eyes. She felt trapped and helpless.

"Geneva, I've come to get you, to—" began Howard Graves.

But Wayne suddenly broke in.

"Well, Geneva, thanks to you, we've got plenty of company today. John, good to see you. Have you met these fellows? That there's Howard Graves." He indicated the smooth-looking man who stood with his arm around Geneva's waist.

John stepped forward politely, but he seemed to have grown taller and broader in the past few seconds.

"Hello," he said, offering his hand to Howard, who gave him one suspicious glance, his eyes narrowing at John's bare chest. "Hello," he said smoothly, "I'm Howard Graves, Geneva's fiancée."

Geneva felt as well as heard his arrogance, but even more evident was the general growing level of tension and piqued male competitiveness. Testosterone seemed to be suddenly manufactured by the bucketful by every man there. Geneva swallowed hard, correcting him with an unsteady voice, "Ex-fiancée."

John's voice was smooth, too, but Geneva heard the mockery in it as he broke in. "Glad to meet you, Howard. I'm John Smith, Geneva's ardent admirer." He gave Howard a handshake that must have been uncomfortably firm. She saw the veins standing out in each of their necks as they gripped hands and glared at each other.

Wayne broke in again. "And this is Howard Knight, the fellow who saved Rachel and Geneva up on the mountain."

Howard Knight stepped lightly down the stairs. "Hi. Howard Knight." He said it perfectly, articulating carefully, if self-consciously, then he glanced sideways at Geneva with a little smile and continued, "Geneva's other ardent admirer." He grinned at John.

"Well, I'm just her brother-in-law, but I like her a lot, too," drawled Wayne. "And now that we have so much in common, why don't we all sit down and have a beer?"

Howard Graves remained cool and aloof, apparently confident of his control. Very calmly, he turned to Wayne and said politely, "I'd like to, Wayne, but I've driven a long way to see Geneva, and we have a few things to discuss, if you don't mind." He smiled intimately at Geneva. "Geneva, we have a lot of catching up to do.

Would you like to go for a ride?"

Geneva wanted to scream or to laugh, but she wasn't sure which, she felt so dazed by the intensely masculine rivalry around her. She stood alone in the uncomfortable spotlight for a long time, aware that eight eyes were fixed upon her every move, waiting to judge her actions. The testosterone was bubbling up and swirling around her ankles by now; she felt that she must do something fast or soon she might be drowning in it.

At last she sighed and turned to the men on the porch. "Please excuse me, but I do think I should talk to Howard here." She dared to look at John briefly, pleadingly. She hoped he would forgive her for this.

There was a moment when the tension grew to dizzying heights, and then John Smith leaned against the porch rail, and with an exaggerated drawl, said, "Waaaal, Hard, looks lak we been give the old heave-ho. Reckon the only thang we kin do now is go git drunk and shoot us out a buncha road signs. I got a case of Buds over at the house, and while we're adrankin 'em, we kin listen to all my Wiley Bob and the Bobcats records."

Howard Knight stepped in nimbly, "Yew got Wiley Bob and the Bobcats records?"

"Ever one of 'em," John assured him.

"Well, hell, we'll have us a good time. I got a jug a shine under the mattress in the truck, and a couple twenty-twos there in the gun rack. I reckon we'll jist haveta git blind drunk and crazy now that this here woman has throwed us over fer a city slicker."

John's face lit up with pleasure. He was warming up. "A twenty-two?" he snorted. "Hell, that's a sissy gun. I got me a forty-four down by the hog barn."

Howard Graves smiled tightly, and Geneva could sense the anger rising as Howard and John tried to top one another sounding like hillbillies. "Come on, baby," he said loudly, not to be outdone. "How do you like the little present I brought you?" He pulled a set of keys from his pocket and handed them to her, then gestured to the Jaguar glistening in the drive. "Get your driver's license, sweetheart, and you can see if you like her."

The men on the porch did not seem to hear him. Howard Knight was saying, "Naw. A forty-four? Now at's a gun, by gawd. I had me a sixty-six oncet, but the dang thang blowed up on me. I useta hunt buffalo with it."

Geneva raced into the house to collect her purse, but on her way out, she hesitated, then stopped to look at John full in the face, trying to read his thoughts. "Will you take care of the horses?" she asked, her eyes begging him to forgive her. She remembered his recent kisses and blushed. But she felt the odd sensation that Howard Graves had some sort of claim on her and that she owed him at least one conversation now that he had driven all this way…

"At yer service, little lady," John said grandly. "Anythang yer sweet li'l heart wants is all yorn."

Wayne was boasting, "That's nothin'. I got a eighty-eight, but Rachel made me put it away after we got married. You know these women. They say they like a man with a big gun, but once they get ahold of you, they never let you show it off to anybody."

"Yep. There's no figurin' women," nodded Howard Knight sagely. "And then, no matter how big yer gun is, they allus run after the men with the sissy car."

Fighting the urge to laugh, Geneva slipped into the Jag and inserted the key into the ignition. But she made the mistake of glancing once more at the three men on the porch and nearly hooted at the sight. They had draped their arms around each other's shoulders and stood silently, a picture of cultural solidarity, looking at her with mock mournfulness. It was all she could do to keep from blowing them a kiss. But she turned her attention to the man who sat beside her, then started the quiet, powerful engine and drove away.

Her initial shock at seeing Howard had ebbed, and now she was angry with herself for becoming weak-kneed at the sight of him. In turn, her anger directed toward him. She drove in stony silence, waiting for him to speak.

"God, what a couple of rubes," he said, eyeing Geneva carefully.

"So that's who you've been hanging out with while you've been here."

Geneva had no patience with him. "What are you doing here, Howard?" she asked sharply.

"I told you. I've come to take you back home. Geneva, you can't imagine how miserable I've been without you. And I'm sorry about all that I did and said." He laid his hand on her shoulder, but she pushed it off. Her anger was genuine, but she was not inclined to stop his words, for despite her disgust, she rather enjoyed hearing him apologize so prettily.

"I know you're mad as hell, Geneva, and I don't blame you, but really, I never intended for us to break up. I just wanted to back off for a little while, so we could be sure. You know, marriage is a big step, and I was feeling a little closed in. I just wanted some space for awhile, to see if what we had was real."

"Oh, right," groaned Geneva. "And that's why you wanted to date other people, and why you left and haven't called me for six months. That's an awful lot of space, Howard."

"Geneva, if you remember, you threw me out of your apartment and told me that if I ever darkened your door again you'd yank my teeth right out of my head. I believe those were your exact words." He flashed a flirtatious little smile at her. "Now, sweetheart, as much as I love you, I don't cherish losing my teeth, not after suffering through three years of braces."

Geneva remembered the words she had uttered, but she found it hard to believe that Howard had actually been intimidated by them. She did not soften. "So what made you change your mind? Did you suddenly decide you could fight me off if I attacked you?"

"Oh, I guess you could say I got over being too proud to come crawling back. Geneva, I really am sorry. Come back. Marry me. I love you." He looked out the window. "Okay, maybe it took me six months to get myself sorted out and to realize that I really do need you. This isn't easy for me, you know."

They had been driving on the high ridge that she and John had traveled the night of their theater date in Tucker. Geneva found a wide place and pulled over to the shoulder. She stopped the car and glared at Howard. For a moment she thought about how happy she had been with him, and how much she had looked forward to their life together: a life sparkling with success and glamor, but before long she found herself examining Howard's nose and deciding that the nostrils were, indeed, somewhat large. There was a long silence while she studied him.

"What are you looking at?" asked Howard.

"Oh, nothing," replied Geneva, blushing. "I was just thinking about how happy we could have been…" and suddenly, she began to cry, remembering the hurt that Howard had caused and how much she had loved him. And more than that, she grieved over the realization that the hurt he had caused her also meant that the joy they might have had together was forever and irretrievably lost. It was too sad to comprehend, all that love just tossed away, left in the gutter to languish and die.

At first her tears were pretty little shimmering drops sitting in her eyes, causing them to sparkle, but then they ran down her face in earnest torrents, and her nose began to run so that she had to cry into her hands and hope Howard would give her a handkerchief.

He did not have one, and seemed as distressed by that fact as she. She hated to cry like this in front of somebody. It made her face all red and puffy, and besides, she was sure the mascara was running. She couldn't face Howard like this, all running and smeared. At last she wiped her nose on her sleeve, and sniffling, waving away Howard's attempts to embrace her, dug deep into her purse for a tissue.

It was one of those bottomless purses that held so much that it was unnecessary to ever clean it out. Things simply collected in there and sank to the bottom if they were infrequently used. Geneva knew she had some Kleenex in there somewhere, but in her distracted and blinded state, she failed to find any even after several moments of rummaging.

Still sobbing, eyes and nose running, Geneva finally turned the purse upside down and dumped its contents in her lap. *Yes, there was one—a little tattered and lipstick smeared, but serviceable.* She blew her nose on it then used a remaining dry corner to wipe off the mascara that had run down her cheeks. Then, after checking the mirror to make sure she looked all right, she faced Howard again.

"I don't know, Howard," she began, after drawing a long, shuddering breath. "I really think it's too late for us."

"Don't say that, darling, please. You're hurt and angry. I've thought a lot about this, and I know we can make things right between us again. Don't say anything now, but just give it some time." He looked so forlorn and miserable that Geneva felt herself softening a little. She remembered again how much she had loved him, and for the sake of that, she wanted to give him a chance, but she felt confused, and somewhere in the back of her mind a little voice said, *Do you really want this man to be the father of your children? They might all have noses just like his.*

She began filling her purse, shaking her head and repeating, "Oh, Howard, I don't know. I've been pretty happy here, and I think that maybe I don't want to go back to DC."

"What do you mean, you don't want to go back? Don't you miss everyone? Don't you miss your job? What can you possibly find here to keep you occupied? There's absolutely nothing here! Just look at it!" He gestured at the empty air before him, and Geneva followed his instructions and looked.

The rain clouds that had threatened her and John on the mountain a few hours earlier had rolled away, and now the sky was a clear, perfect, dazzling blue, the color of the sky in storybooks, and the sun, which had begun to think about setting, had turned the air around them into a hazy, golden gauze, gentling around them and gilding the wings of a whole flock of monarch butterflies that bedecked a crop of purple thistles. In this light they looked like jeweled brooches. Far below them a hawk wafted lazily over a warm air current, circling in a long, slow, effortless glide, and off to her left, a groundhog sat perfectly still on a fallen tree and gazed at her. Somewhere in the trees below a mockingbird went through his entire repertoire, and then flew away, leaving her with the silence and the gentle wind, spiced with honeysuckle and wild sage. With shaking breaths she gulped great draughts of it, feeding her senses with its sweetness.

Howard did not speak for a time, then, when he seemed to be sure Geneva had been alone with her thoughts long enough he tossed off his final salvo. "I bet all this silence has been driving you mad."

He did lisp! No, it was not an actual lisp. More of a sibilant "s," but not quite. She turned to him resolutely. "How long are you staying, Howard?" she asked flatly.

He hesitated. "I should go back on Tuesday."

She nodded. Fine. She would give him until Tuesday to win her back. She owed that much to the love that she had felt for him. But already she knew his was a lost cause.

Eight

Thankfully, both Howard Knight and John were gone by the time Geneva and Howard returned to the farmhouse. The afternoon haze had begun to deepen in anticipation of dusk, and Geneva knew that Rachel had already prepared dinner without her help. Guiltily, she rushed into the kitchen to relieve her sister.

"Sorry, Rachel. I lost track of the time."

"It's okay. I'm just glad you haven't thrown yourself off a cliff. I saw everything from the window before you left. I was too chicken to even come out and face everybody myself." She giggled. "Wayne and John and Howard got into fish stories after they felt they had lied about their guns long enough. What did Howard have to say for himself?"

"Shh. He might hear you." Geneva tiptoed to the door to peek into the living room. Wayne and Howard were drinking scotch and listening to music while the children played with dolls at Wayne's feet. She decided it was safe enough to talk about her conversation with Howard.

"Well," she said, drawing a long breath. "It seems he has

decided, in his infinite wisdom, that we should reconcile. He even said he was sorry."

"Big of him," sneered Rachel.

"Several times, in fact," continued Geneva. "He hadn't come before because he was afraid I would beat him up."

"Makes sense."

"Yes. And the Jag's mine—all mine."

"Take it. They're worth a bundle, and you can hock it for some good river bottom land."

"How long did my ardent admirers stay?" asked Geneva.

"Oh, awhile. Howard—Knight, that is—really likes children, and he played croquet with the girls while Wayne and John put the horses up. Then we sat around and drank sangria and made fun of Howard—Graves. Why do you make things so confusing by getting boyfriends with the same name?"

"Very funny," said Geneva with a wry face. I think I hear somebody squalling for you."

"Right," sighed Rachel. "Here. The salad's yours. I'll see if I can't give them a quick fix and be back soon. By the way, Sally Beth and Lilly are coming for dinner. They're bringing it, actually. This is just incidentals."

"Great," groaned Geneva. Just what she needed. Howard, and now Sally Beth and Lilly. Apart, the two silly sisters would be bad enough: Sally Beth would exclaim over the babies all night and the man-crazy Lilly would throw herself at Howard. But together, they would be intolerable with their constant bickering. She just hoped they both would not find Howard attractive and fight over him. *He was just their type,* she figured as she sliced tomatoes. *Rich and male.*

As she had expected, dinner started out miserably and declined from there. True to form, Lilly instantly zeroed in on Howard and began making an enormous fool of herself. Geneva felt the jealousy flare each time she saw her beautiful cousin flip her silky, pale hair off her shapely neck and Howard's eyes dilate with pleasure.

"So, what do yew do, Howard?" Lilly purred.

"I'm a stock market analyst. You know, I try to figure out what the economy is doing. What companies' stock are good—that sort of thing."

"Ooh!" exclaimed Sally Beth, for something like the fifteenth time that evening. Geneva restrained her irritation. "I bet that's *hard!* I bet yew have to do a lot of *math*, don't yew?"

"Not too much," smiled Howard. "It's mostly done by computers now."

"Computers! Ooh! That's worse! I tried to use the one down at the school and couldn't hardly even figure out how to turn it on! I'm just awful at machines!"

Lilly gave her sister a superior smile. "Yew would be, Sally Beth. Yew cain't do anything that requires a brain." Sally Beth stiffened. Geneva could see the muscles in her jaw bunch. Turning cozily to Howard, Lilly asserted, "I've been using computers down at the store for a long time now. I can do all sorts of things on them."

"Yew can not," sniffed Sally Beth. "The store doesn't even have a computer. Yew jist use a calculator. I can do that!"

Lilly's smile grew a shade more maternal. "No, really. I do lots of things." She turned back to Howard. "Inventory and everything," she said in an intimate voice.

"Yew do not! And I do too have a brain!"

Lilly's smile hardened a bit, and inwardly Geneva moaned. Here it came. Ten minutes into the meal, and Lilly and Sally Beth were starting their first argument. She rolled her eyes at Rachel, who looked at the ceiling. "What do yew know, Sally Beth? I have been studying computers for some time now."

"That's a big, fat lie, and yew know it!" countered Sally Beth, sitting up straighter and glaring at Lilly. "Yew couldn't use a computer if yer life depended on it. Yew cain't use machines at all! Yew cain't even use an ATM machine!"

Lilly tossed her silvery hair. "It's not an ATM machine. That's like saying Automatic Teller Machine machine. You're just repeating yerself. And I can, too."

"Ah—" Geneva jumped in, hoping to redirect the conversation, "a redundancy in modern idiom. I've always heard ATM machine, too!"

Howard spoke up. "Well, there are all kinds of computers—and calculators—and some are harder to use than others. Where do you work, Lilly?"

Lilly settled back into her chair, darting her little eyes once toward Sally Beth, then batting her lashes at Howard. "Down at the Toy Boat," she replied demurely.

"Toy Boat?" echoed Howard.

"A toy store."

"Actually, It's ToyBoatToyBoatToyBoat, but Lilly never can say it. They don't even let her answer the phone!" interjected Sally Beth.

"I can, too!" snapped Lilly. "It's not that hard."

"Yeah, well, let's hear yew!"

"Sally Beth, yer such a child. I cain't believe you are acting so stupid in front of Howard and everbody."

"I'm jist askin' yew to say one little thing. Toyboatoyboatoyboat. That's not stupid. Saying yew can when you cain't is. Why don't yew just admit you cain't say it and we'll move on to another topic of conversation?"

"It really is hard," interrupted Howard nervously. Wayne, Geneva, and Rachel sat silently. They knew better than to get drawn in to one of Sally Beth's and Lilly's arguments, and besides, they could almost be entertaining if one were in the right mood. Better than TV, anyway.

"I certainly don't think I can say it," he continued. "Toyboatoyboytoyboyt. How about you, Geneva?"

"Not me," smiled Geneva demurely. "Rachel?"

"Nope. Makes me feel silly to try."

"Wayne?"

"Sure. Toy. Boat. Toy. Boat. Toy. Boat."

"That's not fair, Wayne," laughed Rachel. You have to say it fast. Even Lilly can say it slowly."

Sally Beth giggled. "No she cain't! She can only say it *once!*"

"Why don't yew tell everybody how it took yew three times to pass your cosmetology test, Sally Beth?" said Lilly mildly.

"Well! That was *hard!*" objected Sally Beth. I had to learn *chemistry* for that!"

"Yeah, like, 'What does peroxide do to hair?'"

"I know that!" exclaimed Sally Beth, missing the point. "It bleaches it out and dries it out, and you cain't put in a perm on top of it!" she shouted triumphantly. Lilly rolled her eyes toward Howard. Howard scratched his nose.

The argument slid from subject to subject, and back in time, until the girls had waxed so historical that no one could fathom the circumstances over which they were airing grievances. Yet, even as they squabbled, somehow Lilly still managed to channel an astounding amount of energy toward Howard. Geneva's head ached from grinding her teeth, and as the evening wore on, she felt bone weary and desperate for peace and quiet. At last, after dinner was eaten and the dishes washed, she slipped out of the living room to the telephone upstairs.

Secretively, she dialed John's number. "Hi. Just wanted to let you know I enjoyed myself today," she whispered into the phone. "Sorry I took off like that. I hope you understand that I felt like I had to go with Howard. The last time we spoke, we were screaming at each other."

"Yeah. I don't blame you. Nice car."

"Yes, well. I sort of like my Mazda. It's easy to get out of ditches."

He laughed, then fell silent. "I suppose you still have company?"

"He said he plans on leaving Tuesday." She hesitated. "But I'd be surprised if he lasts that long. There's really no reason for him to hang around unless of course he wants to go shoot at road signs with you and Howard. Did you kill very many?"

"Not so many. We were too drunk on moonshine to shoot straight." They both laughed, then he lowered his voice. "I enjoyed today, too. I don't know what I've thought about more tonight, what nearly happened up on that mountain, or what you were doing with Jim Dandy this evening. It's been a night of ups and downs."

Geneva felt a rush of feeling for John. "I guess you'll leave before I get a chance to see you again?"

"Yes, first thing in the morning. But I'll be back next Saturday. See you then?"

"Definitely. Have fun."

"You, too." There was a pause, then a chuckle. "I don't mean that. Hope you are miserable."

"You're too kind."

"So everyone tells me. Goodnight."

"Goodnight, John."

She hung up and tiptoed back to the stairs. Lilly and Sally Beth were making their good-byes, but Sally Beth glanced up at Geneva and suddenly hurried up the steps toward her. She motioned for Geneva to come into a bedroom.

"Geneva, honey! I am so *sorry!* We acted jist *awful* tonight, and I cain't tell you how bad I feel about it." Her blue eyes swam in unspilled tears. "I don't know what's wrong with me. I jist let Lilly drive me *nuts!* She's always been boy-crazy, but ever since Daddy died, she's jist gotten to be such a *hussy*, and she's about to *embarrass mama to death*, and I cain't do a thing with her, and it jist makes me *so mad!*" Sally Beth stamped her foot in frustration. "Anyway, I try not to git all riled up, but then she starts *flirtin' her head off* with whatever man is around, and it was so *embarassin'* that she was *flirtin' with yer boyfriend right in front of yew*, and I jist lost it!" She glared down the stairs toward Lilly who was giving Howard a particularly warm farewell and shuddered.

Geneva was taken aback. Sally Beth had never apologized for fighting with Lilly before, but then she realized that most of the time, it had been Lilly to initiate—and sustain—an argument. Sally Beth usually treated her sister with nothing worse than that air of condescension that younger sisters find irritating, and Lilly's temper had always been quick. "Oh, don't worry about it, Sally Beth. I know how Lilly can be, and I'm not worried a bit. As far as I'm concerned, she can have him, but I don't think she is his type."

"Well, for goodness sake, I know that! And she should have the sense to know it, too, but that doesn't stop her from actin' like a—like a—*Jezebel* in front of everbody!" She drew a deep breath and turned pleading eyes toward Geneva. "Anyway, I'm real sorry. I should know how she is by now and not git my dander all up and flyin' around and sayin' those awful things I said. And Lilly is really jist pitiful, she jist hates bein' poor, and she thinks some man is going to save her from it. Tell Rachel we're sorry, will yew? And Howard, and everbody?" She looked so miserable Geneva felt like laughing. Poor Sally Beth really did have a good heart. It just seemed that she and Lilly were such a joke that no one could take them seriously. She gave her a quick hug and said, "Sure, sweetheart. I've already forgotten it."

After Rachel and Wayne went to bed, Howard and Geneva settled themselves in the porch swing to watch the big-bellied moon slide behind a silky gauze of clouds. Geneva found herself in the odd position of feeling both comfortable with Howard and alienated from him. The most natural thing in the world would be to nestle in his arms, for she really no longer felt angry with him. And deep inside, she knew she still loved him, loved him as warmly as her heart could beat and still find part of her mind wandering toward the man across the field. She let Howard put his arm around her while she wondered if John were watching this moon, too. It felt strange, this feeling of love for two men at once, and even more strange was Howard's being here, out of context in the mountain night. She had always associated him with his classy apartment and dinner in downtown restaurants. John should be with her now, here in the creaky swing. For her to feel completely comfortable with Howard, they should get back into the gleaming Jaguar and drive for the city lights.

"Penny," he said, stroking her hair.

"Not worth it," she replied. "I haven't had a coherent thought since you arrived."

"I set you all awhirl, do I?'

"I guess you could say that."

"Like your car?"

"Mmmm. Must have cost you a nice little bundle."

"Not at all. The nice thing about being a stock market analyst is that we know how to make money in any kind of economy."

She sighed, weary, but Howard mistook it for romance. He pulled her to him and kissed her, and she let herself sink into his arms, remembering the taste of his mouth, the feel and scent of his body close to hers. A faint response stirred in her, triggered by months of conditioning during her life with him, but after a moment it died, crushed by her weariness and her sense of dislocation. An image of John kissing the palm of her hand flashed in her brain, and she found herself comparing the two men with a calculating coldness she did not like.

Let's face it. Howard was wealthy, and he had just offered her a brand new Jaguar convertible— but that was about it. He had mistreated her, and although he was now returning with his apologies, the fact that he was capable of mistreating her remained. Essentially, he was spoiled and cowardly. On the other hand, John had told her lies, but Geneva now understood that such lies were not a sign of cowardice, but of a romantic nature, and somehow, a self-deprecating sense of humor. He would never be able to buy her the kinds of things that Howard could, but then, what did she really want? The Jaguar looked decadent and overly lavish there in the gravel drive, something like a gaudy bracelet on the arm of a child. She stirred. "I'm sorry, Howard. I'm really tired, and I need to go to bed. Let's please just hold this until tomorrow."

She could feel his disappointment. "Of course, darling. I've been thoughtless. I suppose your arm is bothering you after your ride today?"

She glanced at it. "Yes, I suppose it is. Goodnight. I guess Rachel has already got you set up in a room?"

He hesitated. "Yes. But I was hoping—I mean, yes. I can find everything just fine. Goodnight, sweetheart. Sweet dreams. You go on in. I think I'll just sit out here and gaze at the moon and think about you."

Geneva smiled. She wondered if John were doing the same, and the funny thought struck her that maybe the two of them could get together and gaze at the moon and think of her while she slept. She bet herself that John would start a hyperbole competition. Howard would no doubt be surprised at his command of the language.

"Goodnight, Howard. Don't gaze too long. The moon can drive a man crazy, you know." She went to bed and slept dreamlessly until the Sunday sun lifted her eyelids.

After breakfast, Wayne, Rachel, and all four of the children went to church. Geneva declined their invitation, feeling awkward at the thought of Howard sitting in the plain little sanctuary. He surely would find it primitive, and although he would say nothing unkind, he would feel condescending there among her kinfolk, some of them uneducated and dowdy. She remembered Howard's mother, so sophisticated in her Dior suits, her polished, bejeweled hands clasped gracefully in her small lap. Geneva could not help but compare her to her aunt Dorothy Jean, all two hundred and sixty pounds of her, enamored of polyester pantsuits and Beechnut gum. They would prefer, she decided, to go riding instead, for she wanted to show Howard the best of what these hills had to offer.

He was a capable rider, if a bit stiff in the western saddle, so they took an easy trail to the north. Geneva did not want to go near John's place, so they wound their way up to a little grotto where water tumbled down to an inky pool laced with black stemmed maidenhair ferns and deep, cushiony moss. The mist rose up like fairy dust, nourishing the wet rankness and bejeweling the rocks and banks with droplets like emeralds. Geneva had always loved it here. Her heart thumped with a strange shyness, almost fear, as she looked at Howard and willed him to love it, too.

He found the place charming. "No wonder you've been happy here," he commented, settling himself on a large rock by the pool. "You look as at home here as a wood nymph, and about as delectable." He pulled her down beside him. They talked for a while, but soon, to Geneva's dismay, they ran out of things to say.

She felt more awkward as she showed him the wintergreen and the place where the watercress grew, then with growing alarm, watched him become bored as she explained why the Indian pipes had no color.

He was not interested in Indian pipes, he told her when she chided him; he was interested only in her. He had missed her and yearned for her for so long that he could hardly contain himself now that they were together again. And then, half jesting, he tumbled her into the wet moss and splashed water on her until her thin T-shirt was soaked and clinging.

"Oh, what a fashion statement!" he teased. Wear this on Madison Avenue, and West Virginia will become a mecca for designers." She laughed, but was embarrassed at her transparent garment.

"Shame on you!" she cried, trying to wring out the water.

"Here, let me help you. You can just take it off and it will be dry in an hour or two," he said, reaching for her and tugging at the wet T-shirt.

As Geneva's embarrassment grew, she wished she had never brought Howard here. She was incapable of returning his kisses, for in this context, she felt his passion defiling. Everything was wrong; nothing had been right since he had come here, and now, as his hands caressed her and pushed her into the moss, she began to struggle with him, fearing irrationally that she might drown in its velvety depths.

Suddenly he stopped, sitting up and looking at her with impatience. "Geneva, what is the problem? I know you still love me, don't you?"

She glared at him. "Yes, Howard, I still love you. But I don't think I like you anymore. You haven't been a very nice person lately."

Howard thought about this, looking very sad, but then he lifted his head and asked suspiciously, "This doesn't have anything to do with one of those two hillbillies I met yesterday, does it? Surely nothing has happened between you and them."

Geneva did not like his high-handed tone. She threw back her head and replied archly, "As a matter of fact, a lot of things have happened between me and them. Let's see… the night I met Howard Knight, we had a car wreck, and I got cut up a bit." She indicated the scar, still angry on her forehead. "And Rachel had the babies, and then I went up the mountain with him and got stoned and chased him all around the barn, begging him to strip for me. It was a very interesting evening."

"Very funny, Geneva. I know how you feel about drugs."

"And John—that's the other hillbilly, the one who seems not to like city slickers. By my reckoning, about the time that you were settling on the front porch to wait for me to come home, I was trying my damnedest to seduce him up on top of a mountain."

"That's funny, too, Geneva."

"He didn't think so. Gave me a lecture on the pitfalls of premarital sex. Quite an honorable fellow that John. Both of them, actually. Unlike some people I know. How many women have you slept with in the past six months, Howard?"

He flushed slightly. "I resent that, Geneva. And I resent your treating my question so cavalierly. You can understand why I might be jealous, and the least you can do is tell me the truth."

She sighed. "Okay, he didn't give me a lecture. He just acted like he thought I should know better."

Howard stood up. "Let's go back. I'm not interested in hearing wild tales about your unseemly behavior, and this place has turned out to be not so pleasant after all."

Without a word Geneva climbed on a rock and swung herself up on Fairhope's back. But her anger was dissipating. Poor Howard! He was out of his element here, and he was having a bad time of it. She would not be surprised if he high tailed it out by tomorrow, she thought grimly.

But to her surprise, he did stay until Tuesday morning, and while she remained cool toward him, he behaved nicely the whole weekend, talking prettily about how happy they would be once they were back in DC. together, the clubs they would join, the

Important People they would know. Geneva found herself enjoying his company again, and more than once she was tempted to sigh and give in to him if only to visit the city again and to see how it felt to be there with him. But many things held her back. She understood that Rachel really needed her and that she should stay at least a few more weeks to help out around here.

And there was John. It was confusing to think that she might actually be in love with two men at once, but whenever she tried to sort out her feelings, she kept coming back to the same conclusion. And worse, she found herself missing John while she was with Howard. She missed his sense of humor and the way she felt so easy and comfortable and warm around him. Howard was a bit of a strain. She always felt like she needed to apologize for things. She began to take more care with the way she looked. On Sunday night she polished her nails, but she felt a little foolish doing it.

Tuesday morning, Howard packed the car while Geneva stood aside and watched without helping.

"I wish you'd change your mind and come with me. It will be an awfully long drive without you."

"It's a pretty day. You'll do fine."

He hesitated, then spoke earnestly, "Geneva, I know it hasn't been the best of times while I've been here, but I'm not discouraged. I'll be back. I've made up my mind about this, and I'm not going to give up."

She smiled, glad he had said that. "Okay, Howard. Whenever you're ready to bring my car back to me, you just come on. I'll be here."

He kissed her good-bye and left. Geneva thought about the beaded gold gown she had worn to the last party Howard's firm had thrown and how good she had looked in it. She walked back to the house feeling emotionally exhausted and downright stupid. Life was getting too complicated.

Howard was not out of the driveway before the phone rang. It was Howard Knight, calling to ask if he could come the next day. Her car was repaired, he declared, and he would like to bring her back to get it. She thanked him warmly, apologizing for not having been able to spend time with him the Saturday before. Something about her had been humbled since the night she had met him. No longer did she feel the urge to sniff at his ignorance and his lack of social graces.

"Who was that?" Rachel inquired. "Another boyfriend? Don't you find it a little hard to keep them all apart?"

Geneva smiled. "It was Howard Knight. And I guess you could say yes, he is sort of a boyfriend, considering what I did to him the night the babies were born."

She told Rachel the story, embellishing it with as many exaggerations and flourishes as she could think up, and by the time she had finished the telling, she and Rachel both were sitting on the floor, raking tears from their eyes, screaming with laughter.

It took them through lunch to sober up. Rachel had to hear it again in bits and pieces, and with each retelling Geneva beefed it up more. *"Ooooh, Haaaaaaaaard!* Let me see! And when we went over the side of that loft, I thought we were flying. Didn't even realize my elbow was smashed until the next morning. And then poor Jimmy Lee comes in all thrilled with me braving all that pain while I was burying him!"

"Geneva, you are so awful! And I'm so glad you're my sister. I don't know how I got along with my dull life before you got here. Poor Jimmy Lee! Poor Howard!" She shook her head, picking up baby Lenora to nurse her. Smiling at her child, she spent a thoughtful moment stroking the tiny, downy head. Then she looked at Geneva pensively.

"You know, Geneva, we are awful to laugh at Howard. He really is a good person. Just think how he must have felt, you chasing him around the barn like that after he had gone to all the trouble to save us from that horrible situation."

"I know," sighed Geneva. "If it weren't so funny, it would be pretty sad. I suppose I'll have to apologize to him. And I will when he comes tomorrow."

"Howard's a lot smarter than you think he is," said Rachel. "And he's had a pretty tragic life that I think he's handled awfully well, considering. When we were in school, he was a budding poet. As a matter of fact, do you remember that poetry competition I won in the ninth grade?"

"With the poem about the fireflies?"

"Yes. Well, I really shouldn't have won that. Howard should have. But he had dropped out of school because his parents were in an accident and his mother was killed. His father lost both of his legs, and Howard just quit school. I don't know what happened to him after that."

"Why do you say he should have won the competition?" asked Geneva. "I thought your poem was pretty good."

"You should have seen Howard's stuff. It made my firefly poem seem infantile. Wait a minute. I think I may have something he wrote. Here, hold Lenora, and I'll see if I can find it. It may be in my scrapbook."

Geneva followed Rachel upstairs to her bedroom and her sister rummaged through a box from the closet.

"Yes, here it is," Rachel said, smiling. "I believe he had a bit of a crush on me, and he gave me this just before he left school. It was interesting. I had a huge crush on him, too. I thought he was brilliant, and even though I loved this poem, I don't believe I really understood it until much later. It seemed sort of clairvoyant when I finally figured it out."

Geneva took the scrapbook to examine the sheaf of Blue Horse notebook paper, now well yellowed and brittle, beside the pressed daisies tied with a purple ribbon. Geneva sat on the bed to read the fine, upright script.

April 9, 1965

To Rachel

The eagle flies deep in the heart of night,
Proud of his ancient story,

But before the Sun, he falters in flight,
Trembling before her glory.

And in her brightness, he buries his dreams,
For he cannot eclipse her, and there is no elixir
To lure or enlist her.
He watches her hopelessly, it seems.

Like all, he adores her but he cannot implore her,
For he's only a shadow in her gold light.
To her just a creature, trying to reach her,
He longs for her as he conquers the night.

> Now I tell you this secret,
> So my message is done:
> I am that eagle.
> You
>   Are that
>   Sun.

Geneva read the poem twice. "Howard wrote this when he was in the *ninth grade?* Our Howard? Howard Knight? Hard? Hemp grower extraordinaire?"

"There's more to him than you'd expect, at least there was, and I have a feeling he may still run pretty deep."

"What about that old aw-shucks façade? I mean, the grammar in this poem is better than what he uses now."

"He's been living in the mountains, with no schooling since he was fifteen. When you have to worry about survival, I guess literacy takes a back burner. Beside, Geneva, you know we used to talk like that, bad grammar and all even though we knew better. Remember?"

"I suppose so," sighed Geneva, remembering her first diction classes and how difficult they had been. "Hit's easy to git above yer raisin', ain't it?"

"Hit shore is, honey. And the worst part of it is that sometimes when you do, you lose sight of some pretty important things." She looked at Geneva holding Lenora in her arms. "I don't think you should go back to DC, Geneva. I don't think you'll be happy with Howard. These mountains are in your blood, and if you keep away from them for too long, you'll die of anemia. Some people might be able to live in concrete, but I know I couldn't, and I don't think you can, either."

With a wrench in her chest, Geneva realized that Rachel was probably right. "What do you think I should do? Run off with Howard Knight and help him tend his hemp patch?"

"He may expect it after what you did to him. There's a pretty strong code of behavior up here, you know."

Geneva laughed. "I haven't told you about what I did to John yet."

"Geneva! What?"

"Oh, nothing, really. Tried to seduce him, but he backed off. I think he may be in love with me."

"Yes, I know. You could do worse."

"But not much better, huh?"

"Definitely not."

Geneva looked at her big sister, radiant and glossy with happiness, and she wished she could be more like her. Her heart filled with affection for the woman who sat beside her, so simple in her desires, so fortified against complexity.

"I love you Rachel," she said.

"I love you, too, Geneva." The sound of children's laughter floated toward them on the warm air, and Geneva let her thoughts float with it, until the ringing phone jolted her out of her reverie. Hoping it might be John, Geneva handed the baby to Rachel to answer it. She was surprised to hear Howard Graves' voice, terse and anxious.

"Howard! Are you back home already?"

"No, Geneva, I'm not. I am in some town, if you could call it that, by the name of Hutterton. Ever heard of it?"

Geneva pulled the receiver away from her face and queried Rachel. "Ever heard of Hutterton?"

"Yes. It's a little bitty community east of here. It's a pretty rough place, I think. Lots of moonshiners, and I think they have a branch of the Klan there. Is Howard there?"

Geneva returned to Howard. "What are you doing in Hutterton? Don't tell me the car broke down."

Howard sounded worried. "Did I just hear Rachel say the Klan's here?"

"Howard, are you in some sort of trouble?"

"I sure am, Geneva. Not only does the local sheriff seem to have a grudge against flatlanders who drive too fast in foreign cars, but somehow they've turned up a packet of what may be cocaine. Do you by any chance know anything about a little plastic bag full of whitish powder?"

"Howard! No! They found coke on you?"

"In the floor of the car. I don't see how they could have planted it. I saw it in the floor about the same time he did. Geneva are you sure you didn't have something? Anything at all that might look like coke?"

"Of course not, Howard. You know I never touch drugs. I bet it was Jason or Marie. I told you that you shouldn't to hang out with them!"

"Geneva, neither one of them has been in this car. It's brand new. I picked it up Saturday, just before I left for your place. And besides, I'm not sure it's coke. It's a funny color, although I guess it could be dirty."

"Well, they can't hold you if they aren't sure, can they?"

"Guess again, sweetie. They tell me they're sending it over to Harrisonburg to have it tested, and until the results get back, they're acting like they have a drug lord on their hands. I won't discuss their interrogation methods. They let me talk to a local lawyer, but I'm not too sure about this guy's credentials. But he talked them into letting me call you. Geneva, can you get up here? Call my attorney in DC. It's Greg Ford. And bring all the cash you can scrounge up. I don't know if they'll let me post bail, but I sure do want out of here." He sounded more and more nervous as he talked.

"Of course, I'm on my way," said Geneva. "But Howard, can't—"

"I gotta go, Geneva," he said hastily. "My time's up. Hurry!"

"What is it, Geneva?" demanded Rachel. "You're as white as a sheet. What's happened to him?"

"Howard's been picked up for possession of cocaine, but I know he doesn't use it." Suddenly Geneva felt a cold river running down her spine. *Howard was wealthy! Howard always drove a fancy car. Howard sometimes went away on business trips and always came back throwing money around.* And now he has a brand new Jaguar convertible that he just was going to hand over to her, as if he had money to burn! *Oh, God! It couldn't be!* She put a shaking hand to her mouth. Her knees buckled and her head swam.

"Sit down, Geneva," said Rachel sharply. "What is it?"

"Rachel, do you suppose Howard is involved with drugs? I mean, he has all this money. I always assumed he just earned it or got it from his family or something. I don't know anything about the investment business." She sat on the bed and sobbed violently. *Her ex-fiancé a drug pusher! Deceiver and murderer of little children! Among the most despicable of the human race! It was too awful to comprehend.* And to think, she had almost married him! The thought brought on a fresh torrent of tears.

"Geneva, get hold of yourself. Surely not. I mean, stock market analysts really can make a lot of money. Look at how well your investments have done. Honey, you don't know all the facts." But Rachel looked really worried.

"You're right, I don't know! I don't know him! To think, I've been in love with a dr-dr-drug lord!" she wailed.

"Hold on. Now just think. What did he ask you to do?"

"He-he s-s-said to bring a lot of c-cash. I guess he hopes to br-bribe them!"

After half an hour of sobbing and wailing, Geneva finally let

Rachel persuade her to give Howard the benefit of the doubt and call his attorney. Rachel wrote a check for Geneva to cash in Tucker on her way to Hutterton. She left in Rachel's car with a very heavy heart.

By the time she reached Hutterton, Geneva was a wreck, vacillating between rage, grief, and fear for him. *What if he had been set up? Framed?* Geneva knew how these small town sheriffs could decide to have a little "fun" with an arrogant, rich boy. She bet he had smarted off at them when they had stopped them. Howard did have a way of letting people know he considered them his inferior.

But what if he really did have a stash of coke in his car? What if he did make his money in covert drug deals? The very thought made her nauseated, and then she found herself furious at Howard Knight, too. To think she had tossed off the idea that he was raising marijuana to sell to high schoolers, perhaps elementary school children, children not much older than her own beloved nieces. Tossed it off with a smile and a shrug. *Be cool. Live and let live. I'm okay, you're okay. Do what you want.* "Hogwash!" she snorted.

It was nearly dusk when she arrived. The courthouse/jail sat in the middle of the one downtown block of Hutterton. It was the only building with the lights on, and the soft glow of these lights tinged the nearly deserted town with pink and gold. The little village seemed a quaint picture nestled among the purple hills.

On the porch of the jailhouse lay a forlorn dog, his head resting between his paws. As Geneva passed him, he lifted his head and whined, but she paid him little attention; her thoughts were absorbed in her fears.

Inside the jail, the picture was no longer quaint. The lights were too bright, loud both to the eye and the ear, for they buzzed with a constant, high-pitched whine. Geneva found them exceptionally annoying the moment she stepped inside. She couldn't imagine how Howard had tolerated it since this morning.

The jailhouse/courthouse was a one-room affair, not much different from Andy of Mayberry's jail: two cells, a gun rack on the wall, and a desk in the corner. But it did not have Aunt Bea's touch; the place was grimy and unswept. Cobwebs hung in the corners, and there were grease stains on the walls. She glanced at the desk, where a fat, unkempt fellow wearing a deputy's badge slouched, and then, incredibly, she found herself looking through a set of bars at Jimmy Lee Land, whose mouth had dropped open into an elongated "O."

Through her shock, she could see his eyes, red and bleary, looking at her with surprise and worshipful awe, which, she realized, was beginning to be his signature expression toward her. Simultaneously, in the other cell, Howard jumped off his cot and ran toward her. He looked indescribably forlorn behind the bars.

"Well, I'll be damned. She's adoin' it agin'!" Jimmy Lee shouted. "How'd ye know I wuz here?"

"It's about time you got here. Why did it take you so long?" demanded Howard.

Jimmy Lee did not notice Howard addressing her. He turned excitedly toward him. "Hit's her! Hit's the one I wuz atellin' ye about! My little lady what done saved my life! The one I'm acourtin'!"

A look of horror washed over Howard's face. He stared at Jimmy Lee for a long moment, then cut his eyes toward Geneva.

"Geneva? You know this man?"

"Hell yes! She knows me awright! She's come to bail me outta here, God bless her soul!" He fairly danced with excitement, grinning at Geneva, then Howard, then at Geneva again, until a puzzled look began to spread over his face. "How come yew ta know her name?" he asked Howard.

Howard groaned and sat down on his cot.

"Jimmy Lee…" began Geneva, but she was interrupted by the unkempt man who was coming toward her.

"Hidy, miss. You here to bail this feller out?"

"Uh…" she said.

"I reckon he's sober enough to go on home now, but I wouldn't let him drive fer awhile." He chuckled amicably at Jimmy Lee.

"Got aholt of some bad corn likker, didn't ye, boy?"

"I sure as hell, did, sir," grinned Jimmy Lee. "But the sight of this little lady here would sober up a deacon." He gazed raptly at Geneva, who felt an overwhelming urge to run.

"Well, uh, actually, I..." she began lamely, then stopped herself. "How much to bail him out?"

"Aw, nuthin'. I kin release him in yer custody, if ye drive him on home and make him keep out o' trouble. Boy jist cain't hold his likker." He guffawed. "I'll tell ye, I'll be glad ta git him outta here. He's been runnin' his mouth bad enough to run us all up a tree. Spent the last four hours ever since he come to atellin' us about yew. Ye got ye a man here shore loves yew, honey."

Geneva searched for a chair. She sensed that this was a delicate situation, and she had no idea how to handle it. Glancing at Howard, she realized he would be of no help. He was glaring at her with open hostility. The unkempt fat man unlocked Jimmy Lee's cell.

She cleared her throat and smiled nervously. Brightly, she said, "Umm, actually, I happen to know that other fella, too. Did he get some bad corn likker, too?" She felt the drawl creeping into her mouth as comfortable as fresh bread, and she dipped her head just enough to look at the man from the corner of her eyes.

He scowled at her. "No ma'am. That there fella's in a heap o' trouble. We found a suspicious substance on him, and he ain't goin' nowheres til we git to the bottom of it."

"Oh? I couldn't bail him out, too?" She turned innocent, wide eyes upon him.

He softened a bit. Shaking his head sadly and importantly, he replied, "No ma'am. This here's serious business."

Geneva judged whether or not to press him. He was looking at her sorrowfully. "But what on earth could he have had on him that is so serious? I happen to know that he's real decent." She calculated, then ventured a little white lie, "His daddy's a judge down in Georgia."

He looked at her incredulously. "He shore don't talk like he's from Georgia."

"Well, his mama's from New Orleans, I mean, Metarie. You know, they talk like that there." She laughed a bright, tinkling little laugh. "They all sound like they're from New Jersey."

Howard looked at her as if she had lost every ounce of reason. She prayed he would keep his mouth shut, but she wouldn't have bet on it, for his face held signs of unmitigated rage. Hoping desperately he would keep silent, she turned all her charm upon the fat man, smiling at him as if she felt fortunate to be in his presence. "Could I maybe talk to him for just a little bitty minute?" She expanded her charm to include Jimmy Lee, feeling like she was juggling live hand grenades.

"Jimmy Lee," she crooned, "Why don't you go sit in the car? It's right out front." She batted her eyelashes at him as she handed him Rachel's car keys, then turned her most coquettish face toward the deputy. "But don't you go driving it, now," she winked. "Yew heard what the man said."

Jimmy Lee took the keys as if they were a token from his beloved, then collected his belongings and went out. "I'll wait fer ye, Miss Geneva."

She turned to the deputy. "Could I? Just talk a little bitty minute to him? Surely there's some explanation to this, and maybe we can clear it up for yew."

He wavered, then sighed. "Awright," he said, his eyes narrowing as he turned toward Howard. "But watch yersef. He seems pretty slick ta me." Turning back to his desk, he took out a Louis Lamour novel and leaned back in his chair, feet propped upon the desk.

Geneva approached the cell with trepidation, fearing not Howard's anger, but rather for his good sense. He could mess things up really badly if he said the wrong things to her. She pasted a smile on her face and let it freeze into him before she spoke. "Well, Howard," she said slowly, carefully. "How on earth did yew get yerself into this mess? What did they find on yew?"

His smile was just as plastic. "Well, Geneva," he echoed mockingly and just as slowly. "I don't know. All I know is there was some sort of whitish powder in the floor of my car."

"Your car? I thought it belonged to somebody else. Like your ex-fiancée." She let her smile broaden, but it became no warmer.

"Of course. My ex-fiancée's car. I was just keeping it for her until she comes to her senses and comes home with me. But it looks like I may not get out of here before she ups and marries somebody else. Goes and lives in a trailer and keeps a tobacco crop. Names her kids Wiley Bob and Potato Bug. Do you happen to know what my *daddy* the *judge* down in Georgia might think about all this? Since he's an *attorney*, he surely would have some insight into the situation."

Geneva caught the hint. He was wondering if she had called his attorney in DC. "Well, I'm sure I don't know," she replied carefully, "but I bet he'll be on his way here as soon as he can, provided no one can bail you out in the meantime. All you have to do is give him a call. You know he'll drop everthing and come."

"Well, do you think you might see about getting me out of here? It hasn't been terribly pleasant, and now that Jimmy Lee's gone, I won't have any company." He narrowed his eyes. "He told me all about how much in love the two of you are, but while he was talking, I had no idea the girl he was discussing was you. I understand you saved his life, and then single-handedly dragged him to a cottage and nursed him back to health, and loved him until he was strong again? All those long days and nights up on a mountain with him must have been pretty romantic. Challenging, but romantic."

Geneva felt her face go hot, and she did not trust herself to reply to his accusations. She was too angry with him for even pretending to believe them. At last, she said, "Jimmy Lee's been known to get things confused. We try not to take him too seriously."

"I see," he said, lifting an eyebrow. "And now that you've sprung him, why don't you see if you can do the same for me. Then we can all go home and talk over all our exciting times together."

Geneva glanced at the deputy reading the paperback. She knew there was no way she would be able to bail Howard out. First of all, something told her the deputy had no authority, and secondly, it seemed that he was certain Howard's crime was serious. Nervously, she turned her smile toward him, then, throwing a stony glance at Howard, she glided across the floor and stood demurely by the desk.

"I'm awfully sorry to disturb you, sir," she said, turning her bluest eyes upon him, "but I think there must be some kind of terrible mistake. "This man here—," she indicated Howard, "is about one of the nicest people I know and from a *good* family. Why, his uncle was a missionary in China until the Communists shot him, and his great uncle on his mama's side was Huey Long. His daddy just about single-handedly wiped out a notorious drug ring down in Athens, and I've known Howard here for years."

The man looked at her with interest, more impressed by the minute as she manufactured a biography for Howard. Geneva felt her courage rise. Almost as an afterthought, she added, "He's thinking of becoming a minister."

The minute she had said it, she knew she had gone too far. The fat man's eyes narrowed. "He shore didn't talk like no preacher when I picked him up. Man's got a smart mouth on him." He glared at Howard, who glared back. Geneva feigned surprise while she thought of a reply. Howard probably had insulted him in a number of ways; had probably aimed invective at him which implied low intelligence and perhaps sexual perversion. "Howard?" she exclaimed. "Why that really surprises me, sir! Normally he's a saint. He must be having some—er—personal problems." She stole a glance at Howard, who smoldered.

The door opened. In walked a very large, red-faced man wearing a sheriff's uniform and badge. His frame was covered with mounds of flesh, which appeared to Geneva to have made it halfway through the metamorphosis from rock-solid muscle to pure blubber. Her eye fell from massive shoulders and chest to a belly so large and round it overhung his pants and rode absurdly low around his hips. His gun holster, too, was fairly obscured by the overhanging belly. Idly, she wondered if he could possibly be carrying triplets in there.

As he strode in, he tossed a small plastic bag filled with a pale, buff-colored powder on the desk. The moment Geneva's eyes landed on it, she froze, reviewing a few seconds of her past life. She saw herself falling on the curb outside her apartment in DC, felt the soft cardboard cylinder give way under her knee, saw fine grains of baby formula meant for the dying kitten spilling out over the sidewalk. She saw herself desperately scooping formula into the little plastic ziploc bag and rushing into her apartment.

"Let 'im, go," ordered the sheriff in a rumbling bass. "Soon's he paid his fine fer speedin'. This ain't nothin'."

The deputy eased out of his chair. "What is it?" he asked.

Geneva turned to Howard, hoping she could distract him from hearing the answer.

"Milk," snorted the sheriff.

"Howard, isn't that nice? He said you could go!"

"Milk?" cried Howard and the deputy simultaneously.

"Why in the hell are you carryin' around milk in little plastic bags?" the deputy queried Howard.

"Oh, I'm so glad that's settled. Howard, you can go right on home now! No need to stay here another minute." Geneva rushed over to his cell, rattling at the bars while she spoke, "Sir, could you let him out now? It's a pity he has to stay here another minute! I told you he was a nice fellow. Are those the keys? Here, Howard, I'll help you get everything together. Ha, what a silly thing. Why on earth did you have milk in your car?"

"Beats me," said Howard tersely. "And I wonder if you know something about it, you being a new aunt and all."

Geneva gasped. "Me? Heaven's no! You know Rachel is nursing those babies—my goodness, we haven't even had baby formula in the house!" An idea struck her. "You know what I bet? I bet the workers putting that car together did this as a trick! Oh, isn't that funny! Putting dried milk into a car so somebody will think it's cocaine! Boy, Howard, they really got a good one on you!" She burst into laughter, laughter that consumed her so completely that she had to sit down, laughter so contagious that the two big lawmen joined her, snorting and wheezing, slapping their knees.

"They sure did, son!" chortled the sheriff. "Milk!"

Howard failed to see the humor. Rigidly, he turned to his jailers. "Perhaps you would be so kind as to let me out now, sirs. I am already late, and I have a long way to go."

"Sure, sure," chuckled the deputy. "But don't go exceedin' the speed limit. Somebody might pick you up and find oregano on you." Another gale of laughter erupted from the lawmen. Howard smiled poisonously. Geneva kept her face artificially bright.

"How much does he owe you, sirs?" she asked. "Was he going very fast?"

"Yes ma'am, but I tell ye what. We won't charge 'im the whole fine, seein's how he had to spend the day in jail fer no reason. I reckon we could let him git outta here with around, oh—." The sheriff looked at the deputy then out the window at the fine sports car. He sucked his teeth while he considered, "Oh, mebe three hunnert." He spat on the floor.

Howard surged forward, outraged, but Geneva stopped him with the lightest of touches on his chest. "Whew! He must have been going some fast to get that kind of fine, but guess we all have to pay our dues when we do wrong. Howard, I'll be happy to loan you three hundred dollars, if you need it." She glanced at his face, which was pale but with two red spots high in his cheeks.

"Thank you, Geneva. I think I may have that much on me, although I appreciate the offer." Geneva prayed he would stay in control while he paid his fine and completed the paperwork before he could be released. After he had collected his belongings, he walked out of the door without bothering to tell her good-bye, and stepped into the Jaguar, now covered with road dust. She stood in the doorway of the jail house, watching him drive off, wondering if she would ever see him again; but before he turned to the corner, he called to her, his eyes dark with wrath. "I'll be back, Geneva. You've had your fun, but you won't forget me." He disappeared into a darkening hill.

Trembling, Geneva approached Rachel's car. Jimmy Lee sat in the front seat with the dog she had stepped over earlier spilling out of his lap.

"Lamentations!" she cried, just now recognizing the mongrel. Lamentations gave her a brief glance and a tail wag, or rather, a rear-end wag, for his tail, once bent and broken, was now completely gone. The stump was red and slightly swollen. Geneva suspected that it had suffered mightily when Jimmy Lee was arrested. Lamentations turned his big, adoring eyes back to Jimmy Lee. His tongue lapped out quickly on the young man's chin, then he laid his head on Jimmy Lee's chest, never letting his gaze fall from his master's face. Jimmy Lee looked at Geneva with a remarkably similar expression.

"Where can I take you, Jimmy Lee? Do you want me to drive you back home?"

"Oh, Lord God, no, Miss Geneva! Hit's way too late fer that! I got kin all over up here, and my truck's here. If ye'd jist run me on over to my cousin's house, jist about five mile down this here road, I'd be obliged to ye."

"You got kin here? Why didn't they come get you out of jail?"

"Haw, thar warn't no need. They jist keep me til I sober up—they allus let me go when I'm ready."

"You do this often, Jimmy Lee?"

"'Bout once ever three months." His demeanor changed to sheepishness. "My cousins is a bad influence."

"I expect they are, Jimmy Lee." Geneva remembered how bad an influence his cousin Howard Knight could be as well. "You got some cousins here making moonshine, while Howard is over at Swallowtail Gap growing marijuana."

"Who? Chap?" asked Jimmy Lee, confused. "Marywana?"

"Hemp, Jimmy Lee."

He scratched his head and scrunched up his nose. "Chap don't grow no hemp. Mammaw does some, for Pappaw's eyes, but that's all. Who tole ye that?"

"He did," replied Geneva tartly.

"Haw. Well, he don't. But I'm danged surprised he said that. He don't never lie to nobody, 'cept sometimes when he gits around stuck up town folks and tells 'em that to kindly shake 'em up. I cain't believe he'd tell you that lie, Miss Geneva. Why, he likes you!"

"You mean, Howard—Chap—goes around telling some people that he grows hemp just to impress them?"

"Only when he thanks thera snickerin' at 'im fer bein' a hillbilly. You know, snooty folks."

"I see," mused Geneva, stung that Howard Knight would deem her snooty. She thought she had camouflaged it better than that. "So what does he do?"

At this, Jimmy Lee fell quiet, and he shifted uneasily. At length he said carefully, "Well, he does a buncha thangs. Farms mostly. Sells timber."

He obviously was lying, although he had seemed to be truthful about the marijuana. Silently, she wondered what Jimmy Lee knew about Howard that he did not want to divulge. She thought about cajoling the truth from him, but when she turned her seductive smile upon him to do just that, his face became so transformed by his infatuation that she decided she had better leave it alone. Jimmy Lee could be a problem. And she already had enough problems.

She altered her smile into a less intimate expression. "Where do your cousins live, Jimmy Lee? I should hurry if I'm going to get back home tonight."

She arrived back at Rachel's darkened house well after midnight, but Rachel rose when she heard Geneva come in.

"What happened?" she wanted to know.

Geneva told her the story, detouring to her culpability in the affair when she got to the part about the lab analysis of Howard's "cocaine." She and Rachel laughed so loudly that Wayne got up to join them in the living room.

"Poor fool," Wayne said, shaking his head. "Are you ever going to tell him the truth?"

Both Geneva and Rachel looked aghast. "Are you kidding, Wayne?" Geneva burst out. "Tell him! What do you think I am?"

Rachel screamed with laughter. "A liar!" she choked out, tears streaming down her face.

"But a good one!" assented Geneva, holding her stomach.

Rachel silenced them. "Hush. Is that somebody crying? "Oh, yes," she added, suddenly pressing her palms against her nipples. Feeding time, and here I go squirting milk." She hurried upstairs and returned a moment later with one infant. "Just Genny, the pig. Lenora's still snoozing."

She settled into the rocking chair to feed Genny while Wayne turned out the lights and brought Rachel a glass of water. Geneva yawned. "I guess I'd better get to bed. Hard Knight's getting here early to take me up to Swallowtail Gap to get my car."

"Oh, Geneva, I forgot to tell you," interjected Rachel. "Wayne's dad has decided his eyes are too bad to drive up here, so Wayne's going to take a few days off and we're taking the children to Charlottesville. His mother's been dying to see the babies, and she was so disappointed about Dad's not being able to drive that she begged us to come on over. We're leaving tomorrow. Want to join us for a few days in the big city? Uncle Henry said he'd take care of everything here while we're gone."

Geneva considered. It would be nice to have the house to herself for a few days, but since John would be gone to his conference, it would be lonely. But then, she really didn't know Wayne's parents well enough to spend several days at their house. She sighed. "I guess not. I could use a vacation from this brood, and to tell the truth, now that I'm getting my car back, I really should run over to DC and try to clear things up with Howard. Anyway, I'd like to see what it feels like there before I try to think about what I'm going to do with my life. I should check on my apartment, too."

"Okay, sweetie, if you really want to. But keep a good head on your shoulders, and I'd avoid Hutterton if I were you!"

"Goodnight, big sister," smiled Geneva. "Goodnight Wayne. I'm beat, and I guess tomorrow could be a big day. May have to bail out Hard Knight for illicit drugs."

"Goodnight, Geneva," they echoed, grinning wickedly.

She left them there in the darkness as they bent their heads, smiling upon their new daughter.

Nine

The sun insulted Geneva's eyes. She rolled over, grumbling, feeling tired and vaguely achy all over. Her throat hurt, too, but she forced herself to rise, then took some aspirin, for she was determined not to put off going with Howard Knight to get her car. The late night and a little cold coming on would not cause her to be less than friendly toward him again, she resolved.

He arrived early, before Geneva had finished breakfast. Wayne had left before dawn for his rounds, so Howard filled in at his place at the kitchen table with the women and children, and later sipped coffee while Geneva washed the dishes and packed diapers for the family's visit to Wayne's parents' house.

To finish her own packing, Rachel set the girls at the table with crayons and put the babies in a portable crib. Lenora curled up peacefully, sucking her thumb, but Genny, vocal as usual, bellowed for someone to pick her up.

"Oh for heaven's sake, Genny. Settle down for just a minute while I get this table cleared," complained Geneva. "What a little loudmouth you are!"

Rising from his seat, Howard scooped Genny out of her infant seat, then settled down again, elbows resting on his thighs, with the baby's head cradled in his hands, her body reclining down the length of his forearms. His action surprised Geneva. Never had she ever seen a grown man voluntarily pick up a newborn that was not his own, and she knew that Howard himself was childless. But he seemed perfectly comfortable, smiling into the baby's face as if he had raised a brood already.

"Hey there, yew little bitty thing," he sang in a high, crooning voice, his head bent close to Genny's. "What chew squallin' for? Huh?" He jiggled his legs slightly to rock her. "Yew better quit yer squallin', now. Yer mammy and yer aunt Geneva's got their work to do."

Hannah and Phoebe clambered down from their chairs to crowd around Howard and peer at their baby sister. Genny quieted. Geneva was so taken aback by the scene that she spoke up, almost embarrassed, "Looks like you've got yourself some girl friends, Howard. But just wait until they all get going at once. They can make quite a racket." Sighing, grateful she was only the aunt, she added, "Can you imagine being the mother of four small children?"

Howard's eyes gazed deeply into the child's face. "I wish I was their daddy," he said wistfully, then he jiggled his legs again and murmured nonsense to Genny.

It took an hour for everyone to get Rachel's car loaded. "I'm late," she said breathlessly, pushing the children into the car. "Wayne's expecting me by now, and I bet it will take me at least forty-five minutes to get to the hospital. He'll be frantic. Bye. Love you. Have a good trip. See you Saturday or Sunday—or whenever!" she called, tearing out of the driveway.

As soon as they were settled in Howard's truck and headed out on their own excursion, Geneva felt the expected awkward silence descend. It was the first time they had been alone together since the night in the barn, and she hoped she could find a way to apologize to him. He was the first to break the silence. "Jimmy Lee tells me yew saved his neck again yisterdy. Tracked him all the way over to Hutterton jist to bail him out of jail." He gave Geneva a slow, sideways smile, not making direct eye contact.

Geneva appreciated his desire to put her at ease; she wanted very much to return the favor, perhaps even to make up to him all the trouble she had caused him. Her contrite heart told her she had wronged him with every word she had spoken to him, and now it was time to drop all her façades.

"Jimmy Lee just happened to stumble into a larger drama," she began, then launched into the whole saga of Howard Graves and his rescue, including the part about why Howard had come in the first place, and why the baby formula was found in his fancy car. She did her best to make the story funny, adding her observation about the fat sheriff and the details on her own machinations. Fluttering her eyelids, she drawled, "But sheriff, he's a *good* man, and his daddy's a *judge!*"

Howard Knight laughed so hard he nearly lost control of the truck, and at one point, he actually pulled off the road so he could lean his head against the steering wheel and give himself over completely to hysteria. Geneva felt she had redeemed herself.

"And poor Jimmy Lee is standing there, without a clue. I don't know how he thought I had found out about his predicament. Then I go out to the car, and he's sitting in the front seat, with Lamentations just lying all over him, looking at him with these big mooning eyes, wagging that mutilated stump!"

"Oh, Jimmy Lee!" laughed Howard. "He's got himself a big problem. I guess I oughta warn ye, he's set his cap fer yew. But the poor fool awready has himself a girlfriend, outweighs him by fifty pounds, and she'll have his hide if she hears about him runnin' after yew!" He ran his fingers quickly through his hair. "Poor man. He's a good soul, but he ain't got a lick of sense. She'll chew up his hide good."

By the time they reached Swallowtail Gap, Geneva and Howard

were good friends. She braced herself for the sight of his home, determined not to embarrass him by being haughty when she saw either a trailer resting on cinder blocks or a rickety shack leaning into the mountain. But she was surprised to find a cozy log cabin, newly built, tucked into a neat yard, surrounded by a deep forest. Her pretty little Mazda, sparkling clean and newly waxed, was parked under a spreading oak. The picture was charming. Inside the house, there was a clean, modern kitchen built for the convenience of someone who lived in a wheel chair, with low counters and more cabinets below than above. Geneva hid her puzzlement over the seeming prosperity of the place.

He introduced his father, the occupant of the wheel chair. Jesse was a small, gentle man with Ike's blue eyes and Lenora's energy. The three of them chatted for a while; Geneva appreciated Jesse's eagerness to please his company. He offered her food and drink, he smiled his eager blue eyes at her, and he told her he wished she would come back often. When the talk turned to horses, he said abruptly to Howard, "Why don't ye take the little lady fer a ride, Chap? I bet she'd like to see the view from the Jump-off." He added to Geneva, "Hit's real perty, yew kin see the river from up there."

Howard hesitated. Geneva knew he felt he would be overstepping his bounds if he invited her for a ride, as if she might think he had lured her here on the pretense of retrieving her car, but hoping for something more. She really did not feel like riding. Her headache and sore throat had returned, but this was her chance to show him kindness. She smiled at him.

"Howard, I'd love to go riding. I've never been up to these parts before. Do you have horses?"

"I do, Miss Geneva. They're in the stable, up through the woods back yonder. I'd be pleased ta take ye up to see the Jump-off."

Howard's father fairly laughed out loud in his delight. "Ya'll take yer time, y'hear? I'll be gone over to Pappy and Mammy's when yew git back," he called after them as they struck off through the woods toward the barn.

The barn, too, spoke of an affluence that Geneva did not

expect. It was new, airy, and large, exuding the rich smell of pine and clean straw, but the real surprise came when Howard opened the first stall and led out a beautiful Morgan stallion. Geneva's eyes widened. How could he afford such a magnificent beast?

The answer dawned on her as Howard led the second horse, an equally beautiful Appaloosa mare, from the next stall, and her heart turned cold and hard. Jimmy Lee had been lying or wrong. Howard did have himself a little cash crop up here. More likely a huge cash crop, one which put a lot of dope into the high school pipeline. Nobody could earn the kind of money it takes to build a homestead like this simply by selling off timber and farming legitimate crops. Her pleasant expression turned icy, and she sagged against a stall door, miserable of spirit.

She wanted to go home. There was nothing to say to this man. They were from different worlds, with different values. She would take the quick ride, then get into her little Mazda and ride back home, forgetting him as easily as she could forget the leering pimps and drug dealers back in Washington who shouted at her as she walked downtown. She was immune to such men; they were so far below her that they were not worth becoming upset over. Angrily, she mounted the mare, but as she lifted into the saddle, a sudden dizziness overcame her so that she had to cling to the horse's mane for a moment to regain her equilibrium. Busy with the high-spirited stallion, Howard had not noticed, and determined that she should get out of this gracefully, she waited quietly until he was seated and on his way up a narrow trail.

It wound up through a brushy, steep incline; the narrowness and roughness of it prohibited much conversation, which pleased Geneva. She rebuffed Howard's several attempts to engage her, pretending to be concentrating on the rough trail each time he called back to her. But after they had come a few miles, the trail leveled off in a fern glade surrounded by enormous, widely spaced hardwoods. It looked like virgin forest, and Geneva felt so awed by the cool stillness that her anger abated. *Perhaps Howard had another source of income.*

As soon as the trail widened, Howard dropped back to ride beside her. He glanced at her shyly, waiting for her to speak.

"Nice place," she commented.

"Thanky. Thank yew," he corrected himself. "I'm real proud of it."

"This is yours?" she asked, surprised. They had been riding over an hour. *How much land did he own?*

He looked pleased as he nodded. "Come, on, I'll show ye the Jump-off." Nudging the stallion into a canter, Howard flew up the slope, across the black earth. She followed him up through the trees, across a roaring stream banked with late-blooming laurel, then back down to a rocky outcropping, where he stopped. She drew up beside him, bewitched by what she saw. They were standing on a ledge miles above a river. In the distance below her, she could hear the faint roar from a waterfall, could see the mist rising like a bridal veil shimmering in the late morning sun. As far as she could see, undulating hills gave way to mountains, which gave way to the blue and silver sky. Beyond the blue, in the corner by a far mountain, clouds the color of bruises rolled in, billowing high and angry. Before them rode a rainbow, grand, but somewhat insignificant amid the vastness of the view.

"It's gorgeous," she breathed.

"Yes," he smiled, pleased. "I'll never let it go, not fer any price."

"You own this? How far?" she gasped, incredulous, then sank back in the saddle, dumbstruck as he stretched out his arm and swept it from horizon to horizon.

As far as ye kin see. And more beyond them hills yonder." He seemed taller, the pride emanating from him, like a full-blooded Cherokee from the last century coming back to claim his homeland.

She gaped at him. Despite her doubts of Howard's honesty, she very much wanted to respect him. Hopefully, she asked, "Did you inherit all this?"

"No," he replied, his face still gleaming. "I bought it. Ever acre of it."

Geneva felt like crying. She had so wanted to like him and to give him the benefit of the doubt. She did not want to repay his kindness to her and Rachel with a display of her distaste for him, but she found the ire boiling up from her stomach, causing her throat to constrict painfully and her head to pound. She almost felt nauseated as the angry, sarcastic words snaked, unbidden, out of her mouth. "I guess the hemp business must be pretty good up here. Do a lot of trading with the Mob? Got a lot of grade-school kids trekking up this mountain to get started in the business?"

The light left his eyes as he turned to her, horror-struck. "Oh, Miss Geneva," he gasped, his eyes pained, "I don't grow no hemp. Not even in the garden. Mammaw jist grows enough to keep Pappaw in tea to cure his eyes. No ma'am. I never grew no hemp," he repeated, distressed.

"Really?" she replied archly. "Excuse me for prying, but I would guess it would take more than anybody could make from a tobacco crop to buy all this land. And these horses. And that pretty little house back there."

Howard stared at her. He opened and closed his mouth twice, but did not speak. At last he shook his head sorrowfully, insisting in a soft voice, "No ma'am. I never grew no hemp. Or nuthin' like it. And I'm sorry I told ye that lie. That wuz jist my pride atalkin'. I got money in other ways."

She waited, but he did not speak again. "Bootlegging?" she finally asked.

The quiet voice was insistent. "No ma'am." he replied, his eyes on the ground.

She sighed. "Farming, then? Logging?"

He shook his head. "Not exactly."

She blew out her breath, exasperated. "Okay, Howard, I believe you." And she wanted to believe him, but she felt too irritable and tired to hear any explanation. She was hot, and she just wanted to go home and forget about this. "I don't know why, but I do, and I guess it's none of my business anyway. Now come on, let's go back. It looks like that thunderhead will be on us in another minute."

The thunderhead was indeed approaching at an alarming rate. Already the wind had picked up, swaying the trees and sending leaves and twigs to the ground. Howard looked around him sharply. "It'll be here in less than a minute. We ain't got time to git back to the house. Come on!" He kicked the stallion in the sides and tore up the trail into the howling wind. Geneva took out after him, suddenly aware that this was no small storm approaching them. The warm sky had turned black; wind tore at her hair and clothes, and the air around them had become an eerie green. The rain had not yet reached them, but they could see it in the distance, black against the trees below. The frothy, white river had disappeared.

They had not ridden more than a hundred yards before the rain caught up with them, driving down in torrents, hitting Geneva's face and head so hard they hurt. And then the stinging hail came raining down. The protection of the large trees loomed ahead; Howard and Geneva made the relative safety of their high canopy, then thundering across the springy humus, they continued into the deep woods. But still the rain and hail reached them. Geneva, already drenched, began to shiver in the cooling air as she urged her horse to follow the stallion. She did not know where Howard was taking her, but she felt as if they had been galloping for a long, long time through the falling ice and rain, so long that the thundering of the horses' hooves drilled into her brain. She hurt all over; a burning pain spewed out from her head and left a tail of venom down her spine and into all her muscles. She felt weak and faint, but she held on, throwing away the reins and slumping over the mare's neck, not caring where she was going, but hoping that she would arrive alive.

She did not notice when the horses stopped. She saw Howard beside her in the pouring rain, touching her shoulder and speaking to her. She was shivering violently and aching with a pain that ran from her ears to her legs. It was all she could do to look at him and gasp, "Howard, I don't feel too well."

Alarmed, he looked closely at her, then he put his hands to her cheeks and forehead. "Darlin', yew got a bad chill. Yer downright blue. Yew think ye kin make it just a little farther?"

She strained her burning eyes toward the weeping sky. It hurt to turn her eyes upward. The rain poured into her face. Blinking against the pain and the water, she nodded mutely, then draped herself over the mare's neck. Never had she felt so miserable.

"Never mind. I'll help ye. I got shelter jist up ahead," said Howard, sliding down off the stallion's back, then swinging himself up behind Geneva. Gently, he pulled her upright and wrapped his arms around her, pressing his body, warm and easy up against her. Geneva felt as if they were swimming through a brutal ocean frosted with ice, but Howard's warmth and strength kept her from downing.

They rode at a canter through the deep woods for another fifteen minutes in the pouring rain. To Geneva it seemed like hours with her head and body wracked by pain with each stride, but she stayed grimly mute, unwilling to cry out and let Howard know what a sissy she was. Summoning all she had merely to hang on, she let the sounds of the thunder in the distance and the more immediate thunder of the horses' hooves wash over her as the water ran relentlessly down her head and face. Howard's horse, lashed to her saddle horn, jerked and plunged beside her so that she feared that the saddle would be torn from her mount. She clung to Howard's arms, keeping her head bent away from the drowning rain.

The horses slowed. Geneva peered through the gray sheets of rain to see a cabin nestled in a hollow. Like Howard's house, it was a fairly new log structure, though considerably smaller than the house. A porch ran around three sides; a stone chimney possessed nearly the entire fourth side. A stable stood beyond near a spruce thicket. Between the house and the stable was a clearing where a small garden lay, punished by the hailstones. Howard urged the horses right up the steps onto the wide porch, then dismounted and lashed the reins to the railing. When he turned to Geneva, she slid off her mount and clung to him while he led her inside the cabin and deposited her onto a low stool placed in the center of the room.

She was shivering; her teeth were chattering uncontrollably, and she could do no more than watch as Howard strode to a cupboard and removed several blankets. One of these he wrapped around Geneva and her wet clothes, then he turned to a narrow bed tucked under the eaves and pulled back the covers. Underneath the wool blankets lay sheets and a mattress made of straw and ticking. It was to this he led her, pushing her gently onto the bed. He removed her shoes and socks and tucked her underneath the covers. Without speaking, he spread the remaining blankets over her as well.

Almost immediately the warmth quieted her shivering. A wonderful scent assailed her nostrils. It occurred to her that the mattress upon which she lay was stuffed not with straw but with grasses and sweet-smelling herbs. Vaguely she recognized the scent of wild mint and lavender, perhaps some fennel. Sighing, she burrowed under the covers and hoped that the warmth would seep into her bones.

Howard had turned to the fireplace that took up most of the wall opposite the bed. He was building a fire from an ample stock of wood and kindling stacked neatly in one corner of the room. Another corner contained a rough-hewn table and a couple of stools. All around the perimeter of the room ran a single shelf built into the wall, loaded with clothing, stores of food and equipment, and oddly, a small collection of books. Under the shelf was a row of pegs, upon which hung an assortment of clothing and gear. Geneva's eyes roved on around the room. A number of shovels stood by the front door; the back door, securely bolted with a heavy beam, shared a wall lined with cupboards and some odd-looking wooden contraptions and buckets.

The fire lit, Howard turned his attentions back toward Geneva. She closed her eyes against the burning and tried to pull the blankets closer. As he moved the stool nearer to the bed, Geneva realized it was only a part of a large tree stump, sawed off smoothly on the top and bottom, and it was new enough that the bark still clung all around the outside. The other stools were of the same make. Clearly, this was a camp that Howard had built himself, and despite her chills and aches, she wondered why he had provisioned it so fully. No doubt he spent considerable time here. But why? She had no idea where they were, but she knew they were deep in the forest, and very high in elevation. The trees outside were spruce and fir.

"Ye'll be gettin' warmed up soon, now," he was saying. "I got us a good fire agoin', and in a minute, I kin give ye somethin' ta make ye feel better. Yew just lay there, and let me dry ye off some." As he spoke, he lifted a rough towel to her head, rubbing it briskly to soak up the wetness. Irritably, Geneva wondered how her hair would look when it dried. He did not seem to mind that his method of towel-drying would surely make her look like she was wearing a fright wig. She moved her head away.

"There, yer about as dry as I kin get ye," he said, rising and draping the towel on a peg near the fire. Now I'm gonna brew ye up somethin' to warm ye up. My guess is ye'll git fever, too."

He moved easily, even gracefully, as he collected two buckets beside the back door. Sliding the wooden bolt from its resting place, he stepped out onto the back porch and disappeared. Geneva closed her eyes, and when she opened them again, she saw him standing by the back door, water streaming from him. He set the buckets upon the table. From one of them he dipped a small pan and a larger one full of water and placed them upon the fire.

Then he selected several tins from the shelf and spooned some of the contents from each of them into the small pan. After a few minutes, he picked up a cup and a dishcloth, and placing the cloth over the cup, poured the liquid from the small pan into the cup. He brought it directly to her.

"Here, Miss Geneva. Drink this," he ordered.

For the first time since she had entered the room, she spoke. "What is it?" she mumbled suspiciously.

"Jist some willer bark tea, with a little mint and honey so it don't taste so bitter." He smiled gently. "Don't worry. There ain't no hemp in there."

She smiled weakly, too sick to be embarrassed, and dutifully took the cup from him. It was bitter despite the mint and honey, but she drank it anyway. Granny Morgan had given her willow bark tea before; she knew its benefits.

While she drank, Howard held his hands to the fire, then returning to the bedside, he reached under the covers for her foot, drew it out, and rubbed it with his warmed hands. Geneva was a little disconcerted. As good as it felt, it seemed an awfully intimate thing to do, and it made her uneasy. She became more uncomfortable when he cupped his hands around her toes, then put his mouth to them to warm them with his breath.

"Lordy, yore feet are as cold as them hailstones. I got a kettle on, and soon's the water gits hot, I'll fill ye a hot water bottle." He reached for her other foot and gave it the same firm massage, but since his hands had grown cold, he opened his shirt and placed her freezing foot against his bare chest, wrapping his shirt and his arms tightly around it.

Oh, God, Geneva thought miserably. *Where am I? Who is this man, and what on earth is he doing to me? Oh, God! Will I make it out of this place alive?* She was so frightened and sick she almost cried, but tears took too much energy, so she merely closed her eyes and concentrated on breathing. At this moment, it took all her strength to do just that.

Presently, he stood again and busied himself at the fire, then returned with several quart fruit jars filled with hot water. These he wrapped in towels and packed them around her feet, then he tucked the covers back tightly around her.

"There," he said, smiling. That'll start warmin' ye up. I got plenty of these jars, and I got water goin'. I'll pack 'em all around ye until ye git yer blood warmed." Filling more jars, he tucked them close beside her all up and down her legs and torso. He instructed her to hold one in each hand, and when he finished laying the last jar up in the crook of her neck, he began again at her feet, pouring out the cooled water and filling it again from the pan in the fire. If Geneva had not felt so miserable, she would have been astonished at his ministrations. He was the most solicitous nurse she had ever seen.

Before long, as the willow bark tea suffused her system, she began to feel a little better. She grew warmer, then ultimately, almost hot. Setting the mason jars aside, she threw off some of the blankets, scratching at the discomfort of her soggy clothing.

"I got some dry clothes ye kin put on," said Howard, moving to gather a flannel shirt and a pair of khaki trousers from the pegs in the wall. "Ye kin lay yer wet things over here by the fire, and they'll dry in no time." His eyes dropped to the floor, and for the first time since entering the cabin, he looked uneasy and unsure of himself. "I'll jist step outside and put up the horses," he said quietly.

"Thank you," she said gratefully.

She stripped before the fire, peeling off the miserable, wet clothing, and putting on Howard's warm, dry shirt and pants, much too big for her, but welcome. She threaded her own leather belt through the belt loops and rolled the legs and sleeves up to a comfortable length. The new clothes smelled of wood smoke and sage. She buried her face in the soft warmth of the flannel for a moment before she gathered up her wet garments to hang them on the wall.

Howard knocked on the door. The awkwardness between them rose up again when she admitted him. With her aches and chills abated, she had room in her mind to consider the delicacy of their position. *It wouldn't have been so bad*, she thought, *if she had not attacked him in that barn so many weeks ago.* Neither of them knew how to establish a reasonable ground for a cordial relationship, especially now that they were alone again, stuck in a one-room cabin high in the mountains, with the rain coming down in rivers. Geneva gingerly sat on the edge of the bed and smiled as well as she could. It still hurt to breathe, and she felt so weak, her knees and arms shook.

"This bed smells wonderful, Howard. What a good idea to stuff it with herbs."

He, too, was obviously uncomfortable. The graceful movements of an hour ago gave way to jerky, almost clumsy gestures as he pulled another dry shirt from the wall. He glanced at her and hesitated. Geneva could see that he was deliberating about going outside to change. Carefully, she looked out of the window.

"Do you think it will ever stop?" she asked hoarsely. "It's a good thing you have this place here. We'd have been drowned by the time we made it back to your house—if we'd made it back all. That hail could have killed us."

She glanced at him. His back was turned; he had stripped off the wet shirt. The fire gleamed upon the wet jeans and the coppery skin, giving definition to the muscle and sinew, just as the lantern light had gleamed upon him the night she had embarrassed them both so. Taking a labored breath, she decided to plunge forward and clear the air.

"Howard." He turned to her, absorbed in the buttons. "Howard," she repeated nervously. "I owe you an apology. Several, in fact." She pulled her knees up to her chest and fought the urge to crawl back under the covers. She felt so undignified, so vulnerable, and she was attempting to make things a little more comfortable between herself and this man who barely spoke the same language as she. She looked at him through a mist and wished she was far away, but she knew she owed him far more than she could repay.

"I don't know how to say this, but I… I mean, marijuana makes me a little crazy—well, a lot crazy. I avoid it, actually. I mean, I didn't know that I'd had some, when I drank the tea, you know?" She stopped. It was the best she could do under the circumstances.

Howard continued to button his shirt, slowly, deliberately. Geneva gnawed at her knuckles, waiting. At last he lifted his head, and while Geneva could see that his cheeks were flaming, there was laughter flitting in his mouth and eyes. At last he spoke.

"Miss Geneva—"

"Just Geneva, please."

"Geneva," he began to chuckle, turning his head and covering his mouth. She smiled, grateful.

"What on earth did you think? Honest, I'm not like that, really."

She grew more anxious. She really hoped he would not think her as loose as she had behaved, especially now that it appeared that she would be alone with him for a while, here in this cabin, far, far from civilization. She barely had the strength to sit up, let alone fight him off should he attack her.

"Ma'am—Geneva. I thought," he chuckled. "I thought fer a minute there, old Santy Claus had done come and give me everthing I'd ever dreamed of."

Geneva sat quietly.

He shook his head. "But then I thought that maybe I'd oughta told yew my name was Chap. That, or else I'd better learn to say Haa-ward."

After that, they fell into an easy companionship, where she entrusted herself to his care, and he was gentle and solicitous. He did not touch her again, but kept the fire hot and gave her mild teas to keep her warm. Although she was not hungry, he prepared a lunch of home-canned beans, corn, and baked potatoes from the garden. After she ate, she felt better, so they played cards while the rain drummed down on the little cabin roof until Geneva began to feel an unpleasant pressure in her bladder that she could not ignore.

"Howard, I've been drinking your teas all day, and I absolutely must go to the bathroom," she admitted reluctantly.

He considered this briefly as he looked out at the downpour. "Well," he replied laconically. "Let me git ye a pot, and I'll just step outside and ye can go."

Geneva was aghast. "No, I'll go outside. I just need to borrow your raincoat."

He shook his head. "No, ma'am. Yew got fever. Ain't no way I'm lettin' ye go out in this here rain. Ye kin pee in a pot, and I'll take it right outside and empty it."

"No! You have been an awfully good nurse, but I am perfectly capable of walking outside!" Geneva's face was growing hot.

He was just as adamant. "Ye git chilled again, we may never git ye warm. There ain't nothin' wrong with goin' in a pot. People do it all the time."

"I'd rather go outside," she said, squirming. "Please, Howard. I do not want to go in a pot! I mean it!"

He sighed, giving in. "Awright. Yew take the pot and go out on the porch, but don't git wet. Yew can jist dump it out over the porch rail and leave the pot there for later. That do you?"

She nodded. This would work for now, but as soon as it cleared, she was headed for the deep woods. *This was humiliating.*

It was colder outside than she had imagined. He had made her put on his slicker, even though she promised not to venture past the porch roof, but nonetheless, she found herself shivering again by the time she had stepped back into the warm cabin

He did not scold, but wordlessly threw blankets around her, prepared more willow bark tea and tucked more mason jars filled with hot water around her feet and in her lap. She drank the tea, but this time it did not drive the aches from her muscles, and her throat became more raw as the afternoon wore on. Finally, she gave up trying to be good company and hunched by the fire, feeling sick and miserable.

Howard grew concerned. "Hit's quit hailin'," he said, squinting through the window. "But it looks like the rain may not slack off fer a while." His face was grave. "I don't think yer in any shape to ride back down this here mountain. I could leave ye here and run down and call yer folks, so they won't worry about ye."

Geneva shook her head. The throbbing had begun again, and her neck felt stiff and sore. Her whole body felt awful. It hurt to swallow. "It's okay, Howard. Rachel and Wayne are gone all week. They won't know if I don't go back tonight." She thought about Howard's father. "But you can go on and leave me here. I know your dad will worry about you. Maybe you can come back for me in the morning."

He considered this briefly. "No, my dad ain't home neither. He'll be stayin' with Mammaw and Pappy fer a few days, to help Mammaw with her cannin'. I told him I'd be up here."

"Oh," said Geneva, relieved. As awkward as it might be to stay here with Howard overnight, she found it preferable to staying by herself in this lonely place. She glanced around, wondering where each of them would sleep.

He stood up. "Well, if we're gonna stay here, I reckon I'd better get us some supper." Picking up a rifle from the shelf, he loaded it, and after he had stirred the fire and added more logs, he put on a rain slicker and left through the back door, calling over his shoulder, "I'll be back in twenty minutes."

He returned in less than that. It seemed that he had no more than stepped off the porch than Geneva heard the report of a shot and he returned with a fat squirrel and some vegetables from the garden out back. He prepared a hearty stew, but Geneva's head had turned to lead by the time it was done, and she was too tired to take more than a few bites. As the day wore down, her fever rose, compounding the pain in her muscles and throat. Touching her face, Howard spoke to her in a soft, comforting voice, as if he were speaking to an invalid. "Yew got fever, awright. Yer face is hot as fire. Here, drink this down. We need to keep after this 'un."

Exhausted, she drank the portion of willow bark tea he had pressed on her and crawled gratefully under the covers of the fragrant bed. But she did not find sleep right away. Tired and weak as she was, she felt fully conscious and a little guilty at the knowledge that she had taken his bed.

"Howard, I'm so sorry to inconvenience you like this. I know I've taken over your bed, and you'll have no place to sleep," she murmured.

He eased himself onto the floor, leaning his back against the wall. "Hey, I've slept in worse places than on this here floor. Nothin' makes me feel cozier'n a warm fire and a dry roof in weather like this. I'll sleep like a prince."

The long evening light the color of pewter fought its way through the rain, no longer violent, but now a steady monotonous downpour. Geneva looked out of the window and sighed. *How long would she be like this?* Feeling helpless, she put her hand to her burning eyes and gave a little, whimpering sigh.

A moment later, he was seated on the floor beside the bed, patting her arm and murmuring to her, "Ye'll be alright, Miss Geneva. We got us all we need here, and ye'll git well in no time. Yer young and strong. I bet ye'll be gallopin' right down this here mountain by tomorrow."

She sighed gratefully, this time not letting it betray her despair. She would fight for her strength, and she would inconvenience him no longer than absolutely necessary.

He returned her smile, then settled down with his back against the bed and began speaking in a slow, low voice, full of the rhythms of the ancient mountains. She closed her eyes, listening to the cadence of the Appalachian tongue, mellowed by the ancient Celtic dialect, flavored more with the rich, proud strains of the Cherokee. He was well into his tale before she began to actually hear the meanings of the words.

"Fer every sickness," he was saying, "God has provided a cure, right here in old Mother Nature's lap. There's an old story my Granny tole me 'bout the gift of healin' the spirits of the growin' things have give to folks.

"Back a long time ago, when there was no evil in the world, back when old Lucifer wuz still the angel of light, before his pride ruint him and this world, there was no sickness. No germs, no way to fall and hurt yourself, no plagues or miseries. Then, Lucifer, he got all puffed up with pride, and he decided to be God, and he told all the creatures, all the livin' things of the earth, the plants and the animals, he was better fer 'em than God, that he cared more for 'em than God did. God didn't bother to come down and speak to His creatures like Lucifer did.

"Now, all livin' things have spirits, jist like we do, and at that time, all could talk, and all lived in peace together. Up til the time old Lucifer started makin' trouble, all the spirits of all the creatures and livin' things used their voices to sing praises to God. Oh, it was a good place, this world, because sin had never come here.

"But pride was the first and worst sin. It made the angel of light turn into the father of all evil, and Lucifer tried to put pride in all the creatures so they'd rebel with him. Ye see, he knew that worship brings humility, and ye gotta have humility fer true worship. Once somebody starts thinkin' they're better'n anybody else, there's hell to pay. They start lookin' at themselves and what they want instead of lookin' out to what God wants, or to what others need.

"Anyways, Lucifer, he went to all the trees and the rocks and the creatures and he said, 'Why do yew worship God? He is no better'n yew. Yew got a mind and a will. Yew've got to be 'bout as great as God, because ye can think for yerselves. Yew breed and create others like yerselves, in yer own image. Yew got great strength and power, like God, and God's not interested in yew anymore 'cause yew don't need Him anymore. But I am interested in ye, and I want to make yew even more like God. I kin give ye knowledge and I kin teach yew how to take care of yerselves. Yew don't even have to go by the old laws any more. They don't mean nuthin' to yew. Ye can make up yer own laws and govern yerselves.'

"Now, some of the plants and the animals listened to Lucifer. It had been a long time since God had come to visit with them, and some of 'em thought the old liar wuz pretty smart. He was the most beautiful thing they'd ever seen, and some of 'em thought they understood what he wuz atalkin' about when he told 'em they could do the same things God could—that they could think and know things. And they could throw away all the old rules they really didn't understand anyhow. And so pride entered the world, and things started goin' wrong.

"Th' Bible says that one third of all the angels fell with Lucifer, but it don't say nothin' about the livin' things on earth. The story I heard says that one half of the livin' bein's here fell with him. Lucifer wanted to own heaven and earth, and he told those who follered him that he'd reward them with perfect knowledge.

"There wuz a big battle, and the rebel angels, bein' more'n outnumbered, were kicked outta heaven, but they were not kicked outta earth. The fallen angels and the rebellin' creatures together overcame those who stayed loyal to God, and they struck all their good brothers on earth mute 'cause they couldn't stand hearin' 'em sing their praisin' songs.

"Fer awhile, the earth wuz an awful place. Evil flew around all over the world, growing stronger and stronger, and persecutin' all that give allegiance to God. Spirits turned into germs and viruses and evil thoughts that afflicted and tortured all the holy creatures.

"But God didn't let things stay that way long. While He wouldn't make evil leave the world, He did give those who had stayed loyal to him special powers to push evil back. First of all, He created a new place on the earth free from all evil: the Garden of Eden, and he allowed all the good creatures and things to live there. Then he gave them man and woman to care for 'em in place of Lucifer. And all of the people and creatures and growin' things sang His praises agin' fer awhile.

"Yew know what happened next. Evil got into the garden, too, and Adam and Eve. Old Satan got to them and they fell into sin, and they had to leave, and the garden disappeared. And Adam and Eve and all their children, they suffered from the evil spirits that tormented 'em all their days. Everthing that's bad, it comes from the Prince of the Air and all his minions. Everthing—sickness, bad thoughts, hurts. But God, He give us all some last defenses. He give the trees and the plants who still love him the power to heal. To th' willer, he give the gift to ease pain and bring down fever, to foxglove, a cure for the bad heart. Mint and chamomile bring ease of mind and sleep." He laughed. "Hemp helps the eyes—and helps people git acquainted. Plain old bread mold cures serious infections. Nearly every growin' thing has a good use, whether to sustain life or to use as medicines. And that's the gift God give to 'em."

He fell silent for a time, then reached under the covers with a tentative hand to feel Geneva's foot, but she was feeling too drowsy to mind.

He continued, "My other granny, the Cherokee, used to say that the creatures still have voices and that ye just have to know how to listen to hear 'em. My great-grandpa, he knew how to drive away evil spirits. That's why he was the medicine man of his tribe.

Nowadays, folks say that's a pack of foolishness, but I've seen him heal the sick with jist an incantation, a prayer that rebukes the bad spirits. He called on the power of the Creator Spirit, the God of all who made the world. And my great granny—I never knew her—but they say she used to listen to the spirits of the trees, and she used to dance with 'em when they sang."

"Like Narnia," murmured Geneva.

"Yes," he replied. "Like Narnia. I reckon that's the way the world used to be."

She was growing warm when he eased away to light a lantern and sit by the fire. She noticed him only as one notices a benign bedside presence during an illness. He was there if she needed him, and content with that, she snuggled down into the bed of healing herbs and slept.

But the good sleep did not last long. First, she grew hot, and she dreamed she was standing right in the hot coals of hell, with Lucifer and hideous spirits dancing around her, but then she was transported to a frigid place, and she found herself swimming through dangerous, icy rivers. The fear and pain grew more intense until she finally woke, shivering, to see Howard seated by the fire, reading by lantern light. He was so still that he seemed to be two dimensional, as if he were merely a cardboard figure stuck against the wall. Presently he turned a page. Once he smiled.

"I'm cold."

He looked up, startled, then with his smooth movements, he strode to her and touched her face. "Chills and fever, and stubborn," he said, shaking his head, "and this willer bark tea ain't doin' ye much good. Let's try somethin' else."

He made her another bitter drink. "Boneset," he told her after she had questioned the contents. "Boneset fer the fever, squawroot for the sore throat. A little ginseng ta warm ye in a hurry. And mint and honey," he added. "Bitter as it is, it'd be awful without 'em."

She drank it dutifully, then lay back, huddled in the bed, waiting for it to take effect. Howard returned to his place beside the fire.

"What are you reading?"
"*Gray Bear.*"
"Is it good?"
"I think so. Want to hear some?"
"Sure."

He began reading. He had read for a full minute before she realized he was reading poetry—and reading it well. It made no sense to her, tangled as her brain was with fatigue and fever, but his voice was soothing as it spoke of sky and water and the mighty buffalo. She began to grow sleepy.

"Howard?" she said, feeling the warmth seep into her bones again.

"Yes?"

"Do you live here or something?"

"Why do ye ask?"

"You have so much stuff here, as if you are doing more than just camping. This is almost like a home."

His answer was long in coming. "I suppose I do live here most of the time, good weather, anyway." He laid aside his book and picked up a guitar.

"Why? You can get here easily from your house. Is there something here that makes you want to stay all the time?"

Again he was silent while he strummed chords and gazed long into the fire. At first she thought he had not heard her, or had forgotten her, but at length his voice came to her as if from far away.

"Geneva, I guess yew know about the Greek gods?"

She was getting sleepier. "The gods?"

"Way back, afore Jesus, the Greeks and the Romans had a buncha gods. Not like the Indian spirits, but gods sort of like spoiled people with a lotta power."

She opened her eyes, surprised. "Yes, I know about them."

"Well, there was this one fella, Prometheus, and he did something that made the gods real mad."

"Yes. Gave people fire," she yawned.

"That's him. Anyways, you know what they did to him?"

Her brain was beginning to function very slowly. She looked lazily into her memory, but it was too much effort. "Think so," she droned.

"They chained him to a mountain and made him stay there til they got tired of punishin' him. The gods hoped to make him suffer, but he surprised 'em. When people come by, he'd do what he could to help 'em. And I bet that sometimes he didn't mind being there, on top of the world, even though birds would come and peck at him."

"Oh yes. Prometheus." She yawned.

He gazed into the fire again. "In a way," he said softly. "I'm like him. I'm chained to this here mountain, fer awhile, anyway." He fell silent for a long time. "But I don't mind," he finally added. "Hit sets me free, too." She could not make sense of it, nor did she try. His music made her drift along its gentle currents, and she was feeling warm and downy.

Sometime later, she woke again suddenly, shivering and hurting. The night was deep and still around her. Howard slept by the dying embers, wrapped loosely in a single blanket on the bare floor. She lay still until her teeth began to chatter, then she rose and tiptoed as quietly as she could toward the wood pile. He awoke as she lifted the first log.

"I'll do that, Miss Geneva," he asserted, wide awake and on his feet. "Yew git on back in the bed." Hurriedly, he replenished the fire while she sank gratefully back into the bed. It was so cold up here, even in August, with the dampness seeping through the logs, the fog shrouding the cabin like a clammy hand. It was impossible to get warm, even after Howard brought her more tea and tucked the blankets up around her chin and rubbed her feet with hands he had warmed by the fire. When her teeth began to chatter, he ordered her to sit by the fire while he pulled the mattress off the bed and dragged it to the hearth. She lay on it, and he lay beside her, pulling all the blankets over them and wrapping his arms tightly around her shaking body. Gratefully, she snuggled against him and drifted off into a dreamless sleep.

Toward morning she woke again, lifted so gently into consciousness that it was some time before she was aware she was awake. Opening her eyes, she saw Howard's face above her, his eyes bright in the pale morning.

"Yer fever's gone," he said quietly, touching her cheek.

She stared at him a long time as if through a misty tunnel. She did not recognize him immediately, for seeing him made her forget the present and think of being very young and lying in a moonbeam. The pale morning light fell on his face, which was full of gentle goodness. "You're beautiful," she said drowsily.

He was amused. "Likely that's the first and last time I ever heard that. Yew reckon boneset's got somethin' in it I don't know 'bout?"

"I mean it," she said sadly. "This is twice you've rescued me, and you've spent all night taking care of me. I've treated you so badly. I really am sorry, Howard. I hate to think how foolish I've been." Tears welled up in her eyes.

"Now, honey, yer sick and feelin' helpless. Hit's made ye blue. Yew never hurt me none. I'm pleased to spend time with ye. And hit's the God's truth, yer the beautiful one. I could look at ye all night."

"You really don't think badly of me?"

He chuckled. "Lord no. Matter of fact, ye remind me of my second wife."

Geneva felt worse. "Lenora said there wasn't anything to her. She ran off with a musician."

"Mammaw didn't know the whole story. Aster gave me a awful lot, and she was real good to me when I needed her. She got me through a rough time after my first wife died, and I just begged her to marry me, knowin' she'd never stay."

"Why would she want to leave you?"

He answered her thoughtfully. "She needed more than I, or anybody, could give her. Seems like she was always searchin' for somethin', and it seemed like she couldn't love me but with jist a piece of herself." He stopped, his eyes pained, then he smiled. "I'm kindly like Jimmy Lee's old dog. I love somebody and that's all there is. Cain't help but love a woman with my whole self—heart, liver, brain, gut, all of it. There's nothin' else but to find ways to love her more. I wanted to have a passel of younguns just so there'd be more of her around.

"My first wife, she understood that, and she felt the same way." His face softened with happiness. "It was like she was me and I was her." He fell silent and his eyes clouded as he seemed to look far away into some infinitely sad and desolate place. At last he continued, "When she died, the losin' was so awful. Not just a piece of me was gone. All of me was gone." His voice grew quiet again, more distant. "I was so lost I nearly went crazy.

"Then I met Aster. She was different. Seemed like she loved everthing she saw, and more besides. Like she had to go out and find new things all the time 'cause it wuz all so good." He gazed into the fire and his voice floated to her from far away. "But that was one of the best things about her. She seemed so—," he groped, then found the word he was looking for, "elusive. Elusive, but real. Bright. Fierce, the way she went after everthing. She was kinda like when yew see the reflection of the sun in the water when the actual sun is hid. It's prettier than the sun, and brighter, but it's not really there. Seemed like I spent all our time together jist watchin' her and tryin' ta figure out how to really touch her without disturbin' the water. I didn't have much time with her, but it was enough. She give me back the will to live."

"But she only stayed for a few months?"

"She knew me. She knew the longer she stayed, the worse her leavin' would hurt me, so she took off afore I could git too used to her. I don't blame her. I coulda been the King of Siam, and she still woulda left to whatever called her. I knew the first day I met her I couldn't hold her." He smiled. "Didn't stop me tryin', though."

"You think I'm restless and searching like that?"

"Ye got a brightness about ye, too. Jist the way ye look at the sky, and you ain't content jist to look. You want it. The way ye looked at that car yer boyfriend brought ye. And that other man,

John." His face furrowed as he tried to explain. "It's like ye got a greedy soul," he said, then hastened to add, "but in a good way. It gives ye that brightness, that look of being real alive."

She felt like sobbing. "I don't want to be restless and greedy. I want to just stop and be happy wherever I am. It's like I'm afraid something wonderful is out there, and I might miss it. And sometimes I feel like I'm running away from something as much as I'm running toward something else." She closed her eyes, but the tears squeezed out between her lids. "I don't like the feeling. I want to be content. I want to rest."

He placed his fingertips on her lips. "Awright, honey, yew hush now, and jist rest right here. I didn't mean ta hurt yer feelin'. I like ye the way ye are. And ye kin rest all ye want right here. I bet someday ye'll find something that'll make yew want to sit still."

She wanted to say more, to cry out that she did not know what made her this way. Could he take away whatever it was that made her want so much? That made her so cruel to good people? That thistle in her soul. The tears welled up hot in her eyes and she drew a ragged breath. She felt his arms go around her as she burrowed her face in the smooth hollow of his throat, and she sobbed until she fell asleep.

When she woke again, he was gone. The sun streamed through the open door, and a fragrant morning, suffused with silver light, rose to greet her. Geneva, suddenly famished, lightheaded, and with an enormous pressure in her bladder, got up and stumbled out of the door.

He was just outside, splitting logs. The sun warmed his hair to a deep chocolate brown, the copper skin glistened on his smooth arms as he raised an ax in the air to pause in a high arc before the muscles bunched and brought the ax down. Geneva stopped to appreciate the scene only for a moment before she murmured to him and hurried into the woods to relieve herself.

She felt so weak she had to sit down before she could make it back to the cabin. Breathing hard, her hair hanging in her face, her mouth tasting like dry, moldy bread, she sat, shaking with cold and fatigue, wondering how long she would have to remain here, how long it would be before she would be able to rise and make her way back to the cabin. How much longer would it be before she could ride back down the mountain?

Howard appeared through the spruce like a bright shadow, and without a word he strode toward her and lifted her as effortlessly as if he were lifting a child. There was silence all around; even her eyes and heart were mute and calm like a still, cloudless sky. Her arms went around his neck and she leaned her head into his shoulder, listening to the sweet silence. When he carried her into the cabin and laid her onto the bed, Geneva felt as if she were returning to a plush, much loved home. She rolled over and fell asleep almost immediately.

The morning and early afternoon slipped in and out again occasionally, but never disturbing her rest. She passed the time as an invalid, waking only enough to eat, drink, and go outside to relieve herself. Howard kept the fire hot and endlessly pressed her with what seemed like gallons of water in which he had steeped a variety of herbs, both pleasant-tasting and foul. By the time the sun had crested, she had begun to feel considerably better; by the time the shadows had lengthened, she felt well enough to be bothered by a general feeling of grunginess. Her hair hung limply in strings, and her teeth felt like they were wearing sweaters.

He brought her another cup of tea. Sighing, she took it, then rubbed her finger over her front teeth. "Howard, do you have a toothbrush? I'm just dying to brush my teeth."

"Yeah, I got a toothbrush," he smiled. "Jist a minute." He left and returned presently. "Here," he said, handing her a stick and a few leaves. "Sweet gum. Chew on this. The wood fuzzes up and ye kin brush yer teeth jist as pretty as ye please. Chew on this mint, too. Yer mouth'll be sweet in no time."

Taking this oral hygiene remedy, she walked down to the spring to give it a try. To her surprise, it worked rather nicely. It took longer than a real toothbrush, but that did not matter. Up here time lay languidly in the air; it did not hurry by, and there was no need to run after it. *This place was sweet. Sweet and safe and good.* She wandered back through the cool, dappled shade, chewing the mint leaves, breathing the spruce-scented air, and feeling the healing sun upon her face. It felt good to sit in the clear, thin air and feel her strength welling up in her limbs like an incoming tide rising higher and higher upon the parched sand.

She stayed out too long, and no doubt concerned about her absence, Howard came looking for her. She saw him striding through the branches, searching, and he seemed so much in control, so comfortablein his own forest, at one with the trees, the sky, the very rock upon which he stood that she wished she could be like him. *Real. Connected. Certain in time and place and circumstance.* A sudden tingling pricked her flesh, and she regretted that she had ever left these hills, that she had polluted her mountain spirit with the tawdry glitter of the past few years.

Although she was sitting low amid some rocks in a sheltered place, Howard's scanning eyes found her. He strode to her, concern on his face, but when he saw her smiling, he relaxed and dropped down beside her. Together they gazed into the deep blue spruce and the sparkling, new-washed sky. Geneva wanted to stretch out on the rocks and lie there all day, so content did she feel. They sat quietly, side by side for a long time.

At length, he spoke. "Geneva, I reckon I owe yew an apology. I told ye I had me a hemp patch up here. I don't blame ye fer thinkin' I wuz a outlaw."

He was tense, and his face seemed drawn. "To tell ye the truth, I do have somethin' like a cash crop up here, and I know ye've been wonderin' how I got me all this land, and a nice house down in the holler."

She had already forgiven him his hemp patch. "You don't have to tell me, Howard," she said. "I was just sick and irritable yesterday. It's none of my business."

He took a deep breath, "No. I owe this to ye, cause I lied to ye before. And now, I'm gonna tell ye the truth, and I'm gonna trust ye to not tell nobody, nobody atall, not yer sister, or yer mama or daddy. People find out about this, and all hell will break loose."

"What is it, Howard? What could be worse than a marijuana patch?"

"Not worse. Better. A lot better. Come here. Let me show ye somethin'. Kin ye walk?" She nodded, and he helped her to her feet. Holding her hand, he led her a hundred paces to the creek, then they turned upstream to walk another several hundred yards to a wild, deep canyon where the stream roared through a gash in towering, streaked rock. Huge boulders lay around; large veins of quartz ran through most of them, and just before them lay piles and piles of quartz rocks and gravel gleaming white and fresh in the afternoon sun. Near the rocks, in the stream, lay a contraption just like those she had seen in the cabin. She realized it was a sluice box. A shovel leaned in a grotto nearby.

Without a word he thrust the shovel into the gravel and sprinkled the white stones into the box. The water boiled around the gravel as it rolled downward. He watched the stones bounce, then easily, almost casually, he leaned forward and plucked out one, then two, then three lumps of brilliant gold, the smallest of which was the size of a pea. Taking Geneva's hand, he placed them in her palm.

"This here's my cash crop," he said. "I've hauled out nearly eighteen million in the last two years, but all that's left now is placer gold. Enough, I reckon, to live on and take care of my family, but I won't be buyin' much more land." He shrugged. "Reckon I got enough, anyway."

The sun, glinting on the gold in her hand, swarmed up to her eyes and made her dizzy. Had he just told her he was a millionaire? Eighteen million? The fact would not register. She gazed at the irregular lumps, weighty in her palm, trying to compute their value. "You mean to tell me you've kept this a secret, pulling eighteen million dollars worth of gold out of here?"

He shook his head. "Hit ain't been easy. Only the family knows about it, and they been helpin' me work it. We pulled the last of the big stuff out o' the mine last spring," he said, indicating a dark opening in the face of the cliff to his left. "It warn't a very big pocket, but you'd be surprised how far a little gold will go." He thrust the shovel into the pile of gravel again and sprinkled the stones into the sluice box. "I go down to Harrisonburg ever few weeks to the assayer's, and I set me up a few corporations to turn it into land. Won't nobody know who's bought all of it till I stop, when all this gold's played out." He pulled out two more shiny yellow pebbles.

Geneva was astonished. "But why do you live like this? I mean, you're rich, and you just stay up here, driving a beat up old truck, when you could be traveling the world, living it up."

He smiled his quick smile, which she was beginning to recognize as an integral part of him. "I been in the world, ma'am, and I ain't got much truck with it. Hit's land I want, land that I know I kin leave to my children and their children, all down the line, and they kin live on it, knowin' what the world's supposed to look like. I reckon I'll spend ever dime I kin scratch out o' here on it, or till I buy up ever tree and ever creek left wild." He looked at her, his eyes liquid. "Kin I trust ye, Geneva? I reckon they ain't but a few hunnert thousand dollars worth left, maybe five or six, eight at the outside, but if word gits out, they'll be people crawlin' all over here, for miles, settin' up machines, skeerin' off the game, trashin' the place up. I'll have ta put up a fence, maybe git some guards. Somebody'll likely git shot. Who knows how much more gold this old mountain is hidin' in her womb? And they's still a lot of gold left in the rocks. Folks'll be wantin' it." He indicated the quartz piled high at intervals along the creek bank. "But to git all of it takes a process that'll poison the creek and the ground, and I don't aim to try for it. Maybe someday I'll haul it outta here to a factory where they kin do it safe, but not here, not now. Kin I trust ye not to tell a soul, not a livin', breathin' soul? Not even yer sister? Not yer boyfriend?" His eyes gleamed desperately.

Geneva gazed at the place around her. A hundred feet away stood a high bank of quartz rock, shining white in the late sun. Beyond that was the mine, which violated the pristine cliff. To her, the piles of gravel and rock, the deep gash in the cliff, already looked obscene here in the verdant hillside, fragrant with the smell of spruce and humus. She imagined people running around wildly, dragging wheelbarrows full of rock and gravel into the stream of sweet water, throwing garbage into the chipmunk burrows, pouring chemicals upon the ferns. She vowed reverently that she would never tell a soul, even hint to anyone about the treasure that lay scattered upon the surface of this mountain.

"Howard, I swear. No one will ever even suspect there might be something here. Not from me."

He nodded once, then dropped his serious façade. "Yew ever pan fer gold?"

"I've never seen it done."

"Here, let me pour some more gravel through this here sluice box, so ye'll have enough to pan for. If ye'll help me, we kin go through a lot o' gravel in a little while."

He instructed Geneva to watch the gravel bouncing and rolling down the waffle ridges in the sluice box as he dumped shovelful after shovelful of gravel upon it. "I bust up the rocks, and that kindly separates out the gold, then we sluice it fer the big pieces. Yew watch fer gold as it runs down. It's heavier, so the small stuff gets caught in these here little pockets, but the bigger stuff rolls on down. Yew gotta catch 'em as they slide by."

He demonstrated, and Geneva caught on quickly. Soon she was snatching gold out of the boiling water as quickly as she used to gather daisies as a child. Before long she had collected a handsome pile of heavy nuggets.

"Now we kin pan us some, go for what's trapped in the box," explained Howard as he dismantled the box over a bucket and separated a piece of carpeting, which he rinsed in the bucket.

Retrieving a gold pan from the creek bank, he scooped up the fine dirt and gravel from the bucket and placed it in the pan. Holding it under water, he shook it, swirled the ore, then poured off the rocks, dirt, and water. Three times he repeated the process until the pan was empty save for black sand, and Geneva could see, small chunks of brilliant yellow gold. He washed the gold again, finally eliminating all the sand. What was left was a quarter of a cup of nuggets and fine grains of gold that he poured in a quart mason jar, like so much honey to set on his cabin shelf for winter feasting. Geneva thought of how it would look sitting there, the firelight dancing upon it and turning the grains from the color of the sun to the color of roses. The thought thrilled all of her senses.

He allowed her to pan for half an hour, until they had emptied the bucket of all its ore and had filled the jar half full of treasure. Then he straightened. "Ye look a little tired. We'd better stop," he said. "Here," he added, handing the jar to her. "I reckon I ought to pay ye yer wages fer yer work."

She took it, marveling at its weight and the beauty of its contents. She would put the gold in a special crystal container and set it upon her fireplace mantel, or she might wear some of it in a vial around her neck, or she could have it molded into a special piece of jewelry… She felt the blood rise hot in her face as she contemplated the value of it.

But a second thought niggled, and then shouted at her. She could not show it to another living soul, lest they deduce its place of origin. A battle raging between lust for the treasure and the desire to protect Howard's trust sprang up like a hot and violent holy war. At last she shook her head, half hoping he would insist.

"No, Howard. I'd better not. Somebody will see it and want to know where it came from." Reluctantly, she handed it back to him.

"Oh. Then here, take some of these. Yew kin have something made out of 'em, or sell 'em someplace." He tried to press several of the larger nuggets upon her.

Geneva longed for them. Never had she seen anything more beautiful than the glint of real gold in the late light, newly plucked from where it had lain for millions of years. But she shook her head again, turning away from the precious metal in his open palm. "No," she repeated. "I'd rather remember it this way." She released her breath, feeling righteous and cleansed.

Then she looked down at the swirling waters and felt herself go limp. Sitting down suddenly, she clutched a boulder and let her head hang between her shoulders.

He was all at once solicitous. "I've kept ye out too long, and workin' to boot," he said, chiding himself. "Kin ye make it back, or do ye want me ta carry ye?" He moved toward her.

Her brain was whirling as if she were drunk, or she thought, with a brief moment of illumination, as if she were stoned. The thought of being lifted into Howard's powerful arms, nestled against his smooth chest, to hear his heart beat and feel the way he glided though the forest. The thoughts, the thoughts… She wasn't sure what the thoughts were about or what they were doing to her. She looked at him mutely, appealing, wanting to feel his arms around her and be carried back to the cabin. She wanted to feel his skin on the palms of her hands…

He was standing over her, now bending close. She could smell his sweat, musky and sweet, could see the hard jaw and the stubble there, black against the copper. His cheekbones seemed carved of wood, his nose aquiline and proud. She saw red spirals rushing at her from gold light, and she reached for him.

Ten

They were moving in slow motion through long, undulating waves of sunlight and shadow. Geneva had not fainted: she had not even felt weak when she reached for him and the brightness came spiraling at her. Rather, she had felt powerful and alive, so alive it made her dizzy. Even now the light swirled around her and made her feel like she was spinning through the warm sunshine. She could feel his arms and his heart beating. She could feel the smoothness of his chest through his shirt, the muscles and sinews under his skin. So heightened were her senses that she could even feel the bones as they moved beside her head. Her ear was pressed against his chest. His heart pounded so that it felt almost painful to her, as if the blood coursed through his heart, then warmed and spiced, into her ear and through her own veins. She felt it moving through her, rising to her lips and groin. She could not stop the sound of the blood thrumming through her ears, or the rapid pulsing of her heart. Nor did she want to. It was a wonderful awfulness: she would have wept with joy or fear or pleasure if she had felt it in her power to do so. But she was stunned into immobility, as if his blood mingling with hers had rendered her unable to act on her own emotions. She was no longer her own self, rather she seemed to have become a part of this man who held her so close. They were one: floating, swirling, eddying in the sunshine through the majestic forest.

Howard laid her on the bed and washed her face with a cool, wet cloth.

"Oh, Lord God, Geneva. I'm sorry," he was saying. "I shoulda known better than to have ye out there aworkin' like that. Yew jist seemed a lot better, and I didn't realize that pannin' would strain ye. Kin ye talk? How do ye feel?"

She smiled at him through a golden mist. She was still giddy, still swirling. *What was it? The gold? Howard? It didn't matter.* She sighed and lay back, enjoying the memory of the moment when she felt herself rise and take flight in his arms.

Then something clicked into place. She saw the concern in his face, and shame flooded her. Silently, she prayed that he had not seen what had been in her thoughts when she lifted her arms and clasped them around his neck. "Oh, God, I'm sorry Howard. I'm all right. I just got hot." Her face reddened at the unconscious innuendo. "And all that rushing water. I'm sorry," she said again. "I scared you." She pushed back the hair falling into her face. "I'm fine, really."

He jumped up. "Let me git ye some more water." He handed her yet another cupful of the cold, clear water redolent with herbs.

"What is this?" she asked, sipping.

"Comfrey, a little fennel. Hit cleans out the blood." He stroked her hair. "I thought yer fever was gone, but you're flushed, and ye feel a little hot now. Ye got some bug, and till ye git over it, ye'll have poisons in yer blood. This'll do the trick, this and a little rest. Ye'll be fine by tomorrow."

She believed him, or rather, wanted to believe him. She hoped he was right. She had some little bug, and that, combined with the dizzying water, had made her swoon. That was all. But she trembled again at the smell of him when he leaned toward her.

"*Be careful!*" a voice screamed in her head. She shook herself and schooled her thoughts.

"Howard, how do you know so much about the healing properties of herbs? Did Lenora teach you?"

He settled on the nearest stump. "Some. My mama taught me some, too. But I learned most of what I know from my great-grandfather. He was a healer among his people. My mama died when I was fifteen. That's how my dad lost his legs—they were in a car wreck. I went to live with my mother's people out in Oklahoma fer a year after the wreck. My dad was in a coma for months, and then he had to go to Harrisonburg for rehabilitation. When he was gone, I felt sort of in the way here. Lost, I guess, and I missed my mother. My grandfather asked me to come live with them for a while."

"Your grandfather was a healer too?"

"Mostly my great-grandfather. He was the official medicine man in his tribe. He was real old when I went out there, and he remembered the old ways. His father wuz born in North Carolina at the time when the Cherokee still claimed all the land in the Blue Ridge and Nantahala. When he was five years old, him and all his family wuz run out. They walked all the way to Oklahoma."

"You mean he walked the Trail of Tears?" Geneva had learned about that event in history, not from the classroom, but from *Walk in My Heart,* the third book sent from the Romance of the Month Club she had long been a member of. It was a novel about an Indian princess whose lover had been a soldier in the American army. She had read it twice.

"Yes. My great-grandfather learned healin' ways from his father, and he taught his children, but it was my mother who took the most interest in it. Of course, I didn't pay much attention to her when she tried to teach me. At that time I was more interested in the things of white men: fast cars, hamburger joints. But when I went to live with my grandparents, I found out what it meant to be Cherokee, and it… changed me." He let his eyes drift toward the window and stared at something far in the distance.

She sat up. "How long did you live with your grandparents?"

"Jist a year. As Dad got better, I figured I oughtta be here, takin' care of him. I got an older brother, but he wanted to go to college, and he had stayed with Dad while he wuz so bad off. So I came on back home. Mammaw and Pappy, they wanted me to go back to school, but I'd spent a year livin' outside, bein' in the woods and in the hills. Now I can't stand bein' cooped up. No way I could sit in a school house all day."

"But you've been cooped up here. You've hardly been outside at all, and you haven't seemed to mind. You sat up half the night reading. I'm surprised you didn't want to go to school."

He glanced at her mischievously. "Who wouldn't mind bein' cooped up with you, Geneva? I reckon there'd be men willin' to fight fer that privilege."

She dropped her eyes, cheeks flaming. "I better go shoot us some dinner," he said quickly. "Yew want more squirrel, or maybe a turkey? Or fish. Hit's a regular supermarket out here."

Rising, she crossed to the window. "Fish," she decided. "You have a fishing pole? I'm a pretty good fisherman myself, and I feel like just sitting by the creek."

"No fishin' poles. I catch 'em the fun way. Yew really feel better? Kin ye come to the creek? I'll show ye."

It was a perfect day for dalliance. The mountain trout shimmered silver in the water. The sun rained down gold, and Geneva sat by the creek and combed her hair with her fingers. Howard, his pants rolled up, waded into the water after a big trout lurking in the rock pool. Laughing silently, Geneva pointed to the shadowy place where the creature lay, and quietly, stealthily, Howard crept upon it. Then, with a motion so slow that he seemed to be drifting with the current, he dipped his net into the water and scooped up a fish so big Geneva knew they both could feast on it.

She was feeling stronger, athough a bit shaky, but she wanted to be useful, so she built the fire while Howard cleaned the fish. As they peeled and pan fried potatoes and onions, she felt her appetite return.

Supper, served al fresco under the deepening sky, was tasty and companionable. Afterwards, they dangled their legs off the porch, watching the sky turn from deep blue to black and the moon rise high and round.

"Boy, oh boy," sighed Geneva as she leaned against the support pillar, "I just need one thing to make this a perfect day."

"What's that?" mused Howard. "Dessert? There's huckleberries over yonder. I reckon we could make us a pie."

"Gosh, no. I've eaten enough. What I really want is a bath. And a brush. And some shampoo." She warmed to the memories of personal hygiene. "And a real toothbrush with toothpaste. Those sticks you give me to chew are okay, but I'm beginning to feel awfully dirty. And where do you wash your clothes?"

"Over in the creek, and I bathe there, too. There's a big swimmin' hole jist below here, right by where I git th' mint. Hit grows wild all over, and the place always smells of it. Hit's real perty there." He frowned. "But I don't reckon yew oughtta git in the creek," he added. "No sense in you takin' the chance of makin' yerself sick again. We'll see how ye do tonight. If ye don't chill, maybe ye kin jump in fer a swim in the mornin'." He looked at the fireflies and added. "I reckon we'll head on back down the mountain tomorrow. Ye'll surely be strong agin' by then, and we don't want yer folks to come home and worry."

"That's true," admitted Geneva sorrowfully. She wished she could stay a little longer. It was so beautiful here.

"But if yer set on havin' a bath, I kin heat ye some water up from that rain barrel, and ye kin git right down in it. I ain't got shampoo, but I kin mix ye some soaproot and laurel tea. Just as good. Better."

"Oh, Howard, would you? A bath would be wonderful. More than wonderful," she sighed.

The rain barrel was already full from last night's deluge, so Howard poured the water into a huge zinc washtub, big enough for Geneva to sit in, and built a fire under it to heat it. In the high altitude, it boiled quickly, just at the right temperature to steam in the cooling night.

"This oughtta be jist right," he announced. "Ye cain't git yer coffee hot enough, but boilin' temperature's about right fer a hot bath. Now you git on in before it cools off, and I'll run over to the creek. Bet I git cleaner'n yew do."

The word "pleasure" took on new meaning to Geneva as she sank into the water. Lying back, she watched the steam rise toward the stars and listened to the frogs singing their nightly chorus. They textured the lonely darkness with their cries. A whippoorwill called for his lost love, then called again and again. His voice seemed forlorn and lonely.

She lathered her hair, then soaked in the water redolent with wild ginger and wintergreen until the moon changed from her yellow robe to her white one and the water cooled. When she emerged, feeling refreshed and cleansed, she dressed in one of Howard's flannel shirts, which hung nearly to her knees. Although she was feeling a bit sleepy and ready for her perfumed pillow, she took the time to wash her own shirt and underwear and hang them on the porch railing to dry. She would wear her own things home tomorrow.

Howard had not returned by the time she entered the cabin. She chuckled to herself, thinking of how she would tease him about lingering so long in his beauty bath. Shivering slightly, she wondered how anyone could spend time dawdling in that cold water. She sat down to wait. He would be here shortly.

He did not come. She looked out the window, but saw nothing except blackness, and she began to grow a little concerned. Surely he was on the trail back by now. She would just step off the porch and call to him.

"Howard?" she called from the porch. There was no answer. She walked a little way down the trail and called again into the night. All she could hear were the roaring sounds of the night creatures and the water rushing down the mountain. *She would go as far as the edge of the mint bed and call again*, she decided. *What could be keeping him so long?*

The moon lit her path and gave her confidence as she strolled through the chilly air. The creek lay to her right, but the water was swift here. He had said there was a swimming hole on down. No doubt it would widen and grow quieter. She stopped when she smelled mint. Knowing she was close, she opened her mouth to call to him, but when she lifted her face, her breath caught in her throat; her voice stilled.

He was standing naked on the top of a cliff on the opposite bank at least twenty feet above her head. His arms were stretched out low and slightly behind him; his back and neck were arched, while his face gazed up into the full moon. White light streamed down onto and around him, giving the illusion of a classical statue carved in marble. He was the most beautiful thing she had ever seen, and at that moment she wanted him with all her heart. Wanted him with such intensity that her whole being throbbed and pulsated with the rhythms of the night. Wanted him and knew she could not have him.

Ever. As soon as she felt her desire rising up like warm smoke, she heard again the words he had uttered to her last night. *Ye ain't content jist to look. Ye have a greedy soul. Ye have to have it.* She recognized the truth in them. She was a greedy soul, wanting everything she found beautiful and good, and her greed and her pride had already caused him sorrow. She watched him needfully until he lowered his gaze to the far darkness, and then took one step forward and plunged like an arrow into the water. Noiselessly she fled back to the cabin.

Shortly afterward he returned, cheerful and damp. She watched him sorrowfully, wondering if there was a way she could love him without hurting him and herself. How could she have him and all the other things that she had yearned for all of her life? She felt half mad, trying to work out a plan that made sense. But it always came back to *Impossible. Impossible. Impossible,* pounding in her head.

"Wanna play checkers??"

"No. I—I think I'd like to read."

"All right. I got poetry mostly. And philosophy. I don't go in much fer fiction." He perused the shelves, looking for something suitable.

"On second thought, Howard, I think I'll just go to bed. I feel pretty worn out." She looked around restlessly.

"Sure." Let me make ye up some bay leaf and chamomile tea. Hit'll help ye sleep."

She watched him work, speaking sternly to herself, angry at the way she had felt the lust for him rise up hot and sweet. She remembered the way he had tasted the night she had kissed his mouth; it had been soft and desirable. Shivering with the recollection, she shook herself again. She was terrible. She did not know why she should be feeling so out of control.

Lying tensely in the bed, she listened while Howard strummed his guitar and sang softly. His voice, too, was warm and honeyed as he sang an old ballad she recognized:

> *In the clover, where I found my love*
> *And I lay tangled in her hair*
> *In the clover where we cooed like doves*
> *And I kissed her lips like cherries fair.*
>
> *In the clover, in the clover,*
> *Our hands entwined with sweet flower chains.*
> *But winter winds blew the blossoms away*
> *And she left me full of sorrow and pains*
>
> *When Spring comes again I'll sing my song*
> *Of love so sweet and true*
> *And I'll wait in the clover, it won't be long*
> *Till our love returns, then I'll marry you.*

She thought of fields of clover lying green and white in a high mountain meadow. *Clover and mint. Fields of mint.* She drifted off to sleep somewhere in a field of mint.

When the morning came, Geneva felt wonderful, cleansed of body and soul. Her feelings toward Howard had dissipated during the night, so that she was able to see him as merely a friend again, a good friend. One with whom she could entrust her life. One who had entrusted his most important secrets to her.

"Ye want to leave right after we eat, or wait till afternoon?" he asked. If ye don't think ye'll be too wore out later on, I'd like to show ye around. There's caves up above us with ancient paintin's. Nobody knows about 'em but me, but I reckon I've already shown ye my biggest secret awready, so there's no need to hide the rest."

"Oh, Howard," she breathed. "I'd love to see cave paintings. I'm in no rush to get back. We can leave as late as you like."

Immediately after breakfast, they struck off through the forest, and after a half hour of walking, Howard guided her up a rocky draw choked with impossibly close underbrush. At the top they came to a creek, which widened as they followed it upstream. When they reached a low place where the water was very wide, still, and shallow, Howard instructed Geneva to take off her shoes and socks. "It's straight across here," he said.

Searching, she could see nothing but a sheer rock face on the opposite bank. "Where? I don't see anything."

"There", he pointed, leaning his head close to hers so they would have the same vantage. As his shoulder brushed her cheek, she felt it again—that sudden, sweet jolt that shook her senses and made her tremble. She took a step away from him.

"I don't see a thing," she said brusquely. "Let's just get over there."

They waded carefully across the stream, treacherous with uneven, moss-slippery rocks. Howard reached for her arm, but she waved him away, laughing brightly, afraid for him to touch her. Once across, he pointed above their heads and to the right. "Up there."

"In that little narrow slit? Nobody could squeeze in there."

"Hit's bigger'n it looks. Here, yew go first. There's enough toe holds to git ye up all right. Jist be careful."

Glad that she was not afraid of heights, Geneva threaded her way up ten feet of the cliff to the small fissure in the rock. As he had promised, it was barely large enough for a man to squeeze into. She stood at the opening, waiting for him to come up behind her with the flashlight.

"Watch it right here. There's a little lip jist in the entrance, then it levels out and widens. Jist step careful." He eased his shoulder through the fissure, then his head and the rest of his body disappeared. She followed immediately, treading carefully behind him until the cave widened out enough for the two of them to stand side by side.

"Hit's not far back," he whispered solemnly, as if they were in some sacred place. "Straight ahead." He gave her a tiny push, walking beside her with his hand on her back until they made their way through a natural arch that opened into a small room. At the threshold Geneva stopped, uttering a small cry. Howard's flashlight beam had fallen upon a stunning array of beautiful and intricate paintings, still brilliant and perfectly preserved. There were several scenes ranging from the most simple depictions of warriors hunting strange beasts to large, meticulously drawn patterns that held cryptic meanings indecipherable to Geneva.

"Beautiful, beautiful," she breathed. "Howard, this is a real treasure! How did you find it?"

"I found it years ago, after I came back from Oklahoma. I liked to wander around the mountains, and I found it one day when I was tryin' to scale the cliff. The man who owned it had never seen it, and one day, I saw him out in his field and I tole 'im about it. This land had been in his family for over a hundred years, and none of 'em had ever seen it as far as he knew. After that, we spent a lotta time together, searchin' for more caves. He wuz sorta like a second father to me. He did the things fathers usually did with their sons, while mine couldn't. He wuz a good man."

"Did he leave it to you?"

"Yes. He had no younguns, no family at all, so he left me all his land when he died. The land where the mine is wuz his. He wuz a good man," he repeated.

They explored the cave for another hour. Geneva found it hard not to touch the delicate paint, but she kept her hands to herself and peered at each picture closely under the light.

"I think this one represents a marriage," he commented, pointing to one of the more elaborate drawings. "See, here's a woman, dressed finer'n anyone else, and over here is a man, the only one wearing feathers." He moved the light downward. "This looks like the priest or the medicine man, maybe the chief. He looks like he'd perform the ceremony. And all the people—see the streamin' lines comin' from 'em? I think that must be good wishes."

He moved closer and pointed again. "And look. See here, floatin' between 'em, looks like an unborn baby, curled up like it would be in the womb. It's like it's waitin' to come to 'em."

"It's marvelous." She could not believe she was seeing these pictures, perhaps thousands of years old, painted by people so long dead that even their language was forgotten. And yet their art was more sophisticated than European art of only a few centuries ago. How remarkable was this day! "Thank you for showing me this. You know I won't tell," she said reverently.

"I know, Geneva. Now we should go on back. We'll have us some dinner, then ride on back down. Yew feel all right?"

"I feel wonderful, thank you. Can I come back here some day?"

"Yer always welcome." She could not see his face, but his voice resonated low and husky and held the darkness of a sultry summer night. She caught her breath and felt the flush rise in her face once again. Hesitating, she looked down at the circle of light on the sandy floor of the cave, afraid to lift her eyes, afraid to move. If he could know how she trembled when his hand brushed her arm! She did not know what she would do if he touched her; she feared that he would read her thoughts—that she would leap into his arms and press her mouth against his. Without realizing it, she willed him to touch her. She closed her eyes and lifted her face, leaning toward him until she swayed.

"Are you comin'?" he asked.

"What?" She opened her eyes. He was standing at the cave entrance.

"Do ye want to stay and look some more? Don't ye think we oughtta git back?"

"Oh. Yes. We need to get back." She brushed past him into the brilliant sunlight.

They hurried back to the cabin, speaking little, just concentrating on the rocky trail until they were in sight of the familiar forest. Several times he reached out as if to touch her or steady her, but he always dropped his hand before he made contact. When the trail grew easier, they walked separately, talking about the domestic issues of lunch and horses and how they would simply forget to tell anyone about the days they had spent there. Geneva was especially mindful of the secrets she held.

The sky turned blue and the day grew hot. When they reached the place where the mine lay, Geneva stopped to bathe her face and feet in the rocky stream. Howard settled on a nearby rock and looked into the deep woods. His eyes grew brooding, as if he had moved his soul away into a distant place. Out of the corner of her eye, Geneva watched him, wondering what kind of man he was. He seemed so simple, as if there was nothing more to him than what he presented, and yet, she was growing more and more aware that there might be depths of him that would never be plumbed. She turned to the running water and cupped her hand to drink.

"Ye better not drink that water," cautioned Howard. Hit's too far from the source.

"Oh, I'm not afraid of a little E coli. I've drunk plenty of water from running streams, and it's never hurt me before. We're not downstream from anything that looks dangerous to me."

"There's wild boar in these parts, and they carry parasites that'll make ye real sick. Yew think ye had fever the other day, it'll take more'n boneset ta git ye over Weil's disease. Come on," he said, sliding off the rock. "There's a spring over yonder. We'll slip on over there and git us a good drink."

Dutifully, she followed him into the dappled shade where he brushed through the ferns and led her to a small spring bubbling from a tumble of mossy rocks. The amount of water streaming over the moss was too small for her to capture a drink with her hand, so she held back her hair and laid her cheek into the velvet. The water was cold and pure. When she lifted her streaming face, he chuckled and leaned forward.

"I usually pick out the critters afore I drink, unless I'm real hungry," he said, reaching into the moss where she had just put her face and pulling out a snail and a few small beetles. "But I reckon hit's jist as easy to strain 'em out with yer teeth."

Geneva laughed. "I am hungry. Wish I had known they were there. I'm in the mood for escargot." She bent and drank again, feeling reckless and a little like a wild creature herself, and she thought about how nice it would be to take off all her clothes and loll around in that deep moss. She plucked a long fern frond and tied her hair back with it, then preened a little while he bent to drink. She felt lightness suffuse her being.

The sky was still blue when they returned to the cabin, but as they sat down to lunch, it darkened deep and threatening. A thunderstorm rolled in from the west.

They looked at each other. "It may let up," he offered.

"You think?"

He grimaced slightly. "I don't know. May. May not. We'll jist wait it out."

They waited until nearly dinnertime, then, watching the dark rain beat hard upon the earth, Geneva sighed and commented, "Well, we can stay one more night. Is this Thursday?"

"Friday. When will yer sister be home?"

"Tomorrow night or the next day." She paused, dreading the growing silences between them and what those silences held. She wondered if he could feel her thoughts when she looked at him. Surely he did. They throbbed nearly palpably to her. She was careful to keep her eyes averted. "We can wait. We'll go first thing in the morning."

They ate an early supper by firelight, then Howard lit the lantern and they washed dishes and settled down to cards. They had played two hands of gin rummy when the rain stopped and watery sunlight lit up the windows. Howard moved to the door.

"It's over. Blue sky jist ahead. Yew want to go fer it tonight?"

She joined him at the threshold. The sun had already dipped below the tree line. "No. It will be dark soon. I don't want to chance it." She said it slowly, fearfully. Something bid her to stay. She shivered.

"Yer right. Won't be long." There was a silence; he broke it by asking cheerfully, "Wanna make a pie?"

They gathered huckleberries in the dying light, then Geneva mixed flour, water, shortening, and sugar together while Howard put the huckleberries and water in the pan and set it on the fire. As soon as the juice was bubbling, they dropped the batter by spoonfuls into the boiling berries.

They ate it outside on the porch steps. Already the sky was deepening, and a handful of stars began pricking their way through the dark blue.

"Yew want another hot bath? Plenty of rainwater."

"Can't pass that up. You going for a swim?"

He shrugged, smiling, "Might as well."

He built the fire outside once again, and she helped him set the zinc tub on rocks above it. Then they dipped water from the rain barrel into the tub and waited for it to simmer. Howard mixed up another batch of soaproot and laurel. This time he spiced it with honeysuckle.

She put the concoction to her nose. "It's lovely," she said, smiling, waiting for him to leave.

Her smile met his eyes. He was looking at her with a quiet intensity that made her heart thump. Almost imperceptibly, he tensed. She saw his jaw go taut in the lampshine streaming from the window, and she was glad that she stood in darkness, for she knew he would surely see the quick rise and fall of her breast. She fought to keep her breath steady.

"Bet I get cleaner'n you do," she said lightly.

He relaxed. "Yew kin try. Enjoy yerself." He disappeared in the darkness.

She climbed into the tub, shaking. She washed her hair and her underwear once again, and scrubbed her clothes before she put on the long flannel shirt and brushed her teeth with mint and sweet gum. Restlessly, she hung her clothes on the porch rail and sat down on the steps, her breath unsteady, and waited for Howard.

The darkness sang its caressing songs, and once again the whippoorwill called to her out of the night woods. She thought of Howard standing on the high cliff, facing the moon, dropping into the water so fearlessly. Her heart rose in her throat, and she found it impossible to rid herself of the image in her mind. She wanted to see him again. The thought burned her brain, and before she made herself think of how wrong this could be, she was making her way toward the creek and the smell of peppermint.

She arrived in time to see him climbing up the rock and poising his face to drink in the moonlight. Back and neck arched, he looked like a proud stallion sniffing the wind. Then, just like the night before, he stepped into empty air and dropped straight to the water. She heard the splash and told herself to run, but she wanted to see him so beautiful just one more time. She willed her feet to move; they refused. Her eyes searched the boulders, her ears strained for the sound of splashing, but she could hear and see nothing except darkness and the voices of the night until he rose out of the water and stood before her.

He loomed up large, dark, and silent. Water ran in dark little rivers down his face and body. She thought if she could not touch him, she would suffocate. Very slowly, with a shaking hand, she reached up and delicately traced the line of his collarbone. Water ran over her hand and dripped to the elbow. She wanted her whole hand to caress the wetness, but she stopped, terrified by both his presence and her feelings.

He stood perfectly still while she touched him, but before she dropped her hand, he caught it in his own, and very slowly, as easy as breathing, he brought it to his lips and kissed the knuckles. His chest convulsed. The trembling spread from her hand to every nerve in her body. Looking at her hand as if it were a rare and delicate creature, he kissed her palm and then gently bit the heel of her hand. He kissed her wrist, nuzzling it softly before he leaned close and brushed her forehead with his lips. Somehow, she was in his arms, and their mouths collided.

Geneva had often read about passionate kisses, and she even thought she had experienced a few of them. But this kiss was unlike anything she had ever known. She had heard about the earth moving, had thought it was a metaphor. This kiss enlightened her. The earth not only moved, it danced and leaped. She lost her balance and leaned hard against him to stay upright. Small explosions in her brain and in her loins spiraled upward and outward so that she found herself expanding into something large and luminous, like a sunflower blossoming.

This must be what they call Chemistry, she thought, then her brain simply quit. She became nothing but feeling.

Howard broke from the kiss and ran his hands over her back and shoulders. Then, seizing her shirt at the collar, he ripped it asunder with one smooth movement. Buttons dropped into the mint at their feet. His hands and his lips pressed hot like a brand upon her, and she reveled in the heat in them, the heat in her own flesh. Again came the explosions, the blossoming. She was in a boiling river, being swept away; she was tumbling over and over in water and fire and drowning passion. Gasping, she pulled him down onto the minty leaves where she touched him worshipfully. He tried to speak. "Oh, God. I feel like I'm in an avalanche," he choked out. Her kiss silenced him, and they spoke no more.

Later they picked themselves up and made their way back to the cabin where they slept curled up tightly together until midnight when a caressing hand on her forehead awakened her.

"Wake up," he said gently. "I want to show ye somethin'."

She reached for him, wanting his kisses, but he slipped from the bed, stripping it of the blankets and throwing them around her shoulders. "Better put yer shoes on. It's a little ways."

Hurriedly, anticipating yet another wonder, she slipped into her shoes, then reached for his hand so he could lead her outside into the redolent, velvet darkness.

"Where are we going?"

"Jist up ahead. " He pressed her hand and tugged her gently along until they came to a clearing where the ground was a smooth expanse of exposed granite. There he spread the blankets upon the rock and lay flat on his back. "Come on," he invited. "Lay down here."

She curled up beside him and put her arms around him, but he pointed upward. "Look, there's one now."

She followed his pointing finger and found herself looking at the burning trail of a shooting star. Another one shot off an angle to the first. And then another and another streamed across the sky before her delighted eyes.

"Oh! A meteor shower! Oh! and it's such a clear, beautiful night! How did you know?"

He chuckled. "Yew've lived in a house too long, darlin'. I bet yew don't even know what this is."

She giggled. She felt full of little bubbles of happiness. "It's not a meteor shower?"

"No. It's the tears of Singing Eyes."

"Who?"

"Singing Eyes. A Cherokee maiden who lost her lover and then threw herself off the edge of the world." He swept his hand toward the sky, alive with falling stars. "These are her tears, and she's cried 'em ever year since the earth was new."

"Tell me the story." She snuggled closer to him and pulled the edge of the blanket over herself tightly.

"There wuz two lovers from neighborin' villages, and their fathers had once been close friends, blood brothers, but for many years they were enemies. One of 'em had gone away over the mountains and had come back with a bride he had captured. She was so beautiful that his friend fell in love with her and wanted her so bad he could think of nothin' else. He found out that she was unhappy with her husband because he had stolen her away from her family and that she often cried at night because she wanted to go back to her people.

"So one day, the friend came and stole her, and she went with him because he promised her to go live with her and her people if she would be his wife. They made the long journey, but when they got there, they found out that her family and most of her people had been killed by an earthquake, and the rest had gone to live with a neighboring tribe. Since there was nobody left that the woman loved, she agreed to go back home with the man and live with him and take his family for her own.

"When they got back, her husband was real mad, and he swore that he would forever be enemies with his former brother, and from then on they never spoke or came to see one another.

"Years passed, and both of 'em had children. The man who had lost his bride to his friend married another woman and they had a daughter who had eyes so beautiful and lively they named her Singing Eyes. The other had a son, his name was Smoke on the Mountain, and since the two families never visited, the children never met.

"But one day, Smoke on the Mountain, grown into a young man, wuz huntin' and came across Singing Eyes as she was washin' her hair in the river. They fell in love and wanted to marry, but when her father found out, he swore he'd kill Smoke on the Mountain if he came near Singing Eyes again. So they met deep in the forest, where they planned to run away over the mountain together. Her father followed them with all his kin, and they chased 'em to the edge of the world. One of the men shot an arrow into the heart of Smoke on the Mountain, and Singing Eyes went mad with sorrow, and she threw herself off the cliff.

"She was much loved by her father, and he was so hurt and shamed by what he had done that he asked the spirits to help him find a way to protect other young lovers from the hate of their fathers. The spirits heard him and felt so sorry fer 'im that they turned her tears into fallin' stars, so they could be a reminder to fathers to listen to the hearts of their children."

"That's a very sad story."

"It's a very old one. There's a dance about it. I learned it when I was a boy. It is a dance that the braves of my mother's tribe dance on this night when they want to declare their love to a particular woman, 'specially if he's afeared her father might not approve of him, or if he feels he's not worthy of her. It's both a love song and dance and a sort of pleading for acceptance.

"Do you remember it?"

"Yes, and the song, too. My father, ye know, is white. He learned it to dance fer my mother, 'cause he knew if she married him he'd be takin' her away from the place she knew and loved. When I was little, he always danced it agin' fer her on the nights it rained stars."

Geneva felt a moment of anxious possessiveness. "Did you dance it for your wives?"

He did not move, but she felt him withdraw for a moment. When he spoke, his voice was soft. "No. With Sarah Grace, there wasn't no need. We were young, and so in love, we felt we were already one person, there was nothing that could separate us. And things moved so fast with Aster, I never got the chance."

Geneva was afraid to ask, but her need was great. "Would you show it to me?"

There was a long silence while Geneva and Howard turned their gaze toward the heavens raining white fire, then all at once, as if he had suddenly made up his mind, Howard rose, and lifting his arms toward the sky, began to sing softly. Geneva could not comprehend the words, but she felt the power of his feeling, and she watched with stilled breath as he began to move, slowly at first, then more rapidly until he at last was leaping and spinning around her. Sometimes his eyes held hers for long moments before he broke away and turned to sing to the heavens again, and sometimes he approached her with his eyes lowered, as if he feared or revered her. But always, there was a sense of overwhelming passion, mingled with hope and fear as he approached and fled and danced his mysterious dance around her.

She sat very still, comprehending nothing but the passion in Howard's voice and in his lithe, naked body as he wove among the falling stars. He was so beautiful she could have spent her life just watching him move so sensuously, and then, she felt compelled to stand, to feel herself closer to the stars and to feel the rhythm of his song. Slowly she rose, cold from the damp night, but she flung off the blankets and let the pulse of the sky and the song and the earth fill her until she felt herself grow warm and light, as if she had become part of the music, or as if she had become the chorus to give fullness to Howard's feeling. Breathlessly, she watched him and listened until at last, his voice rising to a painful wail, then softening to a note so low it felt like a caress, he stopped.

There was a silence, then he dropped to his knees before her and flung his arms around her thighs, burying his face in her belly. Slowly, he stood, lifting her high into the air. Without meaning to, she flung out her arms to embrace the night sky and lifted her face to watch the stars fly around her head. She was wearing a crown of stars. She was worshipped, she was alive with love and passion and desire and youth. Her flesh became immortal and her spirit sang like a river.

And then the stars stilled themselves, and Howard lowered her slowly and gently until their faces pressed close together. Hungrily, half crazed with desire, she clung to him, and he gave a little cry before his mouth found hers and the stars began to spin again.

They made love until the night grew pale and the meadowlark sang, then Howard pulled the blankets tightly around her and pulled her close with her face nestled in the hollow of his shoulder.

"Hit's gittin' on toward mornin'," he murmured.

"Hmm," she replied sleepily. "It's too cold to get up."

"You okay on this rock?"

"What rock?" I feel like I'm in a featherbed."

He chuckled. "They's critters out here could eat us. We'd better git on back."

She ignored him. "Howard?"

"Yeah?"

"I just realized, I don't really know who you are. I love what I know of you, but I've never known anyone like you. You seem to know all about me, but every time I think about you, I see so many different people, so many sides to you. I mean, you seem to belong to these hills, but you read philosophy and you know all about things, nature and literature, and cars and horses." She stopped, wondering if she could ever find his definition.

"My grandfather gave me the Cherokee name I carry. 'Anigia Hawinaditlv Tali Hilvsgielohi.' Hit means 'One Who Walks in Two Worlds.' I think at the time, he meant it to mean that I wuz both white and Cherokee, but now I think it fits in more ways than that."

Startled, she sat up. "That should be my name! I mean, I've felt it all my life. I want to be in so many places at once. Anigia—How do you say it?"

He repeated it slowly, " Anigia Hawinaditlv Tali Hilvsgielohi."

"Well, I can't say it, but that is me, too."

He tugged at her until she lay beside him again.

"No, your Cherokee name is 'Digvnasdi Atsilv Hawinaditlv Galvquodiadanvdo,' I'd say, 'One Who Strikes Fire In the Soul.' Fer me, that's your name."

She did not know how to answer. As far as she was concerned, that should be his name. Maybe they weren't so far apart in the things that really mattered. It seemed to her now that all the differences between them were merely superficialities, inconsequential little details. She stroked his smooth chest. "You strike fire in my soul."

He grew playful. "Well, hit's a good thing we got all this fire agoin', else we'd freeze to death out here. Maybe we kin git on back and put somma this fire onto some kindlin'. I don't want ye gittin' chilled again."

Reluctantly, she rose, and before she could begin shivering, he wrapped the blankets around her again. Together they walked back to the cabin where they slept as lovers, clinging to one another, even in the profoundest of sleep, dreaming of the other's touch and the rhythm of bodies, souls and spirits in perfect harmony. Deep into the morning they slept to the sound of all nature awakening and shouting their joy to the heavens.

When she woke, the sun was quite high. Before her eyes had opened and consciousness had come to light in her brain, her heart was singing. Something wonderful had happened to her in the night. She opened her eyes, smiling.

Howard, still naked, still beautiful, crouched before the fire. When he heard her move, he turned his face upon her and his eyes lit up with love. Geneva had never seen such happiness in anyone's face. He radiated joy so that his countenance was nearly unrecognizable as the man with whom she had spent these—how many?— days and nights.

He sprang to the bed and knelt, kissing her eyes and her face and stroking the arm that lay outside the blankets.

"Morning," she drawled, touching his face. She knew she was in love. There was no thinking about it or planning or even considering what it might mean. She was simply a river of happiness, flowing ceaselessly toward her beloved.

"Morning, darlin'."

"Go for a swim with me?"

He shook his head. "Breakfast is goin'. Besides," he added, lifting his arm to his face and inhaling deeply, "I don't want to wash the smell of you off me. Mmmm," he closed his eyes. "Geneva with mint. Makes my mouth water."

Happily, she sprang from the bed. "What's for breakfast?"

"Oatmeal and hoecake. Lord, woman, you make a man hungry. I cain't wait fer breakfast," and he dived for her and buried his face in her neck, making gobbling sounds until she shrieked with laughter and wrapped her arms around him.

She was happy, more than happy. She belonged here and to this man who made her feel so complete. Languidly, she breathed his scent, then suddenly pulled away and asked, "What was that you called me last night? Strikes Fire in the Soul? No, that's not right. That is your name. I'm that other one—Walks in Two Worlds. But not anymore! I just want to walk with you! You're the fire-starter!"

"Oh, no," he chided. "Ye cain't take a man's name away from him, and ye cain't step out of yer own name. Ye'll have to wear it the rest of yer life, now that it's yers."

"Okay, so tell me how you pronounce it, so I can come when you call me."

He crossed to the bookshelf and retrieved a notebook. "Here," he said, taking up a pencil. "Here's you, how it looks in Cherokee," and he wrote:

ᏗᎬᏂᏍᏗ ᎠᏥᎸ ᎭᏫᎾᏗᎸ ᎦᎸᏉᏗᎠᏛᏙᏙ

"Digvnasdi Atsilv Hawinaditlv Galvquodiadanvdo. Easy enough."

"For you, maybe. It's impossible for me!"

"And here's how my name looks," he continued, writing beneath the first:

ᎠᏂᎩᎠ ᎭᏫᎾᏗᎸ ᏔᎵ ᎯᎸᏍᎩᎡᎶᎯ

"Anigia hawinaditlv tali hilvsgielohi."

"And this is us together," she said, taking the pencil from him and encircling the two words in a heart. "But teach me how to say it. I want to know you, in every way. Anigia… hawin…."

"Anigia Hawinaditlv Tali Hilvsgeilohi. How about we shorten it to just Ta li—two? Call me that, and I promise I'll come arunnin'!"

"Ta li. I can handle that. Ok, now I'm off to my beauty bath. I have mud all over me." She kissed him lightly and scampered off to the creek.

She plunged into the water and swam around the large rock pool until she felt she had used enough energy to be able to contain the life surging through her. She stood for a moment beside the mint bed to let the water run and drip down her naked skin, smiling at the crushed and hollowed out place in the shape of their loving bodies. Then, lightly she ran back to the porch and snatched up her nearly dry panties off the rail. A sudden wave of happiness swarmed over her, and she could not help but execute a neat little priouette and glissade as she held up her panties to determine which side was the front.

She did not make that determination.

As she looked up, her vision was pulled beyond the elastic of her panties, beyond the porch rail and the steps and the zinc tub where she had bathed. Beyond it all, right to the ashen face of Howard Whittaker Graves, III.

She blinked, certain that he was an apparition, but when she refocused, he was still there, and behind him stood Jimmy Lee, Lilly, and Sally Beth, all open-mouthed and still as stones. Beside Jimmy Lee stood Lamentations, whining and looking anxiously at his master.

For a second Geneva stood in horrified disbelief, staring at the small crowd clustered at the edge of the forest, then slowly she lowered her panties and let her eye rove until she focused on Sally Beth's hot pink toenails peeking out of open toed, jeweled sandals. The reality of her situation suddenly hit her, and she turned and fled into the cabin, slamming the door behind her.

Howard was dressed, *thank God!* and setting the table for breakfast. He looked up to smile at her when he heard the door, but when he saw her face, the blood drained from his own.

"Oh, God! What have I done!" cried Geneva in a frenzied whisper. *"Oh God! What will I do?"* She grabbed a blanket from the bed and fled through the back door, heading for the deepest thicket she could find to hide from the source of her shame and dread. *Howard Graves!* How did he find her? What would he think of her here with Howard Knight! He would find out what they had done last night! He would laugh with such derision! *And Sally Beth and Lilly! They would tell everyone! Oh God!* How could she have been such a fool? *Howard Knight, of all people! No one would ever understand.* She wrapped herself tightly in the blanket, rocking

herself and wishing the earth would swallow her up. *Death would be preferable to this humiliation.* Then the hot tears came, and she dashed them away angrily. She did not deserve the luxury of tears! She would merely sit there and suffer until everyone disappeared. Then she could rise and make her way back down the mountain, and then perhaps to parts unknown to her, and more importantly, where she would be unknown to others.

She steeled herself to hide forever, but before many moments had passed, she shifted uncomfortably. The blanket was becoming too warm, and time seemed to be ticking its way by too tediously. How long would she have to sit there before she finally figured out a practical thing to do? Reason began to hint that the mess would not just disappear.

She heard her name. Sally Beth was approaching her hiding place. "Geneva? Geneva honey? Yew can come on out now. Howard explained everthing. We all know it looked a whole lot worse than it really is. Come on out now. I've got yer clothes."

Geneva's grateful ears pricked toward her cousin's voice. *Had she said Howard had made it sound not so bad?* Tentatively, she raised her head and called out, "Here I am. Sally Beth. Over here. Bring me my clothes."

Sally Beth approached her cautiously. "Goodness, you gave us such a *start!* Here we were expectin' to maybe find yew *dead,* and then *Boom!* There yew are, *buck nekked,* holding up your panties like yew had all the *time in the world* to step into them. I liked to have *died!* Your mama would *skin yew alive* if she could have seen yew! It's a good thing Howard told us all about it, or I bet Howard—yew know, the other one, yer boyfriend—would really *be mad!*

"I mean, he *was mad! Fit to be tied!* But he feels real bad now, since he found out how sick yew've been and all. He wants to see yew as soon's yew get dressed."

"He's not mad?" asked Geneva incredulously.

"*Gracious no!* I mean, we had *no idea* yew were sick! Howard just thought Howard—Knight—had *kidnapped* yew or something!

He *pitched a fit* all the way up here!"

"What did Howard—Knight—tell you?" ventured Geneva cautiously.

"*Oh!* He told us how yew'd had a *high fever for days!* How yew *nearly died!* And that yew've been out of yer head for these three or four days, so that he was afraid to leave yew and go get help. Oh, *Geneva!* It must have been *jist awful!* And yew *do* look *jist terrible!* You're just as *white*, and I can see yew've been feeling too bad to even comb *yer hair!* Yew look like a *haint!*"

Geneva's hand instinctively went to her tresses. "Do I really look that bad, Sally Beth?" she asked miserably.

"*Oh, Lord yes!* Yew look like yew've been wallerin' around in the bed for days! I mean, yew must have been in *terrible shape* not to even be able to *comb yer hair!* Now, here's your clothes, honey. Get on in them and we'll just go on back and I'll fix yew up real pretty so yew can face Howard. My goodness, Lilly's *still* tryin' to take him away from yew! Yew should have seen her comin' up here. *All over him,* she was! I jist *hate* how she can act like such a tramp sometimes. I mean, really! Trying to take a sick girl's boyfriend away from her while she's practically *on her deathbed!*"

Sally Beth chattered on thus while Geneva dressed with trembling hands. When she had finished, she made an attempt to pull some of the tangles out of her hair.

"Oh, just *leave* it. I'll fix it for yew when we get back. How yew *feeling*? Yew think yew can make it back down the mountain? It was just *awful* coming up here. It took us since *six o'clock this mornin'* to walk up here, and look, it's nearly *eleven* now! And we've been up *all night!* Howard was about to have the *FBI* out after yew after Jimmy Lee came by the house and told him Howard Knight's daddy had said the last he saw yew, yew and Howard had left on horseback together. And then we went up to Howard's place— that's a pretty little place, isn't it? And the horses were *still gone!* And your pocketbook sitting on the kitchen table! If Jimmy Lee hadn't agreed to help us look for yew, why Howard was going to call in the *FBI! He said so!*"

"Oh, no!" moaned Geneva. She could imagine the place swarming with search parties. "But why are you here? And Lilly?"

"Oh, we had come by the house last night to see the babies, and we saw that *cute* little car of Howard's there, and he was sittin' on the porch, just as pretty as yew please, and nobody home, so of course, Lilly, being the *little hussy* that she is, just had to sit there and talk to him for an hour! Anyway, along comes *Jimmy Lee?* She lowered her voice confidentially, "Geneva, I think yew may have a problem with Jimmy Lee. He was real surprised to find out that Howard was your boyfriend, and do yew know, he had come to court yew! Can yew imagine! His exact words! *Court yew!*

"Anyway, Howard asked him where yew could be and he said he didn't know, he had come by every day and every night to court yew since *Wednesday,* and yew hadn't been home at all! But he said he went up to his grammaw's house yesterday? And Howard's daddy—Howard Knight, that is—had told him he had seen yew take off on horseback with Howard on Wednesday afternoon, and he hadn't seen Howard since!

"So then, Howard—Graves—I declare, honey, this is gettin' confusing! He gets all mad and wants to take out after Howard and yew, and he threatens to *call the FBI* and get a *search party*—I told yew that part already—and Jimmy Lee got *real nervous* and said he thought he knew where yew might be.

"*Well!* By this time Howard's so worked up, he's about to *pop* something, and Lilly's acting all sweet and syrupy and says she'll go with them, and I jist decide to go along to keep an eye on her. I mean, mamma would *die* if she knew she went traipsing out all over the country with *two men!* And then she gets right in that little sports car with Howard, and I have to ride in Jimmy Lee's truck that has a *hole* in the floorboard! Yew get *sick* if yew look down! Yew can see the road *running right under yew!*

"Well, then we got to Howard's house about four in the morning, and of course yew aren't there, and the horses are gone, and Jimmy Lee tells Howard he'll take him to where yew might be if he'll promise not to call the FBI." She assumed the confidential whisper again. "Geneva, I think Jimmy Lee's got a still around here someplace. He was as nervous as a *cat* about comin' up here!"

"Anyhow, we take off walkin', and I had *no idea* we'd be this long in getting here! Seems like we just wandered around for *hours*, circling around and switching back, until Howard starts to act *suspicious*, and then we just came up to a clearing, and there yew were, not a *stitch on*, dancin' with your *panties!*" She giggled. "It was *so funny!* Yew coulda been standin' in your own bedroom, yew jist looked *right at home*, pickin' out your pretty pink panties with the little lace flowers on them!"

"Okay," snapped Geneva. "I get the picture. I'm ready to go back."

"Oh, *great!* But I don't know *how in the world* we're going to make it back with yew *sick* and all, and I'm so tired I could just lay down and die *right here!*"

Sally Beth did not look tired in the least. She looked like she had just walked away from the cosmetics counter at Belks. Her fine, fluffy hair was perfectly arranged into a towering pouf, and her eyes were as bright as a child's. And how had she walked for five hours up a mountain in those minuscule, jeweled sandals? Her feet were even clean!

"I don't feel sick anymore, Sally Beth. Howard's been treating me with medicinal herbs, and I think I'm well enough to get home. We have the horses here."

They took a long time to get back to the cabin. Geneva willed herself to take each step. Howard had done what he could to protect her reputation; now the rest was up to her. She said a silent thank you to him as she opened the cabin door.

They all stared at her, all but Howard Knight, who busied himself at the fire and did not even turn his head as she entered the room. "Geneva!" cried Howard Graves at last. "I've been worried sick about you. How are you feeling? Goodness, you're so pale. Howard here told us how sick you've been. Sit down."

She sat carefully, keeping her eyes down.

"I'm so sorry we surprised you like that. Howard said you'd

been begging for a bath but this was the first morning he'd let you go down to the creek since your illness."

She glanced at Howard Knight. He was concentrating very hard on something in the pan over the fire. The joy she had seen in his face an hour ago had vanished. He looked pale and haggard, and when at last his eyes glanced up and met hers, they were full of grief.

Suddenly, she did not care what anybody thought. She only cared that she was in love and that her lover was in pain. She wanted to run to him and embrace him and see the joy suffuse him again. She remembered the passion from the night before, and nearly cried out in her anguish. She still wanted him! She didn't care who he was or where he lived. No one had ever made her feel like she had felt in his arms last night. Never had she transcended herself, had moved into a sphere where she had stopped thinking and calculating and just let herself be carried along, as if she were riding on flaming horses. Nothing but feeling for him, nothing but happiness and fulfillment flooded her heart when she looked at him. She would tell them all the truth now, and she would stay here with Howard forever. It was enough to know that she loved him and that he loved her.

She looked at the expectant faces. "Everybody, it's true that I've been very sick. And Howard here has taken care of me, but I want you to know that last night…"

Howard Knight's voice broke in. "Miss Geneva, I think it's time for another cup of willer bark tea. We don't want yer fever comin' back, now. And since you'll be goin' back today, I'd like ta give ye some herbs ta take with ye. They're out back. Come on, and I'll explain how ta brew em up." He addressed the others. "Yew all go on and eat. I know yer about starved to death, and there ain't enough room around the table for all of us. Miss Geneva and I've been mincin' since early this mornin' and we ain't hungry right now. Come on, ma'am." He picked up a cup from the hearth, and taking Geneva's arm firmly, he ushered her out the back door.

They stood on the back porch facing each other for a long time before he spoke. Geneva did not like what she saw in his face. *Such sorrow.* She could not bear to see it after the gladness of the morning.

"Howard," she began, but he placed his fingers on her lips and whispered, "Now hush. They believed me when I told 'em yew've been sick and out of yer head. Let it sit at that."

"Howard, I love you! I want to stay here with you. I don't want anything to do with him!"

"Hush. Yes, yes, I know. I know yew love me. Yew loved me last night, and yew love me right this minute, and I can't tell ye what that means to me. And maybe ye'll even love me tomorrow, and when I think of that, I find such hope in here." He put his fist to his chest, then paused, and his face clouded.

"But there'll come a time when I'll be nothin' but an embarrassment to ye. An embarrassment and a regret. I know that. What could yew see in the likes of me? I cain't hold a candle to ye. I can't hold yew. Ye'd be miserable, and I can't live waitin' fer the day."

"No!" she protested.

"Yes. Now, yew just go on down that mountain with that feller and yew fergit about me." His eyes glistened with unspilled tears. "I ain't sayin' ye need ta marry him. I'm just saying ye need time ta figure out what ye want. Ye need a chance ta find yer own happiness."

"Howard, I found it last night. Please."

"You ain't been listening to me, darlin'. We're too different."

"You mean you don't want me? You don't love me?" He was breaking her heart.

He almost smiled. "Geneva, I've wanted yew since the minute I first laid eyes on ye. And I've laid awake nights lovin' yew ever since yew chased me around the barn alaughin' at me. A man kin love a shooting star all day long, but that don't mean he kin have it. He kin grab onto it maybe, for a minute, and he kin feel its flame aburnin' him with such sweetness that he can't think of nothin' else, but that don't mean he kin take it to his heart and make it a part of him."

She fell silent, grieving at his words.

He swallowed hard. "Now, I been thinkin," he began, and his voice shook. "Ye might could git pregnant, and I know ye don't want that, complicate things even worse. Ye kin drink this," he said, indicating the cup filled with a vile-looking liquid, and it'll stop anything that might be started." He drew a shaky breath and licked his lips.

Pregnant? Geneva had not even considered the possibility. Last night had taken her so completely unaware, she had been so overcome with her desire that she had not thought of any possible consequences. Not pregnancy, not Howard Graves, not even any tomorrow. She stared at the cup.

"Take it," he urged. His hands were beginning to shake. "It might make ye a little sick at first, but that's all. Yew won't know one way or the other. Yew kin just think there never was no baby." He saw the pain in her face. "There probly ain't, anyway," he added gently.

She lifted her eyes to his. Tears were streaming down, but his face was impassive, unreadable. It looked like water running over a stone. She felt the wetness of her own face as she stared at the cup in his hands, wondering if she might at this moment be carrying Howard's child. The thought was unbearably sweet, and she felt her heart lift, but when she looked at his face and saw nothing but blank sorrow, she lifted her hands to take the cup. When she touched it, she suddenly felt the weight of a burdened and miserable spirit. Never had she felt so much a sense of sin, the horror of the wrongs she had done to this gentle man and to herself. He still held the cup, then, slowly, as if he were willing himself to die, released it to her. Without a word she lifted it to her lips and drank the bitter death. He watched her drain it, then silently disappeared into the forest.

She was completely alone. So great was her despair that she did not even allow herself the luxury of crying. Tears were for cleansing, and she knew she could never be cleansed of this pain, this guilt which rose up and enveloped her like a slimy black shroud stinking of corruption. She leaned her head against the pillar and felt despair engulf her so completely that her senses finally dulled.

Howard Graves opened the back door.

"Geneva, darling. You look so sick. Come inside and sit down. I've never seen you this pale. Please, come inside. I'm worried about you."

"I'm okay, Howard. Just tired." She lifted her eyes. "I want to go home now. I can't stay here any longer."

"Of course. We'll leave right away. Could you eat a bite first? We could put you on a horse, and the rest of us can walk. We'll make it."

"Yes. Ask Howard if he'll saddle up for me," she said wearily. I'll be fine. But I'm not hungry. Just let me lie down for a while."

She could see the concern in his face. "Certainly. Let me help you inside."

She could not lie down. Her body was not ill; only her heart was sick and heavy with grief, and it made her too restless to lie still. Tossing on the herb-scented bed, all she could think about was Howard's hands on her, and the way they both had been so transformed by joy. The bitter cup and the tears in her lover's eyes loomed before her. She rose and paced the floor.

"Feeling better?" asked Sally Beth.

"Yes, some."

"Well, good. Let me fix your hair a little. You'll feel a whole lot better in a jiffy. Here. I got a brush, and a curling iron, and oh, Lordy, *all kinds* of things in here." She rummaged around in a huge purse, pulling out all manner of beauty aids. Geneva looked at them dumbly.

She started to shake her head, no she did not want her hair fixed, but was startled by a sudden explosion and the "thwak!" of splintering wood.

"*Hey!*" yelled Jimmy Lee. Everyone looked up in time to see several window panes explode. Lilly screamed, looking horrified at her hand, which held only the handle of a cup.

"Oh, hell! Somebody's ashootin' at us! Hit th' floor!" Jimmy Lee shouted. "Git away from the winders! We been ambushed!"

Everyone dived for the floor, everyone except Sally Beth, who simply moved to the center of the room directly behind the big oak front door and sat down on one of the tree-stump stools. She plopped her huge purse in her lap and waited demurely.

There were terrible growling and snapping sounds out on the front porch. Jimmy Lee cursed, then dived for the door, flung it open, and within two seconds had dragged in Lamentations and slammed the door behind him. The dog was snarling and snapping. As soon as Jimmy Lee released him, he resumed what he had obviously been doing out on the front porch: chasing his severed tail with all the frenzy of a maddened beast. Lilly screamed again and huddled beside Howard Graves in the corner of the room. Sally Beth put her fist on her hip and gazed around her, a puzzled expression on her baby doll face.

"What is it?" cried Howard Graves. "What's going on?"

Jimmy Lee crouched by the front window and peered out. "Don't rightly know. Somebody's after us." He raised his head slightly and shouted through the broken window, "Hey! Hey yew!" He waved his hand in the direction of the roaring dog. "Shut up, Lamentations!"

"Hey yersef!" came a female voice.

"Whatcher want?" called Jimmy Lee

"I wanna kill yew, Jimmy Lee Land!" came the voice. "I'll teach yew ta be runnin' around on me!"

There was a silence except for the sounds emitted by the frenzied dog. "Myrtle?" Jimmy Lee said at last. His voice had lost a good bit of its strength.

"I'll kill ye, yew bastard. Runnin' around on me, air ye? I tole ye I'd kill ye, and I meant it. I seen ye with them little yeller haired thangs. Yew cain't git by with that!"

"Lamentations! *Quit it!* Igod, yew are the dumbest damn dog I ever laid eyes on. Somebody gimme somethin' ta knock some sense into that animal." He put his face near the window. "Myrtle!" he shouted. "Did yew foller me up here?"

"Haw. I sure's hell did. Follered ye since early this mornin'. I seen ye with them hussies. And now I'm gonna kill ye!" The last sentence was punctuated with another blast. The windows were gone, so all anyone heard was several pellets embedding themselves in furniture and walls. Lamentations renewed his effort to destroy his rear end. Already there was fresh blood drenching the stump.

Howard Knight burst in through the back door. "Lord amercy, Jimmy Lee," he said, his voice full of disgust. "First ye bring three people up here, knowin' ye ain't even supposed to *talk* about this place, and now ye let yerself be followed by that damn woman. Now git on out there and tell her to quit shootin' at us. Somebody's likely to git hurt!"

"Chap, I cain't go out thar now," whined Jimmy Lee. "Hell, she's mad enough to kill me. Yew heard her!"

"Jimmy Lee, *I'm* mad enough ta kill ye. Now yew talk some sense into that woman before I start shootin' back! Lamentations, *shut up!* Jimmy Lee. Cain't yew shut that dog up?"

"I'm acomin in!" came the voice outside.

"No yew ain't!" shouted Howard Knight. He yanked his rifle from the wall rack and held it loosely. "I got a loaded Winchester right here, and I'm aimin' it right at this here winder, and I swear I'll blow yer head off if yew so much as come into the clearin'." He slapped at Lamentations with a dishcloth. Geneva wished he really would point the gun. This did not look like the time or place to be bluffing.

There was a long silence from outside. Finally Myrtle spoke again. "Awright. I ain't comin' in. Jist send that no good somebitch out here and let me blow his balls off. Yew do, and I won't shoot no more."

Long pause. Lamentations slowed down. Howard whacked at him halfheartedly a few more times with the towel, then turned to Jimmy Lee. "Well," he said. "Yew heard her. Git on out there. She's gonna blow us all to hell if yew don't."

Jimmy Lee squirmed. "Aw, Chap. She might really do it. Yew

see how mad she is." His face brightened. "Yew go talk to her."

Howard's disgust grew. "She don't want me, yew idiot! I go out there, it'll just make her madder. Now quit bein' a coward and go on out there!"

"Chap, I swear, I never seen her this mad. Last time she got mad at me she liked to have broke me in two. What if she shoots me?"

"She ain't gonna shoot yew. She just wants ye ta tell her ye love her and ye ain't been messin' with anybody else. Now go on!"

Another shotgun blast pelted the cabin. Lamentations took off after his tail again.

"Huh uh," Jimmy Lee shook his head. "I'ma waitin' thisun out. *Lamentations!*"

Sally Beth suddenly stood up. "*Well!*" she exclaimed. Looks like we're gonna be here awhile. No need jist sittin' around. Geneva honey, yew jist come on over here, and I'll fix yer hair while we're waitin'."

This is it, thought Geneva. *The most absurd situation I have ever been in in my entire life. I might as well get my hair done. If I get killed, at least I'll look decent.* She sat herself down on Sally Beth's tree stump.

"How about a nice little French braid? Or I've got a curling iron right here in my purse. Oh, my! What did yew wash yer hair in? It smells like *mint!* Oh, Geneva, yew got *knots in here!* It'll take me forever to get all these tangles out!"

"Yew comin' out, Jimmy Lee?" The voice from outside sounded dangerous.

"Now, honey!" shouted Jimmy Lee. "Yew know I won't come out long as yer threatenin' to shoot my balls off. Soon's yew calm down, I'll come out and we kin talk peaceable."

"I ain't gonna talk peaceable! I *am* gonna shoot yer balls off. Goddam man. I leave yew fer one minute and yew take off after ever hussy fer miles around. I know all about that woman yew've been runnin' after. And now yew got her up here, and yew expectin' me not to git mad? Come out here and take what's comin' to ye!"

"I think she's talking about yew, Geneva," said Sally Beth

conspiratorially, working patiently at a troublesome tangle. "Jimmy Lee's said some pretty nice things about yew. Word's bound to get out."

Howard Graves appealed to Howard Knight. "Looks like she could be here for awhile. Any chance we could escape out the back? Did you get the horses ready?"

A shadow of a smile passed across Howard Knight's sorrowful face. "Yeah. I got 'im ready. All saddled up. They're probly halfway back home by now."

"You mean?"

"Nothin like a shotgun blast to spook a horse. I chased 'em more'n half a mile, but they meant business."

"Shit," said Howard Graves. "Lamentations, *shut up!*"

"I think a French braid will be best. Yew need a conditioning *bad*, and I hate to dry it out more by rolling it. These cordless curling irons get a lot hotter than the regular kind. Yew want the braid to go under or over?"

Howard Knight fluttered the towel around Lamentations' head. The dog slowed, then dropped in his tracks, panting. "Good dog," he commented absently.

"Over," decided Geneva.

"Okay. Yew can put on a little makeup while I'm working. Look there in my bag. I think the rose coral lipstick will be best. It will give yew a little glow. And that peachy blush. And yew need eyeliner, bad, girl. Your eyes have jist *disappeared!*"

Lilly joined in. "No, I think eyeliner looks tacky n the woods. Sally Beth, you look all painted up like a Bourbon Street whore. No wonder that woman out there thinks Jimmy Lee's cheatin' on her.

"Jimmy Lee? Yew comin out? I kin sit out here till dark, and then I kin come in and git ye. I do, and they won't be enough left fer chicken feed."

"Lilly, I do *not* look like any *Bourbon Street whore!* Yew don't even know what a Bourbon Street whore looks like! Yew've never even been to Memphis."

"New Orleans, Sally Beth," sighed Geneva.

"New Orleans, either."

"I've seen pictures!"

"Yeah? Where?"

"*National Geographic.*"

"Well, that's not the same! They probly fixed themselves up nice 'cause they knew they were getting their picture taken."

"*Jimmy Lee!!!*" Myrtle's voice had risen to a bellow.

Howard Graves shot a naked appeal to Howard Knight. "Isn't there anything you can do?"

Howard Knight thought for a moment, then sighed. "All right. Jimmy Lee. Yew tell her yer comin' out, but yew don't want anybody to get hurt, so she needs to meet ye down by yer house. Change shirts with me, and gimme yer hat. I'll take off runnin' out the back, and she'll think it's yew, bad as her eyes are, and she'll probly will take off after me. I kin outrun her, and yew caint, so I'll jist lead her far enough away so yew all kin git on away. Knowin' her, she'll git good and lost. Got that?"

Jimmy Lee nodded.

"And make sure yew keep Lamentations quiet till she gits out of earshot." He lowered his voice to an inaudible threat. "Stay off the trail. Cut back and confuse the path, ye hear?"

Jimmy Lee nodded again. "I did that comin' up, too." Geneva knew they were discussing ways to keep her cousins and Howard Graves from ever finding this place again.

Howard, her Howard, her beloved, had not looked at Geneva since he had entered the room. Now he glanced in her direction. "Geneva's gonna be hungry. The rest of yew had a good breakfast." Quickly he gathered up some warm bread, beef jerky, and something from a tin. These he put in a bag, and, eyes downcast, handed it to her. "There's willer bark in there. About a tablespoon to a cup o' water. Steep it five minutes. Or yew kin just chew it."

She did not move, but merely looked at him until he lifted his eyes to hers. His face was a mask, a perfect blank; his eyes looked like dull, black plastic buttons. She searched for the life behind them, desperately, but futilely. Slowly she took the bag from him.

"Now holler at her," he commanded

Jimmy Lee took a deep breath and hollered. "Myrtle, honey, darlin'! Yew know I love ye! And I aim ta marry with ye!" He looked apologetically at Geneva. "I don't mean that, Miss Geneva. I'm jist tryin' ta git her ta stop this shootin'," he whispered. He turned back to the window. "I'm acomin' out! But yer a bad shot, and I don't want nobody in here gittin' hurt if yew go shootin' at me! And I don't want ye shootin' at me neither! I'm atakin' off right now, out th' back, and I'll meet ye t'home! Y'hear?"

Sally Beth put her hand on her hip and narrowed her eyes at Jimmy Lee. "*Shame on yew,* Jimmy Lee! No wonder that poor girl is shootin' at yew. Yew got no business telling lies like that, and then flirtin' your head off with Geneva. Hold still, Geneva," she continued without a pause and produced a can of hair spray from her copious bag. "I just need to spray yew."

Jimmy Lee looked contrite but said nothing.

"Well, I'm gone," said Howard Knight. "Git out quick as ye kin," and he raced out the back door, slamming it hard behind him. Lamentations growled. Jimmy Lee flung himself at the dog and held his muzzle. Through the window, Geneva saw a streak in the forest. It became a woman running around to the back of the cabin. Looking out the back, she saw her disappear into the woods.

"Okay," said Jimmy Lee. "She's gone. If we high tail it now, we'll make it back afore dark. Come on!" he urged, flinging open the front door and racing for the cover of the trees.

Eleven

They traveled in a more or less direct line within the cover of the deep woods for about an hour, then Jimmy Lee subtly changed directions, taking the travelers in large loops and switching back and forth several times. Sometimes he crossed nearly nonexistent trails, then followed them for brief periods before he left them again and cut through wild territory. Geneva admired his ability to confound the others, for no one but she seemed to notice that they were not headed in a direct route toward civilization. She did not mind. The more confused their trail, the safer Howard's secret. She followed Jimmy Lee and Lamentations quietly.

Howard Graves did not speak to her much, perhaps mindful of her illness, she thought, perhaps because he sensed her desire to keep silent. *Or maybe he knew what was in her heart.* Sally Beth and Lilly lingered along behind, bickering but little. Everyone seemed to be wrapped in his or her own thoughts as they descended the mountain.

About mid-afternoon it began to rain. Sally Beth produced a little plastic hat out of her magical purse; the others were forced to slog on miserably through the downpour. Geneva did not care about the physical discomforts; her heart pained her so badly she hardly noticed the water streaming down her face and shoulders. With all of her soul she wanted to go back, back to the waterfall, to the mint bed, to Howard's arms, but her feet carried her forward, farther and farther away from him, down this mountain, and away from her only hope of happiness. Down toward civilization, away, away. She moved through the weeping sky, dreading more and more the end of her journey.

Howard Graves occasionally expressed concern for her; he feared she would chill, would be fatigued, would stumble on the streaming trail, but she ignored him, merely walking on with her head down and her shoulders hunched.

The rain let up, but then a deep, dank fog rolled in, swallowing each of them into their own gray cocoons isolated from one another save for their voices, which called back and forth eerily in the mists. Sally Beth and Lilly caught up, instinctively fearing to lose their way. Jimmy Lee halted until everyone had gathered closely.

"There's a little, narra trail right cheer, and I'm afeered it'll be slip'ry. Innybody skeered o'heights?"

"I am," came Lilly's timid voice. She looked little and miserable, shivering in the damp cold, peering fearfully ahead into the mist. A sheer cliff loomed up darkly on their left, and a thin trail wound beside it. To the right of the trail, the mountain dropped off into nothing but mist.

Sally Beth spoke up. "She really is a fraidy cat, Jimmy Lee, and sometimes she just freezes up in high places. I cain't do a thing with her. If I lead, will yew and Howard help her?"

Geneva realized they were shielding her from responsibility. All they expected of her was to cling to the cliff and get herself across the treacherous part. She felt bad about not being more helpful, but too enervated to offer more. She stood silently.

"Jimmy Lee, you didn't bring us up this way. Why do we have to go across this at all?" questioned Howard Graves.

Jimmy Lee looked away. "This way's a little quicker, and I figured we'd better git on down in a hurry. This bad place don't last long. Mebe thirty feet. Hit widens out agin real quick."

"Okay," sighed Howard. "You lead Lilly, and I'll come behind her. Geneva, will you be all right? Can you make it?"

She felt irritated at his solicitousness. "Of course, Howard. There's nothing to it. The trail's at least two feet wide. Lilly's just got a problem with heights. Just make her close her eyes."

Sally Beth adjusted her voluminous purse and started off confidently, but slowly along the rock face into the mist. The trail was not particularly dangerous; it was level and wide, and smooth enough to traverse safely if one did not step too close to the edge. Geneva kept one hand on the rock wall to her left and peered off to her right into misty nothingness. There was no telling how far this precipice dropped off. Moving closer to the safety of the rock face, she raked her foot through some loose shale and stumbled slightly. She caught herself before she fell, but a rock and some loose dirt had rolled into her shoe.

"Just a minute, Sally Beth, I've got a rock in my shoe," she said, standing on one foot and trying to rake it out with her forefinger. "I can't get it. Here, hold on to me while I take my shoe off."

"Cain't it wait?" asked Sally Beth. "It cain't be much farther."

Jimmy Lee halted. He was holding one of Lilly's hands; Howard held the other. When they stopped, Lilly disengaged her hand from Jimmy Lee's and, turning to Howard, buried her face in his chest. His arms came up automatically, wrapping tightly around her, and holding her close, he leaned her against the solid rock. They all stood quietly while Geneva lifted the irritated foot, but Lamentations, who brought up the rear, growled suddenly and frightfully, the hackles raising.

"No, it's sharp, and it won't take a minute," Geneva replied, unlacing her shoe and removing it. "Here, you get it out. This fog is making me dizzy. And, oh, I've got dirt all over the bottom of my sock. Lamentations, don't worry. I'm just taking a rock out of my shoe. Don't get all bent out of shape." Standing on one foot, she handed her shoe to Sally Beth and bent to dust the gravel and dirt away, then carefully she straightened and reached for her shoe again.

Her eyes looked up, then gazed three feet beyond Sally Beth's shoulder. She gasped and froze in horror, for there, looming out of the mist, seemingly as tall as a mountain, stood a massive black bear, up on his hind feet and clawing at the rock face just beyond Sally Beth's little turquoise plastic hat. The creature opened his ugly red mouth and roared.

Sally Beth whirled, catching sight of the shaggy, wet menace. Within an infinitely small space of time, she screamed, threw Geneva's shoe at the bear, and ran hard into Geneva, who fell back onto Jimmy Lee, who fell over the side of the cliff.

General panic followed as Sally Beth and Geneva, screaming and insane with terror, crowded onto Lilly and Howard. Upon seeing the bear, Howard fled, yanking Lilly after him, and raced back along the trail in the direction from which they had come. No one stopped running until they had reached the safety of the forest and had scattered in all directions. Geneva and Sally Beth each climbed a tree, and Howard and Lilly cowered in a hawthorn thicket. They waited five, then ten minutes, hearts pounding, but the bear did not appear. Lamentations had vanished. No one wanted to mention Jimmy Lee's name.

At last, Sally Beth broke the silence, her contrite voice drifting through the trees. "Sorry about yer shoe, Geneva." She paused, then added, "It was an Eddie Bauer, too."

Geneva looked down at her shoeless right foot. They were in trouble now. What had happened to Jimmy Lee? How could she get down the mountain without her shoe? How could any of them find their way back without Jimmy Lee? She fought to keep the panic from rising past her chest.

Sally Beth was moving along the forest floor, calling out, "It's okay. Ya'll can come on out now. That old bear is long gone by now; Lamentations must've chased him away. Geneva? Where are yew, honey? I really am sorry about yer shoe. Lilly? Howard? Ya'll can come out, now."

Geneva made her way out of the hickory tree. Stepping onto the wet ground, she grimaced as her sock wicked dampness up the sides of her foot. She gritted her teeth, determined to ignore it.

They found Howard and Lilly still crouching under the hawthorn. Lilly was sobbing into Howard's chest, and he was stroking her hair and rocking her like a baby. Sally Beth and Geneva stood watching her through eyes glowing with grief and fear for Jimmy Lee, but neither of them would articulate what they dreaded. At last Geneva sighed, and said in a small, wavering voice, "I guess we'd better go back and see if we can find Jimmy Lee. Maybe he survived the fall," she added hopefully. "The fog's lifting anyway, so we can see a little better."

It was true. The wind had picked up and was blowing away the deep, shrouding mist. They could see the blue sky revealing itself above them, and lambent sunshine filtering through the trees.

"I'm not going back on that trail again!" wailed Lilly. "I'm waitin' right here until somebody comes to find us!"

Geneva considered this. No doubt Howard Knight would find them, although it could take him some time since he would not know the direction they had taken. Jimmy Lee's careful path, which did not even resemble a trail, would no doubt prove impossible to follow. Dogs might work, though, she mused. She winced, thinking of yet another search party after her. *How long would Howard be able to keep his gold mine a secret with people swarming over these mountains?* She furrowed her forehead in dismay. She had caused everyone so much trouble, and it seemed it would never end.

Howard Graves stood up. "I'll go find Jimmy Lee. Geneva, you and Sally Beth stay here with Lilly."

Geneva was moved by his bravery. "I'll go with you, Howard."

"I'm goin', too," announced Sally Beth. "Jimmy Lee may be hurt real bad, and yew'll need all the help yew can get."

Everyone looked at Lilly. She sniffled a few more times, then dried her eyes and looked at them defiantly. "Well, I'll be darned if I'm going to be a crybaby about this. I guess I'll go, too." She stood up and tossed back her wet hair.

They all feared to the marrow the worst about Jimmy Lee, but they murmured hopeful scenarios among themselves as they headed back toward the precipice. Again and again Geneva's mind replayed the scene of his slight body falling through the cold mist. Jimmy Lee surely was dead. Who knew how high that cliff was? No doubt he would not be found for days, his poor body mangled and torn by the awful fall. Geneva shuddered at the thought. Poor Jimmy Lee! His death was her fault! She lowered her eyes sorrowfully to the trail and fought back the tears. *She was a pitiful excuse for a human being.*

Before they had reached the cliff, Lamentations met them, whining and wagging his nub of a tail.

"Lamentations!" cried Geneva, "I'm so glad you didn't go over, too!" The dog licked her hand, then, still whining and wagging, he asked her to follow him back to the place Jimmy Lee had fallen.

Sunshine poured down. The narrow ledge suddenly looked wider and far less treacherous. Lilly hung back, but the others followed Lamentations, half eager to see where Jimmy Lee had fallen, half dreading it as well. Quickly they made their way after the dog.

For the first few paces along the trail, the rock dropped off for a hundred feet or more, but when they reached the spot where Jimmy Lee had fallen, they could look down and see a very large ledge, not fifteen feet below them. It was more than ten feet across and perhaps ten feet deep. Jimmy Lee was lying on his side beside a small pool. Water gushed from the side of the mountain into this pool, and in turn, the pool emptied into a small waterfall cascading silently over the side of the ledge into a vast emptiness. Geneva was so glad to see Jimmy Lee lying a mere five yards away that she nearly forgot her fear for his safety.

Lamentations barked, wagging his rear end furiously. Jimmy Lee moaned and moved slightly. Geneva scanned the rock below her to see if she could find a way to him. Yes. On the trail was an irregular place, and below that was another and another. She felt sure she could climb down to him. Quickly she ran up the trail and swung herself over the side.

"Oh, God, Geneva, be careful!" cried Howard, following her up the trail, then pausing to peer anxiously over the side when she began her descent. Sally Beth sat down and dangled her legs off the side of the cliff.

The way down was fairly easy. Geneva was grateful at the thickness of her sock, which cushioned her shoeless right foot against the sharp shale. She reached Jimmy Lee quickly.

"Jimmy Lee," she said, kneeling down beside him and touching his head. He was warm, but pale, and blood trickled out of his mouth. She took his hand and felt for the pulse. It beat reasonably strong. Moaning, Jimmy Lee turned to her and opened his eyes. A light came on in his face. "Oh, Miss Geneva," he sighed. "Yew really are my guardian angel. Ever since yew come in my life, yer allus there when I'm adyin' or in trouble, and yew allus save me." He grew rapt. "God musta give yew ta me. I'll never stop lovin' yew. Never."

Geneva winced. Twice he had been injured, and both times it had been entirely her fault. And the poor boy could see only goodness in her.

Lamentations was pacing along the top of the cliff, whining and trying to find a place to descend.

"Jimmy Lee, you just lie still." Geneva's voice was shaking with fear and anger for herself. "Where do you hurt?"

"Nowheres," he smiled, the light in his face growing brighter. "Now yer here, I don't hurt nowheres."

"Can you sit up? Does your head hurt? Jimmy Lee. Talk to me! Can you feel your arms and legs?" Her gaze ran down the length of his body and stopped at the shin of his left leg where there was a noticeable bulge underneath the denim. When her hands went to the spot, he yelped with pain and his face grew paler.

"Oh, Jimmy Lee, it's broken, and it looks bad. Have you got a knife so I can cut away your pants?"

"In my pocket," he gasped. He was beginning to feel all of his wounds.

The knife was not in his left pocket, and when Geneva tried to roll him over enough to try the other side, he groaned. Geneva stopped to think.

"How is he?" called down Sally Beth.

Geneva arched her neck upward. "He's got a broken leg, but that's all I can tell right now. Do any of you have a knife?"

"I do," called Sally Beth. She rummaged around in her purse and produced a Swiss Army knife, which she tossed down to Geneva. "Hold on," she added. "I'm coming down. Lamentations, yew stay here. Yew cain't make it down there."

The dog sat whining, while Sally Beth eased herself down the rock face. Geneva knelt by Jimmy Lee's leg and very carefully began cutting at the heavy denim, but he cried out when she tugged the knife upward. Sally Beth joined her presently, and so did Howard.

"Wait jist a minute," cautioned Sally Beth. "I have some scissors here in my pocketbook. They're real sharp, too. I carry 'em with me everywhere in case somebody needs a haircut." She began rummaging again.

"Sally Beth, do you keep a whole life in there?" asked Geneva. "How on earth can you carry all that stuff?"

"Oh, yew get used to it," she answered mildly. "Here they are!" She triumphantly held up a pair of hair cutting scissors encased in plastic, then, very methodically, she removed them from their case and began cutting away at Jimmy Lee's pants. He remained still while she cut a slit to the knee and peeled the denim back to reveal a bulging break at the shin. It was not a compound fracture, not quite, for the bone had not made its way through the flesh, but it was a very bad break indeed. It was obvious Jimmy Lee was not walking anywhere.

Sally Beth sighed. "I cain't set a broken bone. Leastways not a break this bad. Can yew, Geneva?" Geneva shook her head. "Howard?"

He looked stricken at the thought. Sally Beth thought briefly and continued, "Well, Lilly's no good either. I reckon we'll jist have to tie it up best we can so he cain't move it. And I reckon we might as well get Lilly down here. No use leavin' her up there to fall apart waiting for us. We'll need some sticks. Geneva, yew and Howard go get some. I'll go back for Lilly so we can decide what to do."

Geneva's estimation of her silly cousin moved up several notches. Nodding, she moved toward the rock face, but Howard stopped her. "I'll go," he said. You stay here with Jimmy Lee. Didn't Howard give you some medicines? Is there something in there to ease his pain some?" He indicated the bag tied around Geneva's belt loop.

"Of course. Willow bark. If I had a cup, I could mix it in water. It's terribly bitter, especially if you chew it."

"I have a cup," said Sally Beth. "And I have some aspirin, and some Tylenol, too."

Somehow, with much pleading and encouraging, they got the whimpering Lilly down to the ledge, put a splint on Jimmy Lee's leg, and gave him enough aspirin and Tylenol to ease his pain. Geneva wiped away the blood on his face and discovered, to her relief, that it came from a cut lip. He was also bruised and scraped but otherwise unharmed. Geneva began to feel hopeful, but worry descended again when she realized that the afternoon was growing late. Howard, too, was becoming anxious. He glanced up at Lamentations, who lay with his head hanging mournfully over the edge of the cliff. "You suppose that dog could go for help?" he asked Jimmy Lee.

Jimmy Lee grinned. "Why shore! Hey! Lamentations?" Lamentations jumped up quickly and peered eagerly down at his master's face. "Go fer help, boy! Go on home! Bring back Chap!"

The dog responded immediately. He circled around a few times, looking around him, then he grinned and panted back in Jimmy Lee's direction. Excitedly, he tried to descend the cliff.

"No! Lamentations! Go fer help! Go git Chap. Go on, boy!"

Lamentations was puzzled. He sat down, his head cocked to one side, and looked at the group below him. "GO ON!" they all yelled. Lamentations gave them one mournful look and departed.

"Thank goodness," sighed Geneva. "Maybe he'll get home before nightfall and get Howard or somebody back up here. Sure hope we don't have to spend the night here."

"How far is it, Jimmy Lee?" asked Howard.

Jimmy Lee's face clouded. "Not far," he said evasively. He kin git there and back in a hour, I reckon.

Sally Beth stood up. "Well," she declared briskly, "We'd better be prepared just in case. Howard might not be home, and once it gets dark, nobody's going to find us here. Why don't we try to build a fire, and fix us up something to eat."

Geneva, suddenly ravenous, remembered that she had not eaten since the evening before. A cold pain clutched at her as the thought of the jerky and bread Howard had packed for her this morning. "Yes. I have some food," she said, pulling the little bag from her belt.

"So do I," said Sally Beth. "Yew never know when yer going to get hungry." A bag of trail mix and a box of Fig Newtons appeared magically from her purse.

They were just beginning to portion out the food when they heard a whine from above.

"Lamentations!" cried Jimmy Lee. "What are yew adoin' back here? Yer supposed to go git Chap!"

Lamentations wagged his stump pitifully and cocked his head, then tried to scramble down to the small group below him.

"Jimmy Lee," said Howard sadly, "I'm afraid your dog isn't very smart."

Jimmy Lee looked sheepish. "Hit ain't his fault. A eagle caught him when he was jist a pup and dropped him on his head." He gazed at the women with a naked pleading. "He's a good dog," he asserted mournfully. "Jist ain't got much sense."

"Do you think he's capable of getting his own dinner?" asked Howard.

Jimmy Lee grimaced apologetically.

"Okay," said Howard. "It's obvious he wants to be down here with you, so I'm going to see if I can get him down. Anybody want to help? Got any ideas?"

"I do!" cried Sally Beth. "We could make a *chain!* Yew know, Yew and me and Geneva and Lilly can climb up part way and pass him on down to each other?"

"Nuh uh. Not me," said Lilly, shaking her head and cowering as far from the edge as she could. "I cain't believe I got down here myself. I'm not going to climb up anywhere after a dog."

"You don't have to," encouraged Geneva. "We'll bring him down most of the way. You just climb up about two feet and catch him."

"I believe I can get him to one of you, then I can climb down below and catch him again," added Howard. "Shall we try it?"

Somehow they got Lamentations, carried and coaxed, down the precipice. Immediately he ran to Jimmy Lee and began licking his face.

"Yeah, yer a good old dog," murmured Jimmy Lee. "Stupid as hell, but a good old dog."

Lamentations sniffed at Jimmy Lee, then pressed himself up close by his side. He laid his head on Jimmy Lee's shoulder and sighed.

Howard interrupted the reunion, "It looks like we may be spending the night here. I doubt if they will search for us much today, if at all. Howard may not even know we're missing if he went back to his cabin." He bit off a hunk of beef jerky and chewed thoughtfully.

Lilly put her head on her knees and wept softly.

"Oh, Lilly, quit being such a *sissy*," admonished Sally Beth. "We'll get outta here tomorrow anyway, and we can build us up a big fire and pretend we're camping out!".

"I'm jist tired," sighed Lilly.

"I didn't say we couldn't *sleep!*" her sister cried. "And *look!* We've got plenty of water. Shoot, yew can even take a *bath* if yew want to."

Lilly just kept her head on her knees and rolled her head a little.

"Aw, Lilly. Come on, be a sport," she coaxed. "I'll do yer nails fer yew."

Geneva was tired, too, so tired of spirit that she wanted to die. Being here was not horrible in itself. She had spent nights in the woods before, and she knew they were safe perched on this ledge on the high precipice. Surely the bear would not return and venture down the cliff face. But the darkness in her heart overwhelmed her and made her want to cry out for her lover, to call and call, like a whippoorwill, until the echoes reverberated across the mountains and hollows and he came to her. She gazed at the horizon and found no joy in her soul.

Howard Graves put his hand on her shoulder. "You feeling bad, sweetheart? Do you want some Tylenol?"

"No, I'm fine, Howard. I'm a little blue, is all." She smiled wearily. "I appreciate your coming to look for me. Sorry I've caused you all this trouble."

He smiled a strangely gentle smile and followed Geneva's gaze out over the distant blue. "Would you believe me if I said this is no trouble for me? Being out here has been invigorating. I can see why you love it here."

He stood. "But it'll get cold tonight, and we need to see about getting a fire going. Want to help me gather wood?"

"Sure. But everything's wet. I don't know if we can get anything to burn."

"Maybe so. Let's see what we can find up on the trail. If we can get enough dry stuff to get a good blaze going, maybe the damp wood will burn if it's not too wet."

"I'll help," added Sally Beth. "Lilly, yew stay here and take care of Jimmy Lee."

"Yes, I need to find my shoe, too, if I can," said Geneva. "I sure hate the thought of walking all the way home with one bare foot."

They set out in search of wood and Geneva's shoe. They did find reasonably dry wood in the hollows of rocks, but the shoe did not materialize. Wearily, Geneva returned to the ledge to sort through slightly damp pine knots and cedar splinters. Jimmy Lee patiently whittled out enough cedar shavings to lay out a hopeful fire start.

They added some larger, damp, but not soaked, firewood. The rest they stockpiled to last the night.

"Sally Beth, do you have any matches?" asked Howard, winking at Geneva.

"Why, sure. Right in here somewhere."

Before long they had constructed a nice fire, which blazed merrily in the cooling dusk. They ate the rest of their food and drank from the spring gushing out of the side of the mountain, then watched the stars come out and the moon climb over the far ridges. Sally Beth gave Jimmy Lee more aspirin and they moved in close to the fire, huddling together to keep off the chill. Howard stirred the coals and settled back next to Geneva.

"Well, that was a pretty good supper, considering," said Lilly thoughtfully. "But to tell yew the truth, I could go for some real food—even for some of Miss Nancy's pet chicken."

Sally Beth laughed. "Me too. I probly could eat the whole thing myself right here and now."

"Who's Miss Nancy?" asked Geneva.

Sally Beth laughed again. "I don't know if yew ever met her. She was Grandmamma Tate's neighbor for a while, before she *moved!*"

Lilly hooted at this.

Geneva perked up. "There's got to be a story here I haven't heard before."

Sally Beth began, "Well, there was this *chicken…*"

"No, Sally Beth, yew have to start from the beginning," broke in Lilly. "Let me tell it." She turned to the others, her face alight with pleasure. "Well, it all started the summer Sally Beth turned sixteen. She flunked her driver's license test…"

"I didn't know yew had to take a *written test!*" exclaimed Sally Beth. "Shoot, I'd been drivin' since I was twelve, and I could drive better'n anybody in the family, even Daddy!"

"Well, that's what yew get for not tellin' anybody yew was going to take the thing," asserted Lilly. She turned to the others. "She'd been drivin' for so long without a license that everybody sort of forgot that she needed to get one. But the day after her sixteenth birthday, she decides to get one, so she puts me in the car and we go down to the courthouse. And she marches herself in and says, 'I want a driver's license.' And the deputy there says, 'Well, little lady, yew've come to the right place. Where's yer mama or yer daddy?'

"Well, we had to admit that we hadn't brought anybody along with us, and of course he figured out in about two seconds that she had driven down to the courthouse without a license." Lilly began to giggle. "But Sally Beth just stands right up to him and declares she'd been driving better'n anybody in the family since she was twelve, and somehow talks him into letting her take the test, thinking that all she'd have to do was drive around the block. Yew should have seen her face when he tells her to sit down and take a written test!"

"It was *awful*," asserted Sally Beth. "It took me completely by surprise! I bet I didn't get half of them right!"

Lilly went on. "So then, when she ups and fails it, the deputy gets all hot and tells her she'd better never let him catch her driving without a license, or there'd be hell to pay, and then he won't let us drive back, but puts us in the squad car and takes us home himself. Daddy had to go pick up the car down at the station!" At this Sally Beth and Lilly broke into gales of laughter.

"So what does this have to do with Miss Nancy and her chicken?" asked Geneva.

"*Oh!*" exclaimed Sally Beth. "The next day we went over to Grandmamma Tate's. I drove, of course, 'cause it was only a coupla miles, but she wasn't there, so we just decided to wait on her. Then Lilly sees this cute boy next door at Miss Nancy's, come to find out he's her *nephew*, and Lilly, she gets to *flirting* with him, and then she ups and invites him over for *supper* that night! But then we get to thinking about what we'll have, and we have no idea when Grandmamma will be back, and we get to thinking maybe we'd better do something *ourselves*, but there isn't much in the house that would make a company kind of supper, so we decide to drive to the store and get some chicken."

"Now, remember," broke in Lilly. "I'm just fourteen, and Sally

Beth has flunked her driver's license test the day before, but who cared about what that silly old deputy had said? He couldn't stop us from getting in the car and taking off. Well, we get to the end of the driveway and Sally Beth's about to pull out into the road, when guess who drives by. The deputy who had just told Sally Beth the day before that he'd better not catch her drivin'!

"Well, he just about busted something getting his car stopped and gettin' over to us, and he was all red and hollerin', and tells us he's going to arrest us both. And Sally Beth just *sits there* as calm as an ice cube, and when he finishes, she just says, 'Deputy, I'm jist driving up and down my grandmamma's driveway, and this is private property, and yew can't stop me.' Which was true, but that made him even hotter, and he said he was going to park his car right on the road there and make sure she didn't try to drive anywhere outside that driveway, so we had no choice but to go on back to the house."

"By that time it's about three o'clock," added Sally Beth. "And we still didn't have anything for a company dinner, and then Lilly sees this funny little chicken running out in the yard, and she gets the bright idea to catch it and fry it up."

Lilly giggled. "It seemed like a real good idea at the time. But have yew ever tried to catch a chicken?" she asked the group in general. They all laughed, except Howard, who looked askance and asked, "What's so hard about that?"

The others just laughed harder. Jimmy Lee slapped his thigh, then winced and moaned.

"What did you do?" asked Geneva.

"Well, we chased it around for about half a hour," said Lilly, "and then when it was getting obvious that we weren't going to get anywhere, Sally Beth went in and got Grandpa's shotgun and came charging out to shoot it. She missed, of course, but got birdshot in the cow's rump, which she tried to get out with tweezers…"

"I did get it out!" declared Sally Beth. "By that time, yew were too excited to remember anything! I got it out and rubbed it down with alcohol, and Grandmamma never even noticed the Band-Aids

I put on it!"

Geneva stifled a snort.

"Anyway, we ended up catching the chicken," continued Lilly. "Sally Beth got out Grandpa's fish net and caught it on the fly. But catching it turned out to be the easy part!"

"Shoot, the rest was easy for *yew!*" asserted Sally Beth. "After we caught the thing, we didn't know how to kill it. I wanted to chop off its head, 'cause I knew if I shot it up close it would be full of birdshot and not fit to eat, but Lilly wouldn't hold it, and she wouldn't chop, either, so finally I had to put my foot on it and try to chop it off all by myself. But just as the ax came down, it jerked away, and I only got about *half* of its neck chopped."

She began laughing uncontrollably and slapped her knee several times. "Oh, it was *awful!* Blood was *squirting* out *everywhere*, and the chicken took off running with its head sort of *flopped over*, jist sorta hanging on by its skin! And Lilly started *puking*, and then she *passed out* right there in the back yard! I was afraid the chicken would get away, and I didn't know what to do about Lilly, so I jist grabbed the chicken, and honey, blood was just *squirting* out! And Lilly was laying there, dead to the world, so I had this squirting chicken in one hand, with its little legs moving like they was still runnin', and Lilly in the other hand, and me trying to bring her to! Yew can *just imagine!*"

Lilly took over again. "By that time, I didn't care if we ever ate again or not, but Sally Beth just threw water on me then told me to go lay down, but I couldn't even make it to the living room, so I just laid on the kitchen floor, and Sally Beth, she set about to plucking this chicken because she said she'd be damned if a scrawny little chicken got the best of her. It had these real long, downy feathers, so she decided to save them and make a pillow, so once she plucked it, she put all the feathers in a bag, and then she skinned it and gutted it and cooked the thing. Made a chicken pot pie with mashed potatoes and gravy and all the fixin's. She was real proud of herself."

Sally Beth laughed. "It really did turn out right tasty. And this boy just *bragged* on it all through supper, and then I made the mistake of telling the story of how we got it."

"'Course we all just laughed and laughed, and then Grandpa got real quiet for a minute, and then he said, *'That wasn't our chicken!'* Lilly screamed with laughter and she and Sally Beth leaned against each other and laughed until they had to wipe their eyes.

"And of course that made us laugh all the harder," choked out Sally Beth, "until this boy, what was his name, Lilly?"

"Charles," her sister prompted. "Charles Harris. How could yew forget his name?"

"Oh, yeah. Charles. Anyway, all of a sudden, he stops with his fork halfway to his mouth, and he says, 'Was it a Silkie chicken?'"

"We just looked at each other. We'd never heard of that kind before, and he said, 'Long, fluffy feathers, more like fur than feathers?' And we had to say 'yes', and he turned just as white, and he put his fork down, and said, 'That's my Aunt Nancy's pet chicken, Geraldine! She's been searching all day for it.'"

Both girls broke into mighty gales of laughter again, and Geneva and the men caught their hysteria. "And then, the worst thing was," chortled Lilly, "that Sally Beth got up and gave him the bag of feathers she had plucked off it and said, 'Here, I know yer Aunt Nancy will be wanting this!'"

They all laughed until their sides and faces ached, and then they continued to giggle for several moments as they calmed and the fire burned low.

Sally Beth sighed deeply and started to say something, but instead she gasped. "Look!" she cried, pointing up. "A *shooting star!* Oh, and there's another one! And another! It's a *meteor shower!*"

Geneva felt the sudden stab of memory. Howard's long, lean body worshipping her as meteors arched across the black sky. Howard leaping and singing and holding her high as she threw back her head and drank in the wild, sweet night air. Howard loving her and filling her with pleasure and happiness with all that he had to give. She nearly groaned in her agony, but she bit back the tears and listened quietly as the others exclaimed and the night wore on.

Presently, they quieted in the face of the night's splendor, and in the silence, Lilly began humming in her sweet, low voice. Sally Beth joined in with a soprano harmony, and soon they had merged their voices into a lovely old song Geneva remembered hearing at her grandmother's knee.

> *Though the mountain is high and the valley deep*
> *Though there's wind and there's rain and there's snow.*
> *I come to you with my love to keep*
> *On trails through sunshine, starshine, and willow*
>
> *On trails of willow, I'll come to you*
> *Though the darkness blind me and the sunshine burn*
> *Through trails of willow, my heart stays true.*
> *And for your love I'll always yearn*

Howard put his arm around her, and Geneva fought the tears as she thought of the other Howard somewhere in these mountains, watching these falling stars and thinking of her. It was almost more than she could bear, listening to the old, beloved melody and staring into the fire. At last she put her head on her knees and hugged her grief unto herself. Presently, the tears began to roll silently.

"What's the matter, Geneva? Are you sick?" came Howard's voice beside her.

"Oh, Howard, I'm just confused. You wouldn't understand."

"I think I might." He hesitated, then continued, "Something happened up there on that mountain, didn't it?"

Geneva did not answer.

"It's okay. He's a good man. And I haven't been. I guess I have a lot to learn about the people here." His arm tightened around her. "I've already learned that I'm not better than them. I used to think that I was a good judge of people. Now I realize I've had my head up my ass most of my life." He stopped while they both stared at the fire, then continued, "I like it here. If I came here to live, would I have a chance with you?"

This last comment so astonished Geneva that her tears ceased and she stared at him in disbelief. He chuckled.

"Surprise," he sang out softly. "I'm not saying I'd exactly be in my element. Lord knows, I couldn't take up any worthwhile trade fitting for here, but you can be a stock market analyst anywhere. And I'm willing to do it for your sake, if you'll have me.

"You've got to be kidding. You'd never survive here. Besides, I'm not so sure I like you here. You're a city slicker." She rubbed at the dull ache in her forehead.

"I know that. But Geneva, I'm willing to fight for you. If I could get you back to DC, I know I'd stand a better chance, but where things stand now, I'll take whatever comes. Of course, if you would agree to come back with me, I promise you I'll make it all up to you. We could buy a house in the suburbs, or even a nice little cottage in Maine, or here, or wherever you want, so we could get away. We wouldn't have to be city dwellers all the time. Just enough to keep life interesting. What do you say?"

"Howard, this is beyond me. I don't know what to think."

"Me either. I just know that I've changed my priorities over the last few days. When I left Hutterton, I was so mad that I wanted to come back and just lay waste to everything in this state. I even called my lawyer and tried to initiate a lawsuit. And when I came back to find you last night, I was ready to tell you that you weren't good enough for me.

"But when it became evident that you were missing, I had a complete change of heart. I realized how much I love you, and I just started thinking about how fragile we are and how we try to insulate ourselves from really living—and loving. And how stupid we can be," he added. "I had always thought that money is power. Being in these woods makes me realize how silly even the concept of money is." He chuckled again. "I've got about five hundred dollars in my wallet. I'd gladly have burned it if it meant getting this fire going."

Geneva spoke slowly. "Howard, I'm glad to see you feeling sorted out this way, but I have to tell you..." He put his fingers on her lips.

"Hush. Not now, darling. I know I'm competing with a man twice, three times my size. But I also know that he doesn't know how much better he is than I am."

"What makes you say he's better than you?"

He gazed into the darkening night. "He doesn't lie very well, especially about you. I could see how much it took out of him to say what he did to protect you, and yet he did without hesitating. I almost think he would have fought me to the death if I had questioned his defense of you." He smiled. "I remember how I acted that day in Hutterton when I accused you of having something going with Jimmy Lee, and I don't think I compare very well." He let a few silent moments slide by. "Besides," he went on. "The measure of a man sometimes lies in how a woman feels about him. And I saw the way you looked at him." He looked away and rubbed his chin thoughtfully.

"You don't think badly of me?"

He said lightly, "If I made you feel guilty right now, would it help my case? But no. I can never think badly of you. I love you. The thoughts of what happened between you tears my guts out, but I don't blame you."

Sally Beth's pure, high voice floated around them and lent a sweetness to the night. Geneva listened to the sounds and thought about Howard's words. She wanted to tell him how much she loved Howard Knight, but he began speaking again.

"Time and place change things. I'm hoping that once we get back to civilization, you'll see that you really belong with me. I understand the draw this place has for you. Every time I look at the distant hills or come up on another waterfall, I find myself thinking of coming here to live. I could stand it. The work I do seems awfully shallow to me right now. But wherever you are, Geneva, I intend to court you as gallantly as I can. And I hope you'll be able to find some goodness in me to love again."

She did not answer, but let herself be absorbed into the falling quietness. In the drowsy moments that followed, Sally Beth spoke up quietly, "I think maybe we all ought to pray."

Geneva sat up and glanced around. Sally Beth, sitting close by Jimmy Lee, looked expectantly at the others. "It's going to be a long night, and Jimmy Lee could use some healin'. We should pray over him."

Lilly sighed. "Sally Beth, yew are always prayin', ever since you got to be a preacher. Do you reckon it will do any good? I mean, really?"

"Sure it will do some good," answered her sister. "Prayin' always does good."

"Sally Beth, you are a preacher?" asked Geneva incredulously. The girl was full of surprises. "How did that happen?"

"Oh, it wasn't a big deal or anything. Last summer when Ruth Leigh wanted to git married up on Jacob's Bald, the preacher couldn't make it 'cause he'd had a stroke, and so I got ordained so she wouldn't be disappointed. Nobody else wanted to do it. That's all."

"But your church let you do that? They let women get ordained?"

"Oh, shoot, Geneva. Quakers don't care if a preacher is a man or a woman. We're all the same in God's eyes, and He just looks at our hearts. Now, who wants to pray first?"

They all prayed, one at a time, encouraged by Sally Beth. Even Howard lifted his voice up into the night and asked for deliverance and for healing for Jimmy Lee, and Geneva felt her soul quiet as each spoke in turn. Jimmy Lee glowed with gratitude, then, as the prayers ended, each of them settled easily onto the hard ground and listened as Sally Beth and Lilly once again took up their sweet harmonies. Geneva though it was too bad they couldn't get along in life like they did in song. She let the music and the sounds of the night wash over her while stars rained down upon them and the moon rode across the horizon. She fell asleep in Howard's arms, dreaming of the other one.

Twelve

Morning was slow in coming. Geneva woke several times, squirming on the hard rock where they slept and wondering where Howard Knight might be at that moment. She could see him asleep, or standing poised upon the rock and plunging into the deep pool. She saw him riding through the forest in the moonlight, searching for her. She longed to see him riding toward her. She could feel herself being lifted up on the back of the galloping horse, and then together they would ride away deep into the forest where they could love one another far away from the sullied world. When at last the sun rose, she stumbled to her feet, bleary eyed and even more miserable than the night before.

Sally Beth was already stirring. Jimmy Lee and Lilly still slept. Howard Graves opened his eyes the moment Geneva sat up.

"Morning," he smiled. "Did you sleep well on your downy bed?"

She forced herself to smile. "Goodness me, was that down? I kept thinking there was a small, hard lump in there somewhere, and so I hardly slept a wink."

"Well, princess, I'll have to buy you another bed. We can't stand any lumps in your mattresses, now, can we?"

She smiled again wearily and made her way to the rock pool where she washed her face and drank some water. It was cool and good after the hard night, but she wished for one of Howard's sweetgum toothbrushes. Sally Beth joined her at the water's edge. Plopping her kangaroo purse down beside her, she rummaged through it until she pulled out a brush, a mirror, a few items of makeup, some soap and sundry items of personal hygiene. At last she pulled out a toothbrush, which she loaded up from a tube of toothpaste.

"Hey! You've got a toothbrush!"

"Of course I do. Don't yew carry one with yew? Yew know you're supposed to brush after every meal. If yew don't yew can get cavities!"

Lilly appeared on the other side of Sally Beth. "Oh, Sally Beth! A toothbrush! Please, let me use it!"

"Use my *toothbrush?* Lilly, are yew out of your mind? I don't want your *germs* all over it!"

"Come on, please, I'm your sister, for Pete's sake. I'll buy you another one."

"No!" She held it as far out of Lilly's reach as she could get it, which happened to be in front of Geneva's nose. Geneva's mouth watered. She had not brushed her teeth with toothpaste in days. The pristine little brush waved in front of her, all loaded up with the delicious smelling toothpaste, and she could practically taste the fresh, sweet cleanliness of it. It was impossible to resist. She grabbed it from Sally Beth's hand and stuck it in her mouth.

"Geneva Lenoir! I'm going to *kill yew!* Yew give that back this instant!"

Brushing her teeth as fast as she could, Geneva danced away from Sally Beth, who tried to tackle Geneva. They both fell in the water. Lilly shrieked and jumped in after them, fighting both Sally Beth and Geneva for the toothbrush. She wrestled it away from Geneva, then dropped it. Geneva and Sally Beth both lunged for it, knocking heads. Lilly took advantage of the situation, grabbing it away from both of them and hauling herself out of the pool. She stood by the side, dripping, holding the toothbrush high over her heard.

"Got it!" she yelled triumphantly.

Sally Beth narrowed her eyes and tightened her mouth. "Give it back, Lilly! Yew should have brought yer own toothbrush if you're so desperate for one!"

Geneva, easing her way out of the pool, eyes on the toothbrush, inched her way closer to Lilly.

"Yew stay right there!" Lilly cried, but Geneva lunged, and grabbing it, she scurried close to the edge of the precipice, holding the toothbrush over empty air. "Stop, or I'll throw it over!" she shouted at her cousins, who were advancing on her. The sisters halted. "Come on, Geneva, give it here," begged Sally Beth. "I'll *die* if I cain't brush my teeth!" She eased forward.

"Nuh-uh! I'll drop it, I swear I will!" Geneva looked behind her to where the water fell a hundred feet into a rocky stream. "Nobody'll get it down there. You might as well let me use it, and then I'll give it back."

Sally Beth hesitated. "Well, it's already been in your dirty old mouth." She curled her lips in disgust. "And yew've been *sick*. Who knows what yew've got. But go ahead. Maybe I can boil it or something," she grumbled.

"I'm not sick any more, Sally Beth. I haven't had any fever for two days now. I promise, I'm perfectly healthy."

"Please, Sally Beth, can I please have it after you? I promise I'll buy you a new one," wheedled Lilly.

Sally Beth's disgust grew. "Okay. But I cain't believe yew two. Using somebody else's toothbrush. *Ugh!*" She shuddered.

Geneva brushed her teeth in peace, relishing the taste of toothpaste and the feel of slick, clean teeth. She ran her tongue over them and smiled happily. Nothing like basic comforts.

Sally Beth took out her little collapsible tin cup, and filling it with water, placed it in the hot coals. As soon as Geneva relinquished the treasured item, Sally Beth plopped it in the cup and waited for it to steam, then when she deemed it sterile, she shot Geneva a disgusted look and moved to the pool, where she brushed her teeth vigorously. Lilly waited her turn nicely. Jimmy Lee and Howard chuckled at the women, then Howard shook his head and climbed up to the top of the cliff and disappeared.

He returned half an hour later with some huckleberries that he shared all around. "There's more up there, if you ladies want to go looking for them. It wouldn't hurt to get some more firewood, too. Jimmy Lee should be kept as warm as possible, and it feels like it's going to be cool for a while yet." He looked at Geneva's wet clothing and added, "You ladies should dry out, too."

Geneva stretched and rubbed the back of her neck. "Yes. Let's go look for some berries, and get some firewood while we're at it. It could be a while before they find us." She glanced at Jimmy Lee. "You all go on, she added. "I want to make sure Jimmy Lee's comfortable, then I'll join you. Now, hurry," she added as they hesitated. "This wood is getting really low."

She watched them as they climbed up the precipice, Sally Beth and Howard helping Lilly over the treacherous places. When they had reached the top, she squatted down beside Jimmy Lee.

"Jimmy Lee," she said in a low voice. "I know all about Howard's mine, and I swear I'll never tell a soul about it. And I don't know how long it will be before anybody finds us, especially since you went to such great pains to lose the trail. Can you tell me how to get out of here? Is there a trail I can take?"

Jimmy Lee looked at her thoughtfully. "Chap never told nobody about that mine," he said slowly. "Nobody but family. He made me swear I never would, neither."

"I know. But I found out about it, and he told me the whole story. He even let me help him sluice some, and he tried to pay me, but I wouldn't take any gold because I was afraid somebody would see it and figure out where it came from. I swear, Jimmy Lee," she whispered urgently. "Tell me how to get out of here. I'll go alone, if there's a direct route. We're out of food. And your leg needs attention," she added. It was true. His leg was already turning dark, and she could see that the splintered bone had begun working its way through the flesh in his shin. Jimmy Lee could not wait a day or two for help.

Jimmy Lee looked at her with mute, appealing eyes, nakedly adoring. She flinched at the rawness of his feeling. "I cain't let ye go, Miss Geneva. Hit's too dangerous, and there's a hunnert ways to git lost. I think yer about the bravest lady in th' world, but I cain't let ye go. If inny thing happened to ye… Oh, Lordy, I'd sooner die."

"Please, Jimmy Lee," she begged more urgently. "I can take care of myself. What about this stream? If I follow it, will it take me anywhere?" she asked, indicating the white water flowing over the edge of the cliff.

He eyed it carefully. "Yes. This here's the crick that flows down to Chap's house. But hit's hard to foller—hit switches back and forth a lot through thick places and hit branches off in wet weather. I ain't sure I could tell ye how to foller it right." He shifted slightly and winced. Geneva knew his leg must hurt terribly. She could see the suffering in his face.

"Jimmy Lee. If we wait here, how long will it be before anybody finds us? Don't you think that Howard—Chap may not have gone back home, but back up to the cabin? There was no need for him to go back once he led Myrtle away. It could be days before anybody finds us. By that time, your leg could be too bad to save."

He shook his head. "Hit ain't my laig I'm worried about. Hit's yew. Yew git lost up here, or slip on a rock, or fall off someplace. Or, Lord, God, what if yew run acrost another bear?"

"Jimmy Lee, how much farther can it be? Surely I can get there by noon if I leave now."

He shook his head again. "Not follerin th' crick. There's a straighter way, but I don't think ye could find yer way. Th' crick winds around too much. Could take ye hours. No ma'am, he said stubbornly. "Yer safer here. Even if we haveta wait a day or two, we're better off here, together, where hit's safe."

She saw she would get nowhere with him. "Okay, Jimmy Lee. You win. I won't ask you again. Now you just lie here, and I'm going to catch up with the others to look for berries." She rose and made her way to the place where she could climb up to the rocky ledge. She had all the information she was going to get, and she feared for his very life if they waited any longer. She shuddered as she remembered the story of Laurel who had lain in the forest for more than a day with a compound fracture and had died. She would not have Jimmy Lee on her conscience. Resolutely, she hurried up the rocky trail and looked for a way to slip back down below the precipice to where the water fell.

The trail leveled off after a short way, and soon the cliff to her right began to fall off less sharply, and trees grew up out of the loose, rocky soil. She knew if the trees thickened enough to give her hand holds, she could make it down, no matter how steep the incline. Quickly, she walked until the rocky shale gave way to humus and good soil, and the scraggly growth grew lush. Huge trees afforded her secure places by which to make her way downward; their roots sometimes made steps for an easy descent. She left the rocky ledge and struck off downhill, literally running into tress, which stopped her from falling down the incline. Sometimes the going was easy, and it was never exactly treacherous as she worked her way back toward where she thought the stream would be. If she could just get there, she would follow it to Howard's house.

Her heart lightened at the thought of seeing him, and she prayed that he would be home. If only she could see him once more, to have the chance to tell him again how she loved him! Surely he would hear her this time. Surely he would not turn her away again. She thought of the way his eyes gentled when he looked at her, at the feel of his smooth skin under her palms, of the softness of his lips. She flung herself into the next tree. Rounding it, she heard the water straight ahead, and the ground leveled off into a nearly flat little valley. Carefully, she threaded her way through a mighty oak grove toward the sound of running water.

Yes, there it was, just ahead. Surely, it was the same stream by which they had camped the night before. But she should not take any chances. She would work her way back upstream until she could look up and see it falling over the ledge. Then she would hurry downstream as fast as she could and make as much progress as possible before the others missed her. No need to make them worry any longer than necessary. If she made good time, surely she would find help by early afternoon, earlier if Howard were at home. She remembered her Mazda. She could drive for help, but she did not know how to get to Lenora and Ike's house. And it would be impossible to tell anyone how to find the little lost group up high on the ledge. She prayed that Howard would be home. This time her need was more urgent as she thought of Jimmy Lee's injured leg.

She stayed by the creek bank and walked upstream until she found the place she was looking for. Sure enough, above her, the water spilled down a hundred foot cliff of sheer rock face and over the small ledge that had miraculously saved Jimmy Lee. From her vantage, she could not see anyone on the ledge, but she could see the ledge itself plainly outlined against the cliff. Just above it was the scrabbled path they had used to climb up and down, and above that was the scar in the face of the rock that had been the main trail. Assured that she was on the right track, she turned back downstream.

The going along the creek bank was rough, but she knew better than to get into the swift water. A fall could mean a broken leg, and the rocks looked as slippery as oil. It would be better to make her way through the dense rhododendron and laurel, even though it meant slow, torturous going. Sometimes she had to get down and crawl, but she knew she would be better off staying within earshot of the creek. It was her only guide. If she lost it, she would merely have to go back to find it again.

After nearly an hour, the rhododendron hell gave way to a rocky slope, with poor, ragged trees scattered desolately upon its surface. The stream flowed smoothly beside her across the rock, then slipped noisily over the side. Another waterfall. She inched her way carefully forward to peer over the edge. A fifteen or twenty foot drop. She would have to go around. Carefully, she picked her way back up the incline, keeping her eyes open for a good place to veer away and find a more suitable descent.

She turned back into the woods to try to pick her way through the dense underbrush back from the waterfall, but the way continued to be steep for a good while. She walked until she could no longer hear the water, then decided to find a way down the slope without going any farther. If she lost the stream, she would also lose her way.

Leaning against a tree, she peered downward to try to gauge the incline. If she could hang on to low branches and the sturdy roots of trees and bushes, she could make her way without too much difficulty. The earth was soft here; there was no danger of slipping on rocks and plummeting. The worst that could happen would be a bit of a slide. Very carefully, she inched herself downward until her feet could no longer resist the pull of gravity. She sat on her haunches and grabbed for the first tree, then swung herself from limb to root to bush, making her way down the mountain. She reached for a clump of Joe Pye weed, erect and proud, with its blossoms just beginning to burst open, then moved her other hand downward toward a dead limb standing drunkenly askew from an ironwood. Just when she thought her hold was secure, the limb snapped and she tumbled down the hill, grasping desperately at bushes and weeds along the way.

After what seemed like several minutes of plummeting and sliding through the dark, rich humus, she finally managed to get her feet under her. She slid all the way to the base of the slope on her feet and backside.

She looked at her hands. The heels were scraped raw. They stung but did not bleed much. Her shoeless right foot felt terribly strained, but she lifted it and worked it carefully. Nothing bad wrong. It would not be comfortable walking on it, but it was not sprained.

Hastily, she picked her way back toward the direction of the stream, and found it only after having crawled through a cedar thicket so dense and sticky that she thought she would be scratched to pieces before she could find her way out again. By the time she made it to the stream, she was so filthy she could no longer identify the color of her pants. Sap and grime clung to her skin and hair; when she tried to push her hair out of her face, the sap on her hands stuck to it.

But at last she heard, then saw, the blessed stream. She was hot and thirsty. The sticky sap attracted insects, and she was itchy and miserable all over.

Limping, she entered a clearing caused by poor, rocky soil where nothing but butterfly weed and snakeroot grew. Through this the stream tumbled madly. By now she had been gone longer than she had thought it would take to get to Howard Knight's house, and she realized that she probably had not come very far over the rugged terrain. The sun was high, and her shoeless right foot was caked with mud and loose rocks. Wearily, she removed the sock and washed it, then put her foot in the icy water, scrubbing the mud away from between the toes. There was a deep purple bruise and a raw scrape on her ankle, and the whole foot was throbbing and hot. She soaked it in the creek while she splashed water on her arms and face. The sun had turned the day hot, and although she remembered what Howard had told her about drinking so far from a pure spring, she was so thirsty that she was willing to take her chances. If she came down with Weil's disease, she would pay for it later. But she was not certain that wild boar really existed in these hills, anyway. She had never seen one, although Howard had told her about them, and she had heard plenty of mountain folk talk about how they wreaked havoc over the fecund woods.

The clear, cold water was just too tempting, and her thirst emboldened her. As she bent her head and cupped her hand to take the fresh, white water, she heard a crashing in the trees across the stream, and the very beast whose existence she had just denied came trotting across the rocky slope toward her.

She made herself as small as possible and inched backwards,

hoping the beast would not see her. But the wind shifted, and he suddenly lifted his head and poised, listening for noise in the air. His little, vile head with the razor sharp tusks tossed, then paused until he could see her with his little pig eyes.

He was about twenty-five feet away, with the stream between them, and he looked huge and mean as hell. Geneva backed away slowly, hoping it would not cross the water. She did not know how aggressive wild boars were, but the look of those tusks terrified her. She drew in a breath, telling herself not to run unless he made a break in her direction.

No sooner had she thought this, than the animal actually did charge at her. Snorting and growling savagely, it lowered its head and ran straight for the stream. Geneva scrambled backwards and ran for the safety of a medium sized tree just behind her. It would not offer her much shelter, but it was the best to be hoped for on such short notice. She made it in time to see the hog splashing through the stream, still charging straight at her.

Searching ahead of her into the better protection of the fertile soil where the larger trees grew, she darted across the granite earth, leaping over rocks and scraggy little bushes. At one point she stopped just behind a large boulder and glanced back behind her to see if the animal were still chasing her.

It had stopped, but to her horror, it was very close, only about ten feet away—close enough for Geneva to see the short bristles on the top of its head and the small split hooves, caked with filth. The beast stared at her through eyes running with matter. Mucous streamed from its nose, too, so copiously that when he slung his ugly head, she could see it fly from its face and spatter the nearby bushes. Abandoned by all possible sources of help, she stood alone in the clearing. She knew she was lost, and she was more afraid than she had ever been in her life. The forest seemed exceptionally still and silent as she tried to pull her eyes from the terrible face, violent with hatred.

The deep forest was just behind her. Only a few yards away stood a giant tulip poplar, a tree so large that had there been three of her, she could not have circumscribed it with her arms. Gently, trying to glide almost without touching the earth, Geneva took one step away from the small safety of the boulder. Immediately, the boar seemed to explode, charging at her with the energy of a hundred thundering horses, his eyes glaring red and horrible as he anticipated her blood.

She leaped, then ran. The massive tree stood like a beacon of hope against the mindless charge of the raging boar, and to that beacon she fled, offering all her trust to its mighty trunk. She gained safety behind it just as the animal reached her, then it rushed by. Geneva felt its hot, foul breath as it flung its razor tusks at her. There was a resounding thud and a cracking sound as the tusks ripped deep into the flesh of the tree. Geneva's knees turned to water. She leaned against the solid safety of the poplar, and forced herself to turn and discover where the beast had stopped.

He was a scant ten feet away, perfectly still, regarding her with what seemed to be supreme irritation. Geneva could sense it considering, weighing the possible events of the next charge. In the eyes of the beast glimmered a malevolent intelligence that told her she might not be able to dodge him again. Perhaps this time he would circle the tree; he would slice her lovely legs just below the hip. Geneva let her horrified gaze fall to the fresh, deep gash in the tree trunk, wickedly clean, with the bark peeled away, exposing the flesh of the soft, yellow wood. From the wound, sap welled and bled down into the forest floor. The tree could still stand after such a brutal attack. She would not. Already, she could imagine the fragile flesh ripping away from the bone, then the bone itself snapping before the massive weight of that flailing head.

In the pause before the boar took aim to begin its next assault, Geneva felt her blood screaming its anguish with each beat of her terrified heart. She saw the slime running from the beast's snout as he studied her.

Was it possible to outsmart it a second time? A dozen or more feet away stood a ragged pine with a low, solid branch not far above Geneva's head. With her thoughts nearly inaudible above the pounding of her heart, she tried to calculate the distance and the time it would take to reach it, but her brain refused to work. A split second later, the boar charged again, and without hope, but with courage born of the desire to live, she leaped to the other side of the tree, just far enough to be partly visible from the pig's vantage. The animal altered his course instantly, zeroing in on his target with the accuracy of a heat-seeking missile.

Wait... Wait... She forced herself, as the milliseconds ticked by like long minutes, and then, when the boar had come too far to swerve to the other side of the tree, she gathered her strength and switched sides, then sprinted through the clearing. The pine stood solidly, offering its branch like a lover's arms, and as she reached it, she leaped, summoning all her power in her arms and legs to swing herself up and embrace it.

She had bought herself just enough time to stay one step ahead of the boar. It had indeed encircled the tree in anticipation of her ducking behind it the second time and had saved the violent toss of the head until it was more certain of its target. But its cumbersome body had negotiated the turn awkwardly, and Geneva had gained enough ground to make the safety of the high limb.

But her legs, although willing and nimble, were too slow. Just as she felt them swinging upward to embrace the limb, the hog overtook her, running directly under her and lifting its tusks into the deadly, flashing arc. She felt the breath again, and a split second later, a thin, sharp pain in the back of her right thigh. Her leg went limp, then both legs lost their purchase on the limb. For a moment, they hung down, dead weights pulling against the strength of her arms. There was a tickle in the sensitive spot at the back of her knee, and a second later, at the ankle. She dared not look, but she knew that already her blood was wetting the ground below her.

Her hands, clasped together around the pine branch, were wet with fear and pain, and she felt the strength ebbing from her arms. She tried again to wrap her legs around the branch, but her throbbing leg kicked feebly. The bare foot only scraped across the rough bark, then slid downward again. Now she did not know if she had the power to lift her legs at all; this time she must use her arms to pull her body higher.

Before she could think, she heard the snorting animal thundering toward her again. Her brain shut out the sound, and her body, in a last burst of self-preservation, pulled itself up high; her knees tucked up under her chin, and her elbows bent up tight to the prickly safety of the pine bough. The wind rushed under her once more, but this time, there was no responding pain.

There was a long silence while Geneva hugged the tree. The sickening smell of the filthy hog filled her nostrils, but still she was aware of the clean smell of the pine and the less comforting, sharp smell of her own terrified sweat. Sweat darkened her shirt, and she could feel it running into her eyes, blinding her with the dirt and grime it carried. She was afraid to look down, but at last she wiped an eye on her shoulder and peered through the crook of her arm, quivering with fear and fatigue.

The awful thing was standing still, staring at her, dripping at the nose and mouth, and then he tossed his deadly head, snorted once, and very deliberately ran headlong into the trunk of the pine.

The whole tree shook, but not as much as Geneva's arms. Again she tried to sling her legs up and over the branch, but the pain in her thigh weakened the attempt. Her left foot hooked over the branch, but lost its grip and then slithered down again. Adrenaline and lactic acid together made an unholy mix, and as the tree trembled, Geneva felt her own weight, heavier than she ever dreamed possible, pulling against her quaking arms.

The beast charged at the tree again, twice more, three times more. Geneva began to cry, knowing that the muscles in her arms and legs and stomach would surely fail her in a matter of seconds. With each blow at the base of the tree, she felt her fingers slip farther and farther apart.

Oh, dear God! she cried. *Do something! Don't let me be ripped apart by this awful thing!* And she sobbed aloud as she struggled to make her sliding fingers marry.

Again came the thunder of hooves, and the world shook. She

knew she would fall this time, and she peered down to face the demon that was bent upon killing her. She saw him charging; she saw the lifted tusks, and she knew that this time he was aiming for her. Screaming, she begged her stomach to pull her legs up tight, her arms to embrace the tree, her hands to hold steady, but already they were giving away, all at once. Her legs turned to lead, her stomach muscles refused to pull any harder, her fingers, oily with sweat, determined to part. There was an explosion in her ears, and blackness enveloped her as she felt herself falling, falling into the cruel tusks of the wild boar, to his open mouth, to pain and certain death.

There was a violent jolt, and then a strange kind of warmth, and she felt herself no longer falling, but moving swiftly. Dazed, she opened her eyes to look down, and she dimly perceived that she might be flying. The prostrate form of the animal that had surely killed her floated below her. And then she felt another jolt, then a smooth rocking motion. *Odd,* she mused dimly through a swirl of pain and darkness. *Dying feels just like cantering through the forest, only warmer. It's not as bad as I expected...*

Then she lifted her eyes to see ears and a flying mane. Slowly it came to her that she was, indeed, riding a horse, and then eventually, she realized that she was lying in the arms of a man. When her eyes opened again, the sight of the mane streaming toward her face gave her greater joy than she had ever known.

A name came to her, swirling in darkness and confusion, and before it was fully formed in her brain, her lips were already shaping themselves to caress it. "Howard," she moaned, "You've saved me!"

The male arms tightened around her, pulling her close and comfortable against the warm, taut chest. "Not Howard, darling," came the low breath in her ear. "John."

She fainted before she could lift her eyes to his face.

Thirteen

It was cold. Geneva blinked once and whimpered, "Mama, I'm cold."

"I'll get you another blanket, sweetie," came Rachel's voice through a haze. "Mama stepped out for a minute to get a bite to eat."

Geneva blinked again. The light was dim and hazy. She hurt somewhere, but she could not tell where. It just seemed that there was an unhappy feeling somewhere in her body. She tried to move her leg, and winced when the dull unhappiness intensified. She let a tiny moan escape her lips.

Rachel moved toward her with a blanket and threw it over her, then tucked the edges around her shoulders tightly. "There, that should be better. You'll be warm in a minute."

"Where am I?"

"In your hospital room."

"What happened?"

"Oh, the usual. You wandered off from the group like a very bad camper and tried to mess with a wild boar. He was considerably bigger than you, and his teeth a lot sharper. Do you remember?"

Geneva tried to move her leg again and winced. "Oh. Yes. Somebody saved me."

"Yep." All your fantasies come true. The way I heard it, John came charging up on his white stallion right in the very teeth of the murderous beast and swept you right up out of the air. Too bad you were bleeding too bad to appreciate the moment."

"John?"

"Uh-huh. Thank goodness Howard Knight was there. He had enough sense to stop and shoot the thing, or John would have gotten himself killed. Then, too, it was handy to have the carcass. We've sent the head off to see if it was rabid. You'd better hope those thirty-nine stitches is all it's going to amount to."

Geneva barely heard her. "Howard. Where is he?"

Rachel's face registered surprise. "Right outside, with John and the others, waiting for you to come around."

Geneva moved again. The fog was lifting, and the pain was more real. "I want to see him." She felt desperate.

Rachel paused, then said slowly, "All right. I'm sure he'll be happy to hear that. Did... did you two make up or something?"

"No. I want to tell him that I love him." She began to feel the tears well up in her heart and in her eyes. All she could think about was how much she needed to see her lover.

Rachel drew in a sharp breath. "Honey, are you fully awake? I mean, if you really want to see him, I'll go get him. I guess... I mean, I thought you'd want to see John first, at least to thank him."

"Oh, Rachel, I love him! Please go get him! Even if he doesn't want to come! Please, beg him if you have to." She sobbed aloud.

Rachel's beautiful face grew very concerned. "Geneva, honey. Sure. If you want me to, just talk to me for a minute. I didn't know you still felt this way. Are you sure you want to see him? I mean, I know he'll be happy, he told me how much he is in love with you, about how he and the others searched for you all night, and how worried he had been when he found you'd been sick, but Geneva, why have you changed your mind?"

It was too difficult to explain. "Oh, Rachel, he took care of me. And he was so beautiful up on the cliff, and he danced for me, and gave me gold, and he made the stars fall—Singing Eye's tears!" She was crying in earnest now. "But now he hates me because I threw away the baby, and I was ashamed of him! You just don't understand!"

Rachel laid her hand on Geneva's forehead. "Okay, sweetie, try to think straight. You've been dreaming. Let's start over. Who do you want to see?"

"Howard—Chap."

"Who?"

"Howard." She was feeling very focused now. She would have gotten out of bed and found him herself, but it hurt too much to move. "Bring him here," she said weakly. I love him."

"Are you sure? You want me to go get Howard Graves so you can tell him you love him after all? What about John? Don't you want to maybe see him? Or think about it before you—"

"Not Howard Graves! Ta li! Howard Knight!" Geneva's horrified mind raced ahead of her speech. Rachel did not know? How could she not know? She felt very confused again.

Rachel seemed to freeze for a moment, then she sat down suddenly and took Geneva's hand. "Honey, you must have fever. I'm going to run get the doctor. He should have been here by now, anyway. Let's just put off seeing anyone for now, okay? You're going to be okay. You just need to sleep a little more."

The tears welled up again. She felt so helpless, so powerless to make Rachel understand her need. Her tongue felt thick and useless. Miserable, she turned her face to the wall and wept.

She was drifting through sunshine and fog, and stars swirled around her like fireflies, bright yellow and flickering. She felt the sensation of riding again, galloping in slow motion along the forest floor with enormous trees towering overhead. And then the beast lunged at her with its dripping fangs until she screamed and sat up.

Pain shot through her leg. She was in a hospital room, white and sterile. Terrified, she grabbed at the rail of her bed and looked around wildly. Her mother was there. And her father. And she suddenly remembered why she was there and what had happened. She gasped at the reflections in her mind.

People came and went. Many of them poked at her and murmured over her. Sometimes she felt her mother's cool hand and heard her father's voice, low and comforting. She slept in a gray miasma.

It seemed like a long time before she found herself alone with Rachel again. Blue twilight had crept into the room so that Geneva felt nearly shrouded in darkness. She wanted to speak, but she did not know what to say. Rachel laid her hand on her sister's forehead.

"Feeling better?"

"Yes. I'm awake now."

"Good. You look better."

"Where's Mama and Daddy?"

Just stretching their legs. They've both been here ever since they brought you in. I kicked them out just before you woke up. You gave us a real scare, honeybunch."

Geneva sighed and fought back more tears. "I know, I'm sorry. I thought I was going for help."

"Yeah, I know. But you should have known better."

"Jimmy Lee broke his leg."

"Yes, and you could have been killed. This is the third time, in just about as many weeks that you have done something to hurt yourself. If you don't watch it, you're going to be so scarred up, you'll have to join the circus. 'The Incredible Scarred Woman! See the wounds on her elbow! Her forehead! All up the back of her leg!' It's a good thing Joe's here. He's a pain in the ass sometimes, but he's a great plastic surgeon."

"All right, all right. You're making me feel really good."

"So, you feel good enough to see anybody? There's still a pack of people outside in the waiting room, Sally Beth, Lilly, John... and Howard... Graves. All of them have been here all day, and they're all exhausted, but they won't leave until they've seen you."

Geneva lay quietly and watched Rachel. Her big sister returned her gaze anxiously. "What about Howard Knight?"

Rachel licked her lips. "He's upstairs with Jimmy Lee, has been most of the day, except to stop in now and then to ask about you."

"Oh. How's Jimmy Lee?"

"Okay. It was a bad break, and he's in traction, but he'll mend." She paused expectantly.

"I want to see him—Howard."

Rachel nodded gravely. "Yes, you told me earlier. I thought you were dreaming—you were talking out of your head. You... you told me you were in love with him."

"I am, Rachel. And I'm not out of my head." Geneva's eyes blazed with conviction. How hungry she was to see him! "He took care of me while I was sick, and somehow I—we fell in love. There's so much more to him than you know."

"Yes, hush." Rachel's voice grew gentle, and she continued slowly, carefully, "Geneva, I talked to Howard. I asked him why you might be talking like this, why you might thi—say you were in love with him. He said you'd been out of your head with fever for a few days and had gotten him mixed up with someone else, and that you had raved about all kinds of strange things. Honey, you must have been really sick."

Geneva took this betrayal with equanimity. "Yes, I know he probably said that. He's lying," she said levelly, looking at Rachel directly in the eyes. "Rachel. This was real. I did not dream this. Just go get him. And tell the others to go home. I don't want to see anybody else until tomorrow."

Rachel broke eye contact first, and her sigh came after a long moment. "Okay, honey, I'll go get him. You can talk it out with him." She glanced at Geneva's resolute eyes again, then sadly left the room.

She was gone a long time. Geneva lay quietly, wondering what she would say to him when she saw him, how long it would take to convince him that what they had was worth fighting for. She would have to convince him that she would not hurt him ever again. That might take some doing, but she would just start by telling him over and over again how much she needed him and loved him and wanted him. She was sure he would be hers. She almost smiled while she waited.

Much later, Rachel returned. Apologetically, she crossed to Geneva's bed and stroked her arm. "He went home, honey. Jimmy Lee is stable, and there are others there with him, so he left. They said he might be back tomorrow."

"He didn't stop by to ask about me?"

"I don't know. He's been gone awhile. The others left when I told them to, before I went upstairs looking for him. Nobody said anything, though." She looked uncomfortable. "I'm sorry, Geneva. Do you want me to call him at home?"

Geneva felt her stomach sinking. "No. I'll wait. Thanks, Rachel." She attempted a smile.

"I have to go now. Heavy tits," she smiled. "Mama will stay the night. Howard—Graves—is staying at the house for now. The poor man is absolutely exhausted. I have a feeling everyone will be back tomorrow, though, so get some sleep." She gave Geneva a worried smile. "We'll begin sorting all this out tomorrow, okay?"

"Okay, Sis. Get home to your babies."

"Yes. Goodnight."

The night passed fitfully. It felt as if the glare in the hospital halls aimed to penetrate the walls of Geneva's room and mock her lack of peace. Gaynell lay quietly in the cot next to Geneva and came to fuss over her so often that at last Geneva determined to lie absolutely still so that her mother would have no reason to check on her again. Towards morning she fell into a kind of half sleep, where her thoughts intermingled with her dreams so that they took on an unreal shape, and she began to mistrust her memory.

Had he said he loved her? Might it not have been real, what she thought she saw and felt? She remembered the joy in his face, and the anguish. She felt the dewy night caress her skin as he lifted her up into the offering of stars. *Oh, yes, it was real.* And the pain she had caused him was real, too, so real that he wanted her out of his life.

Then she would sleep and see the beast rushing at her, and the terror once again quickened her blood. Sometimes the boar would come right to her so that she would wake with a start, but sometimes it would disappear before it reached her, or she would find herself warm and floating in someone's arms. Over and over again in her sleep she would think of love and danger and sorrow and pain. But sometimes, when the cycles seemed to be spinning out of control, the all-encompassing warmth would come to her, and she would float wordlessly in a kind of unknown bliss.

The nurses interrupted her sleep endlessly. Just when she would find herself at last facing the welcoming unconsciousness, in would come the bustling white figure to check her pulse and take her temperature. She grew more and more weary until at last she resolved to close her eyes and simply stop her brain.

That's when Joe, the plastic surgeon who had stitched Geneva up twice already this summer, came in. It was an indignity to have him strip off the bandages on her leg and leer at it, but when she grudgingly rolled over and let him look at her wound, she vainly tried to gain a peek at her assaulted leg.

She closed her eyes and hoped that he had done as good a job with her leg as he had with her previous wounds. The scar in her hairline was becoming invisible, and the one on her elbow was insignificant. This, however, was a different matter.

"Joe, what does it look like?"

"Yummy. That boar knew you were a tasty treat."

"I'm serious. Let me see."

"Sure, doll." He disappeared and a moment later, returned carrying a large mirror, positioning it so Geneva could see her wound. The sight caused her to gasp. An angry, wide, red line laced up with stitching ran down a ten inch length of her thigh, beginning just under her buttock. The wound was still hot and oozing, and Geneva wondered if she could ever wear a bathing suit again. Putting her face in the pillow, she wept softly.

"Come on, darlin', I think that's going to be about one of the sexiest scars I have ever seen."

"Shut up, Joe." said Geneva.

"You don't like it? Hey, we'll have you posing for *Playboy* by the end of the month."

"You ever been sued for sexual harassment?"

"She means it," warned Gaynell.

"Okay. Sorry. Just trying to make you feel better. Really, though, it doesn't look as bad as I thought it might. If we can just keep infection at bay, we'll be home free. The rabies test should be back this afternoon, and we just have to hope we got all the dirt out."

"Thanks," she muttered grudgingly.

"Sure. And really, Geneva. It won't look bad when it's all over. You've got great skin, and I'll lay odds you'll love this scar when I get through with it."

"Yeah, yeah. What kind of odds?"

"If you don't think I've worked miracles, I'll take you to Grenada with me when I go down there to teach next winter."

"Forget it. You're married."

"Oh yeah. I forgot about that. Sight of a pretty leg like that makes me think I'm available."

"Mom, what's my lawyer's number?"

"Would it make you feel better if I told you that all I find interesting here is this neat little row of stitches?"

"Joe. When can I wear a bathing suit without being stared at?"

He considered this question thoughtfully. "Hmm," he mused. "Twenty years?" He glanced at Gaynell. "How old are you, Gaynell?"

"Seventy-two."

"Oh, then probably fifty years or so. Gotta get a little cellulite on you. Some spider veining." He leered at Gaynell's legs. "People quit staring at you in a bathing suit yet, Gaynell?"

Gaynell smiled. "Doc, you got a way with you. Your wife know you talk like this?"

"Why do you think she married me? Either that or my great prowess in certain parts of the house."

"Joe," warned Geneva.

"Yep, I'm a master in the kitchen, chopping is my specialty. And you should see me vacuum. Comes from all that practicing with the liposuction."

Geneva thought about giving him a break, but squelched the impulse. "You know what I mean. Will this heal up without being too ugly?"

"Ugly? How can you ask that? You don't know who you're talking to! I do things with a needle and thread that other plastic surgeons only dream about. This scar will be so beautiful that you'll be in here next year, asking me to put one on the other leg just like it."

Geneva sighed. "When can I go home?"

"Why do you want to go home? We got every comfort here. Great, greasy, over-salted food, overbearing, pandering physicians, big, ugly nurses."

"I'm telling."

"Three days."

"Tomorrow."

"Two days."

"Tomorrow afternoon."

"Day and a half, if there's no rabies or infection, and if you promise to let Wayne keep tabs on you."

"Done."

"That will be a thousand dollars."

"Go away."

"Can I kiss the back of your knee?"

"No."

"What if I pay you a thousand dollars?"

She considered this, then figured he was kidding. She put her face back on the pillow and waved him away, but before he left, she stopped him again.

"Can I take a shower?"

"Sure." He wrinkled his nose. "I wasn't going to say anything, but I have seen better hairdos on warthogs."

She snorted. "No need to get ugly just because I wouldn't let you kiss the back of my knee."

He smiled, then his expression softened. "Geneva, I'm glad you pulled through this. You're quite a girl." The laughter came back in his eyes. "Now take a shower and wash your hair so I can come back and beg you to nibble your ear."

Geneva suddenly felt confidence and joy shoot through her. She was alive! She had just come through a harrowing ordeal, and only a day later, she was longing for a shower and being flirted with by a handsome, if overbearing, physician. There was hope, after all.

"Come on, Mama. Help me up," she said, struggling to rise. "I want to be beautiful again."

The shower felt glorious. Her mother helped her shampoo her hair, then Geneva gingerly perched on a chair while Gaynell towel dried her hair and combed it until it lay straight and smooth against her cheeks and shoulders.

"Remember when you were a little girl," Gaynell said, pulling the comb gently through Geneva's golden tresses, "and you told me you were going to run away from home and join a band of Gypsies and spend the rest of your life dancing around their campfire?"

"I remember," smiled Geneva. "I was obsessed with Gypsies for awhile. Wonder where I ever heard about them?"

"I reckon you read about 'em somewhere. But I was just thinking—that's exactly what you've done. You really have run away from home, and you're always dancing around the fire. Sometimes, in the middle of the night, I wake up, and I see this picture of you in my head, wildly spinning around a big fire, your hair all golden and streaming in the light, and you're laughing your head off, and you never see how close you are to getting burned. You just laugh and spin and fling your hair toward the fire." She paused, her face wistful. "All I ever wanted was for you to be happy, and I've tried to let you find your own happiness without interfering," she sighed. "But, Lord, honey, you are such a trial sometimes. How did I have a daughter with such a wild streak in her? You court danger at every turn." Her fingers faltered, and when Geneva looked at her, her eyes were shimmering with tears.

"Oh, Mama, I'm sorry. I know I have put you through an awful time. And sometimes I wish I were more like you, like Rachel." She thought about what Howard Knight had said to her on the mountain about her greedy soul, and she grieved that she had caused her loved ones so much pain. Sighing, she took her mother's hand. "Sometimes I wonder myself why I do the things I do. Things seem so right while I'm doing them. I mean, it made perfect sense to go looking for help yesterday. And now I see how stupid it was."

Gaynell laughed and dried her face with the back of her hand, then she hugged Geneva. "Oh, baby, I'm just happy to see you alive and safe. Don't pay any attention to me. I guess I wouldn't want you any other way, but I must say, I'm gettin' awful old to watch you get yourself in so much trouble. I guess I'm afraid I'll die before you learn to take care of yourself, and where will you be when I'm not there to drag you out of the quicksand?" She laughed again, "But then to hear Rachel tell it, she's been there to rescue you a few times when I wasn't!"

It hurt Geneva to hear her mother, always so strong and full of the confidence of her life, to speak so, and she wondered if she, Geneva, were less reckless, her mother would feel less helpless. Deep down, she knew the answer. She had always been a trial to her parents, and yet they had never stopped loving her for a moment. Their love had been fierce, almost wild, protective the way a beast is protective of its young. And yet, they had allowed her to fly away whenever and wherever she wanted, always blessed her, and always welcomed her home again. She took her mother in her arms, and felt her frailty, but she also felt the power of her love, and it felt good.

The day passed in bittersweetness, with Geneva reuniting with her friends and family. She apologized many times for the fear and hardship she had caused, and she was able to thank John for saving her life with passionate gratitude.

"Hey, thank *you*," he said, grinning. "I can't tell you how long I have waited for a chance to do something like that. Straight out of Alexander Dumas."

Geneva smiled. "I don't think so. I think I was supposed to be a little cleaner, maybe dressed a little nicer. I would say the scene was closer to Grotowski."

"Doesn't matter," he said, taking her hand. "I got a chance to be a hero, and it was the best moment of my life. I appreciate it." His smile turned wry. "Of course, it was helpful that Howard was there to keep me from getting myself killed—not to mention a really good horse."

She looked at him long and hard. His eyes were as intense as they were the first day she met him, green and full of that same longing she had seen before that had caused her heart to lurch. But now she only felt sweet gratitude and a gentle hope that he would be happy. "You have always been a hero, John. You go to miserable places and give people hope and a chance to have decent lives. And I'm glad you had a chance to be a knight in shining armor. I've always wanted to be rescued like that, too, but," she laughed, "I thought I'd have on a designer gown when it happened."

His eyes were misty. "I'm glad you're safe, Geneva," he said, and his voice grew husky, "I'd do anything for you. I want to always make sure you're safe and happy. And I want all your dreams to become real."

She felt her own eyes growing wet, and she searched for the words to tell him… what? What could she say to him? What did she want to say to him, so vulnerable and so hopeful here beside her, holding her hand and looking at her with those burning eyes? She drew a ragged breath, and suddenly Lilly and Sally Beth burst into the room.

"My goodness, Geneva Lenoir, you just about scared us half to *death*," breathed Sally Beth, "and girl, we couldn't wait *another minute* to see yew! Do yew know we were here all day yesterday, and half the night, and Lordy, we're not waiting another minute! Don't tell that awful nurse we're in here. They only let in two at a time. Lilly, you run in the bathroom if that nurse comes in. Geneva, honey, you look like you have really been through it! How do you feel? Did that old boar just rip you *all to pieces?*"

"Hello, Sally Beth. Lilly."

John began backing toward the door. "I'll get out of here," he murmured. "We don't want to wear you out."

"Oh, John, don't leave," said Lilly primly. "They'll never know, and Sally Beth can just leave if they come to throw somebody out."

"I will *not* leave! I just got here! *Yew* can just run in the bathroom, and they'll never know! Yew can stay, John."

"I will not run in the bathroom," declared Lilly. "You're the one who should run in the bathroom. I'm surprised Geneva is even talking to you, since this was all your fault anyway. She probly doesn't really want to see you right now."

"What do you mean, *my fault?*" demanded Sally Beth.

"Well, you were the one who panicked when you saw the bear and caused Jimmy Lee to fall over the cliff in the first place. If it hadn't been for you, none of this would have happened, and we would have made it back without any trouble."

Sally Beth's blue eyes grew rounder and she pulled herself up a little taller and put her fist on her hip. "What do you mean, Lilly Lenoir, saying it was my fault just because I got scared when there was this *big old bear right in my face?* What do yew think yew would have done if you'd had the guts to be the first one across that path? Huh? Hey, you never would've had the guts to be the first one, and if that old bear had run into you, you would have run *everybody* over. I did good, considering!"

"I'll see you, Geneva. So long Sally Beth, Lilly." John eased out of the room.

"Now see what you did!" exclaimed Lilly. "Ran him right off, and he's such a nice man. Why do you have to do that?"

"I did not run him off." She turned to Geneva indignantly. "Geneva, did I run him off? Lilly, I declare you are the orneriest girl in the world! Geneva, did I run him off?" Her expression altered suddenly. "I'm sorry, honey," she cooed worriedly. "He'll be back. Do yew want me to fix yer hair or somethin'?"

A nurse entered. "Sorry, girls, I need for you to leave while I check Geneva's dressing. You can just step outside for a minute."

"Sure," said Sally Beth, glaring at Lilly. "We'll be right outside if you need us, honey," she cooed to Geneva. "And I'll do yer hair anytime you want! And yer nails, too! I bet yer hands are a *mess!* And yer toenails, too." She paused thoughtfully. "That was my fault. I shouldn't a thrown yer shoe. I'm real sorry about that." She brightened. "I'll buy you another pair!"

"Forget it, Sally Beth," smiled Geneva. "I'll see you later."

"Sure! We're just outside!" She pointed toward the corridor with her perfectly painted hot pink fingernail as she opened the door.

The nurse peeled the bandages aside and dabbed at Geneva's stitches with antiseptic solution, then taped new gauze over the oozing wound.

"How does it look?" Geneva asked anxiously.

"Not too bad," the nurse replied briskly. "We'll just keep watching it, and you need to get plenty of rest. Be sure to drink plenty of water, too."

Efficiently, she took Geneva's temperature, then gave her antibiotics and left. Geneva stared after her for a few seconds while her mind drifted on the currents of her recent memories, and before she had the chance to really wrap the arms of her mind around Howard Knight and hold him close, Howard Graves knocked, then stepped into her room.

He looked awful. Deep circles darkened his eyes, which appeared sunken and dull in the glare of the fluorescent light. "Hi," he said gently, and his lips brushed her forehead dryly.

"Hi," she returned tentatively.

Taking her hand, he stepped back and gazed at her a long time, then he gave a short, half-sob, half-laugh, and his already dull eyes clouded more. "You're alive."

She wanted him to feel better. "They say I'm too mean to die," she said lightly.

He looked beyond her. "There wasn't anything I could have done. I was just coming over a rise, and the others were already there. We heard you screaming." His voice grew shaky. "I'm not a good enough rider. There wasn't anything I could have done. I can't shoot. I can't ride. I could only stare at you, and watch the others do all that heroic stuff." His eyes came back to her. "Oh, baby, there was blood everywhere, and I couldn't do anything. I couldn't get to you fast enough."

"Hey," she said gently, touching his face. "It's okay. I'm okay. Of course you can't ride and you can't shoot. You're a city dude. I like you the way you are." She smiled brightly. "You look great in a tux. You can dance the Rumba."

He did not return her smile. "The doctors say you're going to be okay."

"Sure am."

"Geneva… do you, could you…" He stopped and began again. "Geneva, I'm going back to DC. I can't stay here. I'm too out of place. I feel worthless. I didn't even know what to do when you were lying there on the ground, and the others were working on you to stop the bleeding. And you were just there, all white and red with the blood pouring out of you. And everybody else was working like mad, trying to stop the blood. Even Sally Beth was cool and was tearing up strips of everybody's clothes, and Lilly and I just stood there and watched, and I was absolutely helpless, watching you die." He gave a dry sob.

"Hush, hush," whispered Geneva, patting his hand. "It's okay. I didn't die. I'm right here, and I'll be fine. Oh, Howard, I'm so sorry to put you through this. It's my fault. Don't be angry with yourself."

"You don't understand. There was *nothing* I could do. I don't even have the right blood type, so I couldn't give you blood. Sally Beth and Howard both gave you blood. I mean, everybody was there to save your life, except for me and Lilly. Both of us worthless. If I had been there by myself, I couldn't have saved you!"

Geneva sat up. "Howard and Sally Beth gave me blood?"

Howard Graves looked more miserable. "Yes. They both matched your type. They wouldn't even let your parents or your sister—they both just acted like they had the right to take care of you, and the rest of us could just go hang ourselves."

She fell silent. She understood how he felt, how impotent he must still be feeling to know there are things to be done, but not to be able to do them. She thought about the night Rachel had her babies, and how she had wandered back and forth between Jimmy Lee and her laboring sister, wondering if they would make it through the night with her incompetent ministrations.

Howard's gaze moved to the window and beyond. After a long moment, he dragged his eyes to her face again and sighed heavily. "Geneva, I have to leave. This is hell for me, knowing how you feel about me, and knowing there isn't much I can do to change your feelings, especially now. I guess you can understand that I feel pretty worthless, pretty undeserving of you, and I need to get away for awhile, just to get to a place where I can feel competent again. I have never felt so out of control in my life."

Geneva smiled. Yes, it would be difficult for Howard to feel out of control. His life had always been so ordered, and here in this place, barely civilized by most any standards, and in the mountains—not civilized at all—he would feel unable to function on any level. Very difficult for one who had always moved effortlessly and gracefully through the seeming labyrinth of his professional life.

He had not stopped talking. "This doesn't mean I won't try again, that I'll give up. This place—you—have given me something, and I don't intend to give it up until I absolutely have to—until you tell me." He smiled, and hastened to add, "and maybe not even then, so don't think you're going to be getting rid of me very easily. I'll be back."

Geneva's heart went out to him. He was so pitiful, so hopeful and yet so hopeless all at the same time. She did not know what she wanted to tell him, whether she wanted him to go away and never come back, or if she wanted him to be her friend (that old cliché!), or if she, somewhere, underneath the layers of her own hope and confusions, still harbored some small flame of love for him that might be rekindled.

No, there was no chance. But old habits die hard, old love dies harder, and there was some of him still in her, no matter how much she longed to be with another. And now Howard Knight's blood was in her veins. She lay back and closed her eyes to trammel the tears that lay perilously close to the surface. In the darkness, she reached for Howard's hand and squeezed it. When she opened her eyes again, he was gone, and she knew the time for good-bye had come, no matter what he had said. He was right. If he could not be a part of this place, he could not be a part of her, no matter how much she might try to deny this portion of her life, the essential roots of her boring deep into this earth, these mountains, giving her shape and definition.

Her parents were there again and then Rachel. Sally Beth and Lilly drifted through a couple of times, and of course, John was always there, lingering just on the periphery of her vision, trying not to be in the way, but always just there, burning her with those eyes. Howard Graves was gone, and Howard Knight did not come. She waited for him as she chatted with her family and with John, always looking eagerly toward the door when she heard a knock. But his continued absence hovered like a sulfurous mist over her head. The longer he waited, she knew, the less she would be able to convince him to love her.

He came at midnight. The others, even her parents, had gone when visiting hours were over, and she had given up hope of his coming, even though she had asked Rachel twice to go and ask for him. She was not asleep when he stepped lightly into the room, but was lying quietly watching the stars through her window, imagining that she saw them streaming across the sky. Although she felt tired and defeated for the moment, she still lay hoping for a way to reach him.

He did not speak, and made no noise, but she felt his presence, and she knew it was him. At first, she felt him in such a quiet and intimate way she did not realize he was really with her, but thought him merely a wish, imagination borne on wings of desire. But presently, she began to feel more intensely the gaze that held her, and she turned to see him standing dark against the door.

"Howard," she breathed.

He did not answer at first, nor did he move. Finally, she heard him speak quietly, "I thought you'd be asleep. I jist wanted to see that yer awright."

Her heart was pounding with both love and fear. Carefully, she wiped her palms against the crisp sheet. "Come in. Please. I've been wanting to talk to you."

Still, he did not move. "I jist wanted to see that yer awright," he repeated.

"Yes, I'm fine. Thanks to you. You saved my life. Twice. I understand you gave me blood, too."

She could see him more clearly now as her eyes adjusted to the darkened end of the room, and she caught the glint of his eye as he moved his gaze to her face. "I didn't do nothin' nobody else woulda done. John wuz really the one that saved ye. I jist got in a lucky shot."

Her voice was shaking. "I know it was you who tracked me. It was you who first came searching for me. I know you would have done anything to keep me alive. Howard. I know you love me." She said this last bit with a little rush of her breath while her courage was still building.

He said nothing, only looked at her.

She rushed on. "And I love you. You know I do. Please come here. I want to feel your arms around me. Please don't be afraid of me. I really do love you. I won't hurt you, no matter what you think."

She could see him shaking his head slowly. "We done been through this all before. Ye jist cain't see ahead like I kin. I kin see ye tryin' ta live up on that mountain—."

"But I can!"

He shook his head again. "I kin see ye gittin' restless and wantin' ta see the city, and ye'd ask me ta take ye there, and I would. And then, I kin see yer shame, and both our sorrow." His voice was pregnant with misery.

For a moment, briefly, she saw it, too. She saw him sitting at a large, shining table with a crowd of her friends, looking lost and uncertain amid the linen and silver. And, regrettably, she saw herself, smiling at him and urging him to fit in, willing him to be a part of her company. She felt, deep down in her core, a tiny knot of embarrassment for him in front of people who would never understand.

She blinked back tears. "Howard, no! We can work it out!" She felt her growing desperation and searched for a logical argument. But there was nothing she could pull from her experience or from her logic that could gloss over the essential differences between them. There was the love, yes, and the passion, but beyond that, the days and months and years, she felt the tremor of his shame and his sorrow washing over her and tainting the hope of their love.

He approached her bed. When he drew close, she seized his hand and tried to pull him to her, but he held back and placed his other hand on her forehead. "I'm glad yer alive. I want ye ta live."

"How can I live without you?"

He chuckled. "Ye kin live through anything. I never seen anybody more alive than yew. Even when I saw ye fallin' in that old boar's mouth, I knew ye'd live. And when ye was alayin' there bleedin', and we couldn't git the blood stopped, I still knew ye'd live."

She sobbed aloud and clung to his hand.

"Shh, there ain't no need to be squallin', now," he said gently. There was a long pause, then he continued, "I sorta wanted to tell ye I wuz sorry for what we done. Ye know, I hope my lovin' ye hasn't caused ye no grief. But I cain't say I'm sorry. I mean, I hate yer hurt, and I hate mine, too. But—," he looked up and breathed deeply, "—but I cain't be sorry fer what happened. I cain't be sorry fer lovin' ye. Never. Yew'll always be a bright spot in me." He stroked her head gently, then disengaged his hand and slowly walked back to the door.

He was leaving! In her misery, she cried out one last time with all her desperate hope, "Howard! Please!"

He reached for the door. "Howard! Chap!" She searched for words to touch him. "Ta li!" she cried out in anguish. And she saw him falter. He dropped his hand, then slowly, as if her will had been thrown around him like a lasso and she was pulling him toward her, he began to turn. She had triumphed! She caught her breath and waited for him to shake off his doubt and fear and come rushing to her. She practically tasted his kiss even now.

But before the turn was complete, before she felt his will succumb completely to hers, before he threw off the last fear and came rushing back to her, the door burst open, and the night nurse came bustling in.

"My goodness!" she exclaimed! "It's way past visiting hours! You shouldn't be here," she chided.

Horrified, Geneva's eyes left Howard for an instant while she glared open mouthed at the nurse. She felt a rush of wind, and before she could cry out again, he was gone.

Fourteen

Late October! Geneva's favorite month, when the autumn trees flamed with a delicious and rowdy self-exhibitionism against the blue heavens. In turn, the sky tried its best to upstage the trees. This was the first day she felt up to a ride, and despite the admonitions from Wayne, Joe, Rachel, and nearly everyone else, she was determined to get away by herself at least one last time before the chill wind blew away the gold in the trees and blew in the leaden winter sky.

She rode carefully, not in any hurry, and favoring the still-tender wound down the back of her thigh. She knew she could not go far, but she did not have far to go. Jacob's Mountain was only two miles away, and she would not even break into a trot. She had plenty of time for travel, for thought, for space to begin to heal her wounds.

Her mother had nursed her during her convalescence; even now Geneva felt guilty as she thought of how she was supposed to have been helping Rachel with her babies, but had instead become a big baby herself. She was not only not doing her job, but also taking her mother's time so she could not be with Rachel's family, either. But no one had complained, and Geneva had to admit it had felt good to be in the bosom of her parents again: indulged, pampered, petted. She had not told her mother or her father about Howard Knight, nor had she mentioned him to Rachel again after the night he came to her room and told her he could not love her. Yet, she didn't give up hope, not until later.

She shook herself and drew her thoughts away, toward the blue sky and the rocky outcropping that marked the final ascent to Jacob's Mountain. What she hoped to find there she did not know, but she knew she wanted to feel loved, completely, unconditionally loved, and she had heard that Love lived there. Of course, her mother and her father loved her, and her sister did, too, and maybe Howard Graves, maybe… and maybe Jimmy Lee, and well, yes, maybe John. She took a moment to add them up. She wondered if there were any other of the men in her past who had once professed to love her whom she could still count in the litany. But no matter how many, still, it was not enough. On this bright day, and all the days that stretched behind her, for as long as she could remember, she had wanted more. She wanted to know what it felt like to be overwhelmed with Love that would never end.

She rode resolutely, aware that there would be no one on top of Jacob's Mountain to meet her, to sweep her up in his arms and begin the beginning of a storybook romance. *Maybe a miracle would happen. Maybe Someone would come.* Maybe she would find Something. Maybe her spirit would quicken with the glory of this day, and she would face the rest of her life imbued with greater joy and purpose. *Maybe.* She had only hope left. Idly, she caressed a memory and nursed the most pitiful of fantasies that she could undo the past. *Silly girl. Don't think about it. Think about something more hopeful, more pleasant.*

She was lying in the porch swing, and she felt a disarming sense of déjà vu as she felt the shadow pass over her and pause. She had the sense of being in that place before, and the sun had come in at just the same angle, turning him into a ghost of sparkling light. She could barely see his face, but she could tell it was John by the width of his shoulders and the certain way he cocked his head to the side and the way the curls of his hair seemed to go translucent in the light. For a moment, she had forgotten all as she sighed and stretched and tried to ease her leg off the pillow so he could sit beside her on the porch swing.

"No, don't bother. Stay comfortable. I'll just sit here on the floor," he said, settling down with his back against the wall at her head.

She felt a little groggy. "I guess I dozed off."

"You deserve the rest. Feeling better?"

He had asked her that before. When? This was an almost perfect replay in the cool afternoon, with the halo of light around his head. How long before had it been that she had seen him just like that and had walked across the flower-laden meadow with him and wished that he would love her? But there was a difference. There was joy before, and laughter. Now there was a desolate yearning in her breast that made her wince when she stared at his bright, light-infused face.

She did not answer, but looked out at the piercing sky and the trees that were deepening into fall. September! She had not seen Howard for two weeks. She wanted to die, she had been telling herself. What use was it to have her senses if they only reminded her of her loss?

He put his hand on the swing and pushed it lightly, and when she closed her eyes and felt the coolness in the motion, he began: "I wanted to come see you at your mother's house, but Rachel told me you weren't up for visitors. I thought I'd give you a chance to recover a little more before I brought on the brass bands."

"I'll live, I guess," she said, answering his first question.

The event loomed up again in her mind, even now.

"I know I was stupid."

"I wouldn't call it stupid. I'd say you were pretty brave. Depends on how you look at it."

"It was stupid. I never think about consequences. I never think beyond what I'm thinking at any given moment."

"That doesn't make you stupid. It makes you you. I'd say it's just part of your charm. If everybody was cautious and thought through the consequences, life would be pretty dull."

She smiled as genuinely as she could. "Thanks. But what do you know? You were stupid, too. Galloping right toward that boar."

He was not put off. "Again, depends on how you look at it. I thought it through for about a twentieth of a millisecond. Live in a world without Geneva or not. That was a no-brainer."

"Exactly what you had. No brain. So what have you been up to?"

"Waiting for you to get back. Doing some thinking. Pretty hard with no brain, but that's never stopped me before."

She did not want to hear what he had been thinking about. She felt certain his thoughts had involved her, and she was too tired to be involved in anything. And she did not want to see his eyes. If she saw that awful yearning again, no matter how fleetingly, she feared she would be too reminded of her loss. She closed her eyes against him.

He was silent a long time, but at length, he said, "Remember when I went to New Orleans?"

She had forgotten. Not a month before, she had wished he would ask her to go with him. Now she was afraid he would ask her. She nodded without looking at him.

"Well, while I was there, I was asked to help with a project in Ethiopia. I told you about my breeding program—more milk from cows who get very little water?"

"Yes. I remember."

"Well, there's a group wants to try it out. The drought has been going on for years, and everyone is starving. They can't keep livestock alive long enough to breed, hardly. These people think we might be able to improve living conditions if we can introduce these cows there. I'd go down for a few months and get them started, then go back a couple of times a year to help refine the processes."

"I see."

"Anyway, I thought I'd go." He had paused, with feeling. "It's a really good project. I guess I think I could make a difference."

Something touched her memory then, and she remembered how good he was. "You make a difference everywhere you go."

After a silence, he said, "I'll take that as a compliment. And maybe a bit of hope."

She did not look at him, but she spoke to him softly. "You're a decent person, John. More than decent, and I wish you every happiness. Go, and God be with you. Make a difference." It was hard to keep back the tears, although she did not know why she wanted to cry. She also could feel his distress, but she did not know how to comfort him. She needed too much comforting herself.

"If I go, will you be here when I come back?"

"I wish I could know the answer to that. Right now I don't feel much like going anywhere."

"I know. Otherwise I might have asked you to go with me." He faced her silence. "Of course, that's a stupid idea. There aren't too many fun things to do in the Ethiopian countryside, except wish for rain and see all the misery."

"Yeah. It's nicer here."

"Or maybe in DC?" He said it so softly she barely heard him.

She smiled. He still thought Howard Graves was his rival. What would he say if he knew of her feelings for a hillbilly miner who sang about tears and stars falling from the edge of the world? "I doubt it. I've decided I'm not built for the city."

When he had absorbed this, he moved to his feet. "Good. I have to leave tomorrow." He touched her face until she looked at him. "I want you to know this was a hard decision. I mean, I have no claim on you, but I wish I did, and I only want to know that I won't be sorry for having gone, now, of all times. Can I write to you? I won't have access to a phone very often."

He was a good man. She never wanted to hurt him. "I may not write back much."

Shrugging, he replied, "I read A Tale of Two Cities *four times. I bet your letters will be even more compelling. One or two a day will be plenty. And just get well. When I come back, I want to see the old Geneva we all know and love so well." With that, he touched her face again and kissed her lips lightly, then he was gone into that dazzling sun. The meadow and the light seemed to swallow him as he strode* away. Feeling the tears squeezing out between her lids, she let herself become lost in a moment of total self pity.

Again, she shook the painful thoughts away and muttered a strong reprimand to herself. This was not making her any happier. *Think about the trees and the late flowers. Look, there's a turk's cap still blooming,* and there, she could see clumps of wild ginger. *Just breathe and don't think about anything. Just look and be glad to be alive. Something good will happen.*

She half reclined in the same swing, her left leg propped up on a pillow, her right dangling on the floor and idly pushing so that she swung gently. She might have been comfortable, except for the cats lounging on her stomach and up under her chin. She pushed them away several times, but Petrarch especially would not take no for an answer.

Damn cats. She stepped out of her reverie to wonder where the kittens were. She had not seen them since she had moved back to Rachel's house after her convalescence. Carefully, she avoided a low hanging branch in front of her face. The saddle creaked under her, and a bird sang among the flaming maple trees. For some reason, the singing pierced her heart with the sharpest of hurts.

That day, the day he came to say good-bye for good, the radio was tuned to a country station, and Crystal Gayle sang about heartbreak, and she let the words tumble her around until she felt dizzy with the hurt and the longing.

She moved slightly in the saddle and half closed her eyes, seeing herself in a cabin high in the mountains before the dying fire and gazing into the deep, liquid eyes of Howard Knight.

She remembered his scent and the way he touched her. She remembered how the passion had leapt up between them like a living thing and how he had lifted her to the black and silver sky and she had flung her arms wide to embrace freedom and ecstasy.

She had held and caressed the memory so often that it had been worn to a smooth, gleaming patina.

The music flooded her with bittersweet yearning until a glint of sunlight on a vehicle turning into the drive caught her eye, and she watched with a pounding heart as Howard's old truck made its way toward her in slow motion. She heard the crunch of the gravel and the coursing of her blood. She held her breath and ran her fingers through her hair.

Yes, it was Howard. And Jimmy Lee was with him. Both of them got out of the truck, but Howard hung back while Jimmy Lee, with the aid of a crutch, made his way slowly toward her.

He was wearing a clean, starched white shirt, crisp black pants, and shining new shoes. Obviously, he had just gotten a haircut. His pink, bare ears and his face shone with scrubbing.

She winced when she remembered the plaster cast, then again at the memory of his paleness the morning she had bent over him and felt his body for injuries. *Don't think about it. See how still the afternoon is, how bright the sky.*

Jimmy Lee looked at her, but Howard kept his eyes downcast. Geneva's mouth went dry, and she swallowed, wishing her insides would stop lurching.

Lamentations jumped out of the back of the truck and tucked his head under Jimmy Lee's free hand as the pale, thin man hobbled toward her. No one said anything for a moment, but Petrarch and Evangeline suddenly jumped up, backs raised, fur leaning backward up their necks.

Remembering, she almost smiled at the image of Lamentations growling and looking over his shoulder, his eyes rolling and showing their whites, and how Jimmy Lee had pleaded,

"Oh, hell, Lamentations! Please don't start now!" But Lamentations growled louder, and when the cats jumped up and scattered in every direction, he cut loose on his poor stump of a tail. Jimmy Lee looked like he wanted to cry. Glancing miserably between Geneva and his dog, he made futile little clutching motions, trying to stop Lamentations' fit. Finally, he gave the dog a light backhand slap, which stopped the canine in his tracks. Lamentations dropped to the ground, panting.

Then Jimmy Lee grinned, looking almost dapper, and addressed her, "Hidy, Miss Geneva. How ye feelin'? We come ta see ye," he said, rather formally, as if the previous scene had not taken place, but his hands clutched one another, seeming to gain courage from one another. With an effort at dignity, he labored his way up the steps.

But Howard stood still in the driveway.

"Hello," she smiled, feeling the hope surge through her. "Come on up. I'll get us some lemonade." Struggling to her feet, she pleaded. "Howard, come on up."

He shook his head, looking at the ground and letting his shoulders sag. "No, ma'am. I gotta git. Uh... Jimmy Lee, he's come ta court ye."

At this, Jimmy Lee's face flamed and he gave a short, embarrassed laugh. "Well, don't spill the beans all over the place, Chap!" Rubbing his chin nervously, he added apologetically, "I jist come on to pay my respects. I ain't seen ye since... since ye saved my life... fer the third time. And I jist..." The sentence trailed off lamely.

"Jimmy Lee cain't drive with that leg," offered Howard. "I jist run him on over to sit with ye a little. I'll be back direckly. Hour or so." He looked so miserable, Geneva longed to rush down the steps and throw her arms around him, but she stood frozen, willing him to come to her. Jimmy Lee made his way to the porch swing to perch on the edge; the

foot encased in plaster rested awkwardly on the floor. Lamentations tried to scramble up beside him, but he pushed the dog back down.

"Naw. Yew set down right here. Yew cain't take up the lady's seat." Lamentations sat, his whole body pressed closely against Jimmy Lee's good leg, his miserable stump thumping against the floor. Quivering slightly, he tried to press himself closer, casting his mournful eyes up into the face of his master.

"Howard, please stay awhile. I… never got a chance to thank you for what you did for me. You saved my life."

"Naw. John done that."

"Hell, Chap, yew shot the hog!" interjected Jimmy Lee. "Right between the eyes at a hunnert feet!" He turned excitedly to her. "They tole me all about it. Right between the eyes! From a runnin' horse!" He was as proud as if he had made the shot himself.

"Don't matter. Fergit it," said Howard evenly. He shifted his weight and glanced at Geneva before he let his eyes rove over the horizon.

"It does matter, Howard," she said pointedly, "and I can't forget it. Any of it. Won't you stay?" She blinked back tears and pleaded with her eyes, but he would not look at her. At last, he moved forward a step, then thrust his hand into his jacket pocket. "I fergot. Ye left this. I figured I'd git it back to ye," and stepping forward, he laid his closed fist on the porch rail and opened it carefully, palm down. Then he backed off and walked briskly to his truck. "I'll be back direckly, Jimmy Lee. Ya'll have a nice visit." Springing into the wreck of a vehicle, he turned in the drive and drove away without looking at her again.

Fairhope gave a little shudder and flipped his tail across his back, bringing Geneva back to the bright October day and to the rhythm of the briskly stepping Morgan. She reached inside her shirt and held the lavaliere suspended on a chain around her neck, remembering again how she had made her way to the porch rail. Walking was still painful then, but she had felt nothing except a dull ache in her soul as she reached for the offering Howard had laid there.

When she picked up the heavy object, she knew she had never seen it, yet she recognized it immediately: It was a comet, made of solid gold, his gold, no doubt (or perhaps hers, the gold she had snatched out of the foaming water on that day of delirium), and layered over with various shades of red, yellow, and orange enamel. About the length of her little finger, the small globe with its multi-hued tail seemed to streak across the palm of her hand even as she held it. She held it aloft by the gold chain and looked at it closely. Engraved along the side was her Cherokee name, the one he had given her.

ᎫᎬᎾᏉᎫ ᎠᏍᎲ ᏆᎾᎾᎫᏢ ᏚᏛᎥᎫᎠᏓᎧᎥ

"One Who Strikes Fire in the Soul." As she beheld this thing of beauty, she heard his voice in the moment of her misery and her shame, "A man can love a shooting star, but that don't mean he can take it to his heart and make it a part of him." And as she listened again for his voice, she searched for a moment of hope in this magnificent gift, but all she could find was his anguish and her own rejection. This was his purging, his goodbye. This was the moment he could lay One Who Strikes Fire in the Soul to rest and begin to mourn her loss. Before long, the healing would smooth over his hurts, and he would be free of her forever.

Or, could it be an offering of love? Could he be asking her to accept his gift as a token of what she meant to him? What did she mean to him? Something he could not hold to his heart, something he could never make his own. She tried to find hope in the moment, but it had vanished as hastily as he had driven away. Perhaps, if he had been wearing the object… but he had not worn it. It had held no warmth from his body. He had kept it casually in his outer jacket pocket, as if he claimed no ownership. She knew then, even as he drove away that already he was feeling the first tremulous freedom, the beginnings of catharsis. She was something from which he needed to flee to save himself.

Slowly, she turned and made her way back to the porch swing. Despite her profound sadness, she tried to smile at Jimmy Lee as she settled beside him. "Well, Jimmy Lee, we are a pair, aren't we? This front porch looks like a rest home for accident victims, or maybe war heroes. What do you think?"

"I think, Miss, Geneva, that yew are about the purtiest thang I ever slapped my eyes on."

She would not cry, but she allowed herself the indulgence of opening her palm and looking down at the shooting star in her hand and wishing with all her strength that the man would turn around and come back to her. The sun streamed in warm and soft. Jimmy Lee let his adoring eyes rest full on her face, while Laminations lifted his mournful face toward Jimmy Lee, wagged his stump, and wriggled closer to his master.

She was approaching the last rise before the grassy bald broke out of the trees, and she gave Fairhope his head as she scanned the horizon to watch how the sun turned the long grass soft and golden. A breeze picked up the moment she found herself in the open, and with a start, she realized she was there. Jacob's Mountain, where Love lived. Where, at one time, she had entertained the fantasy that she would meet The One who would be her all, her past, her future, her dreams and her reality. She thought maybe she should hear music, like the soundtrack of a movie, but all she heard was the empty wind as it rifled through the grass and swirled around her with desolate whisperings.

The sky was still glorious, and far below, she could see the reds and golds of the trees undulating across the hills. It was so lovely, and so empty. There was nothing here but herself and her sorrow and her longing. Slowly, she dismounted, and dropping the reins so Fairhope could graze, she limped to a boulder and sat, turning her face to the sun as it slipped down into the field of grass. The grass looked like wheat, with fuzzy little tops that glowed in the afternoon light. It made her think of a sea of twinkling lights stretching up a long meadow and melting into the blue sky. Before long, the warmth and the wind made her sleepy. Pulling her knees up under her chin, she laid her cheek on her hand and closed her eyes, feeling the sun and watching the red spirals dance behind her eyelids.

When she opened them again, she saw him coming toward her with a halting gait, but smiling as if he knew she needed comforting. She remained perfectly still until he came all the way to her, far closer than he had ever been before, close enough that she could have touched him if she had reached out her hand. She lifted her head. "Hello, Holy Miracle."

He smiled with his eyes and with his cheeks, rosy and round above the snowy beard. "Hello, girlie. I see yer ahopin' fer Love to come and abide in ye?"

He knew all, this wise old man who had roamed the mountains for a lifetime and more, healing all that he touched. Geneva let her mute gaze tell him what he wanted to know.

He straightened and drank in the view all around him. "Hit's been awhile since I been here. I like the view from this side the best." He stopped and looked farther into the horizon. "But I reckon this'll be the last autumn I kin stand here and listen to the angels still invisible. Lord tells me this winter I'll see 'em with my real eyes, and lookin' back, what I see now will be like I wuz alookin' through muddy waters."

"You mean, you expect to die?" The thought startled and saddened her. How could this piece of her history, one of the few sureties of her life, die?

"There ain't no dyin', girlie, only a little sleep, and then the rushin' upward to the light of the Lamb, where the chaff shall be burned away, and the gold will be refined to be fit."

She could not believe it. He had been a part of her for as long as she could remember. He had given her the joy of healed wings flying to freedom. Now, he looked no different than the day he had first revealed himself to her, when she was nine years old and lay watching the trout flit among the bright shadows of the maidenhair ferns.

"How old are you, Holy Miracle?" she asked with the unconscious curiosity of a child.

His eyes grew round with pleasure. "Old," he answered, and he seemed to have to struggle to contain his delight. That was all he needed to say. He was as old as the rock upon which she sat. He was as eternal as spring. He had been born with the very rising of this mountain. And now he had spun out his life and waited to meet his Creator.

He moved a little closer, and his eyes softened. "I see ye still got that thistle in yer soul. Don't ye reckon it's time ta be agittin' rid of it?"

She felt weary. "What do you mean? A thistle?"

"Why, the pain, in yer soul, the one that's amakin' ye long fer what ye ain't got."

"You mean Howard?"

"No, girlie. It ain't a man, though a man will come fer ye. The Lord's already got him picked out fer ye, and he's jist awaitin' til yer ready, with a clean soul, to take him.

"Ah, I know yer needin' Love, even though ye've had Love dancin' all around ye since the day ye was borned. And yer mighty blessed. Ain't many that yearns so fer the glory of God. Hit's His Love yer alookin' fer."

"But how do I find that? Isn't His Love always here, isn't it supposed to live in us?"

"Oh, yes, but when ye git a thistle in yer soul, and ye leave it there, ye cain't feel nothin' but the pain of that, and it's such a pretty hurt, ye don't want to let it go, either."

Geneva made no effort to hide her misery. "But how do I get rid of it?" She wished he would stop speaking so cryptically.

He reached toward her with the easiest and gentlest of motions, and laid his hand, warm, light, and dry as an autumn leaf upon her forehead, then he lifted his eyes. "Oh, Lord God, this child is aneedin' yer Love, and she's been asearchin' and apainin' fer a long time. Open up yer big heart, Lord, and send yer Love apourin' into her. Let yer Spirit take over her whole self, cause ye made her in yer image, and she's apinin' fer yer glory. Oh, Lord God Almighty, in the name of Jesus, let her be Holy Ground."

Geneva felt a little dazed, as if she had walked into a room where nothing seemed in the right place, and gravity held little sway. Then she felt her being, physical as well as spiritual, being filled and probed. At first, she was shamed because it seemed to her there was so little to plumb, and what was there was superficial and ugly. But before the shame came to light, the bottom of the shallows of her soul crumbled away like stale bread, and she felt the deeper avenues of herself opening, as if there were unexplored caverns to be searched and filled. Again, far into the depths of her soul, the bottom seemed to fall away, and there was more and more, until she felt bigger and deeper than she would have ever hoped or thought possible. All of her was huge, but the being—and it was a being, vast and terrible, and of absolute authority—continued to fill her, until she felt there was nothing left of herself, except small remnants shoved tightly in the corners. So filled was she that she was afraid to inhale, lest she should burst.

Her sense of shame remained, and she knew herself as a sinner who had wreaked harm and havoc, but soon this sense was overlaid with a welling joy so that she wanted to abandon self and let the joy suffuse more than just her heart and soul and body. There was more to her than she ever could begin to know. She extended backward and forward into time and space and possibilities. And as she expanded with the presence of this Being of awful power, she fully desired that the vestiges of her past hopes and fears and sins, which clung like noxious little cockleburs, would release and drop away. And still, the filling and expanding continued, and she did not know if she was in pain or ecstasy as she felt herself growing ever larger, surfeited with this awful, agonizing joy, this horrible pleasure.

Holy Miracle lifted his hand away, and smiling with the light behind his eyes, he looked at her with infinite patience and gentleness. "Yes, girlie, the Lord God Almighty loves you sure, and thistles don't grow in no Holy ground. I'll be aleavin' ye now, but ye got yer life to live. Ye tell yer sister old Holy Miracle Jones has found his last and best healin'."

And with that, he turned, and made his way back up the long hill through the undulating grass, ripe with sun and time. He seemed to take on the qualities of the softest of winds, barely rippling the grasses as he passed. Still stunned, but aware that the power in his hands was leaving her, this earth, for good, Geneva let the tears roll down her face. She fell off the rock and onto her knees in the grass, and lifting her arms high, she called out, "Oh, my Almighty God! Take it all away! Deliver me of all my pride!"

After that, there was no more time or circumstances or hope or pain. There was just the overwhelming sense that the illusion of Self had been stripped away, so that she was free to be pure light and joy and laughter. The rosy light poured into her from the edge of the sky and across the golden grass, and the wind whispered the sweetest of secrets, the answers to the most closely shrouded mysteries. She felt the laughter rise to her lips, and she stood, letting herself be wrapped up in this joy as she watched Holy Miracle Jones crest the hill into that rollicking gold light, and Geneva's love streamed after him.

Fifteen

Geneva perched on the toilet seat and leaned forward to examine the little strip of blue plastic pinched between her thumb and forefinger. Positive! Once again, she counted. Twelve weeks. She had barely dared to allow the thought to take root, even when she had missed her second period, even when she had been carried to the bathroom on waves of nausea every morning. She had simply not believed that she could have been reprieved from the awful certainty that she had drunk the vile liquid from Howard's cup.

She squeezed her eyes against the image of his pained face, the lightless eyes staring at her with despair as she took it from him. How reluctantly he had surrendered it! It had been a test, and she had failed, proving herself shallow and selfish. And he had given her up in that moment, knowing that she would not stand firm, that she was capable of billowing and changing course with the slightest wind.

She had given up on herself, too, when he had told her that he could not love her, could not hold her to him and give her the life he thought she wanted. But that was before her wants changed, before God had told her He would never give up on her. He had shattered all the panes of her brittle self and had replaced them with pure, warm light.

And now, this! At first, she felt nothing, just a numb uncomprehending, then a small tendril of fear spooled upward along the path of her spine, curling and twining around her heart. It was quickly joined by a green vine of joy, which unfurled and grew and flowered, coupling with the first weed of fear until she did not know which was which. She only knew that something bloomed and grew, huge and terrifyingly beautiful. The feeling was too big to name; these things bursting into feathery spirals were too fine and delicate to articulate, to hold long enough to slip into a slot of meaning. But she did know that the pain she had been carrying with her all these weeks had lightened.

Thank you, Lord, she whispered, as the joy crowded out the fear, *But what do I do now?* She didn't care. Howard's child was sleeping in her womb. God had granted her something that she didn't even know she had wanted. Against all hope and possibility, she was being offered another chance to love someone. Not Howard. He had made it clear that was not possible. But his child. Someone to give her whole self to, to delight in, a gift worthy of the Magi. She gave a little gasping chuckle and leaned her head against the wall, letting the wonder of it wash over her.

There was a knock at the door of the bathroom.

"Aunt Geba, I gotta pee!" came the small voice. "Let me in! I gotta pee *now!*"

She jumped up and pushed the blue strip of plastic underneath the tissues in the wastebasket, then opened the door to Phoebe's earnest face. "Gotta pee, Aunt Geba." The child clutched at her crotch and danced a little jig.

"Sure, honey, let me help you," Geneva said, lifting the child onto the toilet. "You're such a big girl, holding it like that. I'm proud of you!" Phoebe teetered on the seat, leaning forward with her elbows on her knees and beaming at Geneva. "I know. I can always hold it now!" She reached for the toilet paper and tucked a wad of it between her legs, then hopped off the toilet. "I am a big girl! I can pull my own pants back up," she said, struggling to do so.

The phone rang, and there was a simultaneous knock at the front door. Geneva heard Rachel talking to someone as she picked up her niece and stuck her small hands under running water, then handed her a towel. "Good job, sweetie! You got them nice and clean!" She carried Phoebe into the living room to see who had arrived, but it was empty. Outside, Rachel was setting the twins into their baby stroller. Hannah stood beside her sisters and poked soft toys at them.

"Hey," said Geneva, opening the door.

"Hey," answered Rachel, glancing up and smiling. "Who do you have there?"

"A little girl I found in the bathroom pee-peeing all by herself."

"No!" shouted Phoebe, "A *big* girl!"

"Yes, you are!" agreed Geneva, kissing her. "A big girl, indeed. I won't be able to carry you around much longer." And she set the child down with a hug. Phoebe scampered over to her sisters. "Who was at the door?"

"Sally Beth. She just popped in to borrow Fairhope. Said she wanted to get in one last ride before the weather got bad. Can you believe it's supposed to snow today? It's so warm now."

Geneva could hold her news no longer. "You got a minute?"

Rachel looked at her askance. "I've got days. What's up?"

Geneva had not intended to sound so serious. She laughed. "Not much. Just something earth-shattering." She lowered her voice. "I'm pregnant."

Rachel's eyes flew wide open and she slapped her hand to her chest and gasped. Then she grabbed Geneva and hugged her tightly. "When did you find out?"

"Just now. EPT."

"Oh my!" breathed Rachel, looking at Geneva with something between delight and shock. Then she hugged her again. "Oh Lord have mercy!"

"I think this is a sign of His mercy. You don't know what I did. I tried to get rid of this baby already, before I even know I was pregnant. But I guess I have been spared the consequences of what I did." And Geneva sat down beside her sister and told her about the dark, deadly tea she had swallowed on that bitter morning. "But I still have that baby! Oh Rachel! It's such a gift!"

They both sat silent for a long while, contemplating what this might mean. Finally Rachel spoke, "Honey, that's great, but what will you do? And how come you haven't figured this out already? You haven't been with Howard for months."

Geneva could not stop the giggle. "I know! I can't believe it!" She rushed on breathlessly. "I was so out of it after the attack, I didn't notice that I had missed a period, and then, 'cause I just assumed I couldn't be pregnant, when I missed the second one, I figured it was because so much had been going on, and then, I started thinking I had some sort of stomach bug that wouldn't go away. It wasn't until last week that I started getting suspicious, but I was scared I would jinx it if I thought about it too much…" She giggled again, and then tears sprang to her eyes. "Oh Rachel! This is just so amazing! What on earth am I going to do?"

Rachel caught her giggles. "I don't know, girl! But you'd better do something soon! Three months gone already, so you don't have a lot of time. Oh! By the way! That was Lenora on the phone. She wants to come see the babies again, and, of course Jimmy Lee is coming, as usual. Seems like she just can't get enough of them, and I guess Jimmy Lee isn't going to give up, at least not until he finds out about this!" She tapped Geneva's belly. "I'm going to call her back and tell her to bring Howard with her this time instead of Jimmy Lee!" she laughed. "And bring a ring!" She clapped her hands with delight. "Oh, hot dog! We have to start planning a wedding! Geneva, you're going to have everything you wanted!"

Geneva recoiled. "No! Don't you dare!" She sobered and dropped her eyes. "Rachel, I won't marry him. I can't."

"What? Of course you will marry him! Once he finds out, he'll sweep you up and take you straight to the church. I know he's just looking for an excuse to get you back, and this will be the perfect opportunity."

There was a time when Geneva would have joined Rachel in this fantasy, thinking furiously, planning, figuring out a way to make things turn out in the way she wanted, but today, she did not try to think or plan or maneuver. She simply allowed herself to be, to revel in the gratitude and peace she felt when she thought about this baby. She tried not to think of Howard; it hurt too much to switch the light of her memory onto the little cabin on the mountain and the bed of mint and the streaming stars. God had promised to direct her life, and there was no need for her to try to do it herself. She might not have Howard, but she would have his child forever. She smiled, even as the ache settled into her bones. Would she ever stop this ceaseless yearning for him? She hoped so, but she knew it would be a very, very long time.

"No. I won't." She had not thought about how Howard would react to the news about this miracle, but as the words came out of her mouth, they brought with them resolve. "Of course he would marry me, but I can't do this to him—trap him, or at least make him feel trapped. He has made it clear he doesn't love me, doesn't even want to love me, and I can't put him in that position. We'd be a classic hillbilly shotgun wedding couple, and he would spend the rest of his life resenting me and the baby. I can't do that to him, to us. To this baby. What we had was perfect, and I won't ruin it."

"Geneva! What makes you say he doesn't love you? After what you told me about your last conversation, it seems that he does love you, but he's afraid you will hurt him. This will give him the opportunity to learn to trust you. At least give him that chance! And besides, you love him, that's perfectly clear. This can make things right between you."

"No," she said, cupping her hand at the place she imagined the baby lay. "This baby doesn't need to grow up under that shadow. It's going to be the good part of what I have of him."

"Geneva!" her sister wailed. "You can't do that! I can't believe I am hearing this from you! Why would you run away from the man you really love? What about this baby? Do you want it to grow up without a father?" Her eyes narrowed. "Is this your pride talking? Because you told me you had gotten rid of that."

Geneva sighed. "Let's talk about it later, Rachel. I'll go talk to him, and we'll see how it goes, ok? And I don't have to tell you not to tell anybody, not even Wayne until I say you can." She grimaced. "Or Mama and Daddy, either. Gosh, this will kill them."

"No it won't," growled Rachel. "You aren't the first Lenoir girl to get knocked up. Maybe the first not to marry the daddy, but they can take it." She sighed and took Geneva's hand. "I promise I won't tell, but it's not going to be easy." And then the twins began to wail, and the conversation ended. Geneva fell silent, wrapping her turbulent thoughts around her like an untidy shroud.

The balmy morning wavered and turned. By ten o'clock, the temperature had dropped suddenly. Rain fell like birdshot on the last of the fall vegetables, and by the time Geneva and Rachel had closed all the windows, the rain had turned to ice, then to snow. Geneva stepped out onto the porch to call her cats, but when they didn't show up, she shrugged and went back inside. They knew how to find the barn if they needed it.

Storm clouds began to pile up, thrown high and tumbled like a bed hastily departed, the sky darkened, and the temperature continued in free fall. Snow swirled in tiny white tornadoes against the pewter sky. Wayne came home.

"I was afraid I couldn't make it over the pass with this snow coming down. The weatherman says that we could get six to eight inches before it blows over. I've never seen it snow this hard this early in the year," he said, stamping the snow off his shoes.

Rachel stood at the door. "Wayne, I am worried about Sally Beth. She took off on Fairhope early this morning, and she isn't back yet. "Do you think you ought to go looking for her?"

"Oh, no," groaned Wayne. "Doesn't that girl have enough sense to get out of the weather? Where did she go?" Rachel shook her head and shrugged. "Did you see which way she took off?"

"She went west, so she could be headed toward a dozen different places. Should I call Uncle Henry or Jackson to come help look for her? The snow is already sticking pretty bad."

"Yeah, you better call them both. I'll change clothes and saddle up. If there are three or more of us looking, we shouldn't have any trouble finding her before it gets dark. Did she say when she might be back?"

"No, but she was in a hurry, and she had a big bag of stuff with her. I don't think she was planning to picnic, though. We talked about the storm coming."

Wayne stopped long enough to kiss his girls, then he disappeared upstairs to change his clothes. Geneva looked out the window. "Oh, I wish you had another horse! I should have gone looking for her when it started to snow. Now I am no use to you at all!"

"Shut up, Geneva. You need to take care of yourself. You can't go riding those trails when they are slippery." Rachel looked at her sternly before glancing out the window. "Oh! Here comes Sally Beth! And boy, is she moving fast!" They both bolted out the back door in time to see their cousin pushing Fairhope hard across the field to the west. She galloped right up to the back porch and reined in hard, leaping off his back and rushing up the steps.

Sally Beth, white with terror underneath the chill on her cheeks, her hair wind-whipped and tangled, grabbed Geneva by the shoulders. "Geneva, Holy Miracle is real sick! He is unconscious, and I cain't bring him to! We got to get to him! Oh Geneva, Rachel! I think he's *dying!*" She dashed away a tear that streaked down her cheek and wiped her nose on her sleeve. Geneva had never seen the usually composed and polished Sally Beth look so disheveled or upset.

Wayne appeared on the porch. "Where is he, Sally Beth?" asked Wayne.

"About three miles from here, up past Jacob's Mountain. He lives in a cave there, and, oh, Wayne! He's *real bad!* I tried to get him down to the horse, but he passed out, and it was all I could do to get him back in out of the snow and warm him up!" Her eyes were eloquent in their pleading. "Oh, *please* hurry! I think he's dying!"

Wayne turned away from her to think. "I don't know how we can get up there and get him out with horses, if he can't ride. Maybe we could make a litter…"

"Oh, no! You have to go up over the rocks there. The horses cain't even make it, you have to walk the last half mile. You'll have to carry him out. Or get a *helicopter!* Oh, Wayne! Get a helicopter! Oh, please!" She was fighting hard to hold back the tears.

Wayne looked at her closely. "What does he look like, Sally Beth? Is he hurt? Anything broken? Bleeding anywhere?"

"No, he's just *sick!*" He's real pale and skinny, and he's *cold!* I was taking him some clothes and food 'cause I knew the storm was comin', but when I got there he was just layin' on his bed and shiverin', and I got some soup into him, and then I tried to get him out to the horse, but I could only get him partway down and he just *passed out* on me. It took me forever to get him back up over the rocks and into the cave. He's real *sick,* Wayne!" Sally Beth ended with a sob.

Geneva was taken aback. Sally Beth knew where Holy Miracle Jones lived? She had merely caught the barest glimpses of him on dappled summer days. Why did Holy Miracle let Sally Beth share the remote corners of his life, and not her or Rachel? Geneva had never worried much about his physical comforts; it had never crossed her mind to deliberately take supplies to fortify against the cold. A momentary stab of jealousy pierced her, and then waves of guilt cascaded and foamed. She stared at her cousin, wondering about this girl who nearly everyone had considered insignificant, and she was ashamed. Holy Miracle saw something in her that no one else, including Geneva, had, and Holy Miracle's eyes looked deep.

"Okay," Wayne was saying. "The hospital at Tucker doesn't have a helicopter, but I have a friend over in Harrisonburg who has one, and he was a medic in the army. If I can get in touch with him, maybe he will fly out here. I'm sure he can land it on the bald there on Jacob's Mountain if he can fly in this storm. Rachel, you call Jackson and Uncle Henry, and tell them to bring the horses. I don't suppose John is back yet, is he?"

"No. He's due back tomorrow, I think," Geneva said as Rachel went back inside to make the calls.

Wayne paused to think. "The chopper is too small to carry more than the pilot and one crew member with a patient on board. I'll ride out with Uncle Henry, and hopefully, Jackson can come, too. We'll ride as far as we can, and between us, we can carry him. You say the cave is about a mile from the bald, Sally Beth?"

"Yeah, but there is another flat, bald patch jist above his cave. Don't helicopters have a litter? You could just have them lower it and put him in it right at his cave. You won't have to carry him so far."

"Good thinking, Sally Beth. But we'll have a hard time finding the place. If we have the chopper come here first, James, my friend, can land in the field and you can ride with him to show him the way. Once Uncle Henry and Jackson get here, we'll head on out. Geneva, will you go saddle up Redneck and help Sally Beth put Fairhope back in the stall? I'll go put on my boots and call James."

"Wait!" exclaimed Geneva. "Who knows when Uncle Henry can get here? If it's only three miles, Fairhope isn't tired, and you and I can go ahead."

Wayne hesitated, then nodded. "That's not a bad idea. We could head out now, and it might make a difference if we can get there quickly. The others can catch up. Sally Beth, get Fairhope warmed up, and give him some water. And saddle up Redneck for me." Rachel appeared at the door.

"I can't get hold of anybody," she informed them. "Absolutely no one is at home, or at least not answering the phone. I even called Daddy, but they aren't answering either. I'm betting everybody is out tending to livestock right now. What do you think we should do, Wayne?" she asked her husband.

"Geneva and I are going on. We shouldn't lose any time, and if you can reach anybody, send them on after us." Rachel started to speak, but Geneva broke in. "I'm going, Rachel," she said through tight lips. But when she saw the worry in her sister's eyes, she softened. "And don't worry, I'll be careful," she added. "I know how to ride in the snow."

Rachel narrowed her eyes. "There's ice underneath the snow," she began, but Wayne broke in.

"It would be helpful if she came along. If we take off right now, it might make a critical difference. The others can catch up, if they can even travel in this storm." He looked apologetic. "If it doesn't let up, the chopper won't fly, and I don't even know when or if James can come, and the others may not be able to get out, either. And if the storm doesn't let up, we may not be able to get him out. I'm going to need help if he's as bad as Sally Beth thinks. I'd feel better if she comes." He put his arm around his wife's shoulders. "Will you go help Sally Beth with the horses?"

Rachel glared at him, then at her sister. "You both had better be careful!" was all she said before she turned on her heel, and brushing roughly past Wayne, followed Sally Beth to the barn.

Not long afterward, Rachel and Sally Beth led the horses back to the house, where Wayne and Geneva were prepared to ride. Wayne hurriedly added supplies to his medical kit. "I got hold of James," he said. "It isn't snowing at Harrisonburg. He said he will come, but he can't fly here until there is a break in the storm, and I don't know how long that will be. We need to get there as soon as we can. Holy Miracle might not make it without some intervention. Rachel, keep trying. Get anybody you can to meet us up there in case we have trouble. We'll see you there, Sally Beth."

Rachel nodded and turned slowly back to the door. Suddenly, she spun back and hugged Wayne tightly, and then Geneva. "You be careful!" Geneva could see the sudden redness bloom around Rachel's eyes and felt a tug of tender remorse for her sister. She was glad she was going, and not having to sit at home, impotently waiting for others to rescue Holy Miracle.

"God bless you! And *hurry!*" said Sally Beth. She wrung her hands and added, "Please don't let him die!" as Wayne boosted Geneva into the saddle, then sprang onto Redneck's back. The two were off into the face of the angry snow, disappearing into the white violence within seconds.

The going was rough. Wayne rode ahead at first, but after a few minutes, he fell back and offered to let Geneva go ahead. "I can't really see much in this. You know the way better than I do. Do you think you can find it okay?"

"Yeah," replied Geneva grimly and moved in the lead position, carefully picking her way through the snow-crusted grass. They had not begun moving uphill yet, and it was harder to know the right direction with such poor visibility as they moved across the pasture. It could be difficult to find the trailhead leading up to Jacob's Mountain. After a few minutes, Geneva was relieved to see a line of trees. Now it was just a matter of picking her way along the edge of the forest until the trail presented itself.

"It will be along here somewhere," she called back to Wayne. "Keep a lookout for that big willow oak, and watch out for the creek. If we get to it, we've come too far and we will have to backtrack a little ways." The wind was howling by this time, and Wayne rode closer.

"I couldn't hear you. Do you know where you are?"

"Wait! There's the oak. The trail should start just up here." She nudged Fairhope forward, and Wayne followed closely.

The trail opened to them with a tenuous hope. Now it was just a matter of staying on it, up past the laurel field, beside the ravine, and then over the top of the bald. Geneva said a little prayer, and confidence filled her. *Yes, God would help them,* she thought, settling back and letting Fairhope have his head, for she knew that the horse could keep to the trail better than she could.

It was bitterly cold. Geneva pulled her scarf up around her mouth and her hat down low on her head. Her hands were cold inside the leather gloves, but her seat was warm from Fairhope's steaming back. A rush of love for the steady horse came over her, and she uttered a hymn of thanksgiving for his sure-footedness. Then she offered another prayer for Wayne who was riding the much more spirited Redneck.

It occurred to her that Redneck did not like not being behind, and he was likely to nudge and nip Fairhope if they were not moving fast enough to suit him. That would be a danger when they came to the path along the ravine. She shuddered, remembering another narrow path perched above an abyss on that awful day three months ago, and the sight of Jimmy Lee disappearing silently into the mist after she had bumped into him.

She began to wish she had been the one to take the fall, but soon realized that she might have missed the solid ground and fallen to her death, and that would have meant the death of this baby. *Why had it happened the way it did? Had God had a hand in that?* Maybe at the very moment when Jimmy Lee fell, a tiny cluster of cells was attaching themselves to the wall of Geneva's womb. Maybe that baby was the reason she had lived through the ordeal of the moment, of the ordeal of the boar. She smiled, imagining a guardian angel standing sentry over that little speck of life. Surely God had plans for this little one. He or she—certainly a she—females outnumbered males in the family by about twenty to one. Yes, *she* had started life against terrifying odds, and still hung on. Already, she felt a swell of pride for this tenacious little being. *A tough little survivor!* Maybe she would name her Boudicca, after the warrior queen who wouldn't give up, even in the teeth of the Roman army.

Pulling aside, she called back to Wayne. "You'd better go ahead for awhile. The ravine is just up ahead, and Redneck might get pushy. Unless you want to switch horses."

"No, I'm good. The snow seems to be slacking off a little, and I can see better. It occurred to me back there that I should just give him his head anyway. He's smarter than I am."

Geneva laughed, "I came to the same conclusion. Made it a lot easier, didn't it?"

Wayne did not need to nudge Redneck. As soon as the gelding saw an opening ahead, he lunged for it, brushing Geneva as he trotted by. It would not be long now. The worst of the trail lay just ahead. Again she prayed for their safety, for the safety of the baby, for Holy Miracle who lay shivering behind a black fold in the granite above them.

Redneck paused as he considered his first steps onto the slender collar along the neck of the ravine. Geneva held her breath as his front hoof slid slightly on the ice beneath the snow, but then he steadied and began picking his way carefully upward. This ledge was much wider than the one that had failed Jimmy Lee, but still, one slippery patch could mean a serious tumble down the mountain. She waited for a moment before following, not sure that Fairhope would be a gentleman, docilely following Redneck's rear as the wind howled and the snow stung the eyes. She felt her own eyes filling with tears, and she squeezed her lids against the brutal, icy flakes.

She looked down the side of the mountain. *Here was the place Rachel had slipped and fallen those many years ago and broken her arm.* She wondered if Holy Miracle and his father had seen her lose her footing and slide, or if they had happened upon her after Geneva had gone for help. If they had witnessed her fall, why had they waited for Geneva to leave before they rescued Rachel? She shook her head. All this time she had assumed they shunned all outsiders, but Holy Miracle had let Sally Beth know where he lived, had let her into the confines of his personal life. Her own brief moments with him when he had given her his cryptic insights had seemed like precious treasures to her. How much more had he given to Sally Beth? What was it about that girl that made her special to him?

The path curved upward into the last patch of pines just below Jacob's Bald. They made their way through the restless trees, then picked a careful path through the heath, and they found themselves exposed on the empty, high meadow. Here was the spot where Holy Miracle had blessed her and the Holy Spirit had descended upon Geneva that bright October day. She had been back twice since then, and each time, she had felt the Presence hovering nearby, filling her with peace. Even today, with the snow coming down into the devouring cold, the place felt serene. The wind sang hymns to her in deep harmony with the earth and sky. She pulled up alongside Wayne.

"Do you feel that?" she asked him. "Does it feel like God lives here to you?"

"Oh, yes," replied Wayne. "There is no question this is holy ground."

"As am I," smiled Geneva.

"What?"

In October, when I came here and Holy Miracle blessed me, he asked God to make me 'holy ground.'"

"We all should be so blessed."

They turned west, toward the cliffs that towered beyond Jacob's Bald. The storm picked up, howling through the empty space around them, and the horses put their heads down and pushed against the wind. Yet, despite the storm and the snow, Geneva felt at peace, guided and protected. They rode within the silent, white shell of their own thoughts.

At length, Wayne said, "Come on. I see the cliffs up ahead," as he gave Redneck a slap. They broke into a fast trot across the snow blanketing the sleeping meadow. Riding fast to the edge of the field and over a rise, they came upon a tumble of boulders as high as a man, piled thickly at the base of a sheer cliff.

"She said there was a path off to the left here," Wayne said, pausing to pull out two flashlights. He handed one to Geneva, who switched hers on, but it did nothing to help with visibility. The beam bounced helplessly off the veil of snow streaming from the sky. Geneva took the lead, knowing that Wayne would have difficulty seeing with his less-than-perfect eyesight. Carefully, they scanned the ground as they wound their way around the base of the cliff, but all they could see were the impossible obstacles. They continued alongside the boulders, searching for a break.

At last, Geneva found it. They had walked in a wide arc beneath the cliffs, and just as they rounded a corner, the rocks suddenly gave way to a wide trail bordered by brooding pines. It led them back up behind the wall of boulders, then narrowed and cut its way upward. When it became impossible for the horses to advance further, they dismounted and led them back into the safety of the trees, where they unsaddled and draped blankets over the animals, then they tied the reins to trees and turned back to challenge the rocky ascent on foot. It was rough and steep, and the footing was precarious. Before long, they had to pull themselves upward on hands and knees, and the arduous climb into the face of the buffeting wind exhausted them quickly. Geneva's tired body gasped for oxygen in the thin air as she pulled herself forward and upward, and her lungs ached as they drew in the icy wind. She thought of her baby and placed her hands and feet more carefully. Thankfully, this part of the trail ran no more than a hundred feet, and before too long, they found themselves in a narrow space close to the face of the cliff, suspended high up in the air with the snow swirling around them and nothing but white death below them.

The wall of rock gaped at her left, and the path backtracked into a deeper gloom before disappearing into a black hole inside the cliff. "I think this is it," she called over her shoulder.

"Wait!" he called from behind. "Sally Beth said to be very careful at the entrance. She said there's a big dip in the floor at the extreme left, and she has nearly broken her leg a dozen times going through." He moved ahead of her to enter the dark slash in the wall first.

A dozen times? How many times has she been here? thought Geneva. She brushed aside the ever-present feeling of jealousy and guilt.

"Right in through here. Yeah, it's pretty bad. Just stay right."

They stepped around a rocky breach in the floor of the cave and could see a comfortable wide space opening up to the beams of their flashlights. A pale, rosy light glowed from not far into the interior. A few more paces led them into the space where they found Holy Miracle lying on a narrow bed, his thin body barely visible under a pile of blankets. A fire burned low in a rough fireplace tucked into an alcove beside him. Wayne dropped to his knees to examine the unconscious old man. "See if you can get the fire built up. We need to get him as warm as we can," he said as he checked his pulse and temperature and pulled up an eyelid, shining the light into the sightless eyes. Then he looked at his gums. Finally, he pulled out a blood pressure cuff from his bag and strapped it onto a thin, pale arm.

Geneva piled wood onto the fire, then, remembering Howard's ministrations to her when she was cold and ill, she looked for jars to fill with water to warm him. She found none, so she placed rocks near the coals, taking care not to get them too close, for she knew they could explode if they got too hot. Then she took a pot outside to scoop up snow and hung it over the fire to make coffee.

When she was certain there was nothing more she could do to help, she gave herself the luxury of looking around at this secret place, the home that had sheltered Holy Miracle and most likely his father all these many years. It looked almost like a real home, not exactly what one would expect from a hermit's cave. There were actual furnishings, and even a sort of rug made of burlap sacks on the floor. The bed upon which Holy Miracle lay was made of tree limbs and lined with straw ticking. Tree stumps served as stools, and in the corner, a couch made of bent and twisted willow boughs sat covered with another straw tick. A rough table filled a good portion of the middle of the room, and a bookcase made of slabs of coarse wood held a small assortment of ragged volumes. The tidy fire pit and a good supply of cut firewood took up most of one wall. Geneva could see a hole higher up that served as a chimney, and the smoke curled upward and out into the night rather than escaping into the cavern. It was cozy, she thought, and clean, and homey, and for a moment, she envisioned another place with a table and stools made of tree stumps and a bed filled with fragrant herbs. The hollowness of her loss saddened her beyond description.

"How is he?" she asked.

"He's unconscious, and he's in shock, but there's no fever, so it doesn't seem that there is infection anywhere," he replied as he pulled a bottle of clear liquid from his bag and tied it to the tree limb that served as a kind of bedpost. "Come hold this flashlight for me. I'm going to give him some Ringer's lactate, and it's going to be hard to find a vein."

Geneva moved to Holy Miracle's bed and shone the light as Wayne searched both arms for a visible vein. He was extremely pale, and she could see tiny red spots and larger bruises on the inside of his arm. "What are those?" she asked.

"Petechiae. That's little dots of blood under the skin. His blood vessels are leaking, and that's led to acute anemia." He picked up Holy Miracle's hand. "I might find a vein here. Now, get me sterilized. He's so low, an infection would kill him. Pour some alcohol on my hands. All right, good. Now break open that package and hand me some gauze." Geneva ripped open the packet to remove several squares of gauze. "That's good, now pour some more alcohol on that, and—be careful not to touch it—open that package with a needle in it. And see that tubing? I need that, too."

Geneva carefully followed his instructions. Presently, Wayne had pierced the back of Holy Miracle's hand with a needle and had hooked up the IV solution. Geneva moved to the fire, and wearing her insulated gloves, scraped rocks onto some of the sacking. "Here," she said. "You can warm him up with these." She wrapped them tightly and handed them to Wayne.

"That's great. If we can warm him up, it will help." He tucked the rocks around Holy Miracle exactly where Howard had tucked mason jars around her to warm her on that cold, rainy night. Then he sat back and waited.

"What's wrong with him?" asked Geneva.

"Not sure, but my guess is some bone marrow disorder that is causing anemia. He's bleeding internally, and I see some evidence of bleeding in his gums, but I don't see any other bloody discharge. See, here's a bowl where Sally Beth fed him soup, so he has some liquid in him, and there is no vomit, no blood. Everything around here is clean. But it looks like he needs a blood transfusion." He looked at Geneva sadly, "Honey, we may not be able to save him. I don't know when that chopper will get here, and I don't know if he can last through the night. And even if he does live, the long-term prognosis doesn't look good. I'm thinking myeloblastic anemia or leukemia, and both are pretty much fatal at his age." He paused before adding gently, "And neither is going to be pleasant for him. He probably is ready to go."

Geneva squeezed her eyelids against the tears. "I'm so glad you're here, Wayne," she said, grateful for her brother-in-law's skills and his compassion. If Holy Miracle were to die here tonight, she was glad to know everything possible had been done to save him. She grasped the old man's hand. It was cold, except where it had lain against a warm rock. "Holy Miracle, please just hang on a while longer," she whispered to him. She didn't know why she so desperately wanted him to live if only to face a protracted dying. Maybe she needed to have time to let him go, or maybe she didn't want to let Sally Beth down. Whatever it was, she prayed with all her soul that he should at least last until they had a chance to say goodbye.

They passed the evening murmuring softly so as not to disturb the stillness of the place or Holy Miracle's slumber. It was comfortable here in the cave, with the gentle color of the firelight flickering against the walls of the granite and the wind humming in the distance. The place was warm and dry, and Geneva could not help but think of the cave that Howard had shown her. Wondering if there were cave paintings in here as well, she wandered into the interior with her flashlight and there found, not ancient paintings, but evidence of years of Pwyll and Holy Miracle.

There were drawings of trees and flowers, and of angels, and pictures of what might be heaven. Further in, a steaming pool of still water filled most of a room. Skirting it, she stepped close to the walls ringing it and saw that lines of scripture were etched into the smooth stone. In one section, a good portion of the Psalms graced the rock surface, and in another, nearly the whole of the epistle of First John. She traced her finger along the words of certainty and love.

And this the message we have heard from Him and announce to you, that God is light, and in Him there is no darkness at all.

Later, in another section, she found this from Peter:

"This is my beloved Son with whom I am well-pleased." And we ourselves heard this utterance made from heaven when we were with Him on the holy mountain. And so we have the prophetic word made more sure, to which you do well to pay attention as to a lamp shining in a dark place, until the day dawns and the morning star arises in your hearts.

Geneva's heart felt peace stir and eddy upwards as the holy words permeated her being. Holy Miracle surely would not live long, but she was certain that death would not fully claim his flesh tonight, and it would never claim his soul. His voice would live long enough to give her one last blessing, and his spirit would rise to live forever. And she would see him again one day in the fullness of perfect health. She smiled and turned back to the fire and humanity.

Wayne had settled himself beside the bed, his head leaning back against the lumpy mattress. He smiled at Geneva as she came into the light. "Have a nice explore?"

"Yes. This cave is full of Scripture. Holy Miracle has been here a long time, and probably his father, too. You should go back there and see it."

"I'd like to, but I don't want to leave him. He might wake up, or I might need to resuscitate him."

She nodded and sat down beside him. He sighed and stirred. "Wonder what Rachel is doing right now?"

"Probably on her knees, praying for us. You know she's worried. I'm so glad I am here, knowing as much as there is to know about the situation, and not stuck at home, worrying about the unknown."

"Yeah, it's tough, being a woman. I'm very selfishly glad I am a man, getting to be the one who goes out, has the adventures, when women have to stay home and do the really hard part—waiting and tending and just being patient."

"Wait a minute," Geneva flared. "A woman can do anything a man can do. This is nineteen seventy-seven, Wayne. Things have changed."

"Not that much, and especially here. Women *can* do anything a man can do, but in rural West Virginia, they *may* not, if you understand your grammar school use of the words."

"Like what? Look at Dianne, running the theater, and there's…" she stopped, realizing she had run out of examples.

"Yes, 'there's…' exactly," he said, waving his hand vaguely. "And it's not really just here. There were only two women in my class in medical school, and everybody gave them a hard time. Some of the professors flat-out told them they were taking up space that would be better used by men who wouldn't drop out of the profession to have children."

Geneva fell silent. She had to admit that the world still placed limits on women. Even in DC, she had gotten her job only because her boss was a rabid feminist who had lobbied hard to hire a woman.

Wayne continued, "Just last month we interviewed an excellent nurse practitioner who was really pretty and not married, and my director didn't want to hire her because he was afraid she was wanting the job just so she could find herself a doctor for a husband. He actually said she would be trouble if she were on staff. If that had been a man, his being single or good looking wouldn't have been an issue."

Geneva swallowed the lump of desolation she felt rising in her throat. How was she going to make a living for this baby if she were not able to find a job? Even in DC, it would be difficult to raise a baby by herself, and she knew in the core of her heart she wanted her child to live here, among her own people, among her own hills and clouds and rocks. She did not know how to answer Wayne, and she wondered if he would remember this conversation when he found out about the baby. She rose. "I think I'll go get a breath of air. You okay? Can I get you anything? Coffee?"

"No, I'm fine. Don't fall off the cliff. I don't feel like rescuing anyone else tonight."

"I'll be careful." She threw another log onto the fire and put on her coat and gloves, then moved toward the entrance to the cave. Darkness had completely enveloped the face of the mountain, but the snow and wind had stopped, and the stars spilled into the now-clear night sky in riotous exuberance. Breathing in the frigid air, she looked upward as her hand found its way to the pendant she wore around her neck, and she grasped it tightly, comforted by its warmth as she scanned the sky in the hopes of seeing a shooting star. The spangled heavens looked back at her, silent, still, and cold, with no echo of her hope. Yet, although she was alone, with the little gold comet resting within her fingers, imbuing her with an optimism she should not feel, she was not lonely. *Love has a way of filling in gaps*, she thought, as she leaned her head against the cold stone.

Thank you, Lord, for the life of Holy Miracle, and for saving him, at least for now. And thank you for Wayne. Please let Holy Miracle live long enough so that he can say goodbye to Sally Beth. And then, unbidden, her thoughts rode across the mountaintops, leaping through the ebony and silver night to Howard. She imagined him coming to rescue her, of finding her in this snug cave, and they would stay and live here by this holy mountain, far from the tarnished world, and raise their child in peace and ever-present love, free from pain or want. Then she scolded herself for her vain foolishness. Howard had chosen not to love her, and she should accept that. *Please God, take this impossible desire from me. Let me be content with what I have, with Your love, with this child. Help me to find my own way, to lose my hopes for Howard.*

A reply came in rhythm with the throbbing of the stars: *For as the heavens are higher than the earth, so my ways are higher than your ways, and my thoughts higher than your thoughts… For you will go out with joy, and be led forth with peace; the mountains and the hills will break forth into shouts of joy before you, and all the trees of the field will clap their hands.* She smiled despite the wounding loss that pulsed through her veins and her heart. Her joy lay just under her belly button.

The distant whine of a motor came to her on the wind, and she strained to listen. *Yes, the sound of the approaching helicopter.* She turned and rushed back into the cave.

"Wayne," she whispered, motioning to her brother-in-law. "The chopper is coming!"

He was on his feet immediately, flashlight in hand, and they rushed outside. Standing at the entrance, perched high above the wild tumble of boulders, they waved their lights at the approaching bird.

There was no hesitation. The pilot easily skimmed over their heads and landed in the flat space twenty feet above them. Within seconds, they saw two flashlights waving beams at them. "Hey!" came Sally Beth's voice.

"Hey!" yelled Wayne back. Can you make it down here?

Sally Beth's voice came from the distance. "No, there isn't a path. We're jist gonna lower the litter down, and you'll need to put him on it."

A man's voice broke in. "Hey, buddy."

"James. Thank you for coming. I owe you."

"Nah. I think this is just a payback for what I owe you. Is he stable?"

"Yes," Wayne shouted back, "but his vitals are weak, and he needs more Ringer's lactate right away. And oxygen. Do you have that on board?"

"I've got 'em both, and we'll get to the hospital pretty quick. Your wife is one smart cookie. She called the ER and had Sally Beth talk to the attending, and they are going to be ready for him."

"That's great. Shall I come back with you?"

"No, I don't have the equipment to get you up here without

jury-rigging the harness. Actually, the harness is jury-rigged to get this gurney in place, and it will take too long to get it back to normal. Don't worry. I may be retired, but I know how to take care of a patient in the field. Now, I have to get airborne before I can lower the stretcher, else we're likely to damage it. Then I'll land again and take care of him. You ready?"

"Ready! Bring her down!"

There were a few moments of silence, then came the sound of the helicopter's engine firing up. It flew straight up, and presently, an object descended from it. Geneva and Wayne reached over the abyss to pull a litter in and settle it on the ground in front of the cave, and Wayne uncoupled the lines while Geneva held it steady. "Let's get him out here!" he shouted above the roar of the chopper. Working quickly, they carried the gurney and, running into the cave with it, gently lifted the old man onto it and brought him back outside, where Wayne secured the harness again and waved his flashlight. The pilot switched on the winching system, and Holy Miracle rose into the black sky, into the piercing lights beyond, as if he were being taken up into heaven. The helicopter sailed upward and landed again, then after a few minutes, James called out, "Okay, all secure, and I have the IV going. He's warm, and bp and pulse are not too far out of range. Don't worry, we'll get him there."

"Thank you, James! I probably won't be able to get there tonight, but I sure appreciate this. I owe you a hunting trip!"

"I'll collect next fall! See you!"

"Bye! Thank yew!" shouted Sally Beth. The motor started up, and the chopper took off.

They watched the lights ascend and move off to the east. Within moments, Geneva and Wayne found themselves alone in the still, spangled night in front of the holy cave.

"That's it," said Wayne. "Time to pack up and get out of here."

Sixteen

It would have been nice to have flowers from the garden, but the snow storm had crushed all hopes of anything blooming again before the spring. Hothouse flowers would have to do. She had ordered a nice fall arrangement, but when she picked it up, she was disappointed. Holy Miracle certainly would find this controlled and sterile bouquet alien, and probably not very pretty. But she didn't want to go empty handed. She knocked softly, then pushed open the door to his room.

He was asleep, but Sally Beth was sitting in the chair at his bedside singing softly. When Geneva walked in, she put her fingers to her lips and whispered, "Shh. He just dropped off." She got up while Geneva put the flowers on the bedside table, and the two went back out into the hallway.

"How is he, Sally Beth?" Geneva already knew the larger answer. Wayne had informed her that the old mystic was dying. He had been revived by infusions of glucose and Ringer's lactate, so he had been lucid when they told him he needed a blood transfusion, indeed would need weekly blood transfusions just to stay alive.

He had simply laughed and said, "I'm bound for heaven. Ye cain't make me stay," refusing the blood and all other medications and life-prolonging measures, including the glucose IV. And he had chafed against being in the hospital.

As his physician, Wayne nodded and signed the order for Holy Miracle to be moved to hospice care immediately. "He's not in pain, and he has the look of those who are ready to go. There's no need to upset him by trying to talk him into anything. I don't blame him." And so Geneva knew his hours were limited.

"He's okay," said Sally Beth, wiping a tear from her cheek. "I jist can't bear to lose him. He is my best friend."

Geneva was silent for a long moment. She had no doubt that Sally Beth spoke the truth. She was, no doubt, his best friend as well. "I know, Sally Beth. I'm so sorry. He has been a part of us since we were little."

A young, good-looking physician came down the corridor. He smiled broadly when he caught sight of Sally Beth.

"Sally Beth! I am glad to run into you. Thank you for what you did for Mrs. Halverton. I haven't seen her this perky since her grandson graduated from college." He hurried on, but looked back over his shoulder, "If you have a free minute sometime this week, would you bring Kit and Caboodle over to see Mrs. Jameson? She was asking me for them."

"Sure, Dr. Sams," smiled Sally Beth.

"Kit and Caboodle?" queried Geneva.

"My Yorkies. There were only two in the litter, so I got the whole kit and caboodle. I bring 'em over sometimes and the old folks here jist love 'em."

"And what did you do for Mrs. Halverton?"

"Oh, nuthin'. I jist come over here a couple times a week and do the hair of the ladies. It gives them a little lift." She smiled. "Literally."

"A couple of times a week? Sally Beth, you live forty miles from here. And your car is in worse shape than mine is." Geneva felt herself growing more and more ashamed of herself over her past judgments of Sally Beth.

Her cousin shrugged. "Aww. I don't have anything to do on my days off, anyways. Besides, I like these old birds. They give me a good time every time I come over here."

They continued strolling down the hall. An elderly man stepped out of his room and motioned to them. "Hey, girls, will you come and sing to me?"

"Why sure, Mr. Hawkins," said Sally Beth. "Come on, Geneva. You'll see what I mean."

They entered the old man's room and he got into his bed. Sally Beth perched on the bed as well, and Geneva, feeling a little silly, climbed up beside Sally Beth, who looked happy and right at home. "What do you want us to sing?" Sally Beth said brightly.

"Whatever you want," he replied, nodding eagerly.

"Ok, how about *On Top of Old Smoky?*" Sally Beth nodded to Geneva, and the two launched into the old ballad with the sad words but lilting melody:

> *On top of Old Smoky, all covered with snow*
> *I lost my true lover a-courting too slow.*
> *Now courtin's a pleasure, and partin's a grief*
> *A false-hearted lover is worse than a thief*
>
> *A thief he will rob you and take what you save*
> *But a false-hearted lover will send you to your grave.*
> *Your grave will decay you and turn you to dust*
> *Not a boy in ten thousand that a poor girl can trust.*
>
> *Now come all young maidens and list to my plea,*
> *Never place your affections in a green willow tree.*
> *The leaves they will wither, the roots they will die*
> *You'll all be forsaken, and never know why.*

"How's that?" asked Sally Beth, grinning broadly. Mr. Hawkins looked disappointed. "Well," he drawled, "it was all right—I guess."

"Just all right? What would you rather hear?"

He brightened. "Do you know *Lucille?*"

"No," both Sally Beth and Geneva shook their heads. "How does that go?"

Mr. Hawkins settled back and launched into the song with full voice:

> *"Have you seen Lucille make water?*
> *She can pee a mile and a quarter,*
> *And if you don't duck, you surely will drown.*
> *And if you want to f—"*

"Mr Hawkins!" exclaimed Sally Beth. "Yew know Jesus don't want you singin' those dirty songs! Nor Mrs. Hawkins, either!"

Mr. Hawkins looked sly. "Well now, they ain't here, air they?"

"Jesus sure is. I was talkin' to him jist this mornin', and if yew don't mind your manners, I might let him know what you've been up to, and he might up and tell Mrs. Hawkins. And yew know what she'll have to say about that!"

The old man's eyes flew open. "Oh no! Please don't tell Him! If He tells the Missus, she'll be on the warpath!"

"Okay, Mr Hawkins. I won't tell Him this time. But yew need to mind yer manners," she warned, shaking her finger at him, "'specially around ladies. Yew ought to know this."

"Yes, ma'am," he replied, sheepish. "But will yew come back and sing to me tomorra?"

"If I can. Now, we need to go on. Yew remember what I said, yew hear?" Sally Beth sailed out of the room, Geneva close on her heels. When they got into the hall and closed the door, Sally Bell giggled and leaned into Geneva. "He used to be a deacon, sober and a perfectly nice man. Now he has the Alltimers, and yew wouldn't *believe* the awful things that come out of his mouth! The only way I kin keep him in line is to threaten to let his wife find out. She's been dead for eight years, but he's scared of her. Yew ready to go back and see if Holy Miracle is awake?"

Geneva nodded.

"All right, I've been with him all mornin', so yew go on. I'm goin' to visit one of the old ladies down the other hall. She used to be a fashion model, and she's particular about the way she looks, so I brush her hair and put a little lipstick on her every time I come in. And we talk about what's happening on *All My Children*." Sally Beth drifted down the hallway with a wave.

Geneva pushed open the door of Holy Miracle's room, then stopped short with a gasp. Howard Knight was sitting at the sleeping man's bedside. When he looked up, the blood drained from his face, and she felt the echo of his faintness in her own wobbly knees.

"Howard," she said, as she recovered from the shock.

He stood up. "Miss Geneva."

She almost wept at his formality, but forced herself to smile calmly. "I'm so glad to see you. I've missed you."

He stood silently, gazing at her with something like grief in his face, then his eyes darted toward the door. He was about to bolt, and Geneva willed him to stay just a little longer.

"Actually," she continued, rushing on. "I was thinking about coming to see you—I need to talk to you about something. Won't you sit?" she pleaded, motioning to one of the chairs. He hesitated, then sat, his eyes downcast. He looked supremely uncomfortable.

She sat beside him, heart pounding as hope danced and sparred with despair. This was the moment to tell him, perhaps the only moment she would have to give him the frightfully wonderful news, but her nerve was failing her. Her breath came in short gasps, her face flushed, then drained again. Dreading his scorn, she plunged ahead. "I'll get right to the point. I wanted to tell you—that is, well—" She took a deep breath to steady herself and started again. "Do you remember that tea I drank?"

A brief light flickered across his face, then disappeared. He looked directly at her, puzzled. "Yes."

"Well, I—I mean, it didn't exactly work like it was supposed to."

The light came and went again. A shadow of a smile fluttered at his mouth. Geneva didn't know what to say next. Why did he smile? Was he happy about it?

"Well, I reckon yer right about that. I never saw hemp work on anybody that way." He looked at her directly. "But yew don't have to go apologizing to me again about that. It's all water under the bridge." He stood up.

Geneva understood his misunderstanding. "Oh, no, that's not what I meant! I—" but the door opened, and John walked into the room. She had not seen him for three months, not since he had left for Africa, and he strode into the room with confidence and an air of authority that made her want to make herself as small as possible. The last thing she needed was him thinking he had some sort of claim on her.

He lit up at the sight of her. "Well, Geneva! I was hoping to find you here. Hey Howard," he added, giving a wave. How's he doing?" he nodded his head toward the sleeping Holy Miracle.

Howard used John's entrance as an excuse to flee. "Good to see ye, John. I gotta run now. Tell Holy Miracle I said hidy when he comes to." He ducked his head at Geneva. "Goodbye, ma'am." And he was gone.

Geneva lashed her flailing emotions down tightly as she turned to John. "Hi," she said quietly. "He's been asleep for awhile. I was hoping he would wake up while I was here." She placed her hand on Holy Miracle's shoulder. "How was your trip?"

"Really good. The experiments are going well, and it looks like we're going to get the funding we need to set up some field stations." He hesitated. "I guess I'll be going back in a few months," he said, looking at her and smiling tentatively. She did not want to see his eyes, for she knew she would find the longing in them, and she did not know how to tell him she could never love him, could never pick up that old hint of a beginning that she had felt for him, dust it off, and wrap it around their shoulders. That early stirring of her heart was in shreds now, worthless to warm or comfort either of them. She wanted to cry for him and his hopeless hope.

They chatted quietly and awkwardly for a while, and Geneva ached for John and his thwarted eagerness and confusion. How could she tell him all that had happened to her heart and spirit since that day of wine and honey when they had lain in each other's arms on that hazy mountaintop and hoped for a future together? Torn between hoping Holy Miracle would wake and the desire to flee John's longing eyes, she felt an onrush of gratitude at Sally Beth's return.

"Hi Sally Beth," said John.

"Well hello, John! You're *back!*" she replied with an enthusiastic smile before she moved to Holy Miracle and grasped his hand.

He woke at her touch. "Hey, Holy Miracle," she murmured softly. "We were beginning to think yew were never going to wake up. How you doin'? Kin I git you something? There's orange juice here." She picked up the package of juice and poked a straw into it, then brought it to the parched and pale lips.

He drank greedily, then relaxed into the pillow. "Sally Beth," he smiled, taking her hand. "I dreamed about ye. Yew were cavorting with the angels, and I heard yer laughter ringin' all over heaven."

She chuckled. "I reckon I would laugh all over heaven. And dance, too. What did the angles look like?"

"Yew kin see fer herself. They're right over there." He motioned to the corner of the room. "See how much they love us?"

"Holy Miracle, I sure wish I could see them. Yew have better eyes than I do."

His eyes roved around the room, smiling at persons unseen. As he glanced toward Geneva, he brightened. "Why little girlie! I didn't see yew there with all that crowd standin' around. Come here and take old Holy Miracle's hand. I want to see how ye've growed since I last saw ye."

Geneva did not remind him that he had seen her only a month ago, but she was profoundly disappointed that he had not remembered how he laid his hands on her head and called down the Holy Spirit to her. It had been such an important moment to her, but he obviously had no recollection. She moved to his bedside.

His voice, honeycombed with frailty, came to her weakly, and she had to lean over to hear him.

"Oh, yes, I see ye have growed. Jist a month ago, ye had that thistle still lodged in yer soul, and now that's withered and died; now ye are full of the honeysuckle. God has his hand on ye fer sure."

Relief washed over her. *He remembered that great moment!* She blinked back the tears.

His gaze ran over her face and his smile broadened. "And yer womb has come to life!" His voice strengthened, "Oh holy God, ye have given this girl a babe!" Placing his hand on her stomach, he splayed his fingers wide over her belly button. His face began to glow, creasing like a bellows as he smiled. "This child will be blessed. Holy God, thank ye for the babe, thank ye for the life you have preserved, for the life that will grow and bloom in the spring. Bless him, my dear, Holy Father." He gave Geneva's belly a little pat, then his hand suddenly grew limp and fell back onto the sheet.

Silence filled the room. Geneva could feel John's confusion behind her, and Sally Beth's sudden sympathy. She expected shame to press against her in the deep stillness, but instead, joy welled up. A blessing for her baby! This is why she had so desperately wanted Holy Miracle to live, and now he had fulfilled her most earnest desire. Laughing with delight, she turned to meet Sally Beth's eyes, which were filled with questioning, and then she let her gaze shift to John. He looked stricken. Her joy did not flee, but underneath the happy gauze that enveloped her, she felt his pain and shared his sorrow for the briefest of moments.

"I'm sorry," she began. "I didn't mean for you to find out this way, but I must tell you that I am full of joy right now. Holy Miracle is right. I am pregnant. John, I know I'm hurting you; I'm sorry. I didn't know that was going to happen, and the truth is, I am in love." She turned her eyes inward. "I am a different person now."

That was all she said. Sally Beth moved to her side and took her hand. "I think I do see angels in the room," she said. John was silent. His eyes, filled with desolation, were more eloquent than any words he could have spoken. He rose to go.

"Ah, boy, I see ye carry the pain of loss with ye, but be of good cheer. There's no loss, only happiness right here with ye. All ye have to do is look." He turned to Sally Beth, reaching toward her. "My own sweet child. Bringer of light and laughter. Yew lift the burdens of all you meet. I bless ye with all my heart. I bless yew all." His face grew brighter, his eyes grew round with surprise and delight, and suddenly he gasped, "Oh my Father! Oh! To see your glory! I never dreamed yew could be so complete!"

His chest rose and fell, and the light of his eyes was shuttered; suddenly the room grew cool. Holy Miracle was gone as quickly as his breath.

The parking lot was empty this early in the morning, so Geneva parked right next to the entrance of the cafe and made a dash for the door. The cold rain had not let up for two days, and she was feeling its misery creep into her bones. Sally Beth was already inside, perfectly coiffed and made up. She was wearing a sky-blue dress with a deeper blue sweater that made her eyes look like a summer day. Geneva chuckled to herself. *Of course Sally Beth would dress joyfully for Holy Miracle's funeral.* She looked down ruefully at her own black ensemble.

"Hey! *Geneva!*" came the sunny voice. "Can yew *believe* this rain? My grandmama used to say it was the angels cryin', but I am sure there's no cryin' in heaven right now. They're all happy as larks to be finally gittin' old Holy Miracle home!"

"Hi Sally Beth. You look beautiful," she said as they sat in a booth. "Are you feeling all right?"

"I am *jist fine*. I cain't begrudge him leavin' us, not after seein' how happy he was to be goin' home." Her voice grew solicitous. "How are *yew?*"

"I'm fine. I just wanted to talk to you before we were around a lot of people, about what you found out on Wednesday… about the baby, I mean. I wanted to explain to you…"

Sally Beth smiled conspiratorially. "Geneva, it's okay. I'm really glad for yew. You sounded so *happy* when yew told us!"

"Yes, well, I am, but no one knows, not even the baby's daddy, and I wanted to make sure…"

Sally Beth grasped her hand. "Don't yew worry about *that!* I won't tell a *single livin' soul!*" She sobered. "But what do yew mean the daddy doesn't know?" Her pale forehead wrinkled in confusion and concern.

"I haven't told him, and he, well, Sally Beth, he doesn't love me, although I love him, desperately. We just had a few days together, but, oh, Sally Beth!" The tears rolled down her face suddenly, before she even knew they were lurking behind her eyes. "I'm so sorry! I'm just upset over Holy Miracle, and I feel really vulnerable right now."

"It's okay, honey." Sally Beth moved to Geneva's side of the booth and drew her close, wrapping her arms around her. "I know yew love him, love both of them. Yer jist feelin' real lonely, aren't yew?"

Geneva nodded and gave in to her sobs. "You just don't know the whole story. No one would understand."

Sally Beth patted her back and stroked her hair. "I do understand. I know how much yew love him. I could see the love in yer eyes the mornin' we found yew on that porch, dancin' with yer panties."

Geneva sat up, shocked. "You knew? You could see?"

"Why, honey, it would take a *blind* person to miss it!" She paused to think. "Although Lilly did, but Lilly sees nothin' but herself. And Jimmy Lee, but then, Jimmy Lee is so *crazy* about *yew*, he wouldn't see on purpose. But yew know, Howard, yer city boyfriend, he wasn't blind."

"Oh, no! I mean, I know Howard—Graves—saw it, but I didn't think it was that obvious to you! I mean, you never let on!"

"Well, it wasn't none of my business, was it? The last thing yew needed was somebody winkin' at yew and actin' all silly about it. I could see the pain yew both were in, yew and Howard." She looked directly into Geneva's eyes. "And honey, he sure loves yew, too. He hid it worse than yew did."

"Oh, I know he did love me, but, oh, Sally Beth! I did something so awful! He gave me this… this potion! He gave me an out, in case I got pregnant, and like a fool, I drank it! And that just killed it for him. He would have loved me, I know it! If I just hadn't let him down like that! He so wants children, and I was a selfish fool." She stifled more sobs, and then the smile broke through. "But it didn't work, obviously." She placed her hand on her belly that cradled the child. "So, now I have the baby, but not him."

Sally Beth leaned her elbows on the table and cocked her head. "Miracles happen all the time, yew know."

Geneva nodded her head. "Miracles have already happened. I'm overwhelmed by the fact that God loves me so much, despite the fact that I am so miserably flawed. I don't deserve such mercy."

Sally Beth snorted and leaned back. "Why, that's the *silliest* thing I ever did hear! To say God shouldn't love us because we are flawed or broken is like sayin' He shouldn't love us because we have blue eyes or knock knees! Of *course* we're broken! That's part of bein' human, and if God didn't love anybody who wasn't, then He wouldn't love *anybody!* Git over *that,* Geneva Lenoir!" She sat up and patted her hair demurely. "Yew just need to accept His grace and be happy for it," she said primly, before adding, "and *expect* miracles. God *wants* us to be happy! And I bet He wants you to be with Howard. Yew need to tell him as quick as yew can and see what God provides."

"I don't know. I'm thinking it would be best if I don't even tell him. You know, he will think he has to make an honest woman of me, and I don't want him to marry me under those conditions. Our marriage would be a miserable farce."

Sally Beth looked at her directly and seriously. "Don't be a fool, Geneva Lenoir! That would be the same as lying to him, and yew have *no idea* what is the best thing for him. He's not a child, so don't treat him like one."

Geneva sighed. "Yes, but I know the only right thing to do is to let him go."

"*Mmhmm!* Yer sure about that?" She cocked her head and scrutinized Geneva. "Lemme ask yew this. Did God tell yew this was the right thing to do? Or did Howard?"

Geneva was taken aback, "Well, yes, I guess so. I've had this really strong feeling about it ever since I found out. I think that's God telling me."

"Well, did yew *ask* either one of 'em?"

"I…"

"Uh-huh," she said again.

"Okay, you're right," said Geneva, chastened. "He's not a child. I should tell him."

"He's comin' to the funeral, so you jist march yerself up to him and *tell* him!"

Geneva nodded, humbled by Sally Beth's rebuke. "But please, Sally Beth! You cannot breathe a word about any of this to him, or to anybody! Promise me that!"

The waitress arrived to take their order. Sally Beth slipped back to her side of the booth and smiled brightly. "I'll have the early bird special with black coffee and a glass of water, please." Then she beamed at Geneva. "I bet yew are as hungry as a *horse!* The Mexican omelet is real good. And I can keep secrets as good as anybody."

Geneva relaxed. It was good to have Sally Beth's blessing. Never would she have dreamed that she would disbosom herself to her "silly" cousin, but now that she had, she felt safe and hopeful. She ordered the Mexican omelet, then held Sally Beth's hand as they blessed the meal.

They buried Holy Miracle in the old graveyard near the ancient apple orchard where the hills billowed up to the sky in brown, undulating waves. While there was only a simple graveside service, many dozens of people braved the freezing rain to say goodbye to the old holy man. It was over quickly, but people were reluctant to leave so soon, despite their discomfort. Someone lifted his voice in a hymn:

> *When the trumpet of the Lord shall sound, and time shall be no more,*
> *And the morning breaks eternal, bright and fair,*
> *When the saved on earth shall gather over on the other shore,*
> *And the roll is called up yonder, I'll be there.*

Others joined in until the air was saturated with music and water, and the grief was honeycombed by a deep undertow of love. The thankfulness of all the people Holy Miracle had blessed rose up like the flame of a hundred candles illuminating and glorifying even the gray and black clouds.

Howard was there, joining in the singing, but when Geneva made her way toward him, he folded himself into the mist and the people, and although she searched for him, she could not find him. There was nothing left to do but shrink into the enveloping gloom of the rain and her own grief. At last, when the weeping day drew to a close, Geneva went home alone, tired and empty. Such loss as hers has a way of damping even the most ardent coals of the heart. She fell into bed and alternated between prayers and tears until she fell asleep.

Thanksgiving was two days away. The morning dawned bright, the harsh winter light bleeding the color from the faces of people and revealing all the hunger of the sun-starved land. She needed to do something. Her waistline had already begun to thicken, and in a few more weeks her pregnancy would begin to be evident to anyone with a discerning eye. *Today she would go to see Howard and tell him about their tiny miracle,* she resolved. She had already imagined all the possible scenarios that could be precipitated by her news, and even dared to hope for a moment of luminous joy, where he would laugh and shout and wrap his arms around her and all would be well. But other thoughts crowded into her tangled brain, whispering that he could explode with fury, or most likely, he would turn dull eyes to her and, with lead in his voice, offer to give her his name. Somehow, that seemed the worst scenario, for fury would at least show feeling, and feeling might eventually mean the hope of something more.

She dressed carefully, ate breakfast with Rachel and the children, then got into her little old Mazda and headed out toward Howard's father's house. She hoped he would be there, but if not, she would borrow a horse and make her way up to the cabin on the mountain, or she would wait for him to return. Today she would tell him, no matter what.

Halfway there, she stopped for gas at a country station. An exceptionally beautiful woman wearing jeans, a leather jacket, and cowboy hat and boots was just finishing filling the tank of a shiny, new Ford pickup truck as Geneva pulled up to the pump. The woman flashed a dazzling smile at Geneva, then hopped in the truck and drove away. There was something unsettling about her in the long, dark hair, the sparkling eyes, the self-assured, fluid movements. Geneva felt a stab of jealousy for no good reason other than the fact that the woman was stunning and Geneva felt decidedly not. She sighed and replaced the handle of the pump, then got back into her car and headed uphill.

Not long afterward, she found herself on the road above Jesse's cabin. As she began the descent toward his driveway entrance, she was surprised to see the blue Ford truck that she had seen earlier at the gas station. It turned at the mailbox. Geneva slowed, pausing before following, until the Ford disappeared around a curve in the drive.

Feeling guilty and full of trepidation, Geneva rolled along the driveway until she caught sight of the truck as it stopped in front of the house. Her line of sight was mostly obscured by a grove of beech trees, so she got out of the car and walked until she had a clear view of the driveway and the front of the cabin. Suddenly, Howard bolted out of the front door, followed closely by this father in his wheelchair. The beautiful woman opened the truck door as Howard leapt off the porch, and she ran to him, jumping into his arms. As he caught her up into a tremendous hug, spinning her around and laughing, she wrapped her arms around his neck and threw her head back. The cowboy hat blew off, and her long silken hair lifted, whirling behind her. When Howard set her down, she bounded up the steps and threw herself onto Jesse's lap, where he drew her into his arms, nestling her close, and he kissed her on the forehead.

It was exactly the scene she had imagined in her own hopeful heart that morning, except that the woman laughing and spinning in Howard's arms was the wrong one. Despair scythed raggedly through her being. No wonder Howard had been uninterested in her! This woman had already insinuated herself into his family, was loved, not only by Howard, but by his father, and no doubt the rest of the family as well. Sick and wounded, she crept back to her car and backed out of the driveway.

An hour later, she dialed Howard Graves' telephone number. When he answered, she did not bother with small talk, but got right to the point.

"I'm coming back to DC. My tenants have a lease until June, and I need an apartment at least until then. Can you find me one?"

He hesitated, but his voice was strong and kind. "Yes, as a matter of fact. One of my friends lives on the floor below me, and he's on sabbatical in Italy right now. I'm keeping an eye on his place and feeding his parakeet. He'll be gone until July, and I'm sure he won't mind if you come and stay. Peanuts is lonely. Jeff probably will be glad you're there to keep him company." He thought for a second. "He probably won't like it if you bring the cats, though. That could be an embarrassing disaster."

Despite her compounded grief, Geneva laughed at the thought

of her cats being driven mad by a caged parakeet. "Thanks, Howard, I really appreciate it. I'll try to be up there soon, and I have a lot to tell you." With that, she said goodbye and hung up the phone.

"What's this?" came the voice behind her. "You're going back?" Rachel hoisted Genny higher on her hip and brushed a golden strand of hair back from her forehead. "What on earth happened?"

Broken with misery, Geneva told her sister of her encounter on the mountain, of the beautiful woman whirling in Howard's arms, of how she had flung herself into his father's lap and had been received like a beloved daughter. "There's nothing for me here, Rachel. I have to leave."

"Wait a minute! You don't know for sure what that was about! And you can't just leave! You have to at least tell him and let him make up his own mind."

Geneva turned wearily to her sister. "Rachel, it's plain. He does not love me, but he is an honorable man. He's happy with this woman, and if I tell him about the baby, it will ruin his chance of a good life. He'll feel responsible, and he may even insist on marrying me. It's best I just get out of here, out of his life, go someplace I can make a way for myself."

"Geneva, you have to tell Howard. It just isn't right that you don't."

"It won't be right if I do. I'm not going to saddle him with the burden of this child, or me."

Rachel fell silent to think for a moment. "But how are you going to keep it from him? Everybody a hundred miles around will be talking about this. He can add and subtract, you know."

She ached as she found the words to explain. Howard would delight in the fact of this child, but then he would be bound to her through his sense of honor, and such a binding would weigh him down, cause him pain and sorrow, now when he was finding his own happiness without her. She could win him, but at what cost? No, she would give him his freedom. "I'll go away for good. I have a home in DC, and I can get another job. Nobody here has to know at all."

"You can't just leave here! What will you do, never come back? Try to hide this baby from your family? Your friends? That would be just awful, Geneva! You mean you'd just give us all up?"

Geneva felt the tears well up, but she brushed them aside. This was the price she would have to pay to protect Howard from herself. She shook her head.

"Okay, I know what you are feeling, and I understand. But you can't just leave! You can't tear yourself away from here and from everybody you love, Howard included! Geneva, it isn't right! We love you! We need you here! This would kill Mama and Daddy!

She continued with desperation, "Look, how about this? What if the baby wasn't yours? Now, hush, just listen, and hear me out. We can do this. You stay here until you start to show, and then run back to DC until the baby comes. Meantime, I'll pretend to be pregnant. I hardly ever go anywhere, and when I do, I can stuff a pillow under my dress, and I'll go to DC when the baby is due, and we can all come back together, and everybody will think it's mine!" I can spend the next—how many months?—August, right? That means—May? Oh, Geneva, a May baby! That would be perfect!"

"I'll not give up this baby, Rachel," gasped Geneva, "even to you!"

"Oh, no! You won't have to! You can live here with us, and, oh, we'll work it out later. Maybe I'll decide I have too many children or something and let you 'adopt' it. But this way you can keep it here and you can be here, and Howard won't know. Oh, please, Geneva!" Rachel burst into tears. Hannah and Phoebe ran into the room, alarmed, and threw their arms around her legs. Lenora woke up in the next room and began to cry, and Geneva rushed to her own room to be alone. Steeling herself against her family was not going to be easy, but she knew what was right, and no one would sway her from this decision.

Seventeen

Post holiday dead of winter was not a good time to be in the nation's capitol. Lighted buildings and traffic noise did little to sweeten the bitter season, and although Geneva had found some solace in reconnecting with old friends and a new church, she found herself wondering if her move back had been a wise one. She prayed constantly for guidance, but none came. Even God seemed to be withholding His warmth from her in this damp, inhospitable place.

On this January evening, sodden with icy rain, she was so lonely that she once again sorted through the letters she had received from home over the last few weeks. She did not want to read John's or Rachel's letters again. They were too awkward, too artificially cheerful, and too full of poorly-hidden disappointment—and of bad news. Sammy had been hit by a car and killed. Moe had developed feline leukemia. Only Sally Beth's letter felt comfortable, although she found it difficult to pick her way though it. Her handwriting was typical of the untutored dyslexic: illegible and full of misspellings and scratch-outs. She seemed not to know the difference between b's and d's, or q's, p's, and g's. Sometimes she would write a number in the place of a letter. But the sentiment conveyed was warm and friendly, full of the most inane details of daily life, as comforting as warm, fresh bread on an icy morning. She puzzled her way through some sentences that had stumped her earlier.

> "I've deen learning how to braw, and I think it would 5e fun to desiqn cloths. Mrs. Halverto3 and I are learming to seew. Mr. Hawkinns has a new sonp, it's even detter than Lucille!"

But the real shocker was that Lilly had up and moved to Las Vegas in search of a Sugar Daddy.

> "Mama was fit to de tieb at first, but she's 3k now."

There was a knock at the door, so Geneva set the letter aside to answer it. A pale and worried Howard Graves stood in the doorway. He clung to the door frame, leaning his head against his hand.

"Howard?"

"My mom has been in an accident. Will you come with me? I don't want to face this alone."

They were at the hospital within half an hour. She sat with him during the four hours of surgery, and although more of his friends gathered to be with him, she knew how alone he felt. His father had died five years earlier, and he was the only child of two only children. Her own vast, backwoods family seemed like an embarrassment of riches, or—she couldn't help herself the small pretension—sometimes just an embarrassment. She tried to share the joke with Howard, but he didn't find it funny. "I love your family, Geneva," he said solemnly, just as the doctor came to give him the good news that his mother would live—without a spleen and with a metal plate in her head and four screws in her leg—but she would live. Howard put his arms around Geneva and wept.

They returned to their apartment building at two in the morning. The rain had frozen in puddles in the parking lot. "Careful," said Howard, taking her arm. "You could break your neck," he warned, just as she felt her feet slide underneath her. He grabbed her to steady her. She did not recoil at his touch; he was warm and reassuring, but when he kept his arm around her waist as they navigated the frozen parking lot, she began to feel uneasy. He was vulnerable now, and she did not want to give him any false hopes. She pulled away as soon as they were inside.

"Thank you for coming with me," he said at her door.

"I'll pray for her," she replied.

"Oh, yes. Please do. And Geneva? Please pray for me, too." He touched her hand briefly and left.

The weeks that followed were the happiest of her winter. Geneva stopped bothering to look for a job. Howard still kept his eye on her investment portfolio, and since her living expenses were next to nothing, she seemed to be making more money than she was spending. Now she began Lamaze classes, and she spent her days with Howard's mother who was healing slowly. She came to understand how being around people in need appealed to Sally Beth: it was nice to be a source of comfort to someone in pain and to appreciate the subtle dignity in her suffering. The two women grew close during the bleak hours.

Howard was proving to be a steady and helpful friend. When she finally worked up the nerve to tell him about her baby, he looked saddened, but he took her hand and kissed it before smiling and shrugging. "I guess this takes me out of the picture, then, doesn't it?" She dropped her eyes. "But I knew that anyway. Nothing wrong with hoping, though." He stood up briskly and suggested they go for pizza. When she hesitated, he put up his hands. "No strings. Friends can hang out together," and so they fell into an easy camaraderie that suited Geneva just fine. But sometime later she caught him looking at her in a certain way and a tickle of unease crept across her skin, and when he sent her twenty-five roses for her birthday, she could no longer deny that he still had feelings for her. His mother, too, had become attached to her, and showed it by making subtle suggestions that the two get back together. Mindful that she had already hurt enough people with her selfishness, she tried to distance herself by asking her mother to come for a visit and serve as a buffer between herself and them.

Gaynell came to monopolize her time for a week, but after she left, the loneliness descended again and the long darkness settled into her spirit. She closed herself off, waiting for the spring thaw to dissolve the thorns of winter and for her womb to reaffirm the season of blooms.

By February, she was feeling homesick, lonely, and disconnected, but the baby grew and quickened and gave her a solitary joy. She often reminded herself that she was not going back to the hills, that return would be impossible, but she couldn't stop imagining her little girl running through the meadows, and finally she began to beg God to take away the awful desire to go home. God's voice remained inaudible, and the Scriptures did not comfort. It seemed that she could not get away from the verses proclaiming the fulfillment found in the land, the abundance of the hills. She copied out the verse from Genesis, *Behold, I am with you and will keep you wherever you go, and will bring you back to this land,* and taped it to the refrigerator, then took it down again when she realized the impossibility of the promise it seemed to imply.

Spring came at last, bringing song and scent upon the crest of the warming breezes, and April ripened into May. Geneva's child grew, and with the swelling of the buds and the child, her spirits lifted. Her mother would be back in three days, and after the baby came, Rachel would come for a weekend. She thrilled with the anticipation and tried not to think about the challenges of the next year, the challenges of the rest of her life. God had been providing all this time, and He would surely continue to do so. She counted the hours until she saw her mother's face again.

The ringing telephone startled her. "Hi, honey!" came Gaynell's voice, brittle and too bright. "Mama!" she exclaimed. "Is something wrong?"

"Oh, honey! My bursitis is acting up, and my shoulder is just frozen up." Geneva groaned. "I know. I'm going in for a cortisone shot on Monday, but I won't be able to lift a thing for a while, and I can't drive." Geneva felt the misery in her voice. "I'm so sorry, sweetheart, but I will be worse than worthless. But Daddy can come, and Rachel might be able to get away for a few days. Sally Beth said she would take some time off to take care of the children."

Geneva fought back the tears. "Oh, mama, I'm so sorry!" and the brutal homesickness severed her heart. She missed her mother, and the only thing she wanted was for her to be with her when her own baby came.

Gaynell's voice wavered. "It would be really nice if you just came on home. Daddy will come up to get you, and we can move a bed back into the den, like we did when you were hurt. Daddy even said he'd build you your own wing if you'd come home and stay. And Rachel keeps arguing with me because she wants you there, too."

Geneva thought. "Does anybody know about the baby, mama?"

"No, just Sally Beth and us. But, Geneva, you've been away long enough now that people will probably think the daddy is in DC. We can tell them you had a boyfriend, or a husband, and things didn't work out." She pleaded, "Come on home, baby. You can't be happy there all alone, and we really want you here."

Behold, I am with you and will keep you wherever you go, and will bring you back to this land. The words rippled under the surface of her mother's voice. Her capitulation was sudden and complete.

"Okay, mama, I'll come home. But I can drive. Don't be sending Daddy up here to get me. I need my car, anyway.

"No, indeed! You are nine months pregnant, and I won't have you driving all by yourself all the way here. Daddy can be up there tomorrow."

"I'll think about it. Maybe I can drive just behind him, but I really want a car if I'm there."

She got off the phone, then went to Howard's apartment. He was just leaving for work when she stopped him in the hallway.

"My mom called. She's having a bout with bursitis, so she isn't coming after all. Dad's coming to get me, so I wanted to tell you goodbye, and to thank you for all you've done for me. You've been a good friend, Howard, and I really appreciate that."

"You're leaving? Just like that?"

"Well, yeah. Daddy will be here tomorrow. I wanted to let you know so you can take care of Peanuts. I probably won't be back for a while, and when I do, I'll be moving into my old place."

"Wait a minute. Your dad is driving out here to get you?"

"Yeah, they don't want me driving by myself this far along."

"I can drive you."

"What? No! There's no need for you to do that. And I really want my car."

"No, really. I have business in Chicago next week. I can drive you home, then catch a plane out of there, and I can fly directly back here from Chicago, so you can use my car for as long as you want." He chuckled. "Your car. I haven't forgotten that it's really yours," he said, referring to the Jaguar. "If you can get me to the airport closest to Tucker sometime on Monday, that will work out just fine. Besides, it would be nice to spend the weekend in the mountains. Hey, free place to stay, and I could use the fresh air." He smiled in a friendly way, and Geneva wanted to believe he no longer loved her. *If she accepted, would this be taking advantage of him?*

He seemed to read her mind. "Don't worry. I really do just want to get some good mountain air. I got to where I like it. And there's nothing wrong with letting a friend drive you somewhere when you are nine months pregnant, okay? You've done plenty for me over the last few months."

Despite her concerns, it seemed like a sensible solution, so Geneva accepted the offer, with the exception that they take her Mazda rather than the Jag. She spent the rest of the day packing and finding a sitter for Peanuts while Howard called his travel agent to change his itinerary. It all happened so smoothly that early the next morning, they threw suitcases into the car and headed west. Both

Geneva and Howard were in high spirits, and somewhere along Interstate sixty-six, she remembered why she had been in love with him. He was fun and funny and considerate.

"Thank you," she said.

"You're welcome. I'm having a good time."

"Me too, but thank you for more than this. Thank you for being such a friend, despite all I've put you through. Thanks for sticking with me."

"I'm the one who should be thanking you, and I'm the one who screwed up. You have been my friend too, and good to my mother. She loves you, you know."

"She's a sweet lady. With emphasis on the lady."

"Yeah." He drove silently. "I had a good long talk with her last night. She's doing really well." He was still for a short time, then spoke again. "Geneva, are you going to marry Howard?"

"No. I'm not even going to tell him about the baby."

"Why not? If I can ask," he added hastily.

She looked straight ahead. "He's in love with someone else. It wouldn't do any good to complicate his life."

"He's in love with someone else? Uhmm, I don't think so. If he is, he got over you awfully quick."

"Yeah, well, he did." Her back was beginning to ache, and she wanted the conversation to end, so she shifted away from him and looked out the window. The houses and fields drifted by.

"So you're going to do this all alone?"

"'Fraid so."

"And you'll be coming back to DC soon?"

"Yes. I'll need to find a job one of these days. Or maybe I'll sell my place and move somewhere else. It's a cinch I won't be living in Tucker. Not too much call for retail designers in the backwater."

"I'd hate to see you go." He paused. "You don't have to."

"Maybe not. We'll see. It would be nice to get my old job back, or something like it."

"No. I mean, you could marry me. And stay, and not bother with getting a job, if you don't want to."

She looked at him, incredulous, and a rush of warmth filled her. "Oh, Howard! You are such a gallant darling! Here I am nine months pregnant with another man's baby, and you are offering to marry me! You deserve a medal or something."

"I'm serious," he said. "If I hadn't been such an idiot and let you go, this could have been my baby." He shrugged, then glanced at her. "I can make this one mine. And Geneva, I still love you. I realized that I had never stopped loving you when I saw that boar rushing at you. Even before then, really. You'll never know how I felt when I saw you on that cabin porch, so full of life and all lit up. I had spent the night stumbling around in the dark, worrying about you, wondering if you were alive or dead, and I knew then that I really loved you, that I would always love you. Why don't you marry me and let me prove it to you? This baby deserves a father and a decent life."

She wanted to weep for him. "Howard, I love you, too. I always will, as a friend. But there is only one man who has my heart, and even though he doesn't want me, I guess I will live out the rest of my life hoping for him, at least until God gives me some sort of release from him. But right now, just having his baby is enough for me." She searched for the words to say it without hurting him too much. "I finally know what real, deep love is, and I don't even want to think about sharing that with anyone but Howard. Can you understand that?"

He nodded grimly. "My mother will be disappointed. She's jealous that you're having a baby and she doesn't get to be a grandmother."

"She is welcome to claim being a granny."

"And how about me? Can I claim anything at all? Honorary Uncle seems kind of tawdry, considering our past."

"Maybe you can be best buddy."

He glanced over and smiled. "I'll take it."

The May morning dawned milky and soft. Geneva rose early—

it was impossible to sleep late with her bladder making incessant demands, and her back still ached from yesterday's ride. She tried to stretch it out, then slipped into the bathroom just as the eastern sky blushed a lovely rose-gold. *Thank you God for this day! Thank you that my baby is healthy and strong. Thank you for life!* She couldn't stop humming lullabies as she brushed her teeth and her hair, grown long and vibrant steeped in pregnancy hormones.

In a sudden fit of girlish preening, she put on her prettiest dress and applied a hint of makeup. There was only so much she could do to detract from her huge belly and her swollen ankles, but she felt she owed it to everyone to try not to look too hideous. Smiling into the mirror, she decided she wasn't too bad, considering. *Wouldn't it be wonderful if Howard suddenly showed up and declared his undying love to me?* came a whisper. But she set that fantasy aside and went to make breakfast. Might as well give everyone a chance to sleep a little longer.

She had a big breakfast nearly on the table when Wayne wandered in carrying Phoebe. "Up early, I see. How do you feel this morning?"

"Just great. Of course, I'll be tired as all get-out by this afternoon, but right now I have enough energy to run a marathon. Want some bacon and eggs?"

"Smells good. A burst of energy is a good sign you're ready to deliver. When you start moving furniture around, we'd better head to the hospital. I'll pour orange juice."

"Rachel up yet?"

"Yes, she'll be down in a minute," he said, just as Rachel and Hannah made their appearance, sleepy-eyed and tousled. They were beautiful.

"Hey, sis," smiled Geneva. "Sit down. Orange juice, bacon, eggs. Oops! Toast has popped up. Butter it, will you? Hannah, Phoebe, I made Mickey Mouse pancakes for you."

"Howard still asleep?"

"Guess so. He had a hard drive coming through the rain, so I bet he's pretty worn out."

"So what are you going to do today?" asked Rachel.

"Could be eventful. Geneva is full of energy this morning," teased Wayne.

"Uh-oh. I'd better get dressed," commented Rachel. "Has she been chopping wood or anything?"

"Not yet. Say, didn't you want the closets cleaned out? Now might be the perfect opportunity. We could turn Geneva loose on them, and maybe you and I can go riding. Geneva could watch the children, clean the house, chop the wood, and oh, I dunno, maybe wash the cars?"

"Oh, you had to mention the babies! That woke them up." Rachel set her orange juice down and jumped up, followed by Wayne. "Go ahead and start, Geneva. We'll be right back."

Geneva took the hands of each of her nieces and said, "Who wants to pray for us this morning?"

"I do!" said Hannah, beaming at her. She closed her eyes, then opened them. "Phoebe! Close your eyes!" Her little sister squeezed hers shut, and Hannah prayed, "Thank you Jesus for this food and my aunt Geba and Mommy and Daddy and Ginny and L'ora and Phoebe, and for everybody in the world. Amen."

"Amen" repeated Geneva and Phoebe, then they tucked into their breakfast. Geneva thought her heart would burst with gratitude.

There was a knock. Geneva looked up to see John standing behind the screen door. She felt a sudden, heavy shame when she saw his earnest face. "Hey," he said genially, opening the door and easing inside. "Didn't mean to startle you. I saw your car in the driveway last night and figured you were back." He glanced at her belly, and she folded her hands over it protectively. She couldn't help but wallow in a moment of self-pity. The last time he had seen her she was beautiful. Now she was a blimp, dowdy, slovenly, grotesquely pregnant, unwed. She lifted her head and smiled defiantly.

"Hey yourself," she said. "Come on in. You're just in time for breakfast. If you want to eat well, just have a pregnant woman cook for you."

He did not hesitate, but got himself a plate and silverware and sat down at the table beside Phoebe. "Hey, Pheebs. Can I have a bite of that pancake?" The little girl nodded and offered him a forkful. "I am eating this with relish," he said, his mouth full of pancake. "Do you know what that means?"

Phoebe shook her head.

"Relish. Like pickles and olives and things. But it also means that I like it a lot. So it means two things. One is kind of funny. Pancakes with pickles." Phoebe giggled.

"Geba eats pickles," spoke up Hannah, and John laughed. "I bet she does!" and he smiled directly at Geneva, flashing her that look she once found dazzling. Now she found it painful. She decided to get it over with.

"I came home to have the baby. Mama's pretty crippled up with bursitis, so she couldn't come, and well, Rachel has her hands full."

He nodded. "You need your loved ones with you." He paused, toying with his eggs. "I take it you aren't going to marry Howard?"

She shook her head. "No, it's pretty clear he doesn't want me." She shook off the pain and smiled.

John sat quietly for a moment. "Looks like you're getting close. What's the word?"

"Any day now. I'm so close I can't even drive. Howard—Graves, that is—drove me down."

"Oh," he said. "Nice of him." The silence deepened, and he shifted in his seat. Ever so slightly, he began to swing his leg nervously. "So, what are your plans?"

"Don't really have any, at least for the moment. Guess I'll just have this baby and get on with my life."

"You're okay with not having a daddy around?" He looked at her earnestly.

"Not really, but I guess I've made my bed, as the saying goes."

The leg swung a little more vigorously. "Uh, Geneva, I know this is sudden, but you don't have a lot of time. I just want you to know that, well, I've been thinking, and to tell you the truth, I have been pretty selfishly hoping that you wouldn't marry Howard. The fact is, I…"

"Save yourself the grief, man," came a voice from the hallway. Howard Graves walked into the room. "I've already been through the same song and dance, and the lady is smitten."

John seemed to grow larger in the chair. "I think it would be appropriate if the lady told me that herself. I don't need any advice from you." He glared at Howard.

"Come on, you two," sighed Geneva wearily. "The last thing I need is for you to get all macho on me." They both looked at her with such sternness and concern that she suddenly laughed. "Oh my goodness! You both are such darlings! I am blessed in that I have not one, but two gallants looking out for me! Thank you for making me feel cherished. But Howard, you are right. I am in love with Chap, and this is his baby, and even though we will never marry, I am going to raise her all by myself. I won't have either of you making the big sacrifice here."

They both deflated suddenly, and Howard smiled ruefully. "I know it's tough, man, but we just have to live with it. You'll get used to it. In the meantime, let's agree to play second fiddle." He stuck his hand out to John.

John looked at him for a heartbeat, then capitulated. "Yeah," he said, smiling warily, "I guess we both lose, huh?" He grasped Howard's hand firmly, then punched him in the arm.

Wayne entered the room with Genny. "I see your fan club has arrived," he said mildly.

Geneva laughed. "I'm the fan of these two. You've never met two more extraordinary gentlemen, gentlemen in the classiest sense. They both are looking out for my honor, and my welfare. I'm a lucky girl."

Wayne put Genny in a high chair and sat down. He forked bacon and eggs into two plates just as Rachel came in with Lenora. She put Lenora into a high chair and attacked her breakfast. Howard took a plate and began as well. Geneva suddenly felt overwhelmed with love as she looked at the faces around the table.

I am complete, she thought, *or nearly so. I should not ask for more!*

Wayne spoke up, "Since you two are here, I need some help. Part of the barn roof got torn off in the storm last night. Care to have a go at it with me?"

John brightened. "Sure," he said, but Howard looked doubtful.

"Come on, dude, we farm boys will show you how to patch a roof," John said, slapping him on the back. "We'll take a look at it with you, Wayne. Need us to go to the lumberyard?"

"Yeah, a whole section blew off. If you go to the lumberyard, I'll start on trimming it back," he said between bites.

"Great," spoke up Rachel. "Mom and Dad are on their way. Daddy's made a kettleful of his Brunswick stew, so we'll have a big crowd for lunch. I'll make some cornbread, and there's plenty of stuff for a salad in the garden." She turned to her girls, "Are you up for a big party today? Want to see Granny and Grandaddy?"

"Yea!" shouted the little girls. They jumped up from the table to throw their arms around their mother.

After breakfast was cleared, the men went to the barn to assess the damage, then John and Howard left in John's jeep for the lumberyard. Geneva took a basket to the garden where there were plenty of greens for a salad, and the squash was already ripening. She gathered enough for a crowd, then, since there were a fair number of weeds making serious headway, she stooped to pull a few until, after wrestling with a particularly stubborn oak seedling, her back began to really hurt again. *Shoot*, she thought. *I don't like this! I am taking the rest of this day off!* And soon, she found herself lying in a nest of pillows, watching the sun shimmer through the apple blossoms. The last thing she remembered was how soft the air felt and how beautiful the day was, before the gentle rocking of the swing and the motion of the light hypnotized her into a cloudy daze.

She did not hear the car in the driveway, or the car doors slam, nor the voices murmuring on the spring breeze, but she felt something niggling in the corners of her consciousness, and she opened her eyes drowsily. Lenora had just stepped through a swirl of dust motes dancing in the May light. Jimmy Lee was right behind her. Lamentations trailed along, nudging Jimmy Lee's leg and trying to push his head up under his hand. Geneva heard the bees buzzing in the apple tree, and enveloped in the warm haze of the morning, she smiled lazily at Lenora as the old woman reached the top step and paused. Jimmy Lee bumped into her, then he caught sight of Geneva, and he suddenly sat down on the porch step, staring, all the color drained from his face. In her drowsy state, Geneva felt like she was in a dream where she had no control, but she did not care. She was happy to see Lenora, even happy to see Jimmy Lee. A fuzzy notion that Howard might be close by crept over her like a soft fleece.

"They Lordy, girl! You done surprised the whiskers offa me," said Lenora, smiling broadly. "I did not know you wuz in the family way!"

"Hello Lenora, Jimmy Lee," Geneva smiled and blinked. She glanced around, hoping Howard was just out of sight. "I didn't know you were coming. I would have…" she trailed off, seeing Jimmy Lee's sad state. She wondered if she ought to apologize to him.

Lenora looked at Geneva compassionately. "Sorry. We shoulda called first. We wuz jist in town, and thought we'd drop by, see them babies." She looked crestfallen, embarrassed. "We're intrudin'. I'm truly sorry."

"It's okay, Lenora," Geneva said, as the fuzz began to retreat from her head. "Have a seat. Jimmy Lee, can I get you a drink of water? Really, come and sit down. You'd be finding this out sooner or later anyway," she added, indicating her mounding belly. When neither of them moved, she thought about standing up, but she was too comfortable. "I'll get you something to drink," she said, but she didn't move.

"No, child," said Lenora, suddenly gentle. She came close to Geneva and patted her on the shoulder. "We're jist fine, and we're real sorry we jist dropped in like this. Ike about cut his thumb off this mornin', and we tuk him to the hospital to git it stitched back on. Chap's there with him, and me and Jimmy Lee, well, we just thought we'd run by since we wuz in town and see th' babies. Yew stay settled, and we'll plan on comin' back another time..."

"No," interjected Geneva, glad that the comforting old woman was here, glad that some connection to Howard had arrived, glad the news was broken. "I'm happy you're here. Maybe you can give me a few pointers. She laid her hand on her stomach and smiled. "This one will be along any time now."

Lenora's face lit up. "Law, girlie, I gotta tell ye, it does me good to see another life about to come in the world. Your sister's babies, they was the last I delivered, and seems I cain't git enough seein' 'em and watchin' 'em grow. Now maybe I git to see another 'un." She laughed her clear, childlike laugh, then added wistfully, "Maybe I kin even be here when yer time comes?" She caught herself. "Oh, of course, ye'll be havin' this in a nice hospital, won't ye?"

Geneva did not know what made her speak. The words were out of her mouth before she even thought them. "Lenora, I'd love for you to be here for me, for this baby. After all, it is your great-grandchild." She stopped, suddenly wide awake, the dream vanished in a vapor. Had she really said that? Her hand flew to her mouth and she shrank back into the pillows.

Lenora gasped, then gaped, and blinked twice. Then she turned toward Jimmy Lee and suddenly whacked him over the head with her purse. "Jimmy Lee Land! I am ashamed of you, boy! What do yew mean, gittin' this girl in the family way and lettin' her git this far gone and never a by-yer-leave!" She hit him twice more before Geneva could react and before Jimmy Lee gained the presence of mind to throw up his arms to shield himself from the blows.

"Ow, Grannie!"

"No!" shouted Geneva. "Not Jimmy Lee! Oh, stop it! He's not the one!"

Lamentations grew fidgety, growling and looking over his right shoulder.

"Grannie! Ow! Stop it! Lamentations!" Jimmy Lee was torn between cowering beneath Lenora's blows and stopping

Lamentations before he could go into a full frenzy. He kept one arm over his head and gingerly reached out toward Lamentations with the other.

"Who, then?" demanded Lenora. "By God, I'll see he does yew right. Which one of my boys has got you in this shape?" She stood up to her full height, and although it was just short of five feet, she seemed huge and formidable. Her face blazed with anger, and Geneva could swear her hair stood straight out from her head. She swallowed, deeply regretting her lapse. *Oh Lord, please get me out of this!* Wide eyed, she cowered before Lenora's wrath.

But Lenora was not moved. She was so mad she hit Jimmy Lee several more times with her voluminous pocketbook, and although it was made of soft, quilted fabric, Geneva grew more alarmed as Jimmy Lee tucked his head under his arms and howled. Lamentations started to bark and snarl.

"Which one of those good fer nuthin's wuz it?" She turned back to her grandson. "Jimmy Lee?" Lenora's face shone red with rage.

Panicked, Geneva jumped up, blurting out, "Oh, stop hitting him, please! It's not Jimmy Lee! It's… it's—" and then she clapped both hands over her mouth. She was too horrified to cry, but she sat down abruptly in the porch swing and cowered in the corner. She was certain Lenora would turn on her.

But the old woman did not. She stopped suddenly, and stood perfectly still for a second, eyes drilling into Geneva's, and then spoke through her teeth while still staring at Geneva. "Jimmy Lee. Yew git on the phone and yew call that there horspital, and yew tell Chap to git hisself here right now. Right *now,* yew hear me?"

"No, Lenora! Please! He doesn't know! And it wasn't his fault. It was mine! Entirely mine. He doesn't know."

Lenora was unmoved. "Yew heard me, Jimmy Lee. *Right now.*"

Rachel came around the corner of the house, babies in their stroller, older daughters trailing behind.

"Oh!" exclaimed Rachel when she saw the scene laid out before her. Then she fell silent. For a few seconds, the only motion in the tableaux was Lenora's nostrils twitching and the only sound was her breathing. Then, without a word, the old woman spun on her heel and stormed into the house. Jimmy Lee had moved down a step and had flung an arm around Lamentations' neck. He looked at Geneva with a pale and mournful expression that tore at her heart. Would she never stop hurting people?

Wayne appeared and assessed the frozen spectacle briefly. "Well, Jimmy Lee, looks like you have stumbled into quite a drama here."

Rachel demurred. "I think they may have brought the drama. Geneva? You okay, honey?" She moved up the steps to enfold Geneva in her arms. The children, oblivious to the situation, had discovered a kitten in the yard and were teasing it with a twig. Geneva stared at the kitten, rolling on its back and batting at the twig, and all she could think of was *help!*

The screen door banged open, and Lenora stormed out. "They done left the horspital." Catching sight of Wayne, she directed orders. "Git me the number of that place on forty-four. Heyday Diner. Ike said he wanted to go there."

"No, Wayne," broke in Geneva. "Don't you dare call him. Lenora, please, this is not really Howard's business. He doesn't know a thing…"

"Don't yew tell me it ain't none of his business," spat out the old woman. "If this ain't his business, then I'm the President of the United dang States. Now, git in there, Dr. Hillard. And I ain't pullin' yer laig." She turned to Geneva, softening just slightly. "Girlie, you stop tryin' to protect that boy. Yew jist sit right down, and we'll git this straightened right out." Geneva sat. She simply had no fight left in her. After a brief moment, when Wayne looked questioningly at Geneva, he mounted the steps and went into the house.

No one spoke. They all watched the little girls and the kitten. A tear slipped down Jimmy Lee's cheek, but it was not followed by another one. Geneva gritted her teeth and swore she would not faint or cry or make a bigger fool of herself than she already had. Genny squirmed to get out of the stroller, and Rachel took her out, then sat down beside Geneva in the swing and held the baby's hand while she stood and wobbled. Everyone sat quietly, the swing moved back and forth, squeaking softly. Phoebe and Hannah rolled an acorn in front of the kitten.

The silence was broken by the sound of a car turning into the driveway. It was Howard Graves and John, returning from the hardware store. All eyes turned to them as John parked the car and they got out with the supplies. Howard caught sight of the group on the porch first. He faltered, then stopped. "Did I do something?" he said.

"Come on up," said Rachel. "We have a little situation here. Seems Lenora has found out who the daddy is." That was all she needed to say. Both men looked from Rachel to Geneva. Howard's eyes lingered on Geneva's face for a second, then moved on to Jimmy Lee. He nodded to the younger man.

"Hey," said Jimmy Lee, voice full of misery, but he lifted his free hand and gave a little wave. John strolled over to Jimmy Lee and offered his hand, then sat beside him on the step. Howard's eyes settled briefly on Lenora's marble face before he eased himself up the steps to perch on the porch railing as far away as possible. His face was bright with curiosity.

Geneva wallowed in self-loathing, self-pity, and abject fear. She tried to pray, but her mind, numbed with shame and dread, refused to function more than enough to allow her to breathe.

Wayne appeared at the door. "I got hold of them. They're on their way—but, uhm—they've got Sally Beth with them. Seems she was visiting someone at the hospital and couldn't get her car started. They're giving her a ride home."

"Did you tell them to drop her off first?" demanded Rachel.

"Uh, no. That would take an extra forty minutes, and uh…" He trailed off. No one else spoke for a long time, until Hannah ran up to her mother, "Mama, can I have some lemonade?"

Rachel gently eased Genny into Geneva's lap and stood up. "Sure, honey. Why don't you and Phoebe come inside and help me make it? I'm sure everybody could use some." She took Hannah's hand and carefully made her way across the porch. "Come on, sweetheart," she called to Phoebe. "Come help Hannah and Mommy make some lemonade. I bet everybody is real thirsty." She shot a sympathetic look to Geneva. "Want to help, Geneva?"

"I will," offered Wayne hastily, snatching little Lenora up from the stroller and hastening to open the door for Rachel. Geneva desperately wanted to get away, but she was overcome with inertia, her mind unfocused, as if to distance herself from the surreal scene going on around her. Jimmy Lee looked soft and far away. Howard stared at her with concern in his face, so she winked at him and closed her eyes, retreating into a misty sea of languor. Occasional dull pains intruded into her consciousness that made her think of stones floating in water around her, bumping into her, annoying her. She wished she could say something to ease the tension everyone else was surely feeling, but she was very tired, and the pain in her back kept her from saying anything coherent. She also felt a little nauseated, but she pressed her lips together, snuggled Genny close, and simply waited with everyone else.

Presently, she heard some conversation around her. John was doing what he could to make the situation a little more relaxed. He asked Jimmy Lee about his leg, about Lamentations, and when it became apparent that Jimmy Lee was in no mood to talk, he turned to Lenora, who ignored him completely. Geneva opened her eyes to see Lenora staring at her intently. She tried to smile, but another pain wrenched in her back and the smile evolved into a grimace.

"You awright, girlie?" the old woman asked her, concern in her voice.

Geneva roused herself, "Oh, yes, we just got here yesterday, and the ride was hard on my back. It's bothering me some." She took a breath and stretched, and the pain subsided. She deliberately kept her mind from turning to Howard and how bad things would get when he arrived. She would stop time. He would never come, and soon she would wake up from this nightmare. The swing creaked in the breeze.

Lenora nodded, but continued to watch her closely. Geneva

noticed Howard was doing the same, so she smiled again and made an effort to get up. It was hard to do with Genny in her arms, so she settled back down into the cushions. Howard was at her side in an instant. "Can I help you?" he asked.

"Oh, I thought I would get up, but I can't move with Genny in my arms. Just help me up." She struggled to her feet, Howard's hand at her elbow. There was a sudden pressure in her bladder, and suddenly she was jolted back to reality. *This was real! This was not a dream!* Howard was on his way, and she was totally out of control of her own body, of everything around her. In an instant, she was wide awake, urgently needing to pee. She hurried inside to the bathroom, and then, rather than go back and face the drama on the front porch, she wandered into the kitchen, where Rachel and Wayne scurried around, looking frazzled. "Need any help?" she asked, as brightly as she could.

"No, we've got it," answered Wayne. He looked at her again. "You okay, Geneva? You seem a little… off."

Geneva chuckled ruefully, then felt the tears sting her eyes. She made a little joke. "I think I'm doing pretty good, considering that my baby's daddy is on his way here to walk into a hornet's nest. I don't know which will do him the most harm, finding out about this baby, or Lenora, who is spitting mad. You got here after she beat up poor Jimmy Lee. With her pocketbook." She forced a tired smile. "That family is pretty violent with soft things. She beat up Ike with her hat the night the twins were born."

Rachel snorted. "You're taking this pretty well."

"Yeah, I'm sort of resigned. And I've got this awful pain in my back. I hurt it this morning pulling weeds."

Wayne walked over and put his hand on her stomach. "You might be in labor," he said. "Back labor can feel like muscle spasms sometimes."

"No, it's just a muscle spasm. I felt it when I was weeding and pulled too hard." She moved toward the tray of glasses. "I'll take this lemonade outside. No need for you to have to be in on this. I'll send Howard and John in, too. They've been the unlikely heroes in all this, and they don't need to be subjected to any more." She faltered. "This will probably be ugly."

"No, let me," said Rachel. That's heavy, and I need to be there for moral support. Wayne, I'm leaving you in charge here. If you want, you can give them some *Sesame Street*. She hoisted up the tray and led the way onto the porch. Walking behind her, Geneva felt her heart lurch the moment she crossed the threshold and glimpsed Howard's rickety truck turning into the driveway. She had not seen him in six months, but the distance of time had not prepared her for the way her sinews, even her bones, dissolved at the sight of him. She wished she could protect him from what was coming, but for the first time in her life, she felt that her body was not up to the task to shield anybody from harm. She was as weak as one of the kittens, and the pain in her back and in her heart were so intense she had to fight to keep herself from a writhing collapse.

The truck stopped. He had not seen her standing in the shadows. She held her breath as Ike, then Sally Beth, then Howard got out of the truck and made their way toward the house. Sally Beth was in the lead, walking beside Ike and talking earnestly. Ike's left hand was swathed in a bandage and bound up close to this chest. Howard hung back, making his way more slowly, but he was the first to see her. When she saw his eyes fly open in surprise, she stepped backwards, trying to hide her belly, but when the color drained out of his face, she knew he had seen all of her, even in the gloom. She closed her eyes against the tears and clung to the door, swaying as all the substance in her head seemed to evaporate.

Sally Beth and Ike also stopped at the bottom of the steps. Rachel sang out, "Hey, y'all. Welcome to the party. Come on up and have some lemonade."

No one moved for a moment, then Sally Beth took a deep breath and stepped forward. "Why, that's real sweet of you, Rachel, And *Geneva*, you're here! And my goodness, just *look* at yew! About to *pop* with that sweet little baby. I was hopin' yew'd come home for the birth, 'cause we all want to see it jist as soon as it gits here!"

Geneva did not know whether to be upset or grateful with Sally

Beth's immediately addressing the elephant in the room. At least the preliminary awkwardness was not going to be drawn out. Now the fireworks could begin. She smiled wanly and sank into the swing.

Howard's eyes were riveted to her belly, but he eventually dropped his head and looked away, and the color came back into his face in a rush. She could see the high cheekbones bloom with anger, and hope fled from her. This was the moment he would walk out of her life and never return. She had lied to him, had failed another test, had done this all wrong. He would never forgive her.

Lenora spoke up. "There's no need abeatin' around the bush here. Missy," she said, looking at Geneva, "let's git this over and done with. Yew tell us all right here and now who the daddy of this baby is."

Silence. Geneva looked at the ground, afraid and ashamed. A tear dropped between her feet.

"We're awaitin', girlie." Lenora's lips were a thin, gray line, but her eyes flashed. "And yew might as well git this over with. We ain't got that much time."

Geneva gave up. There was no way out of this. Both she and Howard were already humiliated, and he was already lost to her forever. She might as well take Lenora's advice and get it over with. She continued to stare at the ground. "It's not his fault," she muttered. "I'm real sorry." She could not look at him.

"Sorry, nuthin'. Who got yew in this shape?"

Suddenly John spoke up. "Don't torture her, Mrs. Knight, and don't make her say it. We all know how much she is in love with Howard, and it is his baby. Now, let's just leave her alone."

Geneva gaped at John, and then she immediately turned to Howard. "I'm so sorry! I tried to tell you…" But he was not looking at her. Within the space of a single breath, he had leaped upon the porch and had moved to the place where Howard Graves sat on the porch rail.

"Yew sorry bastard. I'll kill yew!" he said, and hit him in the face. Howard Graves tumbled off the porch and into the hydrangea bushes below.

"Hey, whoa!" shouted John, as Geneva screamed, "No!" But Howard had leaped over the porch railing, into the hydrangeas, and had picked up Howard Graves by the collar. He shook him like a terrier shakes a rat.

"Yew let her git this far gone and ain't married her? What kind of somebitch are yew?" He was about to hit him again, when the bleeding Howard held up his hand and shouted, "No! Not me, you idiot! You!" And John, at the same time, leaped over the porch railing, completely demolishing the hydrangeas. He grabbed Howard's arm and yanked him backwards.

"Whoa, buddy!" said John. "Take it easy!"

Howard Graves shook his head and pushed at Howard's chest. "Cool it," he said brusquely. "You think I haven't begged her to marry me? And I would, in a heartbeat. You sure don't deserve her."

"Hey, get in line," broke in John. If anybody deserves to marry her, it's me. I'm the only one who hasn't dumped on her. She deserves better than both of you."

Jimmy Lee sat up straighter and tentatively put his hand in the air, like a schoolboy who wanted to contribute to the discussion but wasn't sure he would be recognized. "Hey," he said timidly. "Kin I throw my hat in th' ring?" He looked anxiously at Geneva. "I'd be proud, ma'am."

Geneva had not been able to respond to any of that. A sudden contraction had gripped her hard, and she found herself unable to breath. "*Ohhh!*" she finally gasped. "Howard, Chap! I'm sorry! I know you hate me, but I couldn't tell you!"

Everyone looked at Howard Knight. He glared at each of his rivals, the unspoken question burning a deep red on his face, and John and Howard each shook their heads in turn. "I wish," said John. "Me, too," muttered Howard. Jimmy Lee blushed, but said nothing. Howard swiveled his head toward Geneva, and just as the contraction let go its tentacles, she looked at him with all the love in her being. "I know you're in love with somebody else. I couldn't do this to you." She began to sob.

He leaped up and over the porch rail, and was at her side in five long strides. Everyone stepped aside as he brushed past them, and then closed in again to surround him and Geneva as he sat beside her. "What the hell are you talking about, woman?" he demanded. "Is this my baby?" He looked deep into her eyes, and when she nodded mutely, his face suddenly transformed. Light suffused his eyes, and they glistened with sudden tears. "Really?" A sudden grin spread across his face. *"Really?"* he repeated. She sobbed louder and nodded.

"B-but I couldn't tell you. I know you don't love me."

"Don't love you? Lord, woman, I do!"

"No, I know you don't. You're just sa-sa-saying that."

He threw his arms around her. "Oh Geneva, darlin', I love yew! I've loved you since the minute I laid eyes on yew, and I tried to go after yew, but ye'd already gone back to him." He jerked his thumb in the direction of Howard Graves.

"What are you talking about?" demanded Geneva.

"I went up to DC to beg yew to come back, but yew were with him."

"No I wasn't!" exclaimed Geneva. "Why do you think that? When?"

"After yew left here and went back. I drove up there, and went to yer apartment, but yew weren't there, so I waited outside, and then the two of you drove up and went inside together. I waited all night, and the next morning, you came back out together." His misery was written all over his countenance.

Geneva was stunned. "When was this again?"

"In January. I went up there after yew. On a Saturday, it was."

Howard Graves spoke up. "The night of my mother's accident."

Realization dawned on her. "Oh, Howard! You darling idiot! We weren't together! I live in the same building as Howard. We had gone to visit his mother at the hospital. And the next morning I took him to church with me. We weren't together! Not at all!" She appealed to Howard Graves. "Tell him, Howard!"

Howard Graves shrugged. "It's true, much as I hate to say it.

She's been my friend, and she helped me through a tough time when my mother was in an accident, but that's all there was to it."

Howard Knight looked doubtful, but slowly he seemed to grasp the possibility. He looked hopefully at Geneva. "He had his arms around yew."

Howard Graves gave him a look of disgust. "The parking lot was icy. She was pregnant. Somebody had to take care of her, and you weren't there." He crossed his arms and looked away. His eye was blooming red and purple.

Geneva wanted to get to the real issue. "But it's you who are in love with someone else. I saw you with that woman."

He looked puzzled. "What woman? Honey, what woman?"

"That one at your place, who you hugged, and spun around, and who sat in your dad's lap. When I went to tell you about the baby."

Howard looked baffled. "When was this?"

"Just before Thanksgiving. I went to tell you about the baby, and this beautiful woman came, and jumped in your arms, and you spun her around, and, oh, I could tell you loved her!"

There was a silence while Howard searched his memory. "Do you mean Bethany?" ventured Ike.

All heads swiveled to Ike, then back to Howard, then Geneva, expectantly.

"You mean Bethany?" repeated Howard, earnestly looking into Geneva's eyes. His own were filled with light.

"Who-who's Bethany?" sniffed Geneva, but suddenly she grimaced and doubled over, grabbing her belly. Another contraction had come on strong.

She panted, "I think I'm in labor! Oh no! This is not happening!"

"Oh, yes it is, sweetheart," said Wayne. I could see that contraction from over here. We need to get you to the hospital. I thought I saw one earlier, about ten minutes ago."

Pandemonium exploded in the air. Wayne and Lenora rushed to her. Howard and John ran up the steps and nearly ran over Jimmy Lee, who had jumped up as well. In the melee, someone stepped on Lamentations, and the dog began his pre-hysteria barking and growling. Ike broke out in a loud prayer.

"Lordy mercy!" exclaimed Lenora. "We got us a baby a'comin'! Somebody go git a preacher! I ain't havin' no bastard grandchild comin' in this world!"

"Preacher, nothing!" said Wayne, his hand on her belly. "We need to get her to the hospital, and right now, or else we may have a baby on this porch."

"Wait!" exclaimed Howard. "Grannie's right. Somebody git us a preacher. We'll git to the hospital, and he can meet us there. I'm amarryin' this girl! Right now!"

The contraction eased, and Geneva caught her breath.

"No!" repeated Geneva. "I'm not marrying you. I know you don't love me. You're just doing this because you think it's the right thing to do. You already told me you couldn't love me. Back last summer, when you gave me this." She took the pendant from under her shirt and held it out to him. "And who's Bethany?"

"Oh, darlin', she's my sister-in-law. She and my brother and their kids came for Thanksgiving, but Sam and the boys got here the day before. They were just in the barn when Bethany got there. How did you… ?"

"I went to tell you about the baby, and I got there, and she had just pulled in, and I parked the car above the house, and I saw her. Oh, Howard, she's your sister-in-law? She's so beautiful!"

"Oh, baby!" Howard drew her close into himself. "If only you had stayed another minute. You'd have seen Sam and the boys come out, and you would have seen for yourself. Geneva, I do love yew!"

Sally Beth suddenly spoke up. "Right, yew two. We ain't got time to be foolin' around here. I need both of you to release me from my promise. And *right now!*"

"What?" asked both Howard and Geneva.

"Yew both have been spillin' yer guts to me, and both of yew made me promise not to tell, and we cain't clear this up 'til I can speak. So do you both relieve me of my promise?"

They stared at Sally Beth, and then nodded. "Okay," said Geneva in a small voice.

Wayne spoke up. "Really. We have to get to the hospital."

"Shut up, Wayne," said Geneva. "I want to hear what Sally Beth is talking about."

"Make it quick, Sally Beth," muttered Wayne. I haven't delivered a baby in the usual way in about five years."

"I have," said Lenora. "Speak yer piece, Sally Beth."

"Okay," sighed Sally Beth. "Yew both have been whinin' for the last few months about how much yew loved each other, but both of yew have been jist too darn stubborn to go talk to the other. I managed to talk Geneva into goin' to see yew, Howard, but then she ran into yer sister-in-law, and that stopped that, and then, Howard, I finally got yew to come here to talk to Geneva, but yew dragged yer doggone feet so long, she had *awready* moved back to DC by the time yew got here, and I had to talk yew into going up there, and, oh, *Lord*, he saw yew with that *other Howard*. Then yew both were convinced that yew loved somebody else!" She leaned toward Geneva. "Honey, Howard was *sure* ye'd gone back to Howard over there," she waved a hand in Howard Graves' direction, "and I didn't know who that *Bethany* person was. And my lips were *sealed,* so I couldn't say a word to either one of you." She looked at each of them and drew a deep breath. "Anyways, the quickest upshot of it is that yew both have been pinin' fer each other all this time, and if yew don't git married *right now*, we're gonna have us a baby out of wedlock."

Another contraction came on Geneva in a rush. "*Ohhh!*" she screamed. "Oh, Lord, I am going to have this baby! What am I going to do? Oh, Howard!"

"Lord God!" exclaimed Howard. "Marry me, honey! Right now! Granny'll kill me if we have a bastard, and I want to be this baby's official daddy before he gits here."

"Oh *yes!*" wept Geneva. "Oh Howard! Chap! I want to marry you! And I think this baby is coming! Somebody go get a preacher! Quick!"

"Wait a minute," said Wayne. "This is getting too close for comfort. Lenora, get Geneva in there and check her. I'm calling Geneva's doctor. There will be a chaplain at the hospital."

"Come on, honey," said Lenora, beaming with joy and pride. "Let's see how much time we got. Chap, yew cain't come in here. I don't need yew passin' out on me." She paused to smile at her grandson. "I'm right proud of yew, boy. Rachel, help me git this girlie inside."

Rachel led Geneva to her bedroom, where she helped her onto the bed while Lenora washed her hands and rolled up her sleeves. "Now I'm jist gonna check yew, honey, and see how much time we got afore this baby comes into this world. Jist relax, I ain't gonna hurt yew…" she fell silent, then gave a low whistle. "Honey, yew ain't got the time of a mosquito in the freezer. I think we got us a little 'un that ain't in the mood to wait." Kin ye sit up? If ye walk around a little bit, it might make it a little easier."

"What?" exclaimed Geneva, sitting upright. "No! I'm not having this baby yet! I want to get married first!"

Rachel tried to soothe her. "Sweetheart, there isn't time to go get anybody. Wayne's calling an ambulance right now."

"Howard! I want Howard! *Ti—!*" shrieked Geneva. And suddenly Howard was at her side, crooning into her ear, "I'm here, darlin'. I'm gonna be right here forever and ever. I jist love you so much. And we'll git married, but we got to git yew to a hospital so yew can have our baby…" he stopped suddenly as Geneva grabbed him by the collar with both hands and hauled herself out of the bed and into his face. She was in no mood to be crossed.

"Howard," she said through gritted teeth, because another contraction was coming on. "Yew git us a preacher in here *right now!* I ain't goin' nowhere, and I ain't havin' this baby until yew make me your *wife!*"

There was a stunned silence. Howard licked his lips and said nervously to nobody in particular, "Does anybody know how to git in touch with a preacher?"

"I'm a preacher," came a soft voice from the doorway. "I reckon we can do this, even though yew don't have a marriage license or anything. But I got a Quaker certificate here in my Bible." Sally Beth patted her voluminous purse. "And we can worry about a license later."

Wayne entered the room. "The ambulance is on it's way. Lenora, how are things?"

"I dunno, doc," said the old woman. "We ain't got much time. She's comin' along pretty fast. Come on, let's git up and walkin'."

Geneva was feeling giddy and deliriously happy. She began to laugh and sob. "Rachel, I need a veil. And some flowers. I'm going to marry Howard right now! Oh, Rachel, make me *preeetty!*" A contraction make her shriek the last word.

There was another shocked silence, and then the room suddenly exploded. Rachel ran out, Howard jumped up and shouted, "Innybody got a ring? I need a ring right now! Oh Lord! I'm agittin' hitched and I ain't got a ring!

Ike poked his head in the door. "I'm prayin' fer yew, Geneva," he said softly, and Geneva felt such a rush of love for the old man who held his hat in his hand so humbly as he offered to lift prayers on her behalf. She rushed to him and flung her arms around him. He flinched as she pressed herself against his injured hand, but his pain did not stop him from encircling her back with his good arm.

"Oh, yes, Ike! Pray for me! Pray for us all! We're getting married!" and she danced out into the hallway and screamed for Rachel to hurry. The little girls came running at the commotion, and so did the rest of the crowd. Geneva marched into the living room, meeting Rachel coming down the stairs holding her own wedding veil.

"Girls! Run out and pick some flowers for Aunt Geneva! She's getting married!"

"And get some for yourselves, too!" shouted Geneva after them. "I need flower girls! Oh, Rachel, come on, and fix my hair!" She rushed toward the stairs to Rachel's bedroom, nearly bumping into Howard Graves on her way. He was holding little Lenora in his arms. John was behind him, holding Genny. Jimmy Lee was kneeling with his arm around Lamentations, who trembled amidst the tumult.

Two more faces appeared. Gaynell and Ray stood at the door, looking puzzled. Ray held a huge pot in his hands. "What in Sam Hill is going on?" he demanded.

Geneva threw her arms around both her parents. "Mama, Daddy! I'm so glad you're here! I'm getting married! Right now*wwwww!*" Another contraction had taken hold. That was enough to set off Lamentations who had been simmering for the last hour.

"Git that dog outta here!" shouted Howard Knight, and Jimmy Lee and John both tackled the mongrel and subdued him enough to tie a handkerchief around his mouth. They carted him outside.

Hannah and Phoebe ran into the room with armloads of flowers, and Geneva, recovered from her latest contraction, made her way up the stairs and into Rachel's bedroom. "Hurry, Rachel!" she gasped. I think Lenora's right. We don't have much time." And she threw herself into a chair to let Rachel attack her with a hairbrush and makeup. Gaynell sat beside her, holding her hand, soothing her during the pains that were coming regularly and fast.

Twenty minutes and three contractions later, she emerged on Ray's arm, feeling radiant. She could not believe she was about to be married to the man she had been longing for all these months, the man who had stood before her on the mountaintop and sang of his love and his desire for her. She began to weep for joy, but then realized she was making the mascara run, so she simply thanked God for this glorious moment and turned her smile upon her beloved.

They walked outside into the May sunshine, toward the petals of the apple blossoms floating in the soft breeze. Sally Beth and Howard stood under the tree, waiting for her. He had found a white shirt, tie and jacket in Wayne's closet, and although the jacket was a little too large, he looked gorgeous. His hair had been brushed back, and his eyes were shining. Geneva did not believe she would be able to survive her joy. Already her heart was near to bursting. Rachel had put on Beethoven's *Ode To Joy*, and everyone present wept openly. Jimmy Lee sniffled and wiped his nose on his sleeve. John squeezed her hand as she passed by him. Howard Graves kissed her on the cheek. His eye had swelled shut and was already turning black, but he still had all his teeth. Geneva was glad for that. She was glad for everything. She was in love with this day and everyone present.

As she stepped up to Howard and Sally Beth, she faltered and leaned on her father to get through another contraction, but as soon as it was over, she smiled and straightened, and walked to stand by Howard.

Sally Beth smiled shyly at Geneva and Howard and began:

"The right of joining in marriage is the work of the Lord only, and not the priest's or magistrate's, for it is God's ordinance and not man's. We marry none; it is the Lord's work, and we are but witnesses. So, dearly beloved, we are gathered here together in the sight of God to witness the joining of this man and this woman in holy matrimony." Geneva's spirit sang and laughed. She flung her arms around Howard.

"Not yet, honey," said Sally Beth gently. "We have to git through the ceremony first." She continued, "Now, hold hands, please." Howard snatched up Geneva's hand and kissed it.

"Geneva, say this," prompted Sally Beth. "In the presence of God and before these our families and friends…"

Geneva repeated the words.

"I take thee Howard, to be my husband, promising with Divine assistance…"

Geneva was overcome. She brought Howard's hand to her lips, then touched his face as she spoke his names, "Howard, Chap, Ta li."

"To be unto thee a loving and faithful wife so long as we both shall live," breathed Sally Beth in a rush.

Geneva began the words, getting to "faithful wife" before she had to stop and breathe as the next convulsion began. It wracked her belly and spread throughout her whole body, but it felt like bliss, because Howard held her through it. As soon as she was able to stand alone again, Sally Beth prompted, "so long as we both shall live."

"So long as we both shall live," panted Geneva.

"Now Howard, say this: I take thee Geneva, to be my wife, promising with Divine assistance…"

Howard laughed and cried and pulled Geneva to him. "I take thee Geneva, Digvnasdi Atsilv Hawinaditlv Galvquodiadanvdo to be my wife. He covered her face with kisses as he said the words. "Promising with Divine assistance to be unto thee a loving and faithful husband, and a good father," he added, as he kissed her belly.

"So long as we both shall live," urged Sally Beth

"Hallelujah!" shouted Ike.

Everyone laughed, and there was a chorus of "hallelujahs," before Howard said the final words. Then there were shouts and laughter and tears, but Howard suddenly stopped, "Wait! You didn't do the ring part!"

Sally Beth replied, "Yew don't need a ring, and we don't have one anyway."

"Yes, I do," he replied, and from his own neck he took a pendant exactly like the one that Geneva wore. Her heart lifted high and joyous when she saw it. *He had loved her all this time! He had worn this symbol of her next to his heart, even as he denied his hope for them.* The tears flowed from her eyes as he wrapped the chain around her wrist and looped it around her fourth finger. The little red and yellow comet dangled from her hand. She turned it over, laying the bejeweled thing in her palm. "I give yew this, Geneva, as a sign of my everlasting love for yew. Thank yew for being my wife."

And in turn, Geneva took the pendant from her neck, wrapped it around Howard's wrist and looped it around his fourth finger. "I give you this, Howard, as a sign of my everlasting love for you. Thank you for being my…"

She stopped as a sudden "pop" resounded within her, as loud as a champagne cork leaving its home, and before she could fathom what it was, water gushed from her and spilled all over the ground, baptizing Geneva's feet with the water of new life. Lenora laughed out loud, "I reckon yew've been pronounced man and wife, now and fer certain!" and she hustled the stunned Geneva into the bedroom, leaving everyone else to gasp and laugh and cry. Howard was on her heels.

The ambulance arrived, but there wasn't much the paramedics could do. Lenora had taken control; she did not even let Wayne assist her, allowing only Rachel and Gaynell be on hand to comfort her. But it was Howard Geneva wanted, and she reached for him every time the waves came crashing over her, crying out his name over and over again while he clung to her. She tried to remember the training she had gone through weeks earlier, breathing carefully, concentrating, putting all her energies into her small, tight core, and willed her body to relax and do what it was meant to do. She stared at Howard's face, and she felt herself lifting, rising out of herself, and floating into his eyes, feeling beloved, feeling she knew the answers to the mysteries of life. She delved into his love, and sank there, drowning in beauty. She did not want to move, to even breathe, afraid this moment would pass too soon. But then came the overwhelming need to push, and her body separated itself from her mind, and simply took over. She had no control, nor did she wish it. Her body was performing miracles all on its own, and all she could do was lie back and be awed by it.

Later, when the babe was wrapped in a soft blanket and handed to her, she felt the song of gratitude and praise rising out of her heart, *Praise the Lord! Praise the Lord, my soul! I will praise the Lord all my life; I will sing praise to my God as long as I live.*

The Lord answered her, *Peace and love be unto you, my precious child.*

And when she looked at Howard and their new son, she knew this promise would be kept.

About the Author

Deborah Hining believes that life is pretty much perfect as long as it holds a sense of destiny. Her destiny has led her to be many things: wife, mother, and grandmother, and also actress, award-winning playwright, theatrical director, college instructor, and Certified Financial Planner (or as she calls it, "Financial Fairy Godmother"). Now she is a farmer and author. Deborah lives at Corinne's Orchard, a farm in Durham County, North Carolina, with her husband, architect Michael Hining, daughter Mary Elizabeth, an artist, and son-in-law, Nick, a chef. Her son, George, daughter-in-law, Julie, and granddaughter, Corinne, live just a few miles away. You can find her most days working in one of the gardens, writing, and generally giving thanks for her abundant life.

Reader's guide and author interview available online:
dhining.lightmessages.com

CPSIA information can be obtained
at www.ICGtesting.com
Printed in the USA
FFOW02n0947071115
18433FF

9 781611 530575